DEDICATION

For my Grandma Kramer, who let me work
for baseball cards, and more importantly, let me read
scary stories at night when I stayed over.

3 GATES of the DEAD

JONATHAN RYAN

Premier Digital Publishing - Los Angeles

3 GATES OF THE DEAD

eISBN: 978-1-62467-100-5
Print ISBN: 978-1-62467-099-2

Published by Premier Digital Publishing
www.premierdigitalpublishing.com
Follow us on Twitter @PDigitalPub
Follow us on Facebook: Premier Digital Publishing

ACKNOWLEDGEMENTS

Dear Reader,

Stories may be born in the mind of a writer, but books are born into the world through a team of extraordinary people. Here are the people who delivered this book to you with much sweat, dedication and love. Anything right about this book is their doing. Anything wrong is mine. I couldn't have done this without them.

Italia Gandolfo, a super agent, super friend and a super editor. I would not have a writing career without her. My amazing publishing team at PDP: Thomas Ellsworth, for taking a chance; Elizabeth Isaacs for helping tell the world about my book. Hope Collier Fields for her last minute line edit work. You probably bought this book because you liked the cover. So do I. I thank Shavaughn Murphy and Michael James Canales for chilling me to the bone with your cover work. That's a good thing in the horror world. Alan Atchison, for being a sounding board, reading and providing insight. And, thanks to the home team for putting up with my need to write, have quiet and tell stories.

Written on the Third Sunday of Lent, March, 3, 2013
More to come...

chapter one

I don't know if I believe in God anymore.

I stared at the screen, my thoughts of the past few months boiled down to a single black and white sentence as I typed an email to my best friend, Brian. The thought rocked me back into in my dark brown leather couch, the only nice piece of furniture I owned. Richard Dawkins' book, *The God Delusion*, trembled in my hands. I couldn't bring myself to read anymore and set the book down. I reached for a piece of gooey thin crust pizza.

Bishop, my gray and white Boxer, came over and laid his head in my lap. He looked at me with sad, watery eyes. I rubbed his ears. "I know, boy, I know. After all, believing in God is part of my job description, isn't it?"

My job. I rubbed my head as I glanced down at Dawkins' book. Most of the people at my conservative evangelical church would have a problem with me even reading Dawkins in the first place. I couldn't imagine what they would think of their assistant pastor beginning to believe much of what Dawkins wrote. Many would be mad. Many would be so discouraged they might give up their own faith.

I frowned as I looked at his author picture on the cover. On one hand, Dawkins was a bit of an asshole. While my own faith seemed to be circling the drain, I had no wish to ruin other people's beliefs. Dawkins, on the other hand, seemed like a crazed trucker plowing through a crowded shopping mall. He ran over other's beliefs with a sort of manic glee that made me wonder if he just liked pissing people off.

Bishop gave a soft woof as he sniffed the pizza.

"Sorry, buddy, your mommy wouldn't approve."

He looked up at me with wide eyes.

I sighed. "I know, buddy, not like she's around to say anything, eh?"

Bishop put his head on my knees. He missed Amanda, and so did I. Her leaving had been a punch to the gut for both of us. I figured that she'd at least visit Bishop, but she'd never even asked to stop by to see him. She punished the dog who loved her.

I sat back on the couch she had bought. Amanda had said my old threadbare love seat looked like something from a frat boy's dorm. I looked around the room and realized it was the only thing in my condo that had any style. The pizza box from the previous night occupied the other end of the table, nearly falling over from all the books shoving it toward the stained carpet.

Bishop woofed at me and went into the kitchen. I got up to get him some water and caught my reflection in the patio doors. For a twenty-eight-year-old, who the women supposedly swooned over, I looked like hell. My wavy brown hair was disheveled and shadows lurked beneath my dark eyes. Plus, all the pizza and beer I consumed had added about seven pounds to my former soccer player physique. Sucking in my stomach, I resolved to spend more time at the gym.

I almost bumped into a stack of books heaped on my coffee table, my reading list of the past few months. Dawkins and Christopher Hitchens on one pile, John Dominic Crossan and Sam Harris on another. Each book had been well read, underlined, and pored over as I began to question God's existence after Amanda left. Her leaving hadn't been the worst thing in my life, but it was the final straw.

I sighed and looked at the stack of Stanley Kubrick movies on the floor. *Kubrick and Dawkins*, I thought, *quite a combination for the almost faithless.*

My mind began to swirl, and I grabbed for a bottle of beer. As I opened it, I had to laugh at the irony. The man in my congregation who made beer would never have guessed it might bring some comfort as I struggled with my faith.

"One good thing about being a Presbyterian, Bishop, and not a Baptist ... we get to drink beer!"

Bishop ignored me and dove into his food bowl.

I sighed. "I've got to stop talking to the dog."

I went back to my computer and stared at my words on the screen. An email just wouldn't do it. I had to say the words aloud. I had to speak my doubts so I could sort through them with a real live person.

I picked up the phone and dialed the only person I could talk to at ten o'clock at night, my college buddy Brian. The phone rang, and I heard a click as he answered.

"Hello?"

"So, does the SEC suck by accident or as a general rule?"

"Never doubt the superiority of SEC football, you Big Ten Ass." Brian paused. "So, you must have a reason for calling this late. What's up?"

I hesitated, regretting the decision to call Brian. My doubts had gnawed at me for months, and I didn't want to shock him. Brian never doubted anything in his life, especially not the idea that God existed. He had been like that since we first met in college, a small Christian liberal arts institution in Texas.

"Aidan, are you there?"

I took a deep breath. "Yeah, bud, sorry. I'm just struggling over here and needed a friendly voice."

"Speak to me, boy."

"Well, the whole doubt thing, I think it's progressed further. I'm not sure if I believe in God anymore."

"Okay, as in you don't know if Christianity is true?"

"No, way more basic than that. I doubt God's very existence."

Brian paused. "Wait a minute. I'm going down to the man cave."

I started to pace as I waited for him to get back on the phone.

"Now, lay it out. I'm downstairs with the door shut, so speak freely."

"In other words, cuss freely, because Ashley is upstairs, eh?" I said.

"You got it."

I shouldn't have called him. He didn't need this, the late night ramblings of a pathetic, heartbroken sad-sack who no longer believed in God. I took a bite of pizza and washed it down with a big gulp of beer.

"Aidan? Hello?"

"Sorry, Brian, just sort of regret calling you."

"Shut up, man. Just spill it."

I looked at the stack of books and the flattened copy of Dawkins. "Okay, you asked for it. I guess it starts with the science questions."

Brian chuckled. "Of course it does, science boy."

"Hey, at least I'm not an Unfrozen Caveman Lawyer."

"What kind of scientific questions?"

I ran my hands through my hair. "Part of it comes from the tensions I've always struggled with, the tension between science and faith. One seems to contradict the other in a number of different areas. For example, I have always thought that irreducible complexity destroyed the idea of evolution. But now that I've been reading Dawkins, I'm starting to wonder if that's true."

"Isn't Richard a bit of a dick?"

I nearly choked on my beer. "Yeah, granted, he is a dick. That doesn't mean he's wrong though, especially on irreducible complexity."

"Simplify. Me no speak science."

I sighed. "Take the eyeball, for instance. It's a part of us that can't function without everything in place. So the question would be then, which came first, the chicken or the egg?"

"Thus proving there is a designer," Brian reasoned.

"I'd always thought so until I read Dawkins' explanation. He doesn't deny the complexity but explains it came about through slow, gradual changes until it reached perfection. Therefore, there is no need for a designer. Just give it enough time, and the change will happen naturally."

He sighed. "That makes sense, but there are gaps in our knowledge, right? Maybe that is where God moves."

"See, that's what I would have said, but even a lot of Christians find that unsatisfying. Dawkins points out that just because we don't know certain things, it doesn't mean that God is the answer to fill in the gaps. It's flawed logic."

"I guess the main problem is that God isn't exactly open to scientific investigation," Brian said.

"Yeah, and that's been bugging me. Why isn't He? Why isn't there a sensory test for Him? I want to taste, touch, see and hear Him. I want to draw His blood, pinch Him, and pound on His chest to see if He's real. I want Him to show Himself to me!"

"Bud, you don't have to yell."

Sheepishly, I lowered my voice. "I'm sorry, man; this has all been building up."

"Evidently. You aren't the only one who feels this way, you know. I've felt it a few times. But I also know that His ways are not our ways."

I hated that response. Such a cop out. I wanted to throw the phone across the room. Instead, I took another swig of beer. "See, that is what I've always said. But I'm not satisfied with that answer anymore."

"Aidan, have you ever been satisfied with those answers? Ever since we met, you have had the whole science/faith tension. But you've always dealt with it before. Why are things different now?"

I scratched my day-off beard. "I guess I've always resolved those tensions by accepting the evangelical Christian filtering of what scientists say, rather than checking it out for myself. Stupid, I know. Lately, it's all started to crash down on me. I can't overlook my doubts any longer. I'm tired of it."

I had to be honest, it felt good just to lay out eight years of questions; all the stuff I had thought about but never said. It felt like someone pulled a thorn out of my flesh.

"I wish I could help you on the science stuff," he said. "But you know way more than I do in that area, Mr. Biology Major. It sounds like there is more to your doubts than just the science questions."

That was Brian, always looking for some other answer. For a lawyer, he sure avoided the facts when it came to his faith. I had seen that often enough, intelligent people turning a blind eye to what kept smacking them in the face.

I decided not to take the bait and be a smart ass instead. "Fine, it's not just about the science. How about the history? I guess you could say I have doubts about the Bible being real history, especially the Gospels!"

"What do you mean?"

"Well, my reading has taken me into questions I didn't think too much about in seminary. For example, when, how, and who wrote the Gospels?" Beads of sweat collected on my forehead as I continued to pace around the room.

"You mean you don't think it was Matthew, Mark, Luke, or John?"

I took another swig of beer, and the room started to spin. I sat down. "Not that I can tell. It seems to me that the Gospels were written by different faith communities. They wanted to justify certain aspects of their theology. You know, the Gospels were most likely written at least seventy years after Jesus died."

"Where is the proof of that?" Brian asked, his voice starting to fill with tension. I had gone way past guarding Brian's faith.

"Well, like how some people are named in one Gospel and not named in others. Not to mention we have four different accounts of which women were at the tomb to witness the Resurrection!"

Brian's voice lowered. "I see what you mean."

"Yeah, I mean, I'm sure there are certain historical events in the Gospels, but I just don't know anymore which ones to trust, if any."

"You would know those better than me, Aidan. I'm not much of a historian when it comes to the Bible."

Bishop laid his head on my lap. I paused and rubbed his ears. For some reason, tears welled up in my eyes. I fought to steady my voice. "But beyond all that, there is one reason that's most damning of all, the one reason Jesus himself talked about."

"What's that?"

"'All men will know you are my disciples by the love you have for one another.'" I paused. "Christians are supposed to love one another as evidence that God is real. Don't see a lot of that going around." Tears ran down my cheek.

Brian paused and took a deep breath. "No, that's true. And you see evidence of that more because of your job. You are under a lot of stress with work, and you know, other things."

I gripped the phone. "What other things, Brian?"

"Don't you think your personal life has a lot to do with what you're going through? Maybe, just maybe, your doubts are more emotional than rational? I mean, I hate to bring this up, but you've had a rough year. Your parents dying in the fire and Amanda leaving are big things, bud."

I jumped up and sent the half-eaten pizza flying across the room. "Why the hell do you have to bring all that up? Can't a person have honest doubts about their faith without someone thinking they're having an emotional crisis? A lot of people don't believe in God! A lot of respectable people! Famous people don't! Smart people like Richard Dawkins or John Lennon!"

"But you're a minister," Brian fired back. "You have to believe. That's what people rely on you for, helping them with their own doubt. People in the church won't put up with it."

I kicked over a stack of DVDs. "So they get mad at me, and I lose my job. Big deal. It won't get me stoned or burned at the stake like it might have five-hundred years ago. It's been done, like when gay people come out. It used to be such a scandal, *Time* cover material. Now, it's a yawn fest. Very few people care anymore whether you are gay or an atheist. That is, unless you are running for president."

I paused and grinded my teeth. "The problem with you, Brian, is that you live this fairy-tale life, married to a sweet Georgia peach, have two Christmas-card kids and a huge house in the suburbs. I don't think you've fucking failed at anything in your life!"

A long bout of silence made me think Brian had hung up. My anger had clearly mixed with the beer and delivered a crushing blow. I figured he'd be too upset to reply, but I didn't care. It was about time he got a dose of the sad reality of my life.

"Listen, Aidan," he said in a soft tone. "I know things are horrible. I mean, you just lost your parents a year ago, and Amanda left a few months later. But I'm trying to help, so don't take your frustrations out on me, bro. Plus, how many beers have you had tonight?"

I looked at the empty beer bottles on the floor and on the table. "Ten, I think. I'm sorry, man."

"Aidan, I know it sucks."

"It doesn't just suck, Brian, I-F-S!"

Brian laughed. "Yeah, man, I know."

I was glad our little college phrase brought some humor to the tense situation. We'd developed the acronym for "it fucking sucks" to avoid all the frowns from prettty, virtuous, southern-Christian girls for whom saying "fuck" ranked right up there with taking God's name in vain. That never made any sense to me, and I had many arguments as to why "fuck" is better. Most people in my evangelical school didn't buy it.

I plopped back on the couch. "I shouldn't have taken it out on you. I'm sorry. I feel a little lost. I don't have any direction right now."

"Maybe you read too much, did you ever think about that?"

"Well, yeah, you idiot. When you're not dating, you have a lot of free time on your hands, you know? It's not like I think dating and reading are mutually exclusive. I just don't have anything else to do."

Brian hit a sore spot. I hadn't dated anyone since Amanda broke off our engagement.

"Well, it's not like you aren't good-looking. I remember the girls at school loved to come out and watch you play soccer. All you have to do is man-up and ask someone. Use an online dating service or something."

I laughed, and Bishop raised his head. "Funny you should say that. I did exactly that two weeks ago."

"And what kind of responses did you get?"

"Typical."

"More info, man, more info."

I sighed. "It's like this. Half of the responses I get are from the unbelievably-holy Christian girl who was home-schooled, wants to marry a pastor and spend her life entertaining the ladies of the church. The other half comes from girls who, to put it nicely, wish to deflower a pastor. The joke is I've already been deflowered. Too bad for them."

Brian laughed. "Revenge on God by screwing, eh? Or an unhealthy church upbringing."

"I guess. Both types creep me out."

"Come on, Aidan, I'm sure something will work out. There's no need to give up your faith in God over it. I have a book that might help."

I busted up laughing. "Dude, that's such an evangelical response. Gloss over it and offer them a book. Besides, I've probably already read it."

"Well, have you talked to Mike?"

I closed my eyes. I had thought about it many times, but how do you tell your boss you may no longer believe the main values of the company?

Bishop peered up at me and whined. His boxer-mutt face pained with the look of a full bladder.

"Okay, buddy, I know, walk time."

"Hey, Bri, I gotta run out into the snow and cold. Bishop is whining. Poor neglected dog, product of a broken home. Then I need to get to bed. Long day tomorrow with the meeting, can't wait for that…"

Brian chuckled. "Later, Aidan. You can call me anytime, you know. You also know the Buckeyes have no business being in the national championship game, right?"

"I know, man, thanks. And I think the cheese grits are clogging your brain. You should get that checked out."

I grabbed Bishop, and we went out the door. I felt sorry for my poor dog. An assistant pastor was one of those creatures who got dumped on in hopes he would be able to climb the ladder by learning the ropes in a secondary job. So, we did everything we were asked to, hoping it would earn us a fantastic reference for a head pastor job in three to five years. As a consequence, I worked long hours, and Bishop spent most of his time in his crate. I'd been thinking of giving him to my brother and his kids, but I couldn't bring myself to do it, even though he was a reminder of the worst breakup of my life.

It's the same old story. Guy and girl are dating and buy a dog together thinking it's the start of something permanent. Then, said girl finds someone who is holier than said guy (another pastor, evidently). Suddenly, said girl simpers, "God doesn't want us to be together anymore." The Christian equivalent of the "it's not you, it's me" line. It's astounding how Christians always blame God for the selfish crap they want to do.

I thought Amanda was going to be different. She wasn't. She broke my heart like everything else in my life, including God. I wondered if I had always equated God and girls. Now they were both a big disappointment. I felt like I'd been cast adrift on Lake Erie in a canoe without a paddle.

With that happy thought, I walked Bishop, and then we both crawled into bed. As I drifted off, my home phone rang.

"Hello," I mumbled.

"Aidan?" said a frantic woman's voice.

I sat up, eyes wide. "Edna? Are you okay?"

"No. I'm in the emergency room with Olan. He's been having chest pains for the past two hours. Will you come?"

I heard Olan say something inaudible in the background.

"I'm not having him come for you, you old coot!" Edna shouted. "He's coming to help me!"

"Edna? Are you still there? Do you need anything?"

"I don't know, Aidan. I can't think straight."

"I'll be right there."

chapcer cwo

"Sir? Your change." The fast-food window jockey shook me out of my stupor as he handed me my coffee. I couldn't count the late night coffee runs I'd made since I became a minister. No phone call after nine o'clock was ever positive when you were a pastor. You either ended up in a hospital for an emergency surgery or in the house of a screaming couple with kids crying because mommy and daddy took a swing at each other.

As I sipped the coffee, I realized that despite my crisis of faith, comforting people at their worst made the job worth it. I drove through the abandoned streets of Columbus thinking that no matter how cynical I got, one phone call from people in distress helped to distract me from all my doubts.

I frowned into the rear view mirror as I mourned for the person I had been, the idealistic young minister who left seminary on fire, convinced I would set the church ablaze with the holiness of God. My enthusiasm convinced several churches to call me. I had four job offers, but I took the one at Knox because of Mike Johns, the head pastor. He put on the full-court press to bring me to Columbus and then took me under his wing.

While I hadn't regretted working with Mike, the church became a colossal mess, especially among the leadership. The weekly battles over stupid stuff drained my enthusiasm for the job and then threatened to suck out my faith. The fire that once burned in me was nothing but a barely-lit ember now.

I pulled up to the hospital and parked in the clergy space. The bright orange of the emergency sign glowed out into the night as I walked through the doors.

Most ministers hated doing hospital visitations, but I enjoyed it until about a year ago when I had to identify my parents' bodies after the fire. It took what little strength I had to walk through those automatic sliding doors, but tonight I had extra motivation. Olan and Edna Wilkes adopted me my first day at the church. Their own kids — two in the military and one studying at Oxford — rarely made it home, so I often spent time at their farm working for them or committing the sin of gluttony with Edna's cooking.

I fought the lump in my throat as I walked up to the nurse at the emergency station. She peered up at me, and her eyes met mine. She smiled as she reached up and brushed one of her custard-colored curls back.

"May I help you?"

I smiled as I looked at her name tag. "I hope so, Sharon. I'm looking for one of my parishioners, Olan Wilkes. He was brought in with chest pains."

"Yes, uh, Pastor...?"

"Call me Aidan."

"Okay, Aidan." She smiled as she looked up Olan on the computer.

"Yes, here he is. Room three."

"Thanks." I started toward the metal folding doors.

"Uh, Pas ... Aidan?" Sharon called out. "Do you have your chaplain identification? It says that Olan is only allowed one visitor at a time for the moment, but if you have your badge, you can get right in to see him."

My chaplain badge. You didn't have to have it to visit your flock in the hospital, but it could get you in places not usually allowed to normal visitors. I patted down my pockets. "Ah, Sharon, I don't. I left it at my house in the rush to get here."

She frowned as she twirled her hair. "I'm sorry, Aidan, I can't let you in if you don't have it."

I smiled and leaned over the desk. "Please? You can look me up later, but they need their pastor right now. Olan and Edna are friends of mine. Edna is genuinely scared."

She tilted her head, glancing around. "Go on in," she whispered.

I touched her hand. "Thanks, Sharon. You're incredible."

I went in and found Olan's room just a few doors down. He lay on his bed, his full head of white hair combed to the right. If he'd had on a suit and a tie, he would look like the CEO of a Fortune 500 company rather than a dairy farmer, his chosen second love.

"Aidan, my boy, come in," Olan boomed. He waved me in with an IV-injected arm. "Sorry about all the fuss."

"Hey, Olan, are you okay?"

"I'm fine. Well, my chest hurts, and Edna thinks it's a heart attack."

"What does the doctor think?"

"Eh, he's not saying, but I can tell he's not too concerned. My heart rate is normal, and my blood pressure is acceptable. He still wants to be cautious though, so he's running some tests. Hope to have the results soon, which in hospital language means in the next few days."

I grinned. "No doubt. Where's Edna? I brought some coffee for her."

"Where's mine?" Olan scowled.

"Uh, you might be having a heart attack, Olan. Don't think the doctor would approve."

"Bah!" He waved his hand. "I think it's just gas from eatin' out at Jericho's this evenin'."

"That would do it."

Olan's face fell as he reached out his hand. "Thanks for coming,

Aidan. It means a lot."

I gripped his hand. "No worries, Olan. Truthfully, I just came because I love sitting in emergency room chairs and helping Edna with her husband."

He laughed. "Boy, you're all right! I love it. You aren't bein' all serious with me. Have you no respect for my possible death?"

"If you die, I'll apologize to you in heaven."

Olan laughed again as Edna walked in the room.

She grabbed me in a fierce hug. "Oh, Aidan, I'm so glad you're here!"

Edna was a small, skinny woman, but she gripped me with the strength gained from having raised three boys and running a farm. Her gray hair hung down to her shoulders in wispy curls and framed her Jane Fonda face.

"Whoa, Edna, let the boy breathe," Olan said.

I handed her the red and white cup of coffee.

"Oh, just what I need. You always remember."

We sat in silence for a bit before the doctor, a guy who looked about my age, came into the room.

"Mr. Wilkes, your blood test came back negative. No sign of a heart attack and your EKG looks normal. But I want to keep you a few more hours to run a couple of more tests. I think it's most likely acid reflux, but I want to rule out everything else. I'm pretty sure my medical advice will be to stay away from the sausages."

"No problem, doc. Charge it to the insurance company."

The doctor smiled. "The nurse will be here in just a few minutes to take you for some chest x-rays, and I'll be back after I look at them. If everything is good, I'll give you a Zantac and send you on your way. How's your pain on a scale of one to ten?"

"About a four."

"Good, it's dropped since you came in then. I'll be back in a minute."

Edna heaved a giant sigh of relief and laid her head on my shoulder.

"Well, Olan," I said. "Maybe you'll reconsider eating so much for dinner, like the doctor said. God wants us to take care of our bodies, you know."

Olan rolled his eyes. "You know you are getting old when the people giving you dietary and spiritual advice look like they just started shaving."

"Come on, I have a day's growth here. I'm starting to look like Bigfoot."

Olan smiled as he put one hand behind his head.

"You can go home, Aidan," Edna said as she hugged her husband. "There's no point in you stayin'."

"Nah, I walked Bishop before you called. He'll be good until morning. I'll stick around for a bit."

Despite the doctor's words, no one came in for an hour. Olan and Edna had their heads back, and eyes closed. They snored loudly enough to shatter glass. I decided it would be an opportune time to get something to eat.

Sharon gave me directions to the nearest vending machine. After a few turns, I found myself in a deserted hallway. The fluorescent lights reflected off the lime-colored floor, giving the hall an eerie greenish look. As I approached the vending machine, I realized it had become unearthly quiet. No clanking of metal. No talking medical personnel. No pagers going off. Almost as if I had entered some in-between place where the living, the dead, and the almost-dead occupied the same space.

Amazing the thoughts a tired brain will put into your head, I considered as I shook off the cobwebs.

I turned my thoughts back to my conversation with Brian earlier that night. Despite what I told him about ordinary people doubting God or not believing in His existence, I couldn't shake my main problem: my job security depended entirely on my faith. I guess you could define it as a skill, but it wasn't like being able to type fast or being a great public speaker. You could pick those up easily through training or experience. Restored belief in God was a little harder to recover, and I didn't want to seem like a hypocrite. I figured I just had to work through it, and I would start by talking with Mike in the morning.

I sighed. I knew I'd get no sleep tonight, but I guessed I could nap in my office in the morning.

The vending machine clinked as I put the change into the slot. I had just entered the number "33" when a female voice whispered into my ear.

"Aidan..."

At first, I thought Sharon had followed me, and I turned to smile at her.

"Hey, did you..." No one stood by me. No one was in the hallway.

"Hello, is there anyone there?" A cold brush of air sent goose bumps up my skin, and I raised my voice. "Is someone playing a joke?"

I walked down the hall, looking at the closed doors. I tried each one of the handles, but they didn't budge. I shrugged and went back to the vending machine.

"Aidan, they want to wake him..." the voice whispered.

I whirled around and saw the time on the wall clock: 3:30 a.m.

Someone stood just out of my sight as if wanting to be found, like a game of hide-and-seek. Every nerve in my body kicked into high alert as I felt the presence of a person standing right next to me.

"I know you're here!" I shouted. "Come on out!"

No answer.

"Nurse Sharon, is that you?"

There was still no answer except for the low buzz of the vending machine. I rubbed my head and wondered if I should start taking my medication again. I had no desire to go back to popping the "happy pills" as Edna called them. The drugs messed up my system through sweats, tremors, and nervousness. I had no wish to take them again, no matter what hallucinations I might see.

I bought my Reese's peanut butter cups and walked back to Olan's room. Thankfully, I didn't hear any more voices as I reached the door. Edna's glassy-eyed gaze was fixed on a *Cheers* rerun. Olan must have been taken to have X-rays because his bed was empty.

"Aidan, are you okay?"

"Yeah, fine, Edna. Why do you ask?"

"You just had a funny look on your face."

"Oh right, sorry, I thought I heard someone calling my name, but it must have been my imagination. My tired body and low blood sugar are messing with my senses."

Edna gave me a raised eyebrow but didn't say anything.

They brought Olan in about half-hour later, and the doctor pronounced him fit to leave. After Edna signed the paperwork, I wheeled Olan outside.

"Now, you'll come over for pancakes this mornin', right?" Olan asked.

I yawned. "Maybe. Depends on what I have at the church. Besides, don't you all need your rest?"

"Rest? I don't think Olan knows what that word means," Edna said.

"I'll rest when Jesus comes, honey." Olan patted her hand.

Edna scowled. "You don't take care of yourself, and you're gonna rest long before that."

Olan stood up and grabbed her hand. "Come on, woman, let's go home and sleep."

I smiled as they made their way to their car, hand in hand.

chapter three

As I drove to work, my thoughts scattered around like the snowflakes outside my car. Traffic locked into a nonmoving body of steel as Ohio forgot how to drive in the snow. My road rage usually flared in these situations, but I barely noticed I had not made any progress in the last twenty minutes. I knew I needed to talk to someone else about my faith problem.

But who could I tell? One option was to hide it from everyone at the church. I was pretty decent at hiding my true feelings, a skill that had served me well in ministry. This was especially true in situations when someone insisted that contemporary Christian music was better than secular music. Although, when someone started talking about Kirk Cameron being one of the smartest apologists out there, I had to walk away. No one had *that* much control.

As I gripped the steering wheel, I doubted I could cover up something this momentous. It would get out eventually, either through my looks or side comments during Sunday school lessons. Pastors were sort of like the Lindsey Lohans of the church world. Everything we did, from blowing our noses, to what beverage we drank, was discussed and analyzed. Opinions were formed about you on every subject. People would destroy you even as they loved you.

I arrived at the church and parked. The church — a large warehouse-looking building — loomed in front of me. When I first came to Knox, I took one look at the building and almost got back in my car. Everything had been new: the carpets, the smells, and the coffee bar. The sanctuary looked like a modern college theater. For someone who grew up going to an old gray stone church in downtown Indianapolis, it had been a shock to the system. I loved the smell of aged wood, candle wax, and the musty air of the Sunday School Room. Knox had none of those things, but I came anyway.

This building was supposed to be the height of suburban beauty, but it looked like what would happen if a warehouse and an office building produced offspring from a booze-induced hook up. I could never express that to the people of Knox Presbyterian Church, however, who thought the building was a beautiful example of God's grace to the congregation.

I turned off the engine of my 2000 Dodge, and it shuddered to a stop. My poor car needed a tune-up, but I hadn't had the time. It also needed to be cleaned. Trash from Tim Horton's and Chipotle burrito wrappers littered the floorboard. More examples of my terrible diet of the past six months.

After the conversation with Brian, I knew I had to talk to Mike. Actually, the more I thought about it, the better I felt. Mike had always been there for me. He taught me, mentored me, and had my back when I messed up. There had been the time I pissed off our children's ministry coordinator by not returning one of her emails on some nursery policy. After she spent two hours screaming at me, Mike smoothed it all out and helped me avoid that sort of tongue-lashing in the future. His help seemed like a simple thing, but to me, it wasn't. I had heard horror stories from seminary classmates about how their head pastors hung them out to dry. From then on, I latched onto Mike, drank in his every word and followed nearly all of his advice. I knew if there was one person who could help me figure all this out, it was him. Maybe he would suggest I take some study leave and just get away to the mountains to clear my head.

I got out of my car and walked toward the church. I went inside and right for Mike's office. Mike had become the pastor of Knox ten years before after moving his family from Massachusetts. There, he had been the head pastor at a church that had grown from one hundred members to a thousand in the six years he served them. Knox begged him to come do the same, and after about a year of discussion, he accepted their offer.

After Mike agreed, he rebuilt the church, attracted more members, and was loved by everyone, that is until he dared to quote Anne Lamott in a sermon six months ago. From that point on, it all began to crumble. There had been weeks of emails, confrontations, and late night Elder meetings full of shouting.

I was about to knock when Mike's voice carried through the door. He was talking on the phone. Not wanting to interrupt, I went to my office just down the hall. It was supposed to be my place of refuge, but with my gnawing doubts, sitting in it all day would prove to be nothing less than torture. Too much reminded me of everything I had been doing wrong. The wooden shelves lined with books that I never used. My Hebrew and Greek versions of the Bible gathered dust on the top shelf, despite the fact that I had sworn to use them at every opportunity. The books on two thousand years of church history and theology tended to be the worst. I didn't have a great imagination, but sometimes I felt like the ghosts of St. Augustine, John Calvin and Jonathan Edwards stared at me, their eyes full of flaming wrath at my hypocrisy and doubt.

I sat down in the chair and leaned back to think. Mentally, I tried to rebuild the dam. Maybe I didn't need to leave because of my weak belief. Most of the people I knew worked in jobs they couldn't stand, or they were employed by companies whose mission statements were made fun of in the lunch rooms. It didn't take belief to make you halfway decent at your job. I didn't consider myself any different than those people who started off believing in the company they worked for, only to find out years later the company no longer believed in them. But they still worked there because they were afraid of ending up somewhere worse.

Time to bury this crisis of faith, I thought. Full of new confidence, I went to Mike's office and knocked.

"Come in, Aidan," Mike's deep New England-tinged accent carried to the hall.

"How do you do that?" I asked, opening his door.

Mike's space was what most people thought a pastor's office should look like — full of books on every church-related subject imaginable — but with signs of his personality in key areas. A picture of George Whitefield, the revivalist preacher, hung on one wall, as well as a framed page from an early version of the King James Bible. Above his desk was a page of the Bible from one of the people hanged at the Salem Witch Trials. Mike told me he kept it there to remind him of what Christians are capable of doing when they forget Jesus. Still, it always gave me a strange feeling as it drew my staring attention during our meetings. The stain on the yellowed pages looked like an accusing eye. I always wondered if it was blood.

On his desk, Mike had pictures of his beautiful redheaded wife and three adorable honor-roll children. They all wore smiles and waved at the camera from the beach, Grand Canyon, or other family outings.

"Ah, well, one of the little known facts of aging, Aidan. You develop a magical sense."

"Don't tell the elders. They might fire you over that, or press you with rocks."

Mike gave me a tight-lipped smile. "Funny you should say that. One of the things they want to talk about tonight is my Sunday School lesson on the Magi."

I furrowed my brow. "What was wrong with it?"

Mike rolled his eyes. "Who knows? Maybe my top button was undone, and they thought I was tempting the ladies."

We both laughed. Mike motioned for me to sit. "So, what's on your mind?"

I claimed the seat and took a deep breath. "A lot. Not sure where to begin, honestly."

"Take your time." Mike leaned back in his chair, his six-foot-four frame stretched out and his hands resting on his shaved head. His goatee had a little gray speckled throughout the black hairs. The bald head gave him the gravitas needed to minister to older folks in the congregation, but the goatee told people, "Hey, I'm a bit edgy."

I fidgeted with my hands as I fought to get the words out. "I guess, well, my faith has been a little weak lately."

"So has mine, Aidan."

"No, I mean, I have serious questions about my faith."

He raised an eyebrow. "What kind?"

"I'm not sure I believe in God at all anymore."

"Really? Why is that?"

I laid out everything I told Brian the night before, and he listened without interrupting.

"So, there it is," I said as I stared at the floor. "I guess you can fire me now."

Mike leaned forward and laughed. "I'm not going to fire you for being like everyone else."

I looked up as the rock in my stomach softened. "But what if everyone finds out?"

Mike laughed. "Do you really think I'm gonna tell those guys?"

"It could be your job if you don't, right? Won't they question your integrity?"

Questioning someone's integrity in the church was a death sentence, even if their integrity happened to be intact. They automatically came under suspicion. I didn't want that for Mike after everything he had done for me.

"Maybe, but my job is not the most important thing here."

"Then what is?"

"You trying to figure out what you believe. It's a tough thing you are dealing with. I went through it myself."

I rubbed my head in frustration. "Yeah, that's what I've been trying to do."

Mike got up and came around to sit in the empty chair beside me. He took hold of my arm. "You'll pull through it, Aidan," he whispered.

"I did, and I can help you in whatever way you need. When did it start? When your parents died or maybe when Amanda left?"

I sat back and frowned. "Why does everyone come back to that? My doubts are separate from those things. My doubts are intellectual, not emotional."

He smiled with sympathy. "I'm sure. I'm just asking what started it all."

"I guess I'm just no longer ignoring the questions I have always had."

Mike looked at his cell phone and sighed. "I have a meeting in five minutes. I don't want to leave you like this."

"No, it's okay. I already feel better after sharing this with you. I think I'll try working through it on my own for a bit. If I get stuck, I'll come to you."

Mike stood and looked out the window, his face crestfallen.

"Mike? Are you okay?"

"Yes, I'm just thinking about the session meeting tonight. Maybe you shouldn't come."

"Why?"

"Because it's unlikely to help your situation. It could get ugly."

As tempted as I was to take his offer, I couldn't let him face the wolves alone.

"Nah, I wouldn't do that to you. I'll stand with you, bro."

His smile returned. "Thanks, Aidan."

I stood up and began to walk out, then turned. "Mike, do you still have your doubts? I mean about God, the supernatural, all of that."

He turned to me with a somber look on his face. "No, I totally believe in the supernatural. I have no more doubts."

I nodded. "Thanks. I hated coming in here to tell you all of this. *Dreaded* might be a better way to describe it."

"Don't worry about it, Aidan. Just take some time, and let me know if you need anything. You can talk to me anytime, you know."

"I know."

U2's *Sunday, Bloody Sunday* rang out.

"Excuse me," I said as I flipped open my phone. "Hello?"

"Aidan? Is that you?"

"Olan?"

"How are you, boy? Get any sleep?"

I laughed. "Full three hours. Acid reflux gone?"

"Yep, Zantac worked wonders. It had to be the sausages. Edna got a touch of the runs not long after we got home. Don't think we'll be goin' back to Jericho's any time soon."

I smiled and grimaced at the same time. "Uh, right, Olan. Sorry to hear that."

"Nah, she's okay. Nothing a little Pepto couldn't handle."

"Good. So, what's up?

"Are you comin' to the farm this mornin'? I need to show you something."

"Actually, I thought about staying here to get some work done. Is everything okay?"

"Yes, but I need another pair of eyeballs."

I frowned. "For what?"

"Footprints in the field behind my house."

I tried not to laugh. As much as I loved Olan and Edna, they had a weird side. They believed the supernatural was always just around the next corner. Anything out of the ordinary meant, "Something strange is happenin'." Olan once called me out to the farm in the middle of the night because he thought some unusual shadows on his barn wall were demons. After we investigated a bit, I realized the shadow came from empty chicken feed sacks that had been blown from the trash.

"Well, Olan, I don't know. I have a busy day. Can I look at them tomorrow?" It was sort of a lie. There was nothing I had to do that couldn't be put off. I just felt tired and didn't feel like driving forty-five minutes to their farm.

"Nah, heavy snow's comin' tonight. Saw it on the weather channel. I want you to see them before they get covered up." He paused. "Besides, Edna just made some blueberry pancakes that need to be eaten, so I don't gain another ten pounds."

It was hard to refuse Edna's pancakes. I looked at the clock.

"Okay, Olan. I will be out there in about an hour. Will that work?"

"Awlright den. See you in a bit."

I looked up at Mike. "I have to go out to Olan and Edna's farm."

"What's it this time? Were-chickens? Vampire pigs?"

I laughed. "No, not that serious. Some unusual footprints in the snow he wants me to check out."

He rolled his eyes. "Well, at least you get some of Edna's pancakes. I'm guessing that's the real reason you're going."

I grinned. "Guilty."

"Just be back for the session meeting tonight. I'm going to hold you to your promise."

"No worries."

I grabbed my coat and walked outside. The thought of Edna's blueberry pancakes made my stomach rumble.

chapter four

My tires crackled over the gravel driveway as I drove up to Olan and Edna's farmhouse. A pack of dogs — German Shepherd mutts — barked and ran alongside the car. I took in the scenery of snow-covered cow pastures as my canine escort followed me.

I pulled up next to the house and turned off the car, honking the horn as I did. No matter how many times I'd been here, the dogs only treated me as a friend if Olan was around.

Olan came out on the porch. He mouthed something to the dogs, and they abandoned their attack mode and surrounded him like guardians.

I jumped out. "Hey, Olan. How's things?"

"Fine, preacher, just fine. The Mrs. feels much better. Come in and eat."

I made my way through the house and into their living room. The TV blasted in Japanese as ninjas cut their way across the screen. Olan loved ninja movies and had one of the largest collections I'd ever seen. In direct contrast to the images of ninjas chopping each other in half, Edna's watercolor of the Painted Desert hung above the TV. She sold her art at the local farmers market in the city. The hipsters ate up her stuff and called her a "rustic mustic." I had to assure her they meant it as a compliment.

"More ninjas, Olan?" I said with a smile.

"Oh yeah, new one from Japan, and rare. Just got it yesterday. It's a powerful movie for the ninja genre."

"Nothing more groundbreaking than slicing people in half."

"Ha! That is why I like you, boy; you got a sense of humor. Unusual for a preacher."

I smiled. "Well, it's hard not to take ourselves too seriously as God's Kingdom depends on every little decision we make."

"Thank God that's not true."

I headed back toward the door. "So, footprints. Let's see them."

Olan waved his hand. "Nah, let's eat first. Edna will have my hide if I take you tromping around the farm before your stomach is full."

We went into the kitchen where Edna hovered over the hot pancake griddle. The kitchen was the only expensive-looking place in their house. The décor and contents would have done justice to a Martha Stewart magazine. I smiled at the pots hanging from the ceiling, granite counter tops, and every kitchen appliance that could be bought from the Home Shopping Network. Olan said it was the only nod Edna made to material wealth, and he had no reason to complain when he received all the benefits.

I gave Edna a hug. "Hey, beautiful lady."

She wiped her hands on her apron. "Now, I appreciate the hug from a handsome young man, but I'm covered in pancake batter. Sit your butts down. The pancakes are about ready. Do you want juice? Tea? Olan, could you please turn that bloody mess down?"

Olan grinned at me as he disappeared into the living room.

Edna scowled at her husband and then smiled at me. "Old man hasn't been tamed in fifty years of marriage. Thank you for staying with us last night. Now, juice or tea?"

"Both would be great, thanks." I sat down at the table.

Olan came back into the kitchen and poured himself some coffee. "So, ready for the elder's meeting tonight? Should be a barnburner from what I hear."

"Olan, how in the world did you know…"

"Boys, no unpleasant talk at breakfast." Edna frowned. "I'll not have it." She swiped at Olan with a hand towel.

"Yes, dear," Olan said, giving me a little wink. "Sorry. Still, I hope…"

"Olan!" Edna thumped him on the head with a wooden spoon.

"Ow! Woman, you're gonna kill me one of these days doing that."

"Then I'll have some peace at the breakfast table, won't I?"

I hid my smile under the pretense of wiping my mouth with a napkin. Olan and Edna seemed to be always having a fight of one type or another. If I didn't want to think too deeply about it, I might have called it foreplay.

"No, I'd come and haunt you," he shot back.

"If you did, I would get the house blessed by…"

"Edna!" Olan's face changed from a half smile to a frown.

Her eyes widened, and her face went pale. She covered her mouth with her hand.

"What?" I said, looking from Olan to Edna.

"It's nothing, Aidan, nothing," Edna said. "Eat your pancakes. You are far too skinny."

She wanted to change the subject, and I couldn't help but wonder why. Who would bless the house? It wouldn't have been me or Mike. Presbyterians didn't exactly go around blessing houses.

We ate the rest of the meal talking about the Buckeyes and their chances in the national championship game, a must-have table conversation for anyone living in Central Ohio.

At the end of the meal, Olan pushed back from the table and looked up at me. "Well, let's have a look at those footprints."

As he put on his coat, he handed me a pair of rubber boots that flopped in my hands. "Here, put these on. There are too many cow pies where we are going for your shoes to handle."

We walked out behind the house, and Olan jumped over the barbed-wire fence with ease. My pant leg snagged on the top wire, and I almost fell to the ground face first.

"Sorry, Olan, we ministers aren't used to cow pie boots."

"No, but I bet they would be useful on occasion." He helped me back on my feet.

I laughed. "You're right."

We trudged through the frozen mounds of earth and cow pies. The sky turned from partly sunny to Central Ohio winter gray, which had a tendency to be unrelenting. I was convinced this weather had a heavy influence on Trent Reznor and Marilyn Manson. Both lived in this area of the country at one point in their lives and somehow turned their Seasonal Affective Disorders into lucrative careers.

I looked up. "Here comes the storm."

Olan squinted at the sky. "Yeah, I think you're right. Glad you could get out here before the snow hits."

"So, how did you notice the prints way out here?"

He didn't answer.

"Olan?"

"I want you to see 'em first."

He slowed down. "Over there, by the woods. You'll have to step carefully. They're hard to see at first."

I walked to where the field turned into the woods, the in-between place just like a hallway. I shook my head and realized I had too many Irish legends running around in my brain. Still, I'd always felt a little weird about this part of Olan and Edna's property. Olan always wanted to show me the woods, but each time, I found an excuse not to join him.

When I looked at the ground, I couldn't see anything at first. As my eyes adjusted to the bright glare, I could just make out some light indentations in the snow. I bent down to examine the marks.

No boots. No tennis shoes. Not even sandals. Bare footprints. Not only bare footprints, but small, like the feet of a child.

I traced my finger along the faint impression, hardly touching the outer lines of the heel so as not to upset the imprint, up to the ball and then to the small toes.

I looked up at Olan. "I don't understand. Who would let their kid out in the middle of a snow storm?"

Olan gave me a crooked smile. "No one around here, Aidan. Ain't no one that stupid."

"How did you find them?"

Olan stooped down beside me. "Edna had a bad dream last night ... or early morning I should say ... after we got home from the hospital."

"A dream about footprints?"

"No, not exactly. Her dream was about our son who died." His voice cracked a bit, and he rubbed his hands over his face. I had only seen him get this emotional at the funeral of a close friend.

"I don't understand." I tried hard to remember if Olan had mentioned any children other than their sons. I hoped that in my self-absorbed pity of the past few months, I hadn't forgotten something so important.

"I guess we never told you about Joseph. Don't find it easy to talk about him."

"You don't have to," I said, touching his shoulder.

"Nah, should have told you sooner, and the dream won't make much sense if I don't." He stared off at a car moving along a distant road.

"When we first started trying to have kids, we had a hard time. We tried for three years. Nothin'. Then Edna got pregnant, and we were pleased as punch."

"I bet."

"Everythin' went fine. Remember, there were no ultrasounds then."

I nodded. "Right."

"Well, baby was born, crying was good, but he wouldn't eat. They did a bunch of tests and figured out that the baby had no esophagus." Olan stared at the footprints, tears rolling down his cheeks. "Nowadays, there's a surgery that fixes it pretty nicely. Then, there wasn't no surgery. My boy starved to death. I had to listen to him cry for three days." He paused and rubbed his face again. "There's nothin' more horrible in the world, Aidan."

I opened my mouth, but nothing came out.

"So, we had the funeral. Edna ... I thought she would never be the

31

same. The second pregnancy was terrible, full of fear. But James turned out all right, even if he did go to Michigan." He gave a small smile.

I chuckled. "Well, we are all sinners, Olan."

He wiped his eyes. "So, you asked how I found these. You'll also want to know how I know who made them."

I nodded.

"Edna sometimes has dreams, only thing I know what to call them. Anyway, she had a dream that she was walking in this field, and she saw a little boy walking barefoot in the snow."

He reached down to touch a print. "She called out to him and asked what he was doing there." His voiced cracked again. "The boy turned, and Edna saw his face. She knew him even before he said anythin'."

"But how…"

"The mother thing, Aidan. Anyway, the boy spoke."

"What did he say?"

Olan frowned. "Well, that's the strange part."

I tried not to laugh at that one. The strange part, as if the rest of this didn't border on weird already.

"He said, 'They've begun, Mommy. The dark men have begun. They want to awaken the Grinning Man. He's bad, Mommy. Get the Father.'"

"What did Edna say to him?"

"Nothing. She found she couldn't speak. She was only able to think about how much she loved Joseph."

"How did, um, Joseph respond?"

"I don't cry much, Aidan, never have. But this one, well, could have me weepin' for days." He looked at me, tears running down his heavily lined face. "He said, 'I love you too, Mommy. We'll be together soon.' Then she woke up."

"And she had you come out here?"

"Yeah, she did. I can't refuse her anything. I know I seem gullible to some folks, but even I had a hard time believin' her, especially at five in the mornin' after a sleepless night. I came out here anyway."

"And?"

"I've a strong heart as you found out last night — heart of a man half my age, so the ol' saw bones told me — but I could feel it seize up in my chest when I saw these." He pointed toward the prints. "Exactly where Edna said they would be."

"Olan, I mean ... I don't know what to do with that."

He frowned at me. "Do you think I do?"

"No, but..." I stopped and thought of the other incidents I'd been called out here for.

"You're thinking of the chicken feed bags, aren't you?"

My face warmed. "Um, yeah, to be honest."

"Thought so. I didn't think you'd believe me."

I put my hands up. "It's not that. I mean, maybe Edna just had the dream, and someone was running around in their bare feet. Maybe as a joke or for some odd reason, they liked it."

He cocked his head and looked at me with an almost pitying glance. "Aidan, think about what you just said, boy."

"I know, but the other explanation is just..."

"Too supernatural? I thought preachers were supposed to believe in this sorta thing."

He was getting too close. The thing about Olan was he might've talked like an uneducated country person, but he never missed anything. He graduated from Purdue with honors and then went on to become one of the most successful farmers in Ohio.

"Besides," he went on. "How would they have done it? And where are their footprints?"

"Covered by snow?" I said, searching my brain for a possible explanation.

"Boy, didn't they teach you common sense at that seminary school? If those tracks were covered up, why aren't these?"

He had me, and he knew it. He looked me right in the eye. "Aidan, don't you believe such things are possible?"

"I do, but I mean, not to be blunt, it's hard for me to swallow that your son's footprints are out here in the middle of the snow."

"Why?"

I shifted my feet and wrapped my arms around my body. "Well, because, I just don't think it's possible."

Olan nodded, his head still facing the same row of trees. "Mmm hmm."

"Look, Olan, I mean, God just doesn't allow dead people to walk around the earth. I mean, I hate to be that harsh."

He ignored my lame attempts at pity. "Really? The Bible say that?"

"Well, no, not exactly," I said, avoiding his gaze.

"Not exactly is right. Didn't they at least teach you *that* at seminary school?"

I frowned. "Yeah, but maybe I was asleep when we talked about ghosts."

"Remember Saul talking to Samuel?"

"That was probably a demon or something."

"Bible say that?"

I opened my mouth then shut it. Come to think of it, the passage didn't say that at all. In fact, the Bible told interesting stories of the dead walking the earth. Samuel upbraids Saul for using a witch to call him and then for disturbing his rest.

"No, you're right. It doesn't say that, but it also doesn't say that God sends ghosts to carry messages for him either."

"Point taken."

We both stared at the footprints. I hated to admit it, but I didn't really have an explanation for them. The crazy redneck explanation didn't work. I knew all of Olan's neighbors. It took a stretch of the imagination to picture any of them doing anything like this, much less let their kid walk around barefoot in the cold night. But I also knew there was no way it could've been Olan and Edna's dead son.

Olan patted me on the shoulder. "Let's walk back to the house."

We trudged back over the field.

"So, what do you think?" he asked, holding down the barbed wire for me to step over.

"About?" I turned around to hold it for him.

"Joseph's message. What's it mean?"

I didn't want to think about it. "I have no idea, Olan."

"Don't you think we should find out?"

"How in the world would we do that?"

"Dunno. Keep a sharp eye?"

I wanted to humor him, but despite what I said in the field, I didn't see how their dead son could appear to Edna in a dream and then leave his footprints in a field. There was no doubt about someone's footprints being there, I just thought there had to be other explanations. My doubts needed it. "Then keep a weathered eye, Commander."

Olan smiled. He had served as a naval officer during the Korean War. "Good boy. I thought you'd fight me on this one."

"Not at all."

We walked inside the house and took off our boots. I headed for the front door. "All right folks, gotta get back to the church."

Edna hugged me and handed me a Ziploc bag full of pancakes. "Here, Aidan, take these."

I smiled. "Thank you, ma'am."

Then she handed me another bag containing a large, white bone. "This is for Bishop. Bring him out to the farm as soon as possible to get some exercise."

"I will."

Olan walked me out to the car. "Aidan, one more thing."

"What's up?"

"I want you to remember something." The farmer accent was gone.

"Okay." I stared at him.

"Not everything that is real can be seen."

chapter five

I couldn't get those footprints out of my mind as I drove back to the city. What were they? How did they get there? Olan's comment about preachers believing the supernatural haunted me. Was it true? Did God and belief in the supernatural go together? If I didn't believe in God, did that make the supernatural impossible? It all seemed so vague and confusing, like the scene in *A Clockwork Orange* where Alex is forced to watch image after image in a rapid-fire, violent assault.

I listened to the radio's low drone talking about Buckeye football. I wondered how each elder would react to what I told Mike about my faith that morning. I couldn't imagine any scenario that didn't result in my moving in with my only brother and his family in Indianapolis. They would be happy to have me, of course, but I didn't want to become the mooching little brother.

I sat in the parking lot of the church and stared at the glowing white cross. I hated elder's meetings. Every moment would be painful and every word filled with tension. Every situation seemed like a pile of dry wood covered in fresh gasoline, requiring only a single spark to burn the whole thing down. And most of them dragged on for hours.

The idea behind having multiple elders in a church was to keep each person's power in check. It made sense in a logical, American sort of way. I'm sure it's no coincidence that a lot of our founding fathers were Presbyterians. But there was a flaw in this great, democratic plan. Instead of having to deal with one jackass in charge, you had to deal with a herd of jackasses, or in the case of Knox Presbyterian Church, ten. They brayed, kicked, and bit each other, all in the name of Jesus. Though Jesus did ride into Jerusalem on an ass, so that gave me some hope.

I sighed and went into the building. In my office, I noticed a sheet of paper on my desk. Our secretary still had not learned to use email, a constant source of frustration to me. I lost paper all the time, so I asked her on multiple occasions to send my messages by email, a request she hadn't granted in three years. Apparently, my "way with women," as Brian described it, didn't apply to our church secretary who still believed the place ought to be run like a 1920s Southern institution.

No need to look at this paper now, I thought.

I headed over to Mike's office and raised my hand to knock on his door when I heard him talking. From his low one-sided tone, I could tell he was on the phone. Even with the door closed, his voice drifted into the open hall.

"Baby, I can't be there tonight. I have a meeting."

Baby? Does he call Sheila baby? I wondered. I'd never heard him call her that before.

"I know. I want to be with you too. I can't wait to hold you again. Maybe I can come over after the meeting. I can just tell Sheila everything ran late."

I stood there in the hallway with my mouth hanging open.

"Oh, baby, you know what I like. Yeah, the red one, wear it tonight."

No, it can't be!

"Yeah, you will get what you like. I've been thinking about you all day."

What the hell?

I felt the last vestiges of my faith leave me as if a vampire ninja had latched onto my neck. The room spun, and my legs went weak. The pancakes I ate at the farm were in danger of making an encore appearance.

"I gotta go. No, I really do. I can't talk much longer. Aidan will be here soon. He always gets here early, so stop tempting me."

No more. I didn't want to hear any more. I went outside and kicked at the nearest snow pile, sending white chunks into the air. Each thump of my foot filtered my rage into the helpless snow as it flew all over the sidewalk. I let the words fly as I filled the air with expletives. The foul language filter in my head had obviously shut down.

The session of elders would have to be told. They'd slow-cook him with their fire, feeling vindicated and even more secure in their self-righteousness. Damn them, and damn the whole thing. I no longer wanted any part of it.

As I looked at the ice-chunked snow, it occurred to me that maybe I didn't need to say anything. I could just tell Mike I had resolved my faith issue. He didn't need to know that I had lost my faith completely. I didn't have to tell anyone a thing. No one deserved the truth, not Mike or the elders.

Mike's fall just illustrated what I had seen in just about every elder in our church. I had seen into the dark sewers of their hearts, with all of their hypocrisy, cheating, lust, and now infidelity. Not to mention the people I dealt with from the congregation. It seemed as if their darkness had overwhelmed and become a part of me. Why did I have to be any different from them?

I had spent all of my college years, plus four years in seminary, working to get into my position. Unlikely I would be able to find any other useful job, except maybe teaching. Even then I would have to go back to school for my certification, which would take a few years. That would mean more time working at a local bookstore while I went to school at night.

Yep. Money and security. Good reasons to keep my mouth shut.

If they wanted to play the hypocrites, then so would I.

My phone began to vibrate. I pulled it out of my pocket and saw the yellow envelope blink. Someone had sent a text message, but there was no number or name. I pressed the button to view.

They are going to wake him. Cut my ... cut my ... at the gates ... cut my ....

None of it made any sense to me. I couldn't help but wonder if this might not be some joke or a weird marketing campaign. Or maybe some idiot just had the wrong number.

A car door slammed and diverted my attention. Then another, and another. I looked up to see that the elders had arrived for the meeting. It was time to go back inside.

I looked at the text for a moment and then deleted it.

chapter six

❁

"...And further, I think the position of the pulpit distracts from worship. It should be situated in the middle of the platform."

This was the sort of stupid shit that drove me nuts. We talked about this kind of useless crap for four hours as it slowly went downhill from a false piety session, to pastor-beating hour, and then finally to pompous free for all. It always reminded me of the British Prime Minister's questions to Parliament on C-SPAN. The difference in this case was that most of the Members of Parliament had a sense of humor.

"I don't really think God cares where the pulpit should be, so I think we should leave it."

The discussion about the pulpit had been going on for months. I'd always been amazed at how every little thing in the church was thought to be a significant step forward in God's kingdom, from how the pulpit should be positioned to the snacks kids were getting in Sunday School. Not that I cared anymore, but at least they could make things interesting.

I looked down the long conference table at Mike as everyone

droned on through the agenda. I didn't see any sign he had been sticking his shepherd's staff where it didn't belong.

What did I expect? Signs of guilt? Remorse and fear expressed through a trembling lip? Maybe sweat on his bare head? Mike had obviously been screwing someone for at least a few months. My guess was guilt had long since gone out the window.

His face wore the same fixed expression he always had during these meetings, a mixture of amusement combined with irritation. The twitch in his eye had become more frequent, but not so much that anyone used to it would notice.

When the pulpit discussion finally wound down, Mike spoke up. "Well, if there is no other business tonight, I would entertain a motion to adjourn."

A throat cleared at the end of the table, making a sound similar to a Viking blowing his war horn. Elder John Calvin Eisner had a theological library that would put his namesake to shame. He also had the background of being a frustrated pastor, having been fired after only six months in his first church. The maker of war and a math teaching retiree, he spent his retirement torturing pastors. He had gray slicked back hair and always wore a tie to session meetings. Some people loved his act and called him "the picture of wisdom." John never listened to the good idea of not listening to your own press.

He looked up the table toward Mike with a smug smile — part Rush Limbaugh, part Barbara Streisand — without warmth or real humor behind it. He always wore this smile when he was about to destroy someone verbally. When he did, it made him look like a hungry hyena.

"Mike, I have a serious concern I need to bring before the fathers and brothers this evening."

Mike looked down the table, swallowed hard, and nodded. He braced his body as he prepared for the whips.

"I want to question the content of Sunday's sermon. I am concerned whether you were actually preaching the Word of God or not."

I couldn't count how many times John had made that accusation over the past few months. The other elders around the table shifted. Some would agree with John, some would side with Mike, and others wouldn't have the guts to stand up for anything.

Mike waved his hand. "Okay, John, go ahead."

I had to admire Mike in these situations. He never lost his temper. I wondered how he did it. Maybe the same way he lied to the whole world about being a faithful husband. I guess if you hid something that big, you learned to control yourself pretty well.

John kept smiling. "Well, it has to do with your handling of the word 'wise man' in the story of the wise men who visited Jesus."

Mike furrowed his brow as I stared at John. What in the world could he object to with the words 'wise man?' That part had lasted maybe two minutes and had only been a clarifying point in Mike's sermon, which had been on the subject of worship.

"I am not sure I understand," Mike said, his hands clasped behind his head.

Sunday, Bloody Sunday, Sunday, Bloody Sunday...

All eleven heads turned to me as I reached for my cell phone. I must have forgotten to turn off the ringer. Heat rushed to my cheeks as I fumbled in my jacket pocket.

"Sorry, everybody!" I hit the button to stop the ring and saw it was Olan calling again. *What in the world?*

I looked at Mike. "Oh, it's Olan; I wonder if he's okay ... should I answer it?"

He shook his head. "No, Aidan, just call him back."

"Sorry again, everyone." I put the phone back in my pocket.

John smiled, his expression oozing the oil of condescension. "There is no need to ask for forgiveness, Aidan. Your concern for the flock is laudable."

I wanted to roll my eyes. Only conservative Presbyterians talked like that anymore. They ate this sort of stuff up like pancakes covered in syrupy, false humility and a glob of spiritual pride with the butter of the desire to beat the shit out of anyone who disagreed.

"Mike," John continued. "I'd seriously object to your understanding of the word 'magos,' in that you said it actually means 'magician' and not 'wise man.'"

"That's not quite what I said."

"Yes, it is. I have listened to the recording twice since yesterday."

I'll bet he did. The jerk didn't have anything else to do since he retired. My anger rose.

"Yes," Elder Bill said. "But he also clarified that the term 'magos' in the time of Jesus referred to a person who was both a practicing magician and advisor to an authority figure, usually a king. This is especially true of the wise men that were from Persia."

"But that implies they were astrologers and that God spoke to them through astrology by watching the skies," countered Jude, a lawyer whose face was plastered on half the billboards in the poorer areas of Columbus. In one of those strange ironies that proved God — *if* He existed — had a strange sense of humor, Jude had been named after the Beatles song and not the book in the Bible.

"I think that is exactly what the text says, doesn't it?" Mike pointed out, smiling a bit.

No, Mike, don't smile. They will eat you alive. They can't stand to be laughed at.

Everyone got out their Bibles, and the room filled with the sound of rifled paper.

"My translation says 'wise man,'" John said, smiling again.

I couldn't take it any longer. I wanted to wipe that stupid smile off John's face with one of the large Bible concordances on the shelf behind him. It would certainly give new meaning to the phrase, "Thy Word shut my mouth."

I spoke up. "Yes, John, that's true. The Greek word's literal translation is 'wise man,' but if you look at the history of that word, it is directly applied to magicians. The people in the first century would not have recognized the distinction you're trying to make."

"So, Aidan, what you are both saying is that the Bible encourages magical practice? No wonder you love *Harry Potter*. I'm beginning to wonder about our seminary!"

"Listen, guys," Mike said, holding up his hand. "I can give you my books and all the reference material I used. All of them are from theologically conservative commentaries that say exactly what Aidan and I are saying. And also…" He broke off at the low rumble of my cell phone vibrating in my pocket.

I glanced down. "Olan is calling me again. I think I better answer while you all finish. He was in the hospital the other night, after all."

I didn't tell them that Olan just had acid reflux. I wanted an excuse to get out of the room. I stepped out and answered.

"Olan, is everything okay?"

"Well, no. Edna had another dream."

I sighed. "Okay, what was it?"

"She had a dream of Joseph again. He just kept saying one word over and over again."

"What did he say?"

"He drew his hand across his throat and said, 'Cut. Cut. Cut.'"

I felt as if someone had slid ice down my neck. I didn't want to tell him about the text message. "What do you think it means?"

"Don't know, but Joseph felt strongly about it."

"How do you know?"

"Edna said she could just feel it."

I couldn't reply. The part of me that had just given up faith in the supernatural wanted to write the whole thing off. But doubt about my doubt gnawed in the back of my head like a zombie.

I rubbed my eyes. "Olan, I don't know what to say. I'm too tired to think about it. We were in the middle of a session meeting when you called."

"Oh! Forgot all about that. Sorry, Aidan. At my age, the ol' attic gets full of cobwebs."

"Nah," I said. "I think it's what a Purdue education did to you."

"Ha, you ol' son of a gun. Call me back when you think you have an answer."

"Sure thing, Olan. Have Edna drink some water and go back to sleep. See you soon."

I walked back in the room and heard Mike talking in a raised voice.

"I am just saying that God can use any means He wants to get people's attention. I'm not saying He does it every day, but in this case, He was using something the wise men could understand ... a sign in the sky to point them to Jesus."

John shook his head, his face crunched in a grimace. "So, you are saying the Word of God is not enough? That He uses other means to bring people to Himself?"

"No, that isn't what I am saying. I'm just saying that God uses things in people's lives to help them see the truth, and the Bible puts the final touches on that."

Silence filled the room. John again cleared his throat and spoke in what he probably thought was a grand, serious, and pious voice. "Well, I think I finally understand where Mike is coming from, and I am disturbed. I think at the next meeting, we need to question whether Mike should be our pastor in the near future."

The meeting broke up, but no one stayed to chat, leaving Mike and me alone. He looked at me, shrugged, and started to get up.

"Mike, come on," I said. "Aren't you bothered in the least by all of this? You could lose your job."

"I doubt it will come to that. They've been after my job for months, and they haven't gotten anything. All they have are half-baked complaints that fall apart on close examination. They would have to go through the presbytery anyway."

I nodded. "True, I guess."

"Unfortunately, if they keep on like this, they will destroy our witness in the community," he said, leaning back in his chair, hands behind his head.

No, you screwing another woman will.

"I know. That's a problem," I said, staring at the floor.

Mike cocked his head. "Are the doubts still gnawing at you?"

"No, actually, that's over," I lied. "I think I was just feeling down this morning. Now, I'm just tired. It's been a long day."

Mike smiled and looked at me. His eyes were hollow and disturbing. There was no trouble. No panic. No guilt.

Then I knew. He didn't believe either. He had traded everything that was good about himself for the pleasure of a woman. The guy I looked up to — the one who taught me everything I knew — had no better answers than a woman dressed in red getting something that didn't belong to her.

"Yeah, I could use some rest myself. What did Olan want?"

"Something about ushers on Sunday. He forgot we were meeting tonight."

He smiled. "Wish I could forget about it."

"Yeah."

Mike gathered his things. "See you tomorrow, Aidan."

"Sure."

Enjoy your illicit fuck.

I didn't even remember locking up and getting in the car, but before long, I was on the highway heading south toward the city. My thoughts swirled around in a jumbled mess.

If this was who God was, I didn't want any part of Him or His people. His people were liars, hypocrites, and just downright mean. I always thought Christians should be nice, but they rarely were. And to me, that meant God didn't exist, or if He did, He was just as mean as His people. I realized that Dawkins and Crossan had done their work on me intellectually. My emotional ties had been the only thing holding me to my faith, and now they were gone.

Numbness seeped through me. I always thought the loss of faith would feel more like devastation, like a nuclear bomb going off in the soul. I felt nothing — just an aching, radioactive space.

chapter seven

I arrived home feeling beaten and bruised. Bishop danced in his crate, and I got him out for his night walk. We went down to his favorite spot, the condo complex lake that now had a thin layer of ice covering its surface. I thought he only liked it because other dogs left interesting smells for him to find.

As we walked around the lake, snow began to fall, and I looked up into the night sky. The descending white flakes looked like the hyperspace scenes in *Star Wars* and opened up the thoughtless void I had erected against my feelings. The questions poured through like floodwater, chaotic and messy.

Was everyone in the church like me? Did they all hide their doubts until some crisis set off a cratering of the soul? Why didn't anyone talk about it? Everyone was encouraged to share their feelings about everything else, so why not our doubt? Why hadn't I been warned about it?

I gripped Bishop's leash until it almost cut into my palm. I could understand that sort of attitude in the general population. Doubt wasn't exactly a comfortable conversation. When the subject came up at church, you could practically see the tumbleweeds blow past the altar. Why hadn't I learned about the possibility of losing my faith in seminary? Why hadn't there been any classes on what to do when ministry burned you out to the point of abandoning everything you were taught to believe?

A chill ran up my spine that had nothing to do with the cold. The God I once felt so close to me seemed to have vanished for good. I could no longer call my parents. I wouldn't call my brother. He had too much on his plate. And I didn't want to disturb Brian. Even those who cared about me didn't understand my struggles, or at least didn't understand them enough to help. Brian listened well, but I didn't need anyone to listen. I needed answers. I pulled my coat tight around me.

The snow fell harder, and a solid curtain of white descended from the sky. Bishop pawed around, looking for a place to take a dump or reading a pee message from another dog.

"So, Bishop, any answers in the urine that might help me? What does Josie have to say about the existence of God?" Josie was a little Chihuahua owned by my neighbor, Fred — a gay stockbroker who gave me fantastic investment advice. He dropped by with soup when I had the flu or even the slightest cold. The kind of guy who did what the church should be doing.

"Why? Bishop? Why is that? The church deserves for me to stay. They don't have a right to fire me."

Bishop looked at me with deep dark eyes and droopy cheeks.

"Yeah, I know. No hypocrisy."

I guess I had been fooling myself. I couldn't work at this job very long. Not with the situation like it was. I just needed time to figure out my escape plan. I would have to start looking at the want-ads. Maybe I could find a job where my training and experience in the ministry would be considered an asset rather than a liability.

My shoulders slumped. "All right, Bishop, let's get inside."

I turned to head back when Bishop stopped and stared across the lake. His ears stuck up, and he sat down, his head cocked with a look of expectation on his wrinkled face.

"Bishop, come on, let's go."

He turned to me then looked out over the lake again. As he did, a faint crackling echoed toward us as if something had stepped onto the thin layer of ice.

"What is it, an animal? Cat? Rabbit? Sorry, you can't go after it; you might fall in."

Bishop whined, and it sent an unexplained charge up my spine. Bishop hardly ever made any noises. He didn't bark at strange sounds in the night or even at other dogs. Amanda and I always thought his stillness came from the fact his previous owners had beaten him.

Bishop whined again and batted at the snow with his paw. He hadn't done that since ... no, that wasn't possible.

I knelt down beside him and patted his rump. "What is it, boy?"

The noise of the ice crackling moved closer as if someone was popping a sheet of plastic bubble wrap. I peered into the snow but couldn't see any animal that might be attracting his interest. "Come on, boy. There's nothing there. Let's go inside."

He refused to move.

"Bishop, *come!*" I said, nipping him on the neck with my fingers, trying to assert dominance. I could never quite get him to obey.

He looked at me and gave me a muted woof.

"Come on, I'm freezing my ass off and..."

A loud crack caught my attention. I looked up from Bishop's eyes, and goose bumps erupted all over my body. My heart thumped in my chest, and I took deep cold breaths to slow it down.

Bare footprints appeared in the snow over the ice around halfway across the lake. I looked to see if there was anyone nearby and saw no one. The footprints kept appearing and formed a path in our direction.

I grabbed Bishop by the collar. "Come on, Bishop, let's *go!*"

The damn dog refused to move and woofed again.

"Bishop, I mean it!" My own voice rose to almost a shriek. "Let's go!"

The footprints continued to crunch their way toward us. They were bare feet, just like the ones at Olan and Edna's. They were larger than a kid's but not as large as a man's, indenting the snow with light pressure that barely broke its surface.

"Hello?" I called into the darkness.

No answer. I gripped Bishop's collar. The footprints stopped right in front of him. My legs went into lockdown as my breath came in short gasps.

Bishop whined and got up.

"Easy, boy. It's okay. Can't be what it looks like," I croaked.

Bishop bent his head down as if something was petting him. He let out another little woof.

My stomach clenched, and the goose bumps became an invading army. The hairs on my neck stood up, and I began to shake from a chill that had nothing to do with the temperature. He stared at the footprints, his ears pricked straight up, and his hair bristled. He looked around and began to bark.

"What is it, boy?"

Dozens of bare footprints began to appear on the ice as it cracked with whatever put its weight on the dusted surface. My scalp started to prickle, and when I touched the metal on Bishop's collar, I received a small shock.

Whispers began to my right. I couldn't make out any coherent sentences.

"Hello? I can't understand you. Could you speak up?"

The whispers became more urgent, but they still didn't make any sense.

"Okay, funny joke. You got me. Come on out."

No response — just more whispering.

"Well, I'm going inside. Don't let your feet get frozen or anything."

I tugged hard at Bishop's leash, and he finally gave way with a reluctant walk forward. He bent his head again and tried to lick whatever had touched him.

As I turned to drag Bishop back to the condo, I heard one phrase. "Find the Priest."

"What priest?" I answered.

"The Guardian. Find him. He's the only one who..."

"Who? What?" I called.

No Answer.

"The Guardian? What the hell are you talking about?"

Nothing.

I dragged Bishop back to the condo as he kept staring back at the lake. I shut the door, ran upstairs, and splashed warm water on my face.

What was going on? Hallucinations brought on by stress? If so, Olan must've been stressed out too. No, it couldn't be that. Maybe someone was pulling an elaborate prank on me. If so, I wanted to know how they did it. It was the best I'd ever seen.

That thought made me laugh a little, and I heard the jingle of Bishop's tags as he thumped down onto the floor. He woofed at me as he sat in the frame of the bathroom door.

"What was that out there, Bishop?"

He looked at me and woofed again.

I laughed. "I know it's probably our imagination. Too much stress for the both of us lately, huh? Maybe we should take a vacation. We are both starting to see things. Maybe I will take you to a doggie therapist, and you can tell her what a horrible owner I am. Or maybe we can go on *Dr. Phil* and work out our problems as he calls us both idiots."

He looked up at me with sad eyes.

I patted his head. "Let's go to sleep."

I got into bed and stared at the ceiling. Bishop laid down next to me and whined.

"It's okay, boy, go to sleep."

A few moments later, I heard his loud, slow breathing as his paws stretched out to take over his side of the bed.

I was awake most of the night, the sound of crackling ice in my head and the sight of bare footprints filling the in-between places of sleep and wakefulness.

chapter eight

"Pastor Schaeffer?"

A voice brought me back from the world of invisible crunching footprints, woofing dogs, and worrying about my sanity.

I smiled. "I'm sorry, Julie, just thinking about what you said. Please, go on."

"It's okay. I was just saying I don't feel like Jake listens to me. He ignores me, and well, he hasn't touched me in months."

Jake and Julie Evans, a couple who had only been married for a few years, had come to me for marriage counseling. Why they sought marital advice from a single guy whose last relationship had blown up in his face, I had no idea.

To be honest, I struggled to have compassion in marital counseling. Most of the problems I counseled weren't really problems, just people neck deep in their own selfishness. I thought married people forgot what it was like to be single and alone, so they stopped being grateful for the presence of the other person.

"Jake, how would you respond to that?"

"Well, she's kind of let herself go a bit. I find myself not attracted to her anymore."

I fought the urge to strangle him. Julie was about five foot four inches, curly blonde hair, beautiful blue eyes, and weighed, maybe, one hundred and thirty pounds. I had seen their wedding pictures at a cookout they had at their house. She had probably gained ten pounds since they were married, if that.

Jake had been pushing three-hundred and twenty pounds on his six foot frame. In the past year, he had gone workout crazy and shed eighty pounds, an amount that would have neared a hundred except for the muscle weight he had added. No doubt it improved his looks as women in the church were always fawning over him and giggling at his stupid-ass jokes. Personally, I liked him better when he was fat and not an asshole.

Julie looked at Jake with hurt in her eyes. This conversation could spiral out of control if I didn't get a handle on it. Although a part of me wanted to see Julie claw his eyes out, I thought better of it.

"Jake, here is a good place for us to work on communication," I said. "Do you think there might be a better way to say that?"

He sat back in his chair, crossed his legs, and fixed his gaze on me. "I don't know."

I fought the urge to roll my eyes. "Try speaking in a gentler tone for one, and use words like, 'I feel like' or 'this is what I think.' That way, it doesn't seem like you're attacking her."

"Seems kind of girly."

"There is nothing girly about treating your wife with gentleness and respect, Jake. The Bible says that…"

I couldn't bring myself to finish the sentence. My vacant faith wouldn't permit the words to come out. I had been using the phrase "The Bible says" all my faith-filled life. Now, it felt like a curse. I coughed to cover it up.

"I thought the Bible said that wives are supposed to submit to their husbands on everything."

Not when you are being a total shithead!

"Not in everything, Jake, and it also calls you to gently love your wife." I sighed. "I don't want to put all the blame on you, but any sane person can see that Julie has not 'let herself go.' You have."

He looked down at his flat stomach and back up with a puzzled look.

"I don't mean in body. I mean in your personality and the way you treat your wife. It might be time to put your focus on pleasing her rather than yourself."

You would have thought that I slapped him and called him a bitch. He had this amazing and gorgeous woman who, for some reason, loved a total jackass. He should be thanking, well, *someone*, every day of his life.

"You're a preacher," Jake said. "Aren't you supposed to get her to submit to what I want?"

"I..."

The pager on my desk phone rang, and I answered.

"Sherry, I'm in the middle of a counseling session."

"I know, Pastor Aidan, but this caller is very insistent. She called yesterday, didn't you get the message I left on your desk?"

The printed message. I had forgotten all about it. Damn, I wish Sherry would just use email. "I did, but I just forgot to read it. Who is it anyway?"

"Detective Jennifer Brown from the Columbus Police Department."

Jake and Julie stared at me.

"I'm sorry, Sherry, did you say the Columbus Police?"

"I did." Her tone rebuked me for my idiocy.

"Okay, put her through." I turned to Jake and Julie. "I'm sorry you two, this will only take a moment."

I held the phone back to my ear. "This is Pastor Schaeffer, can I help you?"

"Pastor Schaeffer, this is Detective Jennifer Brown, Columbus Police Department. How are you this morning?" She spoke in a Scarlett Johansson voice. Low but feminine.

"Fine, detective. How are you?"

I smiled at Jake and Julie to assure them.

"Good, thank you. I was wondering if you had any time to come down to the station this afternoon."

What in the world?

"Hold on, let me check." I looked at my schedule. "Sure, but may I ask what this is about?"

"Of course. We think you might have some information we need to clear up some points in an ongoing investigation."

"Can I ask about what you are investigating?"

"I would rather not say over the phone. We prefer to handle this sort of thing at the station because officially we have to record our conversation. Typical police procedure. I'm sure you understand."

I paused. "Sure, just let me know the time and place."

"Say, one o'clock at the main building downtown?"

"Sounds good."

"Great, see you then. Thank you very much, Pastor Schaeffer."

"No problem, detective, talk to you soon."

I hung up the phone and turned back to Jake and Julie. "Now, where were we?"

"Are you sure you want to go on?" Julie asked.

"Yeah, it's no big deal. They just need some advice on some things."

Jake butted in. "So, you were insulting me."

I held up my hands. "Not insulting you, Jake. I'm just pointing out that since we started a few weeks ago, you've resisted any notion that you bear some of the responsibilities for the condition of this marriage. I've tried to be tactful, but that wasn't working."

"Seems to me you're being a pansy."

I gripped the handles on my chair. "I think we are done for the day. Think over what I said."

I did the obligatory end-of-session prayer, following the standard Protestant formula that gives the irony to our hatred of written prayers. "Dear Lord, we know we are broken people, and we confess our brokenness. O Lord, help us to admit our sin and need for You. Show us in Your word how to relate to one another. We ask this in Your Son's name, Amen."

Jake and Julie left the office as Jake took the time to give me, what he probably thought, was an intimidating glare. I'd seen it a million times, guys like him, heavily into compensation when their manhood got challenged in any way. I figured he would just go out and buy a bigger truck or something.

I sat back in my chair to think about the phone call from Detective Brown. *What in the world was that about?* I had enough to deal with right now. Maybe it was the parking ticket I got a few days ago. No, I had another week to pay that. Maybe they needed some sort of theological piece of information? If that was the case, why did they call me? I was an assistant pastor at a fairly small church, not really what you would call consulting material. I always pictured that kind of role to be reserved for pastors of mega-churches or respected scholars.

I worked hard to finish my tasks for the day so I could be out of the office by noon. There wasn't much to do except plan the worship service, write a few emails, and make an outline for Sunday school.

As I made my way out the door, I stopped by Sherry's desk. "Sherry, would you please send my phone messages by email? I lose paper all the time, and it would really help me keep track."

She looked at me over her reading glasses. "I don't like sending email. People might access my private information by email."

"Sherry, no one can get your information by just sending an email."

"Not what my friends at the coffee shop say."

Sherry was a part of a women's study group that Mike and I had dubbed the "Four Horsewomen of the Apocalypse." They didn't really study the Bible. They just sat around and traded conspiracy theories for two hours every Saturday morning.

"Right, got it. Thanks, Sherry."

chapter nine

I parked on the street and walked up to the police station. The white walls and green pyramid roof seemed to breathe authority and warning to anyone thinking of breaking the law. As I passed under the seal of the city of Columbus above the doors, I felt a weird sense of guilt, as if I had just been out committing a crime.

The grim old guard poked and prodded to make sure I had no firearms on my body. I thought about the standard "date" jokes, but the people manning the security checkpoint didn't seem like the joking kind.

I went up to the information desk. "Hi, I'm looking for Detective Jennifer Brown."

An African-American woman with graying hair gave me a warm smile. "I can help you, darlin', but I need to know who you are."

I smiled. "I'm Pastor Aidan Schaeffer. I have an appointment with her at one o'clock."

She looked at her sheet. "Ah, right. Pastor, if you could sign in here. I will give you your visitor's badge."

I signed my name and took the badge.

"Go down the hall, take the elevator to the fifth floor," she said. "There's a lady who will take you to Detective Brown. I'll let them know you are coming."

"Thank you very much."

"No problem, take care."

I followed the directions and was met by a middle-aged white lady in an officer's uniform.

"Pastor Schaeffer?"

"Yes, ma'am."

"Please follow me."

She led me past a group of desks and cubicles. I saw pictures of families, wanted posters, handcuffs, and various other cop materials.

A sign hung over a door that read "Major Case Squad." I had heard somewhere that they handled major murder investigations. That thought made my heart beat a little quicker.

The cop took me to a small room. "Could I get you anything, Pastor Schaeffer?"

"Some water would be nice, thanks."

She left the room, and I pulled out a metal folding chair from a small table. The room had been painted a dull white, and no pictures hung on the walls. A darkened window to my left made me wonder why it had been put there before I realized it was one-way glass, and there might be people on the other side.

This was an interrogation room.

I tried to look calm and not fidget. After fifteen minutes in the room alone, it became hard to sit still. Finally, the lady cop came back with a water bottle.

"Sorry about the delay, pastor. Here is your water. The detective will be in shortly."

"Um, ma'am? I hope it won't be too long. I have some other appointments later this afternoon."

"No problem. Just a few more minutes."

A few more minutes turned into another fifteen. I looked at the time on my phone and decided to play a few rounds of Texas hold 'em.

I finished one hand, then another, and then another.

Where was this detective? This was getting a bit ridiculous.

I began to text my brother when at last, a woman walked into the room.

I missed her initial greeting because I couldn't help staring. Her black shiny hair hung down to her shoulders. Her eyes were a distracting shade of green. Her body reminded me of the curves on a sound wave diagram. A slight hint of coconut wafted toward me as she walked over to the table.

"Pastor Schaeffer?"

I nodded. "I am sorry, detective, a bit distracted this morning. Never been in a police station before, believe it or not."

She looked me over and gave me a polite smile. I noticed a thin ragged scar that stretched from the side of her mouth.

How did that happen?

"And we don't get too many ministers here either," she said as she sat down opposite me. She offered me her hand. I took it and marveled at her soft, yet firm handshake. "It's nice to meet you, Pastor Schaeffer."

"Aidan, please, detective. I don't insist on 'Pastor' very much."

"You can call me Jennifer."

She smiled, and I had the chance to be distracted all over again. I'd bet this woman got criminals to confess to anything just by being in the room with them. I'd probably confess to any crime she wanted.

"Do you mind if my boss joins us?" she asked.

"Not at all."

She motioned at the window and confirmed my suspicion. "Sorry, I'm a new detective. They put us in these rooms so they can observe me. I don't like it much."

"I can relate. I've taken ordination exams."

She smiled and raised her eyes. "Oh?"

"Yep, wrote for fifteen hours and then defended what I wrote for about five hours in an oral exam in front of forty people, all biblical scholars."

"Wow, and I thought preachers had an easy life."

"Hardly."

After a soft knock on the door, a salt and pepper-haired man with an athletic build walked into the room. The guy looked like he probably ran marathons for fun. His suit had a crisp just-back-from-the-dry-cleaners look. He had a pleasant relaxed face, but the intense blue-gray shine of his eyes made me feel like I was being X-rayed.

He held out his hand. "Pastor Schaeffer, Lieutenant Scott Weaver. Thank you for coming in and talking with us."

"No problem, lieutenant. And please, it's just Aidan."

"Great, call me Scott then."

He sat in a chair backed up to the blackened window and waved his hand to Jennifer. "Don't let me interrupt."

Jennifer cleared her throat. "For the record, Aidan, could you state your full name?"

"Aidan Chester Schaeffer." I tried not to grimace. I hated that middle name. It had been one of those old family names that, for some reason, people couldn't let die.

If Jennifer found it funny, she didn't show it. "And your occupation?"

"I'm the Assistant Pastor of Ministries at John Knox Presbyterian Church."

"How long have you been at the church?"

"Um, it'll be two years in March."

"Thank you and your address please?"

"197 North Cove, Columbus, Ohio."

"Good, thank you." Jennifer wrote something down. She took out a picture and slid it across the table. "Do you recognize this person?"

She handed me a picture. I looked at it, and my throat tightened. Amanda.

"Yeah, yeah I do. That's Amanda McDougal, my ex-fiancée."

Jennifer tapped her pencil. "When was the last time you spoke with Ms. McDougal?"

"May 15th, 8 p.m."

She raised her eyebrows. "A bit precise on that one, aren't we?"

I sighed. "It wasn't a pleasant conversation."

"Can you please relate the nature of this conversation?"

I stared at Jennifer's face. It may as well have been a map written in French, full of information but giving none of it away. "I'm sorry, did I miss something? Why are you asking me questions about Amanda? Is she okay?"

She looked at Lieutenant Weaver, who nodded. "Aidan, I'm sorry to have to tell you this, but Amanda is dead."

My vision blurred as though I had suddenly become aware of the earth's rotation. I had not realized how much I still loved Amanda until that moment. What had been a dull ache in the back of my soul now sprung up in a quick, sharp pain, like someone knifing me in the gut.

"Are you okay?" Jennifer asked.

"I'm sorry, I … I just can't believe…"

My throat constricted as tears built in my eyes.

"Take a minute. It's okay," Lieutenant Weaver said.

I fought to get a hold of myself. "How?"

"Before I explain how, you must understand this is a private investigation. The identity of the victim has just become known as of a few hours ago. The family was just informed this morning. We have not released the name of the victim to the press. All they know is that there has been a brutal death. We are trying to let the family have some time."

I thought about Amanda's mom and sister. They had endured so much devastation in their lives already, and this would be the worst for them. Amanda had been the rock in her family after her father had died in a car accident a few years ago.

"I understand." The tears began to build in my eyes again. I fought the urge to let the dam open.

"We have every reason to believe that Amanda was murdered."

I nodded. "I kind of guessed that but how?"

"We'll get to that, but first we need to ask some more questions."

"If you think it will help," I said, recovering some control in my voice.

Jen nodded and wrote something down on a small notepad.

"Where were you on January 6th, at about three in the morning?"

"That was what, two days ago?"

"Yes."

"I imagine I was at home sleeping."

Jen looked at me with her left eye scrunched in a skeptical twitch. "Are you sure?"

"Yes, wh … no! Wait, I'm sorry. I was at the hospital."

"What were you doing at the hospital at three in the morning? Cut yourself doing yard work?"

I got a bit annoyed. "It wasn't for me."

"Then, why?" Jen pressed.

I gripped the water bottle. "Detective Brown, I'm a minister, and like doctors we often get calls in the middle of the night. On that night, or rather that morning, I got the call at about one o'clock. A member of our congregation called to say her husband was having severe chest pains."

Jen traced a finger along her scar. "And you rushed right off to be there?"

"I did. Even if I wasn't on call, I would have."

"On call?"

"The senior pastor and I take turns being on emergency pastoral call."

"Can you describe what that looks like?"

I folded my arms against my chest. "Whenever there is an emergency in the church, for example, if someone goes to the hospital, plumbing breaks, or little Julie has just gotten pregnant … whatever it is, we drop what we are doing and go."

"I see." Jennifer continued writing on her notepad. "Can you tell me their names?"

"Of course, Olan and Edna Wilkes. It turns out Olan just had a bad case of acid reflux, thank God, but it took them about seven hours to get the diagnosis."

"You stayed the whole time? Why?"

"Um, because I didn't want Edna to be alone while her husband might have been having a heart attack."

"You care that much?"

Enough was enough. "I'm sorry, detective, does this have anything to do with Amanda's murder?"

"It could."

"What, are you trying to establish my alibi? Am I a suspect or something?" I stared at them, not understanding the direction the conversation had taken.

"That's exactly what we are trying to do," Lieutenant Weaver said.

I couldn't believe it. Me? A murder suspect?

"You're serious?"

"Yes, we are," Weaver said.

"How did you come up with that?"

"We'll get to that, Pastor Schaeffer," Jennifer said.

So, she was back to Pastor Schaeffer. "No, I don't want to *get to that*, I want to know now!"

Jennifer stared at me. I couldn't figure out how eyes that beautiful could look so cold. "Pastor Schaeffer, we will get to everything in due process. For now, let me ask the questions."

"I'm sorry, but this is all a bit much."

She nodded. "I'm sure it is, but if your story checks out about the hospital, you're in the clear. I'm having an officer call the Wilkes' right now, but in the meantime, I need to ask you some more questions."

I crossed my legs and sat back in the chair. "Okay."

"I want to return to that last conversation with Ms. McDougal. Describe the nature of your relationship about that time."

"Do I have to? It's not really one of my finer moments."

She nodded. "Please."

I sighed. "Well, to begin with, breaking up was not my idea. She met some other pastor. I never found out who it was, and she said she needed someone more spiritual in her life."

"And how did you react?" She wrote on her legal pad, not looking at me.

"Well, I guess I exploded. We were engaged, got a dog together, and were making plans for the future. It was like being punched in the face. I really thought we were going to spend our lives together. I called her every name I could think of."

Jennifer raised her eyebrows at me. "That's not very spiritual of you."

Yeah, well I'm not very spiritual anymore, so stick it up your ass!

"Ministers are people too, as some people seem to forget. Just like cops, I would imagine," I growled.

She looked at Weaver, who gave me a slight smile. "Good point," he said. "And you haven't talked to her since?"

"No, I haven't. I wanted to call her all the time, but my stupid pride got in the way. I didn't want to be the pathetic ex, whining about how good we were together."

"And so you just let her go? Forgot about your love for her?" Jen stared at me in disbelief.

I threw up my hands. "Yeah, that's exactly what I did. It's also why I haven't slept soundly for the past six months or stopped complaining to my friends about how lonely I am now. You can ask them if you like."

"So, no emails? No text messages? Nothing?" Weaver pressed.

"No, not in the least. She didn't even come over to my place to pick up the stuff she had left at my condo."

Jennifer raised her eyebrows. "You two lived together?"

I rolled my eyes. "No, detective. If we did, you can bet your gun I would've been fired. But she did spend a lot of time at my place."

"Do you still have her stuff?"

I ran my fingers through my hair. "Yeah, I probably should give it to Ann, Amanda's mom."

"You will need to give it to us," Jennifer said.

She looked at Lieutenant Weaver again, who nodded.

"Pastor Schaeffer," she continued, "do you recognize the handwriting on this sheet of paper?" She passed a photocopy over to me.

"Yeah, it's Amanda's." I took the note in my hand and forced it not to shake. I cleared my throat and read. "Aidan, he is the one. Find him at the Caves of the Dead. 614-181-0844."

I looked up at Jennifer. "That's my phone number."

She uncrossed her legs and leaned forward. "This note was found on Amanda's body. As you can see, it seems to indicate you are the murderer."

Smartly done, accusing me of murder without actually saying so. I guess I couldn't blame them. But seeing as I was innocent, it didn't worry me.

"You're kidding me, right?"

"No, I am quite serious. In fact, we have thought about arresting you." Jennifer reached for something behind her back. I could only assume it was handcuffs.

I had no idea whether she was bluffing. I didn't watch many police shows, so I didn't know if she could just arrest me because she felt like it. I looked at the note again. "You might want to wait before you put me in handcuffs."

For the first time, she looked puzzled. "Yeah, why?" she said, arching an eyebrow.

"Because of the comma."

"What are you talking about?"

I held up the piece of paper. "Here. Notice what it says. It says, 'Aidan,' comma, meaning, this message is addressed to me, it seems. Or she wanted it to get to me."

"Why would a comma make a difference?"

I let out a little snort. "Because Amanda is … was … an English teacher who was anal about grammar. If she had wanted to tell you that I was the killer, she would have been more precise."

Jennifer frowned. "People forget themselves when they are about to die."

Every horror movie, serial killer, and dissecting video I had seen began to show in my mind. Every dead body had Amanda's face on it. Bodies with arms missing, stab wounds, blank, staring eyes.

"Pastor Schaeffer?"

"I'm sorry; I'm just having a hard time with this. I really loved her, you know." I took a drink of my water to wash down the lump in my throat. "And as for the comma, you don't know Amanda."

"Enlighten me."

I paused with a little smile on my face as the tears began to run down my cheek. I wiped them with the back of my hand. "When I first met her, I preached on a Sunday when our pastor was gone. Amanda had decided to come to our church to visit. She walked up to me after the service and told me my sermon was great, but the grammar was terrible."

"And then what, you asked her out to lunch?" Jennifer rolled her eyes.

I smiled. "That is exactly what I did, actually."

"Gutsy of you," Weaver commented with a small smile.

I shrugged. "Couldn't really help myself."

Jennifer didn't smile and continued to stare at me.

A knock on the door interrupted us before an overweight, mustached man popped his head in the room. "Detectives?"

"If you'll excuse us a minute, Pastor Schaeffer," Jennifer said. They walked out and closed the door.

My muscles ached as if someone had just beaten me senseless. I realized I had been tensed up during the entire exchange. I wanted to cry again, but I didn't want to give the watchers behind the glass a chance to see it. I wanted to be alone at home, and be really, really piss drunk in the grand tradition of my Irish ancestors.

The detectives came back ten minutes later. I noticed their demeanor had changed, and their faces were a bit more relaxed.

"Well, it seems your story checks out," Jennifer said. "The Wilkes' are coming down to the station to file their report."

"Great, so now the whole church will know I've been suspected of murder."

Her unreadable face changed to a wrinkle of disgust. "Pastor Aidan, trust us to handle things a little better than that."

"Trust you? You have me come down here without telling me why and tell me the woman I loved was killed. And then, you nearly accuse me of her murder. Sorry if I don't participate in a trust fall with you anytime soon."

I thought she was going to jump over the table at me, but she leaned forward and pointed a finger at me. "It's my job. There are things I have to do sometimes that I don't like. Surely a minister understands that."

She had me there, but I didn't want to admit it.

"Yeah, well, I don't have the power to ruin people's lives and reputations with a false accusation."

"Of course you do; you're a minister. Don't you do that all the time?"

I about came out of my chair when Lieutenant Weaver broke in.

"Okay, that's enough, Pastor Schaeffer, it had to be done. You can deal with that by knowing that we are just trying to figure out who killed Amanda."

"So what you really mean is, grow up, be a man, and help us any way you can now, is that it?" I said as I ran my hands through my hair.

"That's about right," he said, taking a sip of his coffee.

"Fair enough."

Jennifer remained silent but stared at me with her arms crossed. "I know it's painful, but can you tell us anything about this boyfriend?"

I shook my head. "No, she didn't say much about him, except that he was more mature and spiritual, whatever that means."

"So, maybe older?" Jennifer pressed.

I scratched my arm. "I suppose that's possible. She didn't like me spending time on my PlayStation or watching *SpongeBob SquarePants*."

Jennifer raised her eyebrow. "You watch *SpongeBob SquarePants*?"

"I like cartoons, sue me. I watch it with my brother's kids when I visit. They got me hooked. I also like Stanley Kubrick films, quiet country music, and a nice smooth whisky. Do you want all my hopes and dreams now?"

Lieutenant Weaver interrupted. "What about the message? I'm willing to bet she was trying to tell you something, but what could it be?"

"Truthfully, lieutenant, I have no idea. I know it looks weird. I just don't have any explanation for you. My bitterness would say that 'he' refers to whoever this boyfriend might be. Seeing as I didn't know him, she might be telling me something else." I paused. "May I ask where she was murdered?"

Jen looked at Lieutenant Weaver who nodded. "She was murdered at the Confederate Cemetery."

I scrunched up my face. "Confederate Cemetery? As in where dead soldiers from the South are buried? We have one of those in Columbus?"

Weaver gave Jennifer a thin smile. "Ah, here's another one! You owe me ten bucks, Jen. I told you most people in Columbus didn't know that."

She rolled her eyes. "That's because most people in Columbus are stupid when it comes to their own history."

A bit pissed by their banter, I broke in. "I'm actually not from Columbus. I'm from Indianapolis."

"No excuse," she said.

"Okay, whatever. How was she killed?"

"We aren't releasing details of that right now, not even to the family," Weaver said.

"Why?"

They glanced at each other again. "Let's just say there are elements to this case we prefer the public didn't know as of yet," Jennifer said.

I nodded. "I just want to be helpful."

"We don't have any more questions for you, Pastor Schaeffer." Weaver stood up. "Thank you for coming in. I need to run, so Jennifer is going to finish up."

He left, and Jennifer and I stared at each other.

"Listen, Detective Brown, Jennifer, I'm sorry I snapped. I'm just in shock, and my emotions aren't always in check. I have a bit of a temper."

She smiled, her lips tight. "Me too, and I'm sorry."

"Well, let's agree to forgive each other then."

"Fair enough." She handed me her card. "If there is anything you can do to help us in this case, please call. If we need to talk to you again, may we call you?"

"Of course. I just want you to find the sick bastard or bastards who did this."

"I didn't know that pastors used that word."

"Only me. I have a problem with my mouth."

"Well, thank you for coming in." She offered her hand. The touch sent a sensation through me that I hadn't felt in a while. She took her hand away as our eyes met. "I'm sorry, Aidan, I'm sure she meant a lot to you."

"Thank you, she did." My throat tightened again. "I guess I always thought she would come back to me at some point."

She nodded, fingering her scar. "I understand."

"Let me know if there is anything else you need." I walked out of the room not waiting for her response.

chapter ten

‽

"That's been my past forty-eight hours, Brian, finding out my spiritual leader is having an affair and almost being arrested for murder." I held the phone between my head and shoulder as I stirred my homemade spaghetti sauce for dinner.

"Excuse me, but holy shit!"

"No excuse needed, and I hope your wife is not around to hear your language." Ashley was one of those women who blushed when she said "crap," but since she was one of the kindest, most beautiful women I had ever met, I forgave her for that flaw. For some reason, she loved me like a brother, even though I had been a corrupting influence on her husband.

"Nah, she's at her book club tonight." He paused. "I can't believe Amanda is…" he stuttered, "gone. I'm sorry; that sounded so heartless."

"It's okay, man. Seriously." I added the onion I had chopped up. My eyes watered, though I didn't think it was because of that.

"So, you didn't do it, did you?"

"Are you serious?" I slammed down the wooden spoon.

"I just had to ask. It's good to know I'm not friends with a murderer."

"This is serious, Brian! Amanda's dead!"

"I know, which is why I asked."

"What would you have done if I had confessed?" I wrinkled my brow.

"Come on, it's not like I really believe you did it. Don't get your panties in a twist. But you have to admit, you would have been wondering the same thing if it had been me."

There was an uncomfortable silence. I knew that he really didn't believe I would have killed Amanda, or anyone else for that matter. Still, for a moment, I felt very alone.

"Aidan? Are you mad at me?"

"No, not really. Natural enough question, I suppose." And it was. I had to keep telling myself that. Whenever a woman was murdered, so I had read in P.D. James' novels, the lover or ex-lover was usually the first to be suspected.

"Who do you think really did it?"

I took a sip of beer. "I'm not sure. Maybe it was this guy she left me for, but I never actually met him, of course. I probably would have kicked his ass if I had."

I closed my eyes as I fought another round of tears.

"Most likely." Brian agreed. "So, what are you going to do?"

"I don't know. Try to help in any way I can. I still love her, or loved her, so I feel I owe her something." My voice cracked. Thankfully, Brian didn't notice.

"Even after six months of not talking to her?"

"Yeah, I guess so. Weird, isn't it?"

"No, Aidan, it isn't weird at all."

I stirred the spaghetti sauce. Bishop nosed my leg, and I fed him a dog treat. I guessed Brian was right. It wasn't weird. I still loved Amanda but tried to deny it the way most men did when they had their pride destroyed — by acting as if it didn't bother us at all. Inwardly, we asked pretty much the same questions women did. Did I do something wrong? Could I have made changes to make her stay? Treated her better? I hadn't always been the most considerate person in the world.

I felt a totally irrational desire to prove to her that I loved her by finding her killer.

"I don't know how I can help, Brian. I have no idea where to start looking."

"Did she leave any personal stuff at the condo? Things you might be able to look through?"

"No, there's nothing but a few CD's and other small stuff I have to give to the police. Wait..." I said, closing my eyes as I thought.

"What is it?" Brian asked.

"I just remembered that I have a key to our storage shed. I hadn't gotten around to getting my stuff out because I didn't want to take the chance that I would run into her."

"Well, give the attractive Detective Brown a call and have her personally escort you."

"Who said she was attractive?"

He laughed. "You keep talking about her in 'the voice.'"

"What the heck are you talking about?"

"You make this voice that you use when you think a woman is really good looking. You use it every time you talk about my wife."

"Brian, I..."

He laughed again. "Don't worry about it, man. Can't be married to an attractive, fantastic woman and expect to be the only guy who notices."

I chuckled. "Yeah, she is the total package." I stirred my dinner. "Anyway, I don't think I'll be finding my total package in Detective Brown. We didn't exactly part on good terms."

"Hey, call it romantic tension."

"Right. It really gets me going that she thinks I'm a murderer." I paused. "Besides, Brian, I really loved Amanda."

"I know you did."

I tasted the sauce. It needed a few more minutes. "I don't even know if we'll find anything in that shed. I don't really want to go there."

"Why not?" Brian prodded.

"Because it's near a grave…"

I dropped the spoon on the floor.

"Aidan?"

"Caves of the Dead. I know what Amanda was trying to tell me."

"What?"

"When we first got the shed, we noticed the graveyard right behind it. We made a joke that the storage sheds were like the caves of the dead."

"Wow. Maybe you should call Detective Brown now."

"It's eleven o'clock. I think it can probably wait until the morning."

"I wouldn't wait. Call her. In these types of cases, from what I understand, time is everything."

I poured a glass of wine and took a big sip. "You're right. I do need to run though, the sauce is about ready."

"Okay, but we didn't even get to talk about your faith."

The shift in topic threw me. I was not ready to talk about this subject with him. I didn't want to tell him I had lost it completely. It was still too painful, and I didn't feel like being the object of his pity. There was too much other stuff to deal with.

"It's fine, getting a little better."

"Even with the whole Mike situation?"

"Yeah, I mean, that didn't help, but I got over it."

"Good. I was praying that you would. Keep me posted."

"You bet. See you, bro."

I picked up the phone and looked at the card Jennifer had given me. She had told me to call if anything else came up. I guess this qualified, but I couldn't help being nervous.

Come on, Aidan. It's not like you are calling a girl for a date.

And she wasn't just a girl. She was a detective investigating the murder of my ex-fiancée — a murder I had some sort of link to — so it was doubtful she would ever think about me in any other way. I kept telling myself that, but I couldn't stop thinking of her smile and her body, and the way she smelled. I closed my eyes and shook my head.

This had to be all business.

I dialed her number.

"Hello, Pastor Aidan."

"Caller I.D.?" I asked.

"No, I'm a cop. We have a sixth sense about who is calling us, part of the training."

"Uh, right."

"That was a joke." Jennifer chuckled.

"Right, I know, sorry." This hadn't started well.

"Did you have something for me? I'm kinda busy right now."

I wondered if I had interrupted a date or something. "I just remembered something about Amanda, or rather, something of hers that I have."

"What's that?"

"I have a key to her personal storage shed."

There was silence at the other end of the phone.

"Detective Brown?"

"Yes, I'm here. Why didn't you mention this before?"

"Well, I guess shock would be a good word. I hadn't thought about the storage shed in a while."

"Do you have the key in your possession?"

I walked up to my bedroom and took out the box with Amanda's stuff. The key was attached to yellow receipt paper. "I'm staring at it right now."

"I'm gonna have to get a warrant to get into that place."

"No, you won't. I have the password to get in, and I'm on the lease papers. I had some stuff there."

"What kind of stuff?"

"Just stupid crap. Some books, old CDs, I think."

"I'm on another case right now, but I need to see inside the shed. Can I pick you up first thing tomorrow?"

"Uh, yeah, I have to run to the church in the morning. I could meet you there at eight."

"Eight works for me." Her voice became soft. "Listen, I'm sorry about today. I came off like a bitch."

Well, this is interesting.

"It's really okay; you were just doing your job."

"Yeah, but it wasn't just that."

"What?"

She paused. "This case is creeping me out."

I looked at the phone. Was this the same hard woman I had talked to this morning?

"Aidan, are you there?"

"Yes, sorry, just making sure I heard you. Can I ask why?"

"I think it would be better if I showed you tomorrow. Actually, you might be able to help the investigation. So, see you in the morning?"

"Right. See you then."

I sat down on the couch and rubbed Bishop's ears. My mind went to the soulless Xerox copy that had been Amanda's last words.

"Bishop, what was your mommy trying to tell us?"

He looked up and whined.

"I know, bud. I can't figure it out either." I tried to remember what Amanda told me about the guy she left me for. He was a head pastor at another church. She would not tell me anything about him because she knew I might figure out who it was. Amanda lived alone, so she had no roommate to talk with, and all her friends lived in Cleveland. So, I had little to go on.

I hoped the storage shed would have some answers.

I lifted the box to put it back in my closet when I noticed some photos stacked at the bottom. I pulled them out and saw Amanda's face, smiling at me. I glanced at our pictures. I saw the photos of our trip to Disney World with her family, a friend's wedding, and numerous barbecues. Each picture brought a memory, like the time I told her I loved her or the first time we kissed. Most of all, I remembered when I proposed to her in a boat on Lake Erie. We made love for the first time in the woods on Put-in-Bay Island. Christian guilt followed a desire to do it again and again.

She had almost been my wife, my total package, and now she was dead, murdered in some obscure, horrible way that not even seasoned detectives wanted to discuss.

Tears dropped onto my cheek, and I felt full-on sobs coming. Taking deep breaths, I stood up and stumbled down the stairs. My body shook, and I gasped. Going to the fridge, I opened it and pulled out four beers.

I drank the first one without even thinking. I popped open another and gulped it down almost as fast. The room began to spin as I took the other two with me to the couch.

Hopefully, by the time I got to the fourth beer, I would pass into oblivion and remember nothing. At least, for a little while.

chapter eleven

I awoke to the sound of the coffee alarm. My clothes were rumpled from falling asleep in them around four in the morning. Sleeping in my clothes made me feel as if I had done something vaguely naughty that would earn me the rebuke of my mother.

I sat up on the bed. Normally, at that point, I would have prayed, but that option was out. I just had to face the day alone.

With a sigh, I made my way to the bathroom. I lathered lime-green shaving cream in my hands and applied it to my face. As I stretched my face for the razor, a blast of cold air sent goose bumps up my body. I turned to look at the window and caught a blurred figure out of the corner of my eye. I whipped my head around and saw nothing even though it felt like there had been someone standing right next to me.

"Bishop?" I called out.

A loud crunching noise came from downstairs. It hadn't been Bishop. He was obviously too preoccupied with his bone.

I dabbed more cream on and began making slow, deliberate strokes down my face with the razor. The warmness of the water soothed my skin and nerves as I went back to work on the hard stubble. Another cold blast, but this time it lingered as if I had stepped into a freezer, and a blurry, woman-like figure moved just out of the corner of my sight. Surprised, I dug the razor into my cheek and a red line of blood formed on my skin.

"Who's there?" I yelped as I held my hand to my cheek.

I stopped the water and listened. No one. No sound.

"What's going on?"

I shifted my eyes back to the mirror to see if the image would return. It didn't. The temperature returned to normal, and a light scent of vanilla filled the air. Almost like Amanda's skin cream.

I finished getting ready and took Bishop out for a walk. A growing sense of unease filled the pit of my stomach. *It's just stress*, I kept telling myself. The last few days had been bad, the worst since my parents died in the fire a few years ago. I spent a few days in the hospital after their funeral. The shock caught up with my body and sent me into hallucinations and panic attacks accompanied by a strong desire to die.

The doctor told me the hallucinations might return at points of high stress in my life. This certainly qualified. Maybe I needed to go back to the doctor for a bit of help, but I had hated taking medication. It inhibited clear thought and made me tired.

"Or maybe, Bishop," I said as I returned him to his crate, "I just need to deal with it. What do you think?" A soft woof was the only reply, which probably meant, "I'm only a dog. I eat, sleep, and shit all over the clothes you leave on the floor. Can't help you if you are falling apart."

I drove to the church and went right into my office. I didn't feel like enduring Sherry's disapproving stares at my jeans and t-shirt which had a picture of a dinosaur and was emblazoned with the words "Never Forget."

I answered email and tried to read while I waited for Jennifer. I couldn't concentrate, so I began surfing the Internet. I lost track of time as I read idiotic comments by SEC fans on the ESPN Web site. By their remarks, you would think that no one north of the Mason

Dixon should ever bother picking up a football. I logged in and began writing a crushing argument as to why the Buckeyes were the best damn team in the land. A light knock on the door brought me back to reality.

"Pastor Aidan?"

A whiff of coconut reached my nose, and I turned around. Jennifer stood in front of me in tight gray slacks and a form-fitting black sweater. Her scarred mouth curved into a smile.

"Detective, er, Brown. Just finishing up some work."

"So, it's part of a pastor's job to defend the Buckeyes' honor? And it's Jennifer. Call me Jennifer, remember?"

I smiled. "Aidan then, none of the 'pastor' stuff, and yes, all self-respecting Ohioans must defend the honor of the Buckeyes. And is it part of your job to read over my shoulder?"

We both laughed. Our eyes met for the first time, and then she looked away to my shelves of books. "Have you read most of these?"

"Nah, they're just there to give me credibility. I think I got most of them at yard sales."

She laughed. "Seriously, you've read all of these?"

"Yeah, most of them, but some are just reference books. You know, Bible verses, cultural studies and all that."

Jennifer walked around and looked at the titles. "And you get a space of your own. I have a half-open cubicle down at the station."

"Yeah, saw that. That's gotta suck."

"It's not bad. You get used to it. Besides, I'm hardly at my desk anyway."

I stood up. "Sorry about my clothes. If I don't have appointments, I tend to dress down."

She smiled and played with her scar. "No worries. I don't normally dress this nice, but I need to talk with some families today from the case last night."

I put on my coat and then turned off the light.

"Oh, yeah, what happened last night?" I asked as we walked down the hall.

"Unlike the bloodbath in the cemetery, it was a routine drive by."

She stopped and shook her head. "Aidan, I'm sorry. I'm so used to talking with other cops."

I gave her a small smile. "It's okay. Really, don't worry about it."

"How are you this morning?" She searched my face.

"I'm ... well ... okay, I guess."

"It's tough to take. I know," she said as she touched my arm.

I nodded. "Do you ever get used to all of this?"

"Investigating murder? No, but you learn to deal with it."

"How?"

She frowned. "I don't really know. I try not to think about it much, that's one way. I guess the other is to be flippant and crass. This job can really mess you up. Some of my friends are functioning drunks, and most of us have no personal lives. It's hard to deal with the heart of human darkness and then turn it off, you know?"

"I can understand that. A lot of pastors are not only functioning drunks, but many are porn addicts. They're lonely, depressed, and isolated. Eventually, they crash and burn. I'm guessing between our two jobs, the flame out rate is the same."

"I bet." Jennifer looked away as we exited the church building.

"So, should I follow you?" I asked.

"Well, it would be easier if I just drove, if you don't mind."

The thought of being alone in the car with her got my blood pumping. The "other brain," as my dad, the seminary professor, used to call it, started to take over. At that point, I told the "primary" brain to take a vacation. It had done the work to lead me out of my faith and deserved some time off.

But then I thought about Amanda, how she died, and how much I still loved her.

We got into Jennifer's black Mustang.

"No siren?" I asked.

She smiled. "No, I use my own car, one of the privileges of being a detective." She sat there for a second with the car running.

"Jennifer, are you okay?"

"Yeah, trying to decide something."

"What?"

"Whether I should take you to the place where Amanda was murdered."

I had no desire to go, but I didn't want that tropical depression of unease to turn into a full-blown hurricane panic attack.

We rode in silence until we were on the road.

"There is something I want you to explain to me," Jennifer said.

I furrowed my brow. "What is it?"

"You'll see when we get there."

"I'm not a detective. Didn't Lieutenant Weaver have any ideas?"

"I don't need another detective's opinion. I need a preacher's."

"I don't understand."

"You will." She looked at me as we waited at the light. "What did you do last night?"

I cried myself to sleep.

"Oh, just kind of fell into bed. I didn't feel well, must have been something I ate, or maybe being accused of murder had something to do with it."

I hate when I don't think before I speak.

Jennifer frowned. "I explained why we suspected you, and I apologized."

"I know ... I'm sorry ... I suffer from verbal diarrhea."

She looked at me with a small smile. "My brother says that all the time. It reminds me of that *South Park* episode where everyone crapped out of their mouths, especially the people that had become atheists."

"That's me."

She turned to me and arched an eyebrow. "An atheist pastor?"

"No, I shit a lot out of my mouth," I lied. It was too soon to tell her.

Jennifer let out a full, throaty laugh. "That's just disgusting."

We drove in silence through the gray streets of Columbus as the wind blew snow across the road. I kept fiddling with the threads on my jeans while we entered the cemetery. It had always been a habit of mine to play with something whenever I got nervous. It occurred to me that, as a cop, Jennifer could probably tell all the signs of anxiety, and I didn't want her to interrogate me again.

I cleared my throat. "So, tell me about the Confederate Cemetery."
She smiled. "Not a history buff, eh?"

"Not really. It was actually my worst subject in school. More of a science-oriented guy."

"And so you became a preacher?"

"Yeah, odd isn't it?"

"No. Well, no more than an art major becoming a cop," she said as she parked the car.

"An art major, eh? I bet that makes for good donut talk."

Jennifer wrinkled her nose in disgust. Wow, she was even cute when she was mad.

"I don't eat donuts, and neither do most cops. We are not all Chief Wiggums, you know."

"Come on, not even once in a while?"

She looked at me with what must have been her hard-ass cop look. The muscles on her face tightened, and her eyes bore a hole through me. It would have been convincing if not for the twitches at the corners of her mouth. "Well, maybe," she blurted.

"So anyway, the Confederate Cemetery, tell me about it."

"Well, during the war, there was a large Union training camp in Columbus. They turned it into a prison camp. Most of those camps, both North and South … well, thousands of men lived in conditions worse than a third world country. You can imagine…"

Flashes of sick men shitting in holes came to my mind. I stared at the floor of Jennifer's car. "A very public place for a murder."

Jennifer nodded and looked at me. "Yeah, it is."

As we got out of the car, the sun that threatened to peek through disappeared, replaced with the winter sky. The cemetery had a low gray-rock wall with an iron fence sticking out from the top. A rust-colored state historic sign hung on the stone arch gate, marking the importance of the cemetery as a former Union army training site and Confederate prisoner of war camp. Two uniformed policemen stood guard. They nodded to Jennifer as she showed them her badge.

As we walked into the cemetery, I saw white granite headstones with dark water stains from the melting snow. The burial markers

3 GATES OF THE DEAD

stretched out about twenty-five yards on each side.

"Wow, there are a lot of them," I said. "How many?"

Jennifer responded by pointing to a large boulder with 2,220 chiseled into the rock. I marveled at the number as I looked up to the archway where the word "Americans" was etched into the blocks. On top of the English-style gate, a large gray Ohio cross rose over the gateway. Half-moon slash marks had been scraped all over the cross. At first, I thought someone had vandalized the monument, but as I looked closer, I realized whoever sculpted it seemed like they meant for it to be a part of the work.

"That's a bit unusual," I said.

"What's that?" Jennifer asked.

I pointed up. "Those half-moons carved into the cross."

Jennifer frowned. "Yeah, no one knows why they are there."

"Really?"

She shook her head. "From the stories I've heard, they are meant to be grins."

"Grins?"

I shook my head. "Was the artist on something?"

She chuckled. "I don't know what kind of drugs they had at the beginning of the twentieth century. Sadly, since the cross was donated by an anonymous donor, no one could ask the artist."

I nodded as I turned around to take in the cemetery. "I can't believe I have never heard of this place." I touched one of the cold grave markers.

"My dad used to bring me here as a kid," Jennifer said as she stopped to look. "He loves coming to this place. He is one of those Civil War re-enactors."

"Bet he loves Blue Jacket hockey then."

She smiled. "Nice. Most people in Columbus never make the connection."

"I didn't until just now," I chuckled. "All those games wasted."

The wind gusted, and I shivered. We stood side-by-side, close enough that I could feel the heat of her body. I thought of Amanda.

"Where did they find her?"

She hesitated. "I didn't really bring you here to see that."

I furrowed my brow. "Okay, but I still want to see it."

She looked up at me, her eyes searching mine. "Are you sure?"

"No. I mean, not really, but I guess I need to see what happened."

She nodded as she touched my arm. "I understand. Let's go around the cross."

I started to shake, and my stomach churned. This was it. I would see where Amanda had been murdered. I shoved my hands in my pockets, not wanting Jen to see my trembling weakness. We walked around to the back. I expected to see bloodstains on the ground or the police tape I'd seen on cop shows. Nothing.

"I don't see any blood."

She pointed. "Look at the cross."

I glanced up and clenched my fists. A deep red, almost black, color stained the granite all the way down. Trails of darkened blood snaked down the back of the cross in crisscrossed patterns. My throat tightened. "What the … what did they do to her?"

Jennifer frowned and fiddled with her scar. "Are you sure you want to hear this?"

I wanted to run home and crawl back into bed. But it was too late. I had to know.

"Yeah, tell me."

She pointed upward. "They hung her on the cross dressed in a white ceremonial robe. After that, they slit her throat and let the blood spill down." She spoke in a clinical voice as if she were reading a scientific study. It unsettled me, but then I remembered what she said about detaching herself so she could do her job.

"But wouldn't there have been blood on the ground?"

"That's what we could not figure out. Forensics swept this place clean. It's almost as if…"

"As if what?"

"Well, like the blood ran into the opening below the stone arch and disappeared."

I stared at the dark spots. It did look like the blood had just disappeared. The stain stopped right at the bottom of the stone. I couldn't be as clinical as Jennifer. This had been blood that had once been pumped through the heart of a woman. The same heart I heard when I lay my head on her chest. I closed my eyes and turned my face away.

"Aidan?" Jennifer placed her hand on my shoulder.

I took a deep breath. "Did she . . . did she have the necklace on?"

"The Trinity knot one?"

I nodded slowly. "I gave it to her on her birthday last year."

"It's in her personal affects," Jennifer said barely above a whisper.

"I'm sorry, I ... it's ... I can't..." As I stumbled over my words, a sound ripped through the air as if someone had torn a large curtain. "What was that?"

"We don't know that either. It happened when I first got on the scene as well. The cop on duty told me it happens more often with each hour. I thought about having a scientific team here from Ohio State."

I turned around and looked for a logical explanation. No factories, stores, or any place that would make a ripping sound.

"What's going on here?" I asked.

"There's more."

"It gets weirder?"

"Yeah, it does."

Jennifer led me to the covered pavilion at the back of the cemetery. She pointed down at the concrete floor. A huge black image had been drawn on the gray concrete.

"Smiley face," I said. "Just like the ones on the cross, except someone took the trouble to put on eyes this time."

"Yeah. Whoever did this knew the history of the cross. It's not widely known, but then again, they could have done some research. Although, why they would go through the trouble, I have no idea."

"Couldn't this just be normal graffiti?" I argued.

She frowned. "You don't get it, Aidan. This is a bit of a rough neighborhood, but this place never gets vandalized."

I looked at the houses around the memorial. Most had spray

paint or gang symbols on their siding. "Really? Never?"

"No. It's actually a bit weird … almost like there's an unspoken respect for the dead. This place is checked every day by patrols." She paused. "Plus, it's not paint. It's blood. Amanda's blood."

I leaned against the stone column of the pavilion. The world started spinning, and I took a few deep breaths. "So, maybe it's some serial killer who taunts the police and knows the history of Columbus?"

Jennifer shrugged. "Maybe. Some new weird angle, I would have guessed. That is until I saw…"

"Saw what?"

She waved to the right. "This way."

We trudged toward the back of the cemetery, and she took me behind the last row of graves. I fought the urge to cry out as I saw bare footprints all over the ground, lightly crunched into the snow. They had barely broken the surface.

I stopped walking and bent down to examine them. "I'm guessing this is what you wanted to show me."

Jennifer pointed her finger and turned in a circle. "They are all over the cemetery. It was one of the things the first officer on the scene reported. Everyone thought he was crazy until we got here."

I traced the inside of a print and felt a cold shiver run up my hand. "So, detective, what made them?"

"I have no idea. I was actually hoping you could tell me."

"Why would I be able to tell you anything about them?" I spread my hands, hoping my face hid the truth.

She frowned. "I dunno. Just seems right up your alley I guess. My guys in forensics could give me no explanation. There are no traces of skin or anything that you might expect in a barefoot print in the snow."

I steadied myself with my hand as my stomach churned. "Come on, there had to be something."

"I am telling you, nothing. Don't you think we checked? There's been a brutal murder, the worst I have ever seen. This whole area has been covered like a thirteen-year-old boy goes over a

Sports Illustrated Swimsuit calendar. There is nothing. It's as if the footprints..." Jennifer's face scrunched as she looked around.

"What?"

"As if they rose out of the ground."

I stood up. "You can't be serious."

"I am just telling you the results of the investigation." She dusted the snow off her pants.

"That isn't possible."

"You're a preacher. Don't you believe in all that supernatural stuff? I mean, I would have brought a priest, but you were more available. That's why I brought you here. Our whole team is a bit, uh, unnerved."

I wanted to tell her I didn't believe anymore and explain how all this had a natural explanation. The books I'd read the past six months offered no refuge.

"Well, yes, but there has to be some other explanation for it."

"I can tell you, no one on the squad had any. None of my forensic guys or any of the detectives working the case."

I brushed the snow off my hand. "Do you think the prints are connected to Amanda's murder in any way?"

"No one has any idea. But these only appeared *after* her death."

"How do you know that?"

Jennifer led me back to the entrance. "By the time of death established by the coroner. One of our patrolmen responded to a noise complaint from the apartment building across the street around midnight. He walked over here to look at the cemetery."

"Why did he do that?"

"Just to be thorough, and of course, to see the Gray Lady."

"The what?"

Jennifer gave a half smile. "Supposedly, there is a lady who haunts this cemetery and puts a flower on one of the soldier's graves. I guess the patrolman got curious."

"That's a bit weird."

"Not if it was a slow night. You would be amazed at how boring a cop's life can be sometimes."

"I am guessing he saw no footprints."

"Good guess, preacher. When Josh went to the patrol car to call in the murder, he came back to guard the scene. The footprints were all over the ground. The patrolman swears they weren't there when he first saw Amanda's body."

We stared at the prints. They seemed to mock us with their mystery, the way God had always done to me.

"So, you have no other leads from her, um, body?" I said, looking back at the cross.

"Other than the note?"

"Yeah."

"No. And I can't tell you how much that disturbs me. There were no footprints, no cloth fibers on the body, no fingerprints, no drag marks..."

"Drag marks?"

"Places where they might have dragged her over the snow to the cross. It's almost as if..."

"What?"

"It's stupid, but it's almost as if they levitated her up to the cross." Jennifer stared at the ground.

I looked at her with my best skeptical expression.

She frowned and held up her hands. "I know it sounds crazy. But we have no rope burns on her anywhere other than around her neck. We have no idea how they held her against the cross while they hung her. There were no ladder or scuff marks on the archway."

"How do you know the rope hadn't held her there when they killed her?"

"Because it's only one piece, used simply to keep her there. There's no way she just stood there and let them hang her."

The image of Amanda hanging from the cross forced its way into my mind. I closed my eyes. "Where did you find the note?"

"Inside her vaginal cavity."

"Amanda was clever ... I'm not surprised."

Jennifer paused at the gate. "Do you have any idea what she was trying to tell you?"

"No, and I have been thinking about it since yesterday. I think I even dreamed about it. I can't figure out why she didn't write down his name."

"Yeah, that's got us in a knot as well. You can't imagine how pissed off Lieutenant Weaver is right now. He always has a good idea about the how, except with this case."

"Seems like a good boss."

"He is the best the force has really. He might call in the FBI on this one, which I don't think he has ever done, even when the mayor begs for it."

We began to walk back to the car.

"So, you really have no idea what those footprints might be, like something supernatural?" Jennifer asked.

"I have no idea."

"For someone who is supposed to have all the answers to life's questions, you don't seem to have many."

I grimaced. "I could say the same about you, *detective*. Besides, the longer I've been a minister, the more I realize how little I actually know."

She looked at me with a raised eyebrow. "Just like a cop."

chapter twelve

"So, I have a question to ask you," Jennifer handed me a hot chocolate and turned to grab hers from the drive-thru attendant. We'd decided to stop for before we went to the storage shed.

"Wow, a detective asking questions," I said. I couldn't believe how easy it was to talk to her. Yesterday, neither one of us probably cared to see the other again. Today, we were chatting like old college buddies. I guess my getting cleared of murder charges had something to do with it.

"*Funny*. Anyway, my question is: what does a minister do during the week?" She took a sip of her hot chocolate. "I mean, I always thought they only worked on Sunday and then played golf the rest of the time."

"Well, the older ones do. Guys my age troll the Internet."

Jennifer rolled her eyes. "I'm serious, Aidan."

I smiled. "Well, it depends on the position, I guess. Take mine for instance. As assistant pastor, I see to all the church details, small groups, visit people in the hospital, and counsel troubled people."

"Do you like it?"

I stared ahead as I considered the question. "Most of the time. There are times I get bored, but I love helping people. I hate the administrative part though."

"Yeah, I can relate. Before this case, I was stuck doing a departmental study on revamping investigative procedures."

"Sounds fun."

"About as fun as running the bulletins, I guess."

I laughed. "Yeah, I don't do that. Our secretary does. I think copy machines are from Satan."

We drove for a little while in silence, taking in the sights along Interstate 71. The Crew soccer stadium loomed in front of us.

"Do you ever go to the Crew games?" Jennifer asked.

"Season tickets," I said. "Bought them my first summer in Columbus. How about you?"

"As all natives in Columbus, I'm getting around to it."

"Maybe I'll take you some time." I immediately wished real life conversations were like chatting on a computer, where you could think about what you're going to say and erase it if it didn't sound right.

I glanced at Jennifer who had a little smile on her face. "I'll buy the brats and beer," she said. "Or wait, for you, a Coke."

"Why can't I have a beer?"

"Oh! I thought preachers didn't drink."

"This one does. Our church is cool with that. One of the few things they are cool with, actually."

I checked our progress on my iPhone as Jennifer continued to drive.

"So, are you a Mac disciple?" She laughed.

"Yeah, I light incense to Steve Jobs every night," I said as I followed the glowing blue dot on Google Maps.

"Mac people are nerds."

I gave her a mock bow with the upper half of my body. "That would be me. Get off on Morse Road."

I directed her through a few turns until we arrived at the storage shed.

"Which row is it again?" Jennifer asked.

"Row seventeen, number twenty-three."

We pulled up to the puke-yellow shed door and stared at the other side of the fence.

"Wow, you weren't kidding," she said. "It's right next to the graveyard."

"Yeah, Amanda would never come here alone because it creeped her out."

"I can see why."

I got out of the car and went up to the shed. I unlocked the padlock and slid the rusty door upward as a musty scent hit my nose. Amanda had obviously not been here for a while. Boxes were stacked to the metal roof on the left and right. She'd left a path in the middle that enabled her to get the boxes in and out.

"You were right," Jennifer said. "She was orderly."

I nodded, fighting tears at seeing all of Amanda's stuff. I knew I needed tell her parents about the shed so they could clear it out. Everyone talked about burials being hard, but I thought it was always harder after the funeral. When my parents died, the funeral hadn't affected me much, but going through my parents' personal possessions with my brother required two bottles of Irish whiskey.

"Are you going to take this stuff in as evidence?" I asked.

"Depends on what we find. If there is nothing, we won't." She gazed around at the boxes.

"Okay, so where do we start?"

Jennifer looked up, and her face drained of color.

"What? What is it?" I said.

"We start with that one." She pointed up to a box with black writing on it. Instead of a normal label like "books" or "kitchen," Amanda had written something in Hebrew.

I furrowed my brow. "I didn't know Amanda knew Hebrew."

Jennifer looked at me. "What? You know what these symbols mean?"

"They aren't symbols. Not exactly, anyway. It's a Hebrew word."

"Hebrew?"

I nodded. "I ate, drank and bled Hebrew for a summer in

seminary."

Jennifer played with her scar. "Can you read it?"

"A little. Now I mostly rely on my Hebrew computer program, but I'll give it a shot," I said as I started to climb the boxes.

"No, let me," she said, pulling out two pairs of rubber gloves from her purse. She handed me one and climbed up on a chair. I had to look up so I could get the box from her, and as much as I tried, I couldn't keep myself from checking out her form as she stood reaching above me.

"Here," she said, catching my gaze as she handed me the box.

I put the box down and tilted it up. The letters gave me goose bumps. I'd always loved Hebrew and the inherent mystery of the language. My professor in seminary told us that Hebrew contained all the secrets of God, and I believed him. Amanda's writing on this box only increased that mystery. I traced the letters with my finger as I read right to left.

Jennifer pointed to the lines and dots. "Why doesn't Hebrew use a normal alphabet?"

"It depends on what you mean by normal. The lines are the actual letters. The dots, however, aren't part of the original language. They are used as vowel markers for pronunciation because it's a very guttural language. Hebrew doesn't have any vowels in its alphabet."

"Can you decipher it?"

"Give me a second." I sounded out each consonant with its vowel sound. "I think it says, *Nebo*."

"Nebo?" Jennifer frowned.

My mind went through a thousand Bible verses until I recalled its origin. "Moses, ring a bell?"

"I know who Moses is," she said. "But I'm a lapsed Catholic, which means I have done my best to forget everything I learned in Sunday school."

"Nebo isn't a lesson — it's a place. God took Moses to Nebo, the mountain overlooking the Promised Land before Moses died."

"Wait, Moses didn't get to go into the Promised Land?"

"No, he didn't. He struck a rock to get water when God hadn't told him to. So, his punishment was never to enter the Promised Land."

"That doesn't seem nice."

"Yeah, well, God is like a mean kid sometimes."

Jennifer stared at me with wide eyes. I couldn't tell if she was upset or sympathetic. "Okay, not sure how to take that," she said.

"Just forget I said anything. Let's see what's in the box."

"Allow me," she said, taking a knife in her gloved hand and cutting the packing tape down the middle. Jen opened the box, and we gasped.

The box contained a CD in a plastic case with the word "Nebo," in English this time, written in black marker across it.

"A CD? Can't be music," I said. "More like files, I would guess. I doubt she would go through this much trouble for music."

Jennifer picked it up. "I agree. Wonder what's on it?"

We both stared at the disk as if we somehow had the ability to read what was on it. I looked up at the boxes again. "You are going to have to take this stuff in, aren't you?"

"Yes, I'm afraid so. Her family is just going to have to wait."

I nodded. I needed to call them, but I just couldn't bring myself to do it, especially if they thought I might be a suspect.

"Did you tell him tha-"

"Yes," Jen interrupted. "They no longer think you are a suspect in their daughter's murder from what they told me."

"Good." I breathed.

"Excuse me a second. I need to call in forensics."

Jennifer hurried back to her car and grabbed her cell phone. As she spoke, I saw a small yellow corner peeking up through the flap at the bottom of the box. I worked the cardboard a bit and pulled out an envelope.

I looked back at Jennifer. She was still talking on the phone. I opened the envelope and found a hand-written letter inside.

Aidan,

Find Father Neal. You won't survive when they wake "him" if you don't. Take care of Bishop. The disk contains pictures of the next

place. Will see you again. Forgive me.
   Love,
   Amanda

"What are you reading?" Jennifer walked in without me hearing her.

I closed the letter. "Oh nothing, just some old seminary notes I pulled from one of my boxes."

I didn't want to tell Jennifer about the note until I could figure it out, so I changed the subject as we exited the shed. "Can I ask you a question?"

"Yes, but I can't guarantee I will answer it."

"Fair enough. Why did you pick out the box with the Hebrew writing?"

Jennifer stared straight ahead, looking at the cemetery behind the storage shed. She didn't say anything for a few moments and then looked back at me. "Her head."

"What?"

"Amanda's head."

"I don't understand."

She grimaced. "When I saw her body, there were cuts in her forehead. At first, we thought they were just random knife wounds, products of the attack. When the coroner got a closer look, she realized they were some kind of code, but no one knew it was Hebrew. You filled in that little detail."

I had to brace myself to keep from swaying. My mind swam with images of Amanda screaming as some sick freak carved Hebrew letters into her head. I didn't want to imagine how long it took for that to happen.

"This just gets more hellish."

"You said it, preacher."

"Will you tell me what's on that disk?"

Jennifer turned, her hard eyes examining as she played with her scar. "I'll call you when I know."

chapter thirteen

After forensics arrived, Jen dropped me off at the church before going back to the storage shed. I couldn't help thinking about how boring my life had been up to that point. I had lost my faith and been accused — as well as cleared — of an ex-fiancée's murder, not to mention met the force-of-nature woman detective investigating her murder. There didn't seem to be any rhyme or reason to any of it. I would have thought God moved in mysterious ways, but I was pretty sure that was a lie. Still, I had so many questions. What about Amanda's note? Who was Father Neal? And who was this sleeping guy? Was "he" the same one she talked about in her last letter?

A cold sensation ran through my body as I remembered the voice at the hospital, Joseph's words in Edna's dream, and the footprints in two different locations that didn't seem to have any connection.

The familiar rock in my stomach returned as I entered the office area and saw a woman who was completely out of place for our church. She sat in one of our semi-comfortable couches that made our waiting area seem like a glorified doctor's office, except our magazines were worse. We had reading material like *Christian Living* or *Southern Christian Hospitality* — an addition of our secretary's.

Sherry looked up from her reading. "Pastor Schaeffer, this is Ms. Zoe Othmeyer and she is here to see you."

Zoe looked to be in her early forties and had long stringy gray hair that hung down to her chest. She had earrings that dangled to her shoulders and a stone cross around her neck. Her faded green sweater was probably in style back in the 1960's, and I wondered if she was a hippie who had just recently decided to enter society.

"Pastor Schaeffer?" she asked in a high breathy sort of voice that reminded me of Julie Haggerty from the movie *Airplane*.

"Yes, can I help you?"

"May I speak with you in private?"

"Oh, um, well, to be honest, Ms. Othmeyer, it's been a long day. I was just getting some stuff from my office."

"Please, call me Zoe. It means 'life' you know."

"Yeah, I know."

"Please, Reverend Schaeffer, it's important." She looked at me intently, her eyes moving back and forth as if searching for something in my face.

I stared back at her for a moment in silent tension. "Okay sure, Zoe, I can spare a few minutes. And please, call me Aidan. Right this way."

We went into my office, and I sat down at my desk. Zoe, however, walked around to study my books and let out little exclamations as she read each title.

"Ah, St. Thomas, very profound! Mystical! Made me feel the mystery! Mmm, Mr. Calvin, not so nice. Still, some excellent points about communing with God."

"Um, Zoe?"

She gazed back at me as if she had forgotten I was there. She gave a sheepish grin and sat down. "Yes, I'm sorry. My message."

I turned my chair around to face her and tensed as she grasped my hands.

"It's so wonderful to meet you. I heard about you a bit from Amanda when she was alive. Now, she can't stop talking about you."

She gripped my hands tightly, and I winced. She wasn't strong, but her hands buzzed with some kind of hidden energy. It felt like she was holding one of those cheap joy buzzers you used to be able to get out of the back of comic books. My hands vibrated along with hers, and the tingle began to spread up my arms.

"You knew Amanda?"

"*Know*, Aidan. I know her. You speak as if Amanda has stopped existing."

"Well, she's dead," I said, my throat constricting.

"That she is, but dead doesn't mean what you seem to think. In fact, she is with us right now."

I pulled my hands from her grasp and shoved my chair back to get away from her.

"What did you say?"

She smiled. "Amanda is standing right by you."

I looked and saw nothing. This woman was just bat-shit crazy. "Zoe, I'm guessing you are some nice lady who read about Amanda in the paper? Are you here just to … why are you here?"

"I told you. Amanda has a message for you. She won't let me rest until I give it. They never do, you know."

I looked around the office even though I knew there would be nothing to see. This woman was probably harmless, but I wanted her out of there. I didn't want her to freak out, so I figured I would have to edge her on her way as best I could. "Um, right, she came to you after she was dead?"

"Yes, that's the way it usually works." She smiled, almost like she pitied me for *my* lack of sanity.

"So, maybe you can tell me a little about that?"

"Well, the dead come to me and give me messages."

"Uh, what?" I said, shifting in my seat.

"Yes, it's most unpleasant, but I have been able to see them since I was a little girl."

You mean since your first hit of LSD.

"But this one is different," she continued. "Amanda was my friend. I don't often get people I know. When she appears to me, she keeps slashing her neck. I hope that's not how she died."

My stomach tightened. Jennifer and her team were the only ones who knew about Amanda's neck. "How did you know Amanda?"

She leaned back in her chair, touched her fingertips like a church steeple, and squinted her eyes at me like a mom trying to decide if a son could handle the wisdom she was about to impart. "Well, we were a part of a group together, a group she joined a few months ago."

"What kind of group?" I said, leaning forward, hoping her words might give me some clue about Amanda's murderer.

"A paranormal investigation group."

I tried hard not to stare at her with my mouth open.

"Talk to Father Neal," she said.

I tried to ignore the increase of my heart rate and control my facial expressions. I didn't want Zoe to know anything I'd heard or seen. "Father Neal. Can you tell me who he is?"

She smiled and played with one of her earrings. "He is the priest at St. Patrick's Anglican Church in Clintonville."

"Can you give me the address?"

She wrote it down on a piece of paper and stood up. "Thank you for your time."

"Wait! You're leaving?" I stammered as I got up.

She smiled and touched my arm. "I delivered my message, and now I'm going to let you have the rest of the day to yourself. But, Aidan, Amanda is very insistent. I'm not sure why, but you must see Father Neal very soon."

I raised my eyebrows. I couldn't believe she was just leaving. I expected her to try and convince me, by some obscure logic, of her *gift*. "Um, thank you, Zoe."

She tilted her head. "Do you believe me?"

"Well, I don't know what to believe. I mean, the Bible forbids talking to ghosts."

"It does no such thing, Pastor Schaeffer."

Motioning for her to wait, I grabbed my Bible from my desktop, flipped to Deuteronomy 18, and began to read aloud. "When you enter the land the LORD your God is giving you, do not learn to imitate the detestable ways of the nations there. Let no one be found among you who sacrifices his son or daughter in the fire, who practices divination or sorcery, interprets omens, engages in witchcraft, or casts spells, or who is a medium or one who seeks to master the dead. Anyone who does these things is detestable to the LORD, and because of these detestable practices the LORD your God will drive out those nations before you. You must be blameless before the LORD your God…"

I paused. "So, you see, the Bible forbids contacting the dead or talking to them."

"Forgive me, but you just added to the Word of God."

Her words stunned me. Even though I didn't believe any longer, it was still one of the worst things a Protestant Evangelical minister could hear.

"I'm not doing that. It's the plain meaning…"

"The Bible says you should not make efforts to contact the dead or control information from them. It forbids being a Bone Master."

"A what?"

"Bone Masters are people, magicians if you will, who summon the dead for control, information, comfort, or knowledge of the future for their own, evil intent. But if the dead come to you, it is permitted, even if it's not the norm."

I couldn't believe this conversation or being corrected by this bizarre woman about the Bible. The thing was she'd been right. The passage didn't say anything about the dead coming to us. I picked up one of my pens and started chewing on it.

"So, you're not a master of bones?" I gave a half smile.

Zoe stared at me, lip trembling, and then slammed her hand down on my bookshelf. "Please do not ever associate me with such people. Ever. What they do is an abomination before Yahweh."

"Zoe, I'm sorry. I mean, you might be right about that Bible passage, but it is just hard for me to believe Amanda came to you."

She nodded and held out her hand. "I'm not surprised. Father Neal said you wouldn't believe me."

She turned to leave, and I grabbed her arm. "I'm sorry, you *know* Father Neal?"

"Yes, he is my priest. I attend St. Patrick's. Amanda started coming to the church and having some talks with Father Neal. He also helps out with my group when I need a house blessed. Did Amanda introduce you to him?"

"No, I only just heard his name, um, from you."

Zoe startled me as she reached up and touched my cheek. "Of course you've heard of him. This is all linked, don't you understand that?"

I pulled her hand off my cheek. "It's just a coincidence, that's all. One of those things that happen when we assign meaning to what are really just random events."

She cocked her head and looked at me with pity as she gave my cheeks a squeeze. "So young to be so cynical. Call Father Neal. Talk to him."

Before I could answer, she walked out the door. I sat down, rubbing my cheek. I had thought I was rid of it — the idea of God, the spirit world, all of it. Now, I had to deal with the footprints, weird people visiting me, and Father Neal's name. I'd trained as a scientist not to ignore evidence, evidence that had sprung up so often. My education as a Presbyterian strengthened that resolve. I'd had "nothing but the Word of God" beaten into me. Strangely, the way it had been taught to me helped contribute to my crisis of faith. But even now, I still wondered if part of me just wanted to see a supernatural world. After all, if you looked long enough, you would see something because your mind imposes order on it.

That had to be it. The idea of God, the supernatural, and Amanda still existing in some form had such a hold over me that I kept looking for meaning in random events. I took the Bible in my hands and threw it against the wall, chipping the paint.

Mike walked by that moment and stuck his head into my office. "Hey, why are you here?" he asked. "Are you okay?"

"Um, yeah, sorry. One of my books fell."

"Good. Listen, Aidan, I know this is last minute, but I need you to do something for me."

"Sure, whatever you need," I said, still chewing on my pen.

"I need you to cover for me at the Wednesday night church dinner tonight. I have some personal errands I need to attend to."

Yeah, like sticking your pastoral staff in places where it doesn't belong.

"Sure, whatever."

"Are you okay?"

"No, haven't you read the newspaper?"

"Not in the past two days, been busy with the fallout from the elders meeting."

I let out a deep exhale. "Amanda is dead. She was murdered."

Mike's jaw dropped open. His eyes went wide as he gripped the doorposts. "I don't … I … I'm so sorry, Aidan!"

"I know. It's pretty unreal. I was the first suspect."

"Are you still?"

"No, it happened while I was at the hospital with Olan and Edna."

"How are you handling it?"

I ran my fingers through my hair. "Fine, I guess. I'm just in shock. I don't really feel anything yet."

He nodded. "Tough year for you, my friend."

I ignored the faces of my parents and Amanda etched in my mind.

Mike lowered his voice. "Do you need to talk with Dr. Winter again?"

I shook my head. "No. I'm okay. It's been six months since I've even talked to Amanda."

"I know, but combined with your crisis of faith…" he trailed off.

"No. But I appreciate your concern." Even though Mike was a cheating jackass, he always went out of his way to help me. I owed him a lot.

He stared at me as if trying to process whether or not he should leave me alone.

"Seriously, Mike, it's fine." I changed the subject. "What are you going to do about the other night?"

"You mean with the elders?"

"Yeah."

"Don't worry about it."

"But if they have the votes, which by my count they do, it will go to the congregation."

"Maybe, but that is as far as it goes. It will be my excuse to get those guys out of eldership." He gave me a tight-lipped smile.

"How will you do that?"

"With the same sort of tactics they are using against me."

"Yeah, but come on. You are above all that, right?"

"I will do what I need to do."

I wanted to hit him right there. This guy had been my example of what a ministry-minded man and husband was like for the past three years. All this time, his soul had been rotten to the core. Yet he always treated me like a younger brother. I couldn't reconcile the two conflicting personalities.

Mike looked at me with a smile of pity. "This is a hard lesson for you to learn, but it is the way Presbyterian government works."

I winced. "If that's the case, I don't want any part of it!"

"Aidan, don't say that to anyone but me. Otherwise, you will be in the same trouble. The assistant pastor is supposed to fly low, learn, and then move on to a head position in a few years. You are well on your way, so don't mess it up now by getting involved in this."

"But I'm already involved!" I replied with a harsh whisper.

"No, you aren't. Stay that way. Look out for yourself."

He walked to his office and closed his door. I wondered if he was going to call his mistress for a stress-relief screw. Jackass. I shut my door and sat down. My phone buzzed, and Jennifer's number flashed on the screen.

"Hey, Aidan." Her voice sounded tired and confused.

"Hi, Jennifer, what's wrong?"

"Well, things keep getting more complicated."

"The disk?"

"Yes. It's full of pictures."

I swallowed hard as my mind filled with all kinds of horrible possibilities: Amanda in leather, Amanda doing something bad, or something bad being done to her.

"Something terrible?"

"No, not that I can tell. I can't talk about it much as I'm still at the station. I'll bring it over tonight for you to see."

"Yeah, about tonight, I got stuck doing the Wednesday night supper and Bible study, so you will have to come over later. Is that okay?"

"How about I just come to the church dinner. Do you mind?"

I sat silent for a moment as I tried to grasp what she'd just said.

"Aidan, is that okay?"

"Yeah, yeah. Of course it is. Be here at six. Food's not bad. We get it from a local catering company."

"Sounds good. I haven't had anything real in the past few days, just fast food salads."

"Well, I can promise you better than that."

"I hope so."

"See you tonight."

I hung up the phone, my mind in a whirl. What were Jennifer's motives? Was she into me? Or was this a cop thing, trying to get more information, playing the subject like some hot, James Bond chick. Seduce the guy, get the information you need, and then move on. And did I even really care?

chapter fourteen

I went home and changed into respectable clothing: a blue blazer and khaki pants — the unofficial outfit of Presbyterian ministers everywhere. You could go to a General Assembly of our denomination and wonder if there had been a midnight madness sale at Banana Republic.

I got back to the office and threw together a lesson for the Wednesday night study. Jennifer arrived at quarter to six and knocked on my door.

"Aidan, are you busy?"

I typed in the final words for my lesson. "No, come in, just finished. Let me print this out."

The temptation to stare hit full force. Jennifer wore a red turtleneck sweater and black slacks. Her black hair hung to her shoulders like Solomon's flock of goats, and I dared not even think about the "two fawns, twins of a gazelle." I knew tonight's lesson would be a disaster with my staring at her all evening.

"How is the lesson coming?" She asked as she leaned against my bookcase.

"It may not be very good, but what do you expect with three hours' notice on my day off?"

"How come your boss bailed?"

I fought to keep from clenching my jaw. "Not sure really. Probably family stuff. He didn't really say."

She nodded. "How many people usually come to this dinner?"

"About seventy-five. We have three-hundred in the church, but everyone is busy during the week. Kids' sports practices and all that," I said, standing up. "Usually, our youth minister handles the duties, but he's on vacation. I don't normally have to be here."

"You don't have to go?"

"No, but I usually do anyway if I haven't gone hiking," I said, gesturing to the hiking books on my shelf.

"I haven't gotten into hiking much," she said, standing up straight. She folded her arms across her chest.

"You should. Now, shall we go and feast on processed catered food?"

As we walked to the hall, I realized I probably should have warned Jennifer about the possibility that everyone would think we were dating. But then I figured they'd be discreet and not assume anything. Why would they?

Sometimes, I could be so clueless about people it scared me.

As soon as we walked into the hall, one of our blue hairs, Mrs. Templeton, came up to us.

"Oh, Aidan, such a pretty young lady you have found for yourself! When did you start dating? Any wedding plans?"

I felt my face heat up as if I'd had two glasses of whiskey. "Um, no, Mrs. Templeton. This is Detective Jennifer Brown, from the Columbus Police Department. She is, um, interested in our church." I looked sideways at Jennifer. She had a little smile on her face.

"Nice to meet you, Mrs. Templeton," Jennifer said, shaking her hand.

"Oh! Thank you, dear. You are very beautiful. Did you notice that, Aidan?"

Jennifer smirked in my direction.

"Um, yes she is," I fumbled.

Mrs. Templeton grabbed my hands. "Oh, honey, I'm so sorry about Amanda. It's awful. I saw it on the news."

I always wondered who taught Mrs. Templeton tact.

"Thank you. And yes, it is awful."

I could almost feel Jennifer's eye searching my face. I began to tear up and fought it. I should have expected they would want to talk about Amanda.

Mrs. Templeton walked away as Jennifer put her hand on my shoulder. "Are you okay?"

I didn't look at her. "No, not really. But I'd like to avoid situations like that."

I walked Jennifer over to a table, and she began talking with the Lutzes, a nice family that had just moved to Columbus. As the crowd poured in, I tried to look busy until six o'clock.

"Okay," I called out. "Let's sit down for a moment."

The people came together in good Presbyterian fashion, decent and in order. I took a deep breath. "Before we start, I would like to make a prayer request."

Everyone stared at me in complete silence. I wondered if they knew what I was about to say. Even though I no longer believed in the power of prayer, I thought this was the best way to acknowledge the elephant in the room.

"As most of you know already, my ex-fiancée, Amanda McDougal, was recently murdered." I paused. "There are no suspects at this time, and police are not releasing a lot of details. So I would ask that Bill, if you are willing, please pray for Amanda's family and friends, as well as our time together tonight."

Bill, always in tune with people's emotional needs, stood up next to me.

"Absolutely, Pastor Aidan." He put a hand on my shoulder. "Let's pray."

Everyone bowed their heads as Bill laid out one of the most heartfelt and beautiful prayers I'd ever heard. I felt sick to my stomach and could barely stand.

Why is my grief coming in waves like this? Why couldn't last night have been enough?

"...And be with Aidan and help him minister to us tonight. Amen."

Everyone either gave me a look of sympathy or stared at Jennifer as they made their way to the tables. She whispered to me out of the corner of her mouth, "They all think I'm your date."

"I know, and I'm not going to stop them from thinking that."

"Why is that?" She smiled.

"Because then I won't get fixed up with every single girl they know."

It had become pretty common practice in evangelical churches to think that single people need to be married. That rule was especially true when that single person was the assistant pastor.

I tried to concentrate on my food and talk with Jennifer, but I couldn't focus. I actually felt relieved to get up and start the lesson as the plates were cleared, and the kids were dismissed to their Wednesday night classes.

I stood up. "Okay, everyone, let's take out our Bibles and turn to Acts. Pastor Mike is under the weather tonight so I will be taking over our study. Now, as you might have talked about last week, Peter was thrown in jail. And this week we see his..."

Ernest, one our eldest members raised his hand.

"I'm sorry, Ernest, did you have a question?"

"Yes, I was wondering if you could tell us something."

"Sure, Ernest, what's up?"

"What does the Bible say about ghosts?"

I looked at Jennifer. She stared at me with arms folded.

"I, uh, am not sure ... why do you ask?"

"Well, strange things I've been hearin' lately from some friends, like footprints in their yard and all."

Olan. He and Ernest were hunting buddies.

"Um, well, truthfully, Ernest, that is probably a whole other lesson in and of itself. We need to stick with the text for tonight.

"You avoidin' my question?" He glared at me with green eyes

that still held the authority of an army colonel. I felt everyone staring at me. A few of them bent forward in their seats.

"Oh no, it's just that we need to stick with the text for our discussion."

"It's in our text, right in the verses, talkin' about Peter's ghost. Did they think that was possible?"

He had me. I totally overlooked this verse in my preparations for the night. This sort of thing happened all the time, preachers focusing on the big idea and missing the things people would be most curious about, like Peter's ghost. Or in the case of this passage, what the Christians in Acts thought was Peter's ghost.

I imagined Jennifer could tell I was in trouble because she gave me a little smile. Whether it was of encouragement or mockery, I couldn't tell.

"Ah, right. Good point. Well, let's take a look at this passage. First, it isn't really Peter's ghost. It's Peter himself. He hadn't died."

"Still avoidin'," Ernest said. In spite of his age, I wanted to throw a Bible at him.

"Now, hold on, give me a chance. It wouldn't be good to assume they believed in ghosts just because of their assumptions."

"Why not?" asked Mary, a forty-year-old soccer mom who made studying theology one of her many hobbies. "Seems like it would take some belief in spirits for them to mistake Peter for his ghost."

The conversation started to get out of hand, and some of the elders shifted in their seats. They all had expressions of discomfort and confusion. No one liked the topic at all. I certainly didn't, especially with my newfound disbelief in all of this.

"Well, that may be true, but just because they believed it, doesn't mean the Bible teaches we should believe in ghosts. Luke is merely telling the story as it happened. There are a number of passages in Acts that do the same thing, describe what happened, but do not prescribe it for the life of Christians today."

I gave them the textbook seminary avoidance tactic. My professors would be proud.

"But what does it mean to be asleep in Christ or with him in death? What does that look like?" Mary asked. "Couldn't that leave room open for the dead to visit us?"

The whole room buzzed with an excitement I had rarely heard before. Usually, when Mike taught, the room was full of respectable silence. Now, everyone talked at once. Jennifer looked around and gave a small, sympathetic smile as if she knew I had no answers to these questions.

"Listen, I'll be honest. I didn't have much time to get ready for tonight, so I didn't prepare a talk on ghosts in the Bible. I came prepared to talk about Christ's faithfulness to Peter even when he was being persecuted. That's really the main point of the passage. We have to be faithful to the Word."

The good Presbyterian mantra seemed to pacify everyone, except Mary and Ernest. Their faces wore the expression that all pastors knew too well. A look that said, "We now know you don't have all the answers, so we probably won't listen to anything else you say." I plowed ahead with the teaching that lost attraction for everyone in the room. They listened, but I doubted anyone took in a word I said. I didn't even pay attention to myself. I wanted to be out of there.

At the end of the lesson, the obligatory "good job" and "great word" comments came my way, which I knew were scandalous lies.

After the room cleared out, Jennifer walked over to me and touched my arm. "Good talk. I learned a lot."

"Isn't it against the law for cops to lie?"

"No, because that's how we get half of our confessions. Ready to go?"

"Never been more ready. Let's get out of here."

We drove to my house with Jennifer following me, and I pulled into my parking spot. Thankfully, the snow had buried the footprints.

"Do you rent or own?" Jennifer asked, arms tight around herself as she waited for me to unlock the door.

"Own. Bought it shortly after the church hired me."

"It's really nice. I actually drive by here all the time on my way to work. I've wondered how much these places cost. Do you mind me asking?"

I opened the door, and we walked in. "I got it pretty cheap, and it increased in value until the housing market circled the drain. If I sold it now, I would break even at a hundred and fifty thousand."

She nodded. Bishop barked a greeting. I let him out, and he nearly tackled Jennifer. I grabbed his collar. "Sorry, he is usually better-behaved."

"I don't mind. I love dogs," she said, rubbing Bishops head and patting his side. "Can I take him out?"

"Yeah, of course, go for it. Do you want any coffee or anything?"

"No thanks, too late for that."

"How about a beer?"

"Hmm, what would the congregation do if they knew their sweet, single assistant pastor had beer in his fridge?"

"Probably join me. Heck, most of them brew as a hobby."

Jennifer took Bishop out, and I poured two beers. I sat down in the living room and opened my laptop to check my email. My instant messenger came up, and Brian was on.

Hey, what's up dude? he wrote.

Not much. Jennifer the cop is here.

Right there with you?

No, she's out walking Bishop.

Wow, you have reached walking the dog stage! When is the wedding?

Shut up, you ass. She's here to show me some evidence. It's pure business.

I made a face at the computer screen.

Right, Brian wrote, *I know, but still, you can't deny that you seem attracted to her.*

I'm not denying anything, but yesterday, she thought I could be a murderer.

Footsteps came up to the door with a light thud. *Hey, man, got to run. She is coming back.*

Take care, man.

"How was the walk?" I asked as they came inside. Bishop trotted up to me and put his head in my lap.

"Freezing. I hate when dogs can't make up their mind."

"I know, and Bishop is worse than most."

Jennifer sat down right next to me, her leg touching mine. She had that out-in-the-cold smell. I forced myself to concentrate on business.

"Good, you have your computer up. Put this in," she said, handing me a CD.

"I'm guessing this is an illegal copy?" I asked, putting the disk into the drive.

"Of course it is," she said, smiling. "But Weaver gave me permission to show it to you. I told him about Nebo, and he was more than willing to let you see these. He told me that if you talked to the press, he would personally shoot you."

I chuckled. "I'll keep that in mind. I know the drill. Any leaked information could hurt the investigation. That's the last thing I want to do."

She stared at me. "You still love her, don't you?"

"I did. Do I still? That is more difficult to answer."

I avoided her eyes. With a few taps on the keyboard, the disk revealed a yellow folder entitled *Nebo*. My finger hovered over the mouse. I couldn't bring myself to click on the file.

"Aidan? Are you okay?" Jennifer asked, touching my shoulder.

I took a deep breath. "Just hoping that I'll know what these pictures show."

"Me too. Remember, there's nothing disturbing on them. If there was, I wouldn't show them to you, for your sake and the sake of the investigation."

I nodded, but my heart raced. My hands shook as I clicked on the file. Pictures of oak and spruce woods filled the screen. Some of the pictures contained a gravel crossroads. I squinted at the images. "I don't get it. It's just trees and a road. This could be anywhere in the eastern United States."

"Why do you say that?" Jennifer asked as she leaned closer to the screen.

"Well, the trees are all pretty common in this part of the country. And as for old gravel roads, there are probably hundreds in Ohio alone. One thing is for sure though…" I enlarged one of the pictures.

Jennifer leaned forward. "Wait, what's that?"

I rotated the picture. Someone had scraped a huge smiley face in the gravel.

"More smiley faces," she whispered.

Goosebumps crawled up my arms.

"We've been checking on known serial killings, and none of them had any smiley face connection. This is a new pattern and probably a new killer."

"Killer? A serial killer? I mean, I know I'm not a cop, but this seems to be something else, don't you think?"

"You mean the footprints too, right?"

I ran my fingers through my hair. "Footprints, Amanda hanging from a cross, it just seems, I don't know, ritualistic, I guess."

"Serial killers are ritualistic," Jennifer said in a flat tone as if she was trying to convince herself.

"Maybe, but I just can't help but feel there's something we're missing."

She scoffed. "There is a lot we are missing, in case you couldn't tell."

We sat in silence for a few minutes while we stared at the pictures.

"Wait a second," I said. "Amanda is from Athens, Ohio. She liked to go back there to hike in the hills around the city. It could be a picture from one of those hikes."

"Didn't she hike in other places?"

"No, she didn't. Well, at least not day hikes. She felt that southeastern Ohio was the most beautiful part of the state."

"I agree on that one. My dad likes to hunt in that area," she said. "But couldn't this have been a trip to Pennsylvania or West Virginia?"

I shrugged. "Could be. You'll have to ask her mom whether she took any hiking trips recently." I right clicked on the file and looked at the properties tab. "The date says December 12th."

Jennifer nodded. "We noticed that. Do you see anything else?"

"No, that's about all I can come up with."

She nodded. "I should probably go."

We stood up, and I walked her toward the door. She turned and looked me in the eye. "Can I ask you something?"

"Go for it," I said, trying to avoid her gaze. I stared at Bishop who had lain down on his big pillow.

"Why didn't you answer those people's questions about ghosts in the Bible?"

I shrugged. "They all have a tendency to try and get the teacher off track on silly questions like that." I hoped that would be enough to satisfy her.

"Is that the only reason?" She looked at me with her arms folded across her chest.

"I ... well, I hadn't really studied on it, so I really didn't know."

That's it, Aidan, give a half-baked explanation to a detective.

"I find that hard to believe."

"It's true. And besides, it's not a topic ministers in my denomination easily discuss."

"I think there's something more. I saw a look of panic on your face, way out of proportion than just fearing breaking a minister's taboo or something stupid like that."

"Do you believe in the law, Jennifer?"

"I ... what kind of question is that?"

"Do you believe in the law, right and wrong? You're a cop. That is what you try to do, right? Protect people and obey the law?"

She scrunched her face. "Well, I guess I wouldn't put it in such amateur terms, but essentially, yeah, that's why I became a police officer."

"What if you didn't? Would you still be a cop?"

"Truthfully, probably not. Wouldn't be any point would there?" She paused. "Why are you asking me this?"

"I don't believe in God. I am a minister who doesn't believe in God or the supernatural. That is why I didn't want to answer their questions."

Jennifer stared at me, her eyes wide. She probably thought I was a horrible person with no integrity. That would be the end of it. I looked back up, and her face was unreadable.

"What are you going to do?" she asked.

"I don't know. My boss knows, and he told me to think about it. But I already have. I just have to figure out what to do. There aren't a lot of other job options with a Masters of Divinity degree."

She nodded, and I noticed she kept clenching her fist as if she were fighting for control.

"I'll keep you updated on the investigation. If there's anything else, contact me." She turned and left.

I sat on the couch, a bit mystified by her abrupt departure. The pictures on my computer screen were evidence that Amanda tried to tell me something. What though?

Amanda's words echoed in my head: *I have found someone else.*

That was it! I had to find this "someone else." Whoever she had been dating had to be the key. Maybe someone at the church where she worked would have some information. Jennifer probably already asked there, but I might notice something she hadn't.

I paused as Zoe's words and Amanda's letter came back to me: *talk to Father Neal.* I sighed. Maybe I could do both in one day.

Bishop got up on the couch and stretched out.

"Tired, you big bag of fleas?"

He looked at me with his liquid eyes as I patted his rump. "Goodnight, Bishop. I'm going to watch some TV."

The high-pitched, scratchy voice of Eric Cartman filled my living room as I tried to forget everything I'd seen and heard over the past few days. None of it made any sense as I tried to sort through the jumbled puzzle pieces in my head.

chapter fifteen

❋

I woke up the next morning and called the church as I made breakfast.

"Sherry, this is Pastor Aidan. I've had an emergency come up. I'm going to need you to clear my schedule. Please tell the children's ministry team that I'm sorry. This can't wait."

I could almost hear her mind whirring as to what emergency it could possibly be and when she would be able gossip about it.

"Of course. Is there any message you want me to pass on to Pastor Mike?"

"No, just tell him I'll call him later." I had just given her something to talk about for the rest of the morning with her friends.

"No problem, sir."

"Thanks, Sherry, you're the best. Have a good morning."

I hung up the phone and took a bite out of my chocolate muffin. With a few clicks, I pulled up the website for Fields of the Lord Church, Amanda's former place of employment, on the east side of the city. I wrote down the directions, put Bishop in his crate, and made for the door.

As I got in the car, I remembered Jen already questioned most of the Fields of the Lord Staff. Still, I couldn't just sit around and wallow in my misery over Amanda or the hypocrisy of my life. I had to do something other than look for jobs.

I also wanted to see people's reactions when I started asking questions. My suspicion that Amanda's man had been a married pastor had never gone away, and I had to lay that to rest.

Still, I figured it probably wouldn't hurt to tell Jennifer what my plans were. It's not like she could really stop me, short of arresting me. I dialed her number.

"This is ... Detective Brown," she said, in quick breaths.

"Jennifer? It's Aidan. Are you okay?"

"Running laps. Morning exercise, gotta keep in shape."

"Right. I have a question," I said as I started up my car.

"Shoot."

"Did you send someone over to Fields of the Lord church?"

"Yeah, we did." She paused. "I think Jeremy went there and asked around. Why?"

"Did you turn anything up?"

"No, other than shocked church people. Again, why do you ask?"

I chewed on my frozen lip.

"I'm not sure. Maybe you guys missed something."

"Jeremy is very thorough. There's probably nothing else there," Jennifer said as she caught her breath.

"Well, I'm just going to the church today."

She paused and then spoke in a low, authoritative voice, "Aidan, you aren't trying to be a cop, are you?"

"No, of course not. Just, um, a pastor's conference."

I could almost feel her disbelief oozing through the phone and into my ear. "Is that right? You aren't a very good liar."

"How do you know?" I said, smiling a little.

"Trust me. You aren't. And I'm totally serious. You were just a suspect in this case, and if you ask the wrong questions to get people upset, it could…"

"I know, put me back in the suspect column. I'll be careful."

"What are you going to do after that?"

"Not sure, why?" I hadn't told her about Father Neal yet, and I had no desire to tell her how I even heard about him.

"Thought maybe we could have lunch, talk about your faith thing," she said. "I'm sorry I left so quickly after that. I felt bad, so I thought I would give us a chance to talk."

"Uh, sure," I stammered. "Well, I have a lunch appointment … can we do dinner?"

"Of course, no problem. Want to go somewhere in the Short North?"

"Sure, Northstar Café, around sixish?"

"Excellent, that is right down the street from my condo," Jennifer said.

"Great, I'll meet you at your place then."

My head whirled with thoughts of the lady detective as I drove down I-71 to Fields of the Lord Church. I didn't need to look it up on my GPS as I'd seen the huge church building from the highway. Pulling into the parking lot, I felt like an ant staring up at a house. The rumor around town was that this church could be seen from space on a clear night because of all the lights around the outside. I doubted that story, but the electric bill had to be a bitch.

The design of the building made me wonder if George and Elroy Jetson would come zooming past the "tower of prayer." The building supposedly held five thousand people and reached capacity for each of their three services. The sheriff had to assign a deputy to direct traffic into the vast parking lots, which were now empty as I drove into the complex.

The CEO of this corporation, or rather, pastor of the church, Daniel Mueller, had become a young, rising star in the evangelical world. The man had it all, beautiful ex-model wife, three adorable kids, a book deal and growing political power. All in all, he was the perfect American evangelical minister.

I gripped the steering wheel as I started to have second thoughts. I suddenly realized they weren't just going to let me come in and start asking questions. Still, I'd traveled this far and might as well play the whole hand. The car shuttered to a stop, I turned it off and went inside.

The demon of ugliness had been cast out of Fields of the Lord and cast into the pigs of lesser churches. Everything had a place. Real plants were positioned in the corners and tasteful, if bland, inspirational paintings decorated the walls. The ceiling rose above me, revealing the cold, blue sky through spotless glass panels.

Under these glass panels sat one of the most beautiful soccer moms I'd ever seen. Her short, dark hair slightly bobbed at the neck, and her make-up was applied to perfection. No part of her red business suit was out of place. She seemed like a piece of art placed among the rest of the meticulous lobby.

She gave me a pleasant, if somewhat cold, smile. If I didn't charm her, I wouldn't be visiting the broom closet, much less talking to the pastor of the church. I thought about the scene in *Monty Python and the Holy Grail* where the knights met the bridge-keeper who asked them three questions. I wondered what pit I would be cast into if I answered her questions wrong.

"Hello, my name is Pastor Aidan Schaeffer, and I would like to speak with Pastor Mueller."

She gave me a tight lipped smile. "I'm sorry, Pastor Schaeffer, do you have an appointment?"

"No, um, Jessica," I said, glancing at her name tag. "But I have some urgent business to discuss."

The smile disappeared. I guessed she'd dealt with my type before and wouldn't let me in to save her life. "I'm sorry, Pastor Schaeffer, but Pastor Mueller is a very busy man. The way to see him is by calling his personal secretary and making an appointment."

I tried a bluff. "Yes, of course, Jessica, I understand. But I have not been able to get a hold of his personal secretary in the past few days."

She rolled her eyes. "Yes, well, she is on vacation at the moment. I am sure if you try back next week."

This was going nowhere. I wouldn't get in, and I had been stupid to even try.

"Well, okay, thank you, Jessica. Maybe I will try that."

A voice came from down the hall. A tall blonde *GQ*-looking model appeared, talking on a cell phone.

"Please tell Reverend Graham I am praying for him and that he should get some rest."

I knew I had one chance. With Jessica squealing in protest, I walked right up to him.

"Pastor Mueller? I am Pastor Aidan Schaeffer, from Knox Presbyterian Church. I was wondering if I might have a moment of your time."

He looked at me with a "TV" smile. "Pastor Schaeffer, it's good to meet you."

Jessica caught up with us and grabbed my arm. "I'm sorry, Pastor Mueller, he didn't have my permission to do this. I was just telling him he should leave."

"It's okay, Jessica, I love speaking to fellow pastors."

She threw me a look of church-lady disgust as she went back to her desk.

"What can I do for you, Pastor Schaeffer? I hope you don't feel rushed, but I have a phone conference in about fifteen minutes."

"I want to talk to you about Amanda."

His chiseled face slackened into a look of surprise before he could control it.

"Amanda? There are a lot of Amandas at our church, Pastor Schaeffer. Is she a former member of your church that has started coming to ours?"

"No, I am talking about Amanda McDougal, your head of communications, who was recently murdered."

Once again, an uncontrolled look crossed his face, a look that reminded me of Bishop when he had been caught taking a dump on the rug.

"Oh, yes. Forgive me, Pastor Schaeffer. I talked to the police about Amanda. Sad situation, but I really don't have much more to say."

"I'm sure, Pastor Mueller, and I'm not really here for that. Amanda was, well, my ex-fiancée."

Pastor Mueller smiled and chuckled. "Oh, you are *that* Aidan!

The Calvinist! I would say that God predestined you to be here today."

I hated that stupid joke. Calvinists had to hear it all the time because we believed in God's sovereignty. Even though I didn't believe anymore, the comment still made me want to scream. But I wanted to keep him happy, so I laughed. "Yes, right. Anyway, I just want to find out about Amanda's last days before she was murdered. I thought maybe you could give me some clues."

"Ah, a man still in love, eh?" Pastor Mueller gave me a guy-to-guy pat on the shoulder with a somber expression on his face. He probably never realized how close he came to losing a hand or getting punched in the face.

"I guess you could say that. I just want to see her killer brought to justice." I winced as I said it. I sounded like a bad TV show.

He nodded his head but avoided looking me in the eyes. Instead, he stared just off to the right of my shoulder. "I really can't tell you much. Amanda was a great worker and helped me tremendously. We are devastated by her death."

Really? You sure don't look like it.

"But I don't have anything else to say. Amanda seemed perfectly normal. Nothing out of the ordinary."

"What about the pastor she was dating here, have you talked to him?"

His jaw clenched. "Pastor Schaeffer, I don't get into personal matters like that unless they are sins. If some of my staff are dating, I don't go out of my way to find out unless it becomes a problem."

I had a hard time believing anything went on in this church without this jackass knowing every detail.

"Besides," he continued. "I wouldn't want a member of my staff exposed to any, ah, unfounded accusations by the wrong sources."

"Did you tell the cops that?"

"My conversation with the police is confidential." Even as he shot me down, he kept that smile on his face. He'd begun to edge his way toward his office.

"Of course. I'm sorry I wasted your time."

"Not at all. It's good you have such a drive for justice. I hope the police find her killer."

"Yes, of course. I feel the same."

I began to walk away and then turned around quickly. "Did you ask Amanda to take pictures of some woods, say for a church bulletin or brochure?"

He laughed. "I don't give that sort of assignment. If Amanda had some pictures in her possession, she may have been taking them for a project. She was in charge of all that. I let her do that work without questions. As you know, she was very good at it."

"Yes, well, I will let you get back to work. I have to go work on my sermon on Moses and Mt. Nebo."

Pastor Mueller's jaw clenched, and his eyes bulged. "What did you say?"

"I am doing a sermon on Moses looking at the Promised Land from Mt. Nebo. Just the next sermon in Numbers you know."

His eyes looked me up and down. Then, he smiled. "Yes, of course, very sad passage," he said, his voice lowered. "I hope it goes well. Have a good day, Pastor Schaeffer."

I walked out of the foyer and smiled at Jessica. She didn't smile back. Instead, she brushed her hair over her ear. The light caught on a huge diamond ring on her left hand.

Well, someone must love her, or that's a huge apology gift.

I slowly got into my car and looked up at the church building. Did I just imagine his reaction of anger? Was I letting my feelings dictate my response? I hated mega-churches, even when I still believed in God. They represented everything that's wrong with American Christianity, from their bloated buildings to their bloated budgets and bloated searches for political power. Amanda and I fought about it all the time when she took the job. She said I was just jealous of their success.

I looked at my phone and punched in the address for St. Patrick's Episcopal Church. To my surprise, the church was pretty close to my house. I'd never noticed it before.

From a mega-church superstar to an Anglican priest. Quite an ecumenical day.

chapter sixteen

I pulled up to St. Patrick's Episcopal Church just before noon. My body ached, and I felt weak. I rested my head on the steering wheel. The contrast between Fields of the Lord Church and St Patrick's jarred me. The stone building seemed to flow out of the Ohio turf. The whole of St. Patrick's could have fit neatly in Fields of the Lord's reception area. Yet, I couldn't shake the feeling of some hidden power. I felt nothing but loathing at Fields of the Lord Church. Here, as I stood before the small stone church, the whole atmosphere seemed to pulsate with a hidden secret. The air shimmered, and light danced on the building as if it were alive.

I went inside and found another secretary. This one, an older lady with gray hair and reading glasses, seemed more pleasant even as she glared at a computer screen.

"Cursed computers, minions of the Devil, all of them," she mumbled.

"Hello, ma'am, is Father Neal in?" I asked.

She jumped and then she smiled.

"Yes, just a minute, honey, I am trying to figure out this new email program."

"Um, do you mind if I help? I am pretty good with computers."

"Oh, you are sweet. Thank you." She backed up from the screen, and I showed her how to press the "send" button. She smiled. "Thank you! You are a peach. Now, let me take you back to Father Neal's office. He has gone into the sanctuary for prayer and will be right back. Would you like any tea or coffee, dear?"

"Thanks. Tea would be great, uh…"

"Mrs. Ryder, honey, but you can call me Sue."

"Thank you, Sue."

She walked down the hall to the rectory kitchen, leading me to Father Neal's office.

I sat down in a wingback leather chair and waited. The air in Father Neal's office hit me like the air of a mountain I'd climbed in New Mexico. I'd expected it to smell old and musty. I breathed deep and sighed. I relaxed, my mind stopped buzzing, and my eyelids began to droop. My whole body felt like Jell-O as if I'd inhaled laughing gas at the dentist.

I snapped awake.

Stupid! You can't fall asleep here!

I tried to stand, but my legs felt too heavy. I stayed in the chair as I looked around at Father Neal's office.

Books, the mainstay of any minister's office, lined the wall behind Father Neal's desk. Instead of the theological discourses of a Presbyterian minister, the books looked old, cracked and most likely out of print. A Celtic cross made of solid oak hung over a wooden desk. I couldn't help but wonder if they'd been made of the same tree. I leaned over and knocked on the desk. Solid Oak.

I sat back in my chair. My eyelids started to droop again, and I held them open with my hands.

Come on, Aidan, stay awake.

I looked at the pictures on Father Neal's desk. A stunning, gray-haired woman sat on a park bench surrounded by three adult girls. The girls appeared in other frames on the desk and looked just like the older lady. Father Neal had a group of lovely women, I thought.

I gazed around to other frames and badly cut paper flowers and bugs. Most of them contained variations of "Daddy, I love you" and "You're the best daddy in the world."

I looked at my watch, thinking fifteen minutes had passed. It had only been three.

I stood up and walked around, but I felt dizzy. The whole atmosphere seemed to swirl around me. I knew that I had been in Father Neal's office for at least fifteen minutes. Or maybe ten.

Or maybe I was just losing it.

I sat back down and closed my eyes. As I slipped into a dream world, everything glowed. I looked around for the source, but I couldn't find it anywhere. A woman behind me cleared her throat. I stood up and turned, thinking another church worker had walked in and caught me sleeping.

Amanda stood behind me, smiling and shining with light. She raised her hand in greeting. Her hair appeared almost white, and she moved toward me as if she were made of air.

I tried to speak but couldn't. She stared at me with an expression I'd seen on her face when I first proposed to her. I ached to touch her and reached out to try. As I did, another voice spoke. I couldn't tell what it said, but Amanda turned to the voice and nodded. She looked back at me, gave me one of her half smiles that I'd loved so much, and disappeared.

"Aidan, my son, wake up. Wake up."

I jolted out of my chair and came face to face with who I presumed to be Father Neal. "Amanda. Where is Amanda?" I asked, looking around the room.

"Amanda is not here, son. It's just you and me. I'm Father Neal." He wore all black like a catholic priest. His hair was white and he walked with a gnarled, black cane.

"But ... I know ... I saw her. The room was..."

"I think you are tired. Please sit."

I sat down, feeling a bit embarrassed. "I'm sorry. I don't know what happened. I just felt really sleepy."

"I'm sure you did, lad. It's okay, I understand." He smiled, straightening the deep wrinkles of his face.

The fogginess of sleep passed. "I'm sorry?"

"You are a pastor, aren't you? You're like me then, probably don't get much sleep."

As he sat at his desk, he examined me with bright, blue eyes. I shifted in my seat as I wondered if he could see right through me.

"Well, lad, you falling asleep in my office is not the worst thing to ever happen here." He chuckled. "Though people usually wait until my Sunday homilies."

His voice reminded me of Ian McClellan's, a deep, upper class British accent that had a tone of command. I would have bet money that he never needed to raise his voice to his daughters.

"Now, Aidan, how may I help you?"

I didn't know where to begin or how to start. Father Neal beat me to it.

"I heard Zoe visited you the other day," he said.

"Um, yes, she did."

"And what did you think of what she said?" The corner of his mouth twitched a bit.

"Well, I guess, I don't know, it was a little bit…"

"Unusual?"

"To say the least. I would have dismissed her except for one thing."

"Yes?"

"Well, it's a long story."

"Try me."

I stared at Father Neal for a moment as I figured out what to say. He got up from the desk, limped around it, and sat down beside me. He touched my arm and a jolt of electricity ran through me as if I'd stuck my finger into a light socket. I pulled away from him.

"What have you seen, my son?"

His question startled me. "I … I don't know what you mean."

Father Neal sighed. "Aidan, you have the look all over you."

"What look?"

"The look of a man who has seen things he can't quite believe."

I replied without thinking. "That's for damn sure."

He smiled. "As for damnable, that remains to be seen. I'm guessing, however, you're starting to see what most people refer to as ghosts."

"Ghosts? Seriously?"

He gave me a wide smile. "I know what you're thinking. White sheets. Scooby Doo. But it's not like that at all."

"And how do you know?"

Father Neal paused, and he stared off into space. At first, I wondered if he fell asleep, but his mouth moved.

"Father?"

He started to speak and then abruptly stopped. "Forgive me, my dear boy. Old age is not very kind. My mind drifts from time to time. To answer your question, I'm going to ask you a question. What did you see? Was it Amanda?"

Goose pimples shot up my arm, and I swallowed hard. "Father, I couldn't have seen her. She's dead."

He put a shaking hand up to his head. "I know, lad."

"You saw it on the news?" I asked, perplexed.

Father Neal gave me a sad smile. "Something like that. Now, why do you think I asked you if you saw her a few minutes ago?"

I stared at him. This conversation had veered into weird shit territory.

"I have no idea. I mean, I saw her, but I was dreaming."

He shook his head. "No. I saw her too."

"Um, what?"

"I saw her. She was here with you. She is what you might call a ghost, although that term is terribly misleading."

"Right. Ghost. Sure." I edged my chair back.

"You don't believe me?"

"Not really, no. I don't believe in ghosts."

"Why not?" He leaned forward, his intense eyes boring into mine.

"Well, I mean, come on. Ghosts? Isn't that just something to scare teenage kids around the campfire?"

To my surprise, his face muscles tightened, and his eyes seemed to blaze with fire. "Don't you believe in the unseen world, *Pastor Schaeffer?*"

"Why does everyone keep asking me that? Of course, I'm a pastor, but I don't think believing in ghosts is the same thing."

He gripped his cane and leaned forward. "Don't use the term 'ghosts'. It's not right or proper."

I couldn't help but ask. "So, what *is* proper?"

"Are Presbyterians required to know all of the Bible and the Creeds? Or just Paul's letters?"

I scoffed. "Depends on who you ask. What does that have to do with ghosts?"

He pointed his cane at me. "Everything, dear boy, everything! Your Presbyterian education has made you dull to the seen and unseen world. Do you think it's an accident that the Creeds start off with God is the creator of all things seen and unseen?"

"So, what? When people die, they walk around and see us?"

"That's exactly what they do, Aidan!"

Father Neal stared at me and waited for my response. I struggled for words and decided to change the subject.

"Zoe says she has a ghost group. Are they like Ghostbusters or something?"

"I believe they like to call themselves paranormal investigators. I think they'd find the notion of ghost-busting offensive."

"Who you gonna call?" I grinned.

"Aside from the fact that Ghostbuster's is the last funny movie that Dan Akroyd and Bill Murray made together, it's terribly inaccurate."

"Score one for your pop culture knowledge. What does this group do?"

He frowned. "Did you ever see a show on the Syfy channel called *Ghost Hunters?*"

"Can't say that I have."

"They go to places that are haunted and scientifically investigate them."

"Oh? How do they do that? I didn't think ghosts were in the realm of science," I said as I ran my fingers through my hair.

Father Neal waved his hand. "I can't describe it to you. I think you might just need to see for yourself."

Mrs. Ryder walked in with two mugs of tea. "Here you go, Pastor Aidan."

"Thank you very much," I said, taking the mug.

When she left, Father Neal got up and opened a drawer in his desk. "Would the Irishman like a bit of whisky for his tea?"

I nodded. "Mother's milk, Father."

He tipped a small amount into my cup. I took a sip and coughed.

"Been awhile?" he asked, as he poured himself some in a shot glass.

"Yeah," I rasped, the whisky burning my throat. "Usually I just drink Guinness."

"Aidan, my lad, you're a stereotype."

We both laughed, and I pointed at his pictures. "Your family?"

The lines in his face softened as he smiled. "Yes, the ladies in my life. That's my dear wife, Judy, who passed away a few years ago."

"I'm sorry."

"Ah, don't worry. I will see her again."

The confidence and faith in his voice made me shift in my seat. I didn't want to broach that topic with him. "Do your daughters live around here?"

He paused as he stared at the pictures. The lines on his face tightened.

"No, sadly. They're all back in England."

"Why don't you move back to England to be close to them?"

"Ah, well, I don't feel a release to go yet." He avoided looking at me.

"Sorry, I didn't mean to get so personal."

"No worries, lad. I'm always glad to talk about my angels."

I took another sip of tea. "So, about Amanda. Do you see dead people like Zoe does?"

He smiled. "Not exactly. Our gifts are ... different, you might say."

"How so?"

"Zoe doesn't always see through the veil. She gets breaks. I do not."

"I'm not sure I follow."

Father Neal looked at me. "Not only do you not follow, do think you're ready for my explanation."

I sat the tea down. "Why do you think I came here?"

"I don't know, lad. Tell me."

"Zoe came and talked to me." I balled my fists. "I thought I explained that."

"I heard you the first time. And what did you think about what she told you?"

"That she was bat shit crazy, excuse me."

"No excuse needed. She might be crazy. I happen to think her brain has been somewhat damaged from all the chemicals she ingested in her youth."

His frank confirmation of my suspicions floored me.

"But Aidan, that doesn't mean she is wrong. Besides, if you thought she was so warped by drugs, why did you come to me? You could have just discarded her message."

He had me on that one. I would have to tell him everything that'd happened in the past week.

"Why don't you start at the beginning?" he said as if reading my mind.

I started at Edna's dream and finished with my trip to Fields of the Lord. When I was done, he stared down at the floor.

"Father?"

He mumbled something I couldn't hear and then looked up. "I suppose you're wondering how we all knew Amanda, eh?"

The abrupt change of subject jarred me. "Yeah, now that you mention it. I would like to know when she started with your group."

"She came to me about four months ago. Nervous about something, but she would never spell it out."

"Did she ever?"

Father Neal frowned. "No, sadly. She hinted at boyfriend problems, but she never elaborated. Zoe latched onto her, and they discovered a shared interest in the *other*."

"The other?"

"The unseen realm, my lad. Anyway, Amanda went on some investigations. She disappeared a few weeks ago, and we were wondering what happened. Now we know." He looked at me. "She talked about you all the time, you know."

My throat tightened. "Why didn't she talk about Mr. Spiritually wonderful?" I lashed out.

"As to that, I have no idea. I do know that when she started talking about her most recent boyfriend, she would stop, turn white, and then not say any more."

"And you didn't find that odd?"

Father Neal sighed. "Of course, I did. I still do. Something happened with Amanda beyond just the normal abusive relationship."

"And why do you think that?"

"Because, she was drawn here, to this church and to me."

His words made me shift in my seat. The room began to shimmer and swirl in a variety of colors. The smell of incense wafted through the air. The world seemed to tilt as Father Neal stood up. His black priest outfit morphed into a white monk's robe. Voices started singing in a language I didn't understand. I glanced at Father Neal and gasped. His white hair glowed, and the age dropped from his face. In his right hand, he held a cup that pulsed with a golden light.

My heart started to race, and I fell out of my chair. I crawled for the door.

"Aidan, are you okay?" Father Neal said.

I looked up, and everything had gone back to normal.

"I ... uh ... I ... I don't know. I ... you... What the hell? What is wrong with me?"

Father Neal limped over to me and gave me his hand. I took it lightly, and he pulled me up with surprising strength. "Nothing, lad."

"Then what?"

"Something ... *other*." He smiled.

I had to get out of that room, that church, and away from him. "Father Neal, it's been great. Thanks. I gotta run."

He reached out and grabbed my arm. "Aidan, I want you to come on a ghost hunt with me."

That was the last thing I expected to hear from him. "I'm sorry?"

"A ghost hunt. There's one tomorrow night. I want you to be there. Meet me here at seven."

"But Father Neal, I can't..."

"I won't take no for an answer, Aidan. Seven o'clock sharp, please."

"But..."

"There are things you must understand."

I walked outside and headed to my car. The snow had begun to fall again in slow, lazy flakes.

Crunch. Crunch. Crunch.

I turned around and saw no one.

Crunch. Crunch. Crunch.

I looked down and saw bare footprints appearing in the snow again. Not just one pair but dozens of them coming toward me from the church. The church building itself seemed almost alive, its walls bulging, roof shifting and windows reflecting a shimmering presence that looked right through me.

I stood, unable to move. The snow came down in a torrent now, almost blinding me as each footprint appeared, filling the air with the pop of hardening flakes.

Horror gripped my throat. I forced my legs to function, threw myself into the car, and sped off.

chapter seventeen

"So, that was my day," I said as I ate my High Street pizza full of meat and olives.

"Sounds like an interesting day among the clergy of our city." Jennifer picked at her half-eaten veggie burger. "So, why aren't you going back?"

"You're joking right?" I folded my arms and leaned back in my chair. I hadn't told her about the Amanda dream or Father Neal turning into *Other-World Man*.

"No, I'm not," she said. "It sounds interesting, a ghost hunt."

"Yeah, but there is one problem. I don't believe one word of it, remember?"

She frowned and leaned forward. "Why don't you believe in God anymore, Aidan? We didn't talk about it last night."

I shifted in my seat and picked at my straw. I needed to open up. I couldn't handle bottling it inside any longer. Jennifer seemed trustworthy; at least, she hadn't tried to run me back into jail. She'd seen the footprints and heard my offhand comments about God. But I couldn't find my tongue. "Yeah."

Jennifer smirked. "You know, for a preacher, you don't really have a way with words."

"Sorry. It's just not something I want to talk about, really. You don't have me in an interrogation room now." I hoped she would take that as a joke and drop the subject.

"I'm sorry." Her face flushed a bit. "I'm just curious."

I shrugged. "It's cool. I'm just trying to find the right words. But first, let me ask you a question."

She raised an eyebrow at me and took a sip of her ginger ale. "Ask away, preacher."

"What do you believe?"

"About God? I guess I believe there is one."

"What does that mean?" I folded my arms across my body, the way I did when teaching a Bible study lesson.

"Well, I'm not really sure. I mean, I was raised Catholic, but I don't go to Mass much anymore. I don't hold to most of what the church teaches."

"Doesn't that usually go with being an American Catholic?" I laughed.

"True," Jennifer said. "I guess I have my own religion. You know, I believe in God and spirituality. I'm spiritual, but not religious."

"Okay, let me stop you there. What does that mean, 'spiritual but not religious?'"

She stared out the window, watching the Gallery Hop Art patrons stream by our table.

"You know, I have never really thought about it. I guess it means acknowledging God, being thankful, nice to people, helping in the community and all that. I guess a little praying gets thrown in there too, especially on some of the cases I have to investigate."

"Okay, so this God you pray to, what is He or She like? Can you describe this entity?"

"Well, no, I guess it's more of a feeling."

"Exactly. Why do you need God to be a good person? You don't. People can be nice without worrying about God hanging over their head." I took a sip of beer.

She folded her arms across her chest. "So, who says what's nice? Someone has to enforce the law."

"So, God is a universal cop? That's comforting." I tried to keep the scorn out of my voice.

"No, I mean, laws come from somewhere right?"

"Sure. Society. It's in the best interest of society for laws to be made."

She slowly nodded her head. "I see what you're saying, but I don't buy it."

"What, that there is no God or lawgiver? No God you can't define other than good feelings or 'must be's' that you can't prove?" I leaned in so far that our faces almost touched.

Jennifer backed away. "I guess, but I have a hard time believing there isn't something out there."

"Like what? It could be anything, as Dawkins says. It could be a flying spaghetti monster. You don't know."

"True, I guess, I don't know." Jennifer frowned. "Still, I hardly think that God and a flying spaghetti monster are the same damn thing."

"How do you know?" I pressed.

"Because, Aidan, I'm not a dumbass. God is something you can define. A flying spaghetti monster is a stupid concept some asshole came up with."

"Who says God isn't the same thing?"

"I do, and so does just about everyone else. Anyone could see the difference between your pasta god and the possibility of a real God," she said.

I let out a long sigh. "I guess I don't believe in God anymore because I see no other alternative. I think the whole, vague, spirituality thing is a crock, no offense. Either believe in God, do what he says, or don't. Why try to have both? It's just hypocritical or holding on to the notion of God without any of the responsibilities."

"So, does that go for other religions?" Jennifer played with her empty glass.

"Yeah, pretty much the same concept across the board."

Jennifer wrapped her arms around herself. Her eyes looked at the table, but from her face, it seemed as if something had just broken inside her.

"Listen, Jennifer, I'm sorry. I got a little intense."

"No, Aidan, you are right. I just never thought about it myself. I guess God was a teddy bear I didn't want to let go of. Maybe I just need to grow up."

"No. I mean, if you want to believe in God, it's okay. I just can't do it anymore."

She stared at me. "You really have thought this through."

"Yeah, I guess I have." I paused. "Or I'm trying to anyway."

"Do you miss it?"

"My faith?"

"Yes," she said, staring out at the people walking past our table.

"Of course I miss it. It has been a huge comfort in my life, and now it's gone. There is nothing to take its place." I fiddled with the saltshaker.

Jennifer hesitated for a moment. "Let's go for a walk, look at the galleries."

We paid and headed out the door. The steel archways stretched over High Street, lit with the glow of soft, white light. People filled the streets, walking through the galleries and chatting. A college student band full of white boys with dreadlocks strummed on guitars. People plunked change down into their empty cases. A woman dressed as a groom and a man dressed as a bride twirled in a bizarre, dirty dancing style waltz as they parted the crowd.

"You know," I said. "I once brought my brother to a Gallery Hop."

"What did he say?"

"He said it was crazier than anything he saw on a trip to San Francisco."

"Seriously?"

"Yeah."

"How many brothers and sisters do you have?" she asked.

"One older brother. You?"

"Two sisters. My poor dad never got the bathroom."

We both laughed, and it broke the tension from our dinner conversation. As we walked through each art gallery we talked, and she even touched my arm a few times. It's amazing how much you miss being held by someone, how much you begin to crave it. My skin tingled as it soaked up the lightness of Jen's fingers.

We made our way into a particular art gallery, attracted by the artist's Monet-style self-portrait just outside the door. I picked up a brochure and read it aloud. "My name is Tara. These paintings represent an artistic task that I set out for myself. That is, to paint as much as I could for five days without any corrections. What you see is an honest representation of those days without any visual editing."

Jennifer gave a half smile. "Visual editing, hmm?"

I laughed. "Yeah, well, it's an interesting idea. Let's check it out."

We walked past the reception desk and into the main room. I saw the first painting and gasped. "What the hell?"

The artist had depicted a large footprint, painted blue. A stream of red blood poured out of a wound from the middle of the foot.

"Well, that's a bit disturbing," Jennifer said.

"To say the least."

"Let's look at the next one."

The bloody footprint theme exploded throughout all the paintings. The artist had painted it into buildings, landscapes, and people. The last painting made my heart race and the hair on the back of my neck stand up. A tall, willowy girl who looked exactly like Amanda stood with her arms stretched out in a cross formation. Across her throat, a red slash gushed blood and on her forehead, the Hebrew word Nebo had been painted in what looked like jagged knife marks. Her blue eyes were open in death and bore right through me.

"Jennifer," I rasped. "Look!"

She stared in disbelief. "I don't believe it."

Jennifer walked over to a small, red-haired girl with a ponytail. "Excuse me, Tara? Can I ask you a few questions about that painting?"

"Oh, yes, disturbing isn't it? I haven't been able to sleep since I painted it."

"Yes, I'm sure," she said, her brow furrowed. "But I'm curious, where were you when you painted it?"

Jennifer, who'd been so breezy and relaxed the whole evening, had switched back into detective mode. She radiated tension as she folded her arms. The art gallery had become an interrogation room.

Tara played with her fingers, nervous. "In my studio, of course."

"Do you have anyone who can back that up?"

"Why do you want to know that?"

Jennifer pulled out her badge. "I'm curious."

Tara stiffened. "Do you have a warrant?"

I cringed.

"No, but I can get one if I need it," Jennifer replied, her voice soft but firm. "I hope I won't. I just need to know about these paintings. It's really important. It might help us solve a murder."

Tara went pale and gripped the desk in front of her. "No, that can't be! It was just a picture in my head. Emily was with me the whole time, weren't you?" She turned toward her nose-pierced friend standing a few feet away.

I ignored the rest of the conversation and stared into the blue eyes of the painting. I could almost see Amanda in them. It felt like she had died and been trapped on canvas.

I turned away from the painting, the same way I wanted to turn away from all the things that had been happening to me. I couldn't ignore them, but they were highly inconvenient with my newfound lack of faith. Something kept hitting me in the face. The footprints. The dream. The painting. It almost felt like Amanda was trying to lead me to her murderer from beyond the grave.

But why go through all this trouble? Why not just appear to me and tell me the name of the guy so I could track him down, like she did in Father Neal's office? I couldn't understand it.

I had to get out of there. I left Jennifer to her interrogation and stumbled outside. I sucked in the cold night air. Jennifer came out a few moments later, shaking her head.

"Well, their story seems to check out. At least, I couldn't find any reason to doubt them. But I'm having them come into the station in an hour, just to be sure." She paused. "Sorry to have to cut this short."

I nodded. "It's okay. Bishop needs to go out anyway."

We walked in silence back to Jennifer's condo. She stood in the doorframe, looking at me.

"What?" I asked.

"You still love Amanda, don't you?"

"Why do you ask?"

"That look you had when you saw the woman in the painting."

I paused. "Yeah, I guess I do. I know it's weird. I mean, she's dead now, but I keep feeling as if she is right here with me."

She shook her head. "It's not weird at all, Aidan."

"I was ready to marry her. I still have the ring, actually."

She nodded but didn't say anything.

"Are you okay?"

She pointed to the scar on her face. "Do you see this?"

"Yeah, how did it happen?"

"My ex-husband," she answered in a dry, flat tone. Her voice sent chills up my spine.

"I'm sorry, what happened?"

She gave a slight smile. "I caught him with his girlfriend, and he got mad at me. But let's just say he got worse than he gave. He limped through the whole assault trial." She hesitated and looked at her watch. "Gotta run to the station. Talk to you later."

I squinted. "Wait, why did you tell me?"

Jennifer paused in the doorway. "Love leaves scars, Aidan. Some visible, some not. But they all hurt like hell." She reached out and touched my arm. "But it doesn't mean we stop trying to love."

chapter eighteen

My phone rang as I was getting ready for church the next morning.

"Aidan?"

"Mike? You sound terrible."

"Yeah, I feel horrible. I hate to do this to you, but I can barely speak. Would you mind preaching this morning?"

He had never done this before, but as an assistant pastor, I always had to be ready for something like this. "No, I don't mind. I'll pull one of my old sermons from seminary. It's only seven-thirty, so I should be able to get things in order by then."

"Thanks, Aidan. I really appreciate it."

I showered and dressed, making sure all ends of my shirt tucked into my pants. Old ladies of the church noticed that sort of thing. I sometimes wondered what would cause more of an uproar, going into the pulpit stark naked or leaving my shirt untucked. It would probably be an even tie.

I got to the office and pulled an old sermon on Jonah that I had done years ago. My preacher autopilot took over. Most of the congregation would sleep through the sermon anyway.

Bill led the first part of the service; Opening hymns, confession of sin, and the offering. As the last chords of the Doxology ended, I stepped up to the pulpit and began my sermon.

"As I said before the service, Pastor Mike came down sick, so I'm filling in for him. I chose a passage from the second chapter of Jonah that I thought would be good for you all this morning."

The fluttering of pages in the congregation signaled that they had all brought their Bibles to church, like good Presbyterians. As I began to read from Jonah, I realized my mistake.

Why did I choose this sermon?

Everyone stared at me, so I continued, pausing after each verse. "I called out to the LORD, out of my distress, and he answered me; out of the belly of the dead I cried, and you heard my voice. For you cast me into the deep, into the heart of the seas, and the flood surrounded me."

My breath shortened, and my heart speed up. My vision narrowed as I struggled to form coherent thoughts. I took a few deep breaths to get over the panic. I was in the belly of the dead, the belly of my own unbelief.

I found myself a dying hypocrite preaching to dying hypocrites.

The sanctuary spun around, and I gripped the pulpit to prevent myself from passing out. I excused myself and grabbed a glass of water so that everyone would think I just had a dry throat. The rest of the sermon erased from my brain. In a panic, I went with the old preacher standby of evangelical buzzwords. I flung out "grace," "redemption," "sin," and "repentance." Everyone ate it up. I just wanted to get out of the pulpit and into the solitude of my office. The words kept echoing in my mind, "belly of the dead, belly of the dead."

In a daze, I led the congregation through the final hymn, gave the benediction, and made my way to the door. Everyone gave me the usual, "Good sermon, Pastor Aidan," which told me no one actually listened.

I retreated to my office as soon as I could get away. I slid into my chair and saw my cell phone had two messages, one text and one voice.

I clicked on the text. It was from Jennifer.

I had fun last night. Had to come into the office. Call me when you get home from the ghost hunt.

The ghost hunt. I'd nearly forgotten.

The voicemail message was from Father Neal.

"Aidan, this is Father Neal. Meet me at the church at six-thirty. I will tell you about the Bone Masters tonight."

That did it. Now I would have to go. I sighed and sat back in my chair. My mind began to wander, imagining what the night would hold.

A sudden knock sent me right out of my chair to my feet.

"Aidan?"

"Olan? You scared the shi ... tar out of me!"

"I'm sorry, didn't mean to. Me and the Mrs. want to know if you will come over for lunch."

Olan steadied me with an old but strong hand.

"Of course, I would love to," I said. "Do you mind if I bring Bishop? He needs to run around a bit."

"Course, bring that ol' boy around." His smile fell, and he grew serious. "Edna wants to know how you are doing with everything going on. She won't ask you directly and warned me not to ask. Thought I would give you a heads up." Olan patted me on the shoulder. "Are you doin' okay? You look a little pale."

"I'm okay, or at least, I'm up on two feet, talking and breathing."

He nodded. "But that ain't really livin', son. See you in a bit."

After Olan left, I drove home to change into my jeans and get Bishop. When we arrived at the farm, Bishop pawed at the window, anxious to play with the dogs that ran alongside my car. Edna greeted us as we got out. Bishop bounded off, snapping and playing with his buddies.

"Aidan! So good to see you, dear, and Bishop, too! I think I have an old bone for you."

"No thanks, Edna, broke my teeth on the last one."

"Oh, you! You're as bad as Olan!" She slapped me on the arm with a towel, but her eyes were full of concern as if I would collapse into a puddle of tears.

We sat down to a good Midwestern lunch of meatloaf, potatoes, and biscuits … all the stuff that would most likely kill you.

"So, Aidan, fine sermon," Olan said after a forkful of meatloaf.

"Thanks. I appreciate it. I'm sure it was a bit rough, had to get it together in about three hours."

He frowned. "Yeah, Mike's alleged sickness."

I nearly spilled my coffee. "Why do you say that?"

"Didn't look sick at Graeter's last night, did he, Edna?"

"No, he sure didn't." Edna picked at one of the leftover biscuits. "I even told him that. And Mike said he was ready for the morning."

"Huh. Don't that beat all. Must have had something come on all of a sudden," Olan said, burping.

Yeah, he had something all right. His red-clad lover.

"So, how are things with your young, police lady friend?" Edna asked.

I smiled. "Let's go into the living room, and I'll tell all." Following Olan, I sat down beside him on the couch. "I see the church gossip hounds are well on the case."

Olan frowned. "Yeah, and I am disappointed you didn't tell us first."

"There is really nothing to tell. We aren't dating."

"Why not? Pretty girl, policewoman, and single."

Edna cleared her throat and Olan stopped.

"I'm sorry," Olan said, offering me his hand.

"It's okay. I mean, Amanda is gone, and really, she was gone from my life six months ago."

Edna leaned forward in her chair. "Aidan, don't minimize your grief. Amanda was such a lovely girl. I felt so terrible for you when she broke your heart. Now she is gone, and gone in such a terrible way."

I didn't have the heart to tell them how terrible.

"Do they have any idea who did it?"

"Olan!" Edna shouted.

"I'm just curious, is all."

"It's okay. I don't mind," I said.

I related everything that we had found out, including my conversations with Father Neal and Pastor Mueller. "And so, Father Neal wants me to go on a ghost hunt tonight."

"Are you going?" Edna asked then glanced at Olan.

"At first, I thought, no way. I mean, I'm a pastor with a scientific background. It makes it hard to believe that a ghost hunt is anything but pseudo-scientific spiritual bull."

Olan smiled. "Boy, you got too much mouth for your own good. So, answer the question, boy, you goin' or not?"

"I don't know. I need to catch up on some sleep."

"I think you should go."

"Why?"

"Well, aren't scientists curious folk?"

"Yeah, about provable things."

Olan chuckled. "I might be an ignorant Purdue grad, but it seems to me a scientist should always be curious about a possible source of new knowledge. Aren't they supposed to be open-minded?"

I grinned. "Good point."

"At least you'd have a good story out of it," Olan said, rubbing his belly, a sure sign he would be getting the Pepto pretty soon.

"I guess. I have to say I am curious."

"Ever watch any of them ghost huntin' shows? They try to disprove a haunting before they recognize anything supernatural."

Interesting, I thought. I wondered if Father Neal's group had the same approach. "No, but I guess I'll be having my own real-life experience soon." I stood up. "I should probably get going."

"Guess so." Olan nodded. "Say, Aidan?"

"Yes?"

"Be careful, son. You'll be in danger tonight."

I stared at him wide-eyed. "What?"

"I mean it. You'll not be safe tonight. Guard your heart and your mind."

Okay, now I need to leave. "I'll be fine. Don't worry."

"I hope so, and too late for that."

I looked away and changed the subject. "Can I borrow *Revenge of the Ninja?"*

"Sure, help yourself. Third shelf on the right."

I grabbed the movie and yelled outside for Bishop.

Edna met me at the door. "Here you go, Aidan, dear. Leftovers."

"Thanks, Edna."

"And as Olan said, be careful tonight."

I tried to laugh it off. "I'm sure the only thing I need to worry about will be stubbing my toe in the dark."

Her face went tense and her eyes wide. Her grip on my hand hardened until I flinched. "Aidan, I'm serious," she said. "You might be messing with more than you can handle."

I took her arm and gently removed her hand. "Okay, I promise. I'll be careful."

chapCeR nineCeen

I drove up to St. Patrick's with the clock on my dashboard blinking 6:45 p.m. The church building loomed over me, casting dark shadows on the ground. Tall oak trees stretched across the roof of the sanctuary, and only one light in the office gleamed out into the darkness. Thankfully, I didn't see any footprints on the ground.

I shook my head. I couldn't dwell on thoughts like that. I convinced myself to bring scientific objectivity into this whole thing. There might've been undocumented natural phenomenon that caused people to think they see ghosts. I decided to think of it as an interesting study of people who believed in the supernatural.

With my nerves thoroughly quelled and nothing more to chew, I went inside. The office had been shut down, and there was no Mrs. Ryder at her desk. Everything was quiet. A faint light emanated from under Father Neal's door. I had to admit, I didn't feel too excited about going back into that room.

"Father Neal?" I called out. "Are you there?"

The rustle of papers and thump of a book broke the silence.

"Yes, Aidan, come on in."

I opened the door, and the same sense of peace washed over me. "I'm glad you could make it," Father Neal said as he slowly walked around his desk, leaning on his cane. I failed to notice how tall he was the first time we met. I realized he had about three inches on me.

"To be honest, I almost didn't."

He got out two shot glasses and poured a round. "Why not?"

"I was a science major before I became a preacher. Let's just say I tend to place all of this in the same category as nineteenth-century spiritualist meetings and everyone who listens to *Coast to Coast AM* radio with all the conspiracy theories and ghost stories."

"Yes, interesting program, isn't it? I put it on at night when I can't sleep." He smiled.

"Anyway, I'm really skeptical of all this. I bet they aren't even that scientific in their investigations."

"I would keep your feelings to yourself tonight. Zoe and her team are very serious about what they do. They consider their work scientific first, supernatural second." He pointed his cane at me.

"How do they do that?"

"The group tries to debunk a haunting, to find rational explanations for things."

"What is their success rate on that?"

"I believe about ninety-five percent. Most can be written off as having rational scientific explanations. Squeaky floorboards, drafts, high electromagnetic field readings from unprotected wiring that often cause sickness and paranoia."

"And the other five percent?" I asked.

"That is the rub, isn't it?" He handed me a whisky. I downed it and savored the smoky scorch.

I didn't know how to handle Father Neal's matter-of-fact manner.

"So, you are a member of this group?"

"No, I'm not. I consult for them on some of the more, shall we say, negative cases." He swirled his drink around.

"What, like demons?" I said, failing to keep the sarcasm out of my voice.

"Oh, yes, very much so." He paused as he caught my look of skepticism. "I'm not sure I understand your doubt, my boy."

"Well, as I said, I earned a science degree and was educated in hard-headed Calvinism where the spirit world is not a widely discussed subject. I find it more than a bit unbelievable. I don't think I have ever seen anything that would be described as paranormal or spiritual." *I'm such a liar.*

"A bit ironic, isn't it?" Father Neal said.

"What do you mean?"

"Well, the Presbyterian church has its roots in the moors and mountains of Scotland, does it not? And the last time I visited a small village in Scotland, they were having a serious discussion as to how to protect their houses from Brownies."

I furrowed my eyebrows. "What?"

"A Scottish folk spirit, as it were," he said. "Anyway, it's strange that their theological descendants take such a naturalistic view on things."

Before I could answer, Father Neal glanced at the clock. "We must be on our way. We need to be at the house by seven-thirty, and it's a bit of a long haul, I'm afraid."

"I can drive if you want," I said. I somehow didn't think Father Neal was the speediest driver in the world.

"Ah, I was just going to ask. Thank you."

We sat in silence as we made our way. Father Neal's gray head bowed over his cane. I didn't want to bother him, but I wanted to ask him about the house. I opened my mouth a few times but never quite formed the question.

"So, you want to know more about the house we are going to?"

"Are you a mind-reader as well as a priest?"

"Sometimes. To be a good priest, or minister in your case, you have to be a good mind reader, don't you think?"

"Yeah, I do. Okay then, tell me about the house we are going to."

He didn't move and went silent.

"Father Neal?"

"Sorry, Aidan, lost in my thoughts again." He lifted his head and pulled his cane closer. "Right. The house, then. This couple approached Zoe because their infant daughter had scratches on her body every morning."

"Shouldn't they have just cut her fingernails?" I ventured.

"Believe me, these people never let her nails go beyond dull, much less let them sharpen to the point they might cause injury."

"Sorry, too presumptuous on my side, I guess."

"It was, but don't worry about it. Besides, you have not heard the worst part."

"What's that?" I gripped the steering wheel.

"Well, being that it was an unusually cold winter, their baby, Audrey, was in a sleeper with one zipper down the middle. There is no way for her to scratch herself in this fashion, much less get to the location where the scratches were."

"Where?"

"On her back."

"How is that possible?" I glanced over at him. "Scratchy pajamas? Left over plastic tag?"

"That would make three distinct lines like fingernail scratches?"

"No, I guess not. Is there a human explanation?"

He looked at me. "Child abuse, you mean?"

"Yeah, maybe one of the parents. Terrible, but seems more likely."

"Well, yes, it would seem so, except they put a nanny-cam in the bedroom at night. I have seen the tapes, Aidan. Each morning for four nights in a row, at about three o'clock, the baby would cry. They would run in, and the scratches would be there, fresh each night, blood oozing out of the wounds."

I stared ahead as I drove. I had no category for what I'd just heard. Even when I did believe, I had been raised in a conservative Presbyterian environment where talk of the demonic only happened at late-night drinking sessions.

"Is that it?" I asked. "The scratches?"

"Unfortunately, no. There have been lights flickering on and off, moaning noises, appliances malfunctioning and apparitions."

"This was all determined by the ghost hunter folks?"

"They've seen the tapes and interviewed the family. Tonight is their first on-site investigation. Because of the potential for, shall we say, negative forces, they have asked me to be present at the house."

"What will you do?"

"Observe. Pray. And if needed, fight."

"Fight?" I said, still not bothering to hide my sarcasm.

"Are you telling me that in all your years in seminary and ministry, you have never been taught anything about this?" Father Neal frowned at me.

Something about this old priest gave me the creeps, and yet, made me want to bow the knee at the same time. I shook my head. "Well, no, wasn't really room between Calvin and Berkhoff. I mean, come on, this is stuff that happens with weirdo TV preachers."

"First, you do Calvin a disservice," he said. "He knew way more about these situations than his theological children. And second, this goes far beyond televangelists."

"If you say so."

He thumped my leg with his cane. "Aidan, I can't stress how seriously you need to take this. If there is a fight, you must stand back. You are not ready for this sort of thing. But the group may ask you to help in the investigation."

"How in the world will I do that?" I asked, rubbing the sore spot on my leg.

He smiled. "They will show you. Turn here at St. Michael Road."

I made the turn and glanced over at Father Neal. "So, you don't think I'm ready to fight a spiritual battle, eh?"

He stared out of his window in silence.

"Come on, I'm a minister in a Nicene-confessing denomination, fully ordained by the laying on of hands of the Fathers and Brothers of Columbus City Presbytery."

Father Neal turned to me, his eyes blazing green again. "It would be like sending an infant to fight a dragon. No, you are no

St. George."

I grimaced, stung by his remark. True, I didn't believe in anything he was saying, but he didn't know that. I felt oddly offended. This priest, who I barely knew, somehow seemed to know me.

"You must promise me that whatever happens, you will not get involved. You will be protected to a point, but not if you directly interfere in any way."

My thoughts went straight to the movie, *The Exorcist*. I just hoped I wouldn't get puked on in the process or worse, thrown down a flight of stairs to my death. That usually happened to assistants.

Snow fell hard as we pulled up to the house. A black van sat in the driveway, and a few people stood around it. Light reflected off the vapor from their breath, and steam rose into the night air from the coffee cups they held.

Father Neal pointed toward them. "There's the team. They all know you're coming."

"Do they know I'm a minister?"

"Yes. And not all of them are Christians, by the way."

"Really?" I asked.

"Yes, it does make for some lively discussions at times. But, oddly enough, they all come to me for spiritual advice."

I looked over at the gray-haired priest beside me. He examined me, and I couldn't hold his gaze for very long.

Nothing special about him. Just an old man with a cane.

I looked back up. He still stared at me.

"Guess we should join them, eh?" I said.

Father Neal nodded, wearing a small smile. "Yes, boy, let's go."

We walked up to the group, and they all greeted Father Neal with hugs. As they chatted and laughed, I felt my phone vibrate. I pulled it out of my pocket and saw a text message from Jennifer.

Talk to Abraham Lincoln yet?

I smiled. *No, but Napoleon sends his regards.*

Call me when you are done.

Despite the cold temperature, a warm feeling crawled up my toes to my stomach. "You're damn right I'll call you," I whispered to myself.

"Aidan, come meet the group." Father Neal's commanding voice brought me back to reality. I strolled over and put on my best, fake pastor-smile.

"Hey, y'all, nice to meet you."

A man in a green, Land's End pullover walked up to me. His closely-shaven head gleamed in the van light. A bushy, gray mustache covered much of his upper lip as he smiled. "Y'all? Are you from the south?"

I laughed. "No, went to school in Texas."

"Ah, that would explain it. Name's Reg. From Georgia myself."

"Reg, nice to meet you." We shook hands. "What do you do for the group?"

"Tech manager. I run the motion sensor cameras and take care of the equipment."

"Hello again, Pastor Aidan," Zoe said. "Thank you for coming to lend a hand this evening. We are short an investigator. Melissa is out with the flu."

"Sure, glad to help," I said. "But I have to say, I'm not sure what I can do. Never been on a ghost hunt before."

"Don't worry, we will train you right," she said with a warm smile. She looked more normal with an Ohio State stocking cap on her head.

Father Neal introduced me to the rest of the group, which included a mousy-looking graduate student named Kate with long, straight brown hair, and a wise-cracking guy named Darrin, who walked around with an unlit cigarette in his hands.

"So, what do you do?" I asked Darrin.

"Investigator-in-training. I'm learning this shi … stuff, just like you."

"It's okay." I chuckled. "You can cuss in front of me."

"It's not that, really, just been trying to stop." He ran his fingers through his hair.

"Right, got it. I actually meant, what do you do in real life?"

"Ah, right, grad student. English Literature." He twirled the cigarette through his fingers.

"How did you get hooked up with this group?"

"Well, Kate and I recently had an experience."

"Like what?"

"It's not really polite to ask that question on a first date." Darrin laughed.

I laughed with him. "Fair enough, but you have to at least tell me about the cigarette."

"Help me carry the bags, preacher, and I'll tell you." Darrin handed me two large black duffle bags and then grabbed a couple of cameras. "Follow me."

I fell in behind him as we walked toward the house. It seemed like a fairly typical 1930s Clintonville style building with red brick and a real wooden porch. Certainly didn't seem like the house of doom.

Darrin glanced back at me and saw the look on my face. "Yeah, I know, it's not *Amityville Horror*, is it? Then again, most places we investigate look completely normal on the outside. But it's what goes on inside that you have to watch out for."

"Why do you think that is?"

He fiddled with the cigarette some more. "Nothing is really *normal* if you know what I mean."

"Not entirely, no."

Darrin nodded as he put the cigarette behind his ear.

"Ya probably just need to see what I mean, preacher. I can't really explain it."

Not knowing what to say to this, I pointed to his ear.

"So, the cigarette?"

He led me to the living room and set the bags down by the TV. "I quit smoking. Not hard to do really, but it drove my fingers crazy. I needed something to mess with."

"How long does one cigarette last?"

"About two days."

"So how do you know Father Neal?" I asked.

"Well, Kate and I started going to his church recently."

"Connected with your experience?"

Darrin stopped attaching the camera wires to the computers and looked up at me. "Hole in one, preacher."

Zoe's voice sounded from above. "Pastor Aidan, would you mind helping us upstairs?"

After giving Darrin a pat on the shoulder, I climbed the stairs and found myself in the nursery. Nothing seemed amiss other than it looked like a bomb had exploded, throwing pink sheets, pink curtains, and pink teddy bears all over the room.

I found Zoe in the master bedroom. "What's up?" I said.

She stood with a woman I saw in most of the pictures downstairs. Zoe had transformed from the aging hippy to a serious person with business to conduct. She put her hand on the lady's shoulder. "Pastor Aidan, this is Abby Huron. We're trying to help her family this evening."

"Mrs. Huron, glad to meet you." I offered my hand.

"Thank you so much for helping me." She pressed my hand between hers. Her face radiated the earnest, hopeful expression I'd seen on a number of congregation members in my office over the past few years.

The expression always made me feel useless especially when they found out I didn't have the answers. I hated their crushed looks when they would leave my office.

I forced a smile. "We will do what we can, Mrs. Huron."

"I know you will." She nodded and left the room.

"That poor woman. She is a bit desperate," Zoe said, playing with a long strand of her hair.

"I can tell."

She turned to face me. "Are you ready for your ten minute training session?"

"Yes, I think so. Give it to me, sergeant."

She held up her walkie-talkie. "Reg, the newbie is ready for your wisdom."

"Send him on down!" The radio crackled as Reg replied.

"Be careful tonight," Zoe said, gripping my arm as I turned to go.

"Seems like I've been hearing that a lot lately."

I walked downstairs to Reg, his nearly bald head bent over several electronic devices lined up on the dining room table.

"I see why people get into ghost hunting." I drank in the sight of digital recorders, cameras, and some devices I didn't recognize.

Reg beamed. "A fellow tech geek? Very good, we should get along just fine."

"Geek doesn't even begin to describe it. More like unhealthy obsession."

"Blackberry or iPhone?"

I reached in my jacket and pulled out my black and silver iPhone. "Please don't ever question my geek status, Reg."

He laughed. "Sorry, had to make the secret Apple geek handshake."

I smiled. "I'm assuming you're going to explain all this to me?" I motioned at the tech swag.

"Of course. Each group gets a camera. One of those is actually infrared, and we keep them on at all times."

"And you are hoping a ghost appears for its Andy Warhol?"

Reg smiled. "Exactly."

"And the digital recorders?"

"They capture, at least we hope, a phenomenon known as EVP or Electronic Voice Phenomenon."

"You lost me."

"It's like this; we sit in a room of the house and ask questions."

"To the ghosts?"

"Correct, and the recorders pick up any answers."

"Can you hear the answer out loud?" I picked up one of the recorders.

"Not usually. The frequency is lower, undetectable to the human ear for some reason."

Even though I thought the whole thing was full of shit, it was interesting. I pointed to the other devices I didn't recognize. "What are those?"

"This meter reads electromagnetic fields. It's thought by most in paranormal investigation that when a spirit tries to manifest itself, it sucks up energy, creating a detectable electromagnetic field."

"If that thing spikes and there is no earthly reason for it, it will more than likely mean a ghostie is around."

I laughed and shook my head.

"What?" Reg asked, puzzled.

"I guess I just didn't expect all this high-tech stuff."

"What did you expect? Divining rods? Séance tables?"

"Well, to be honest, I did."

Reg nodded. "Most people do."

"I'm sorry, I didn't mean..."

"No worries, preacher. Most people are skeptical about the paranormal and wonder if what we do is legitimate. That's why we try to be as scientific as possible. I'm a skeptic myself, but since I've been with the group, well, I've seen some interesting things."

"Interesting things?"

He stared at me expressionless. "I only use the word 'things' because I have no other word for it."

I thought of the footprints. "I understand, Reg."

He handed me a voice recorder. "You can pair up with me to start. I'll take it easy on you."

"Do you all go in the same pairs?"

"No, we try to change it up during the night."

"What do you mean?"

"Forces in haunted places often react differently to different people. No one really knows why, but we try to keep mixing it up. Plus, it's an issue of safety." Reg gave me a half smile.

"Safety?"

"Yeah, we don't want the forces focusing on particular people. That can get a bit dangerous."

"How so?"

Reg paused and gave me a tight-lipped smile. "Well, we have had people attacked before."

"Attacked? As in beaten?"

"Yeah. Damnedest thing I ever saw. Last year, Zoe got thrown into a wall. Poor thing received some nasty looking bruises."

"I don't even know how to handle that." I admitted.

"You and me both. I'm a scientist by profession, you know."

"What?" I exclaimed.

He smiled. "Physics professor at Ohio State University."

"Seriously? And you are on a ghost hun ... I mean paranormal investigation?"

He smiled. "You would be surprised at how many physics professors are into some wacky things."

"Enlighten me."

"Well, the nature of physics, especially in the theoretical realm, invites some pretty mind-blowing speculation, which drew me out of atheism. But let's just say my colleagues don't know what I'm doing on the weekends."

"So, you go to Father Neal's church?" I asked.

"Occasionally. I've not made the trip to the ol' baptismal fount though."

"Why not? Wait, sorry, that's probably a little personal."

He chuckled. "Not at all. I guess you could say I'm still being convinced, kind of like Anthony Flew."

I mentally sorted through my famous atheists knowledge from my reading. Flew, a well-known British philosopher and atheist, had converted to deism recently, much to the dismay of many atheists, especially Dawkins. Basically, he came to believe God created the world and then let it go.

"Makes sense," I said.

A voice crackled over Reg's walkie-talkie. "Zoe wants everyone on the porch. We're all ready to go."

"The boss lady calls," I said.

We went out to the porch and all gathered in a circle. As the vapor from our breath rose above our heads, I couldn't help thinking we looked like a bunch of naughty teenagers with a shared cigarette.

I stood next to Kate, the nervous grad student. She had scars near her eyes that looked like they had been caused by long talons. "Hi. Kate, right? I'm Aidan."

"It's nice to meet you," she said, in a low, timid voice, without looking me in the eye.

I tried not to stare at her scars, but I couldn't help myself.

"I was attacked," she said in a dry, flat voice.

"I'm sorry; I didn't mean to stare."

Kate smiled at me then looked away. "It's okay, most people do. No harm in it, really."

"Did they catch the guy?"

She looked at me with the expression of pain I had seen a few times in counseling situations as if she would crumble at the slightest touch.

"No. No, they didn't." She hugged herself and looked away.

"I'm sorry; I didn't mean to bring up bad memories."

She nodded, and I caught the glint of a tear rolling down her cheek.

"Aidan?"

Zoe waved at me. "You are going in first tonight with Reg. Just stick with him." She then paired up everyone else, except for Father Neal and herself. "Now, I know not everyone here is a Christian," Zoe said. "But I hope you don't mind if I ask Father Neal to bless us."

Everyone nodded without hesitation.

Father Neal put aside his cane, stood up straight, and held out his arms. "May the Power of the Father, the Love of the Son, and the protection of the Holy Spirit guard you all, in front of you, beside you, and behind you. May the Holy Trinity send Michael Militant, protector of God's people, to surround you. In the Name of the Blessed Trinity, Amen."

The poetry of the prayer struck me. In my conservative evangelical church upbringing, our prayers were punctuated with "Father" a billion times, and "just do this, God" at least two million.

Reg slapped me on the shoulder. "All right, preacher boy, are you ready?"

"Always."

chapter twenty

"The first thing we do is turn off all the lights," Reg said, walking around the house flipping switches.

"Why is that? Ghosts scared of the light?" I turned off an old-fashioned lamp as Reg headed back to the living room.

He laughed. "I have no idea. But our infrared cameras sure are."

"Ah, right. What's next?" It was hard not to feel some kind of excitement. The streetlights cast shadows on the walls, and the whole house had the surreal quality you felt when you got home late and everyone's gone to bed.

"Let's start upstairs and work our way down." Reg headed to the staircase.

"Fine with me." I strained to find my way in the dark. With the light from outside filtering through the window, it certainly wasn't pitch black. But it was dark enough for my shins to connect with a stray chair. I fought the urge to utter a stream of profanities.

"Are you okay?" Reg said.

"Yeah, just hit my shin. What room do you want to try?"

"Might as well go to the nursery."

We ascended the stairs into a realm of darkness. No light penetrated inside the nursery.

"First, we scan the room with the infrared camera," Reg whispered. He bumped into me as he panned the room, the blue-green glow of the furniture swirling in the screen.

"What are we looking for?"

"Anything that doesn't belong here," he muttered.

"Okay, just what would that be?" I said, trying to figure out what to do.

"Odd heat signatures. Shapes of people. That sort of thing."

"Should I be doing anything?" The dark made me antsy.

"Start asking questions with the digital recorder."

"What, like, *what is your quest? What is your favorite color?*" I fumbled with the recorder as I got it out of my pocket.

Reg chuckled. "No, more like, *is there anyone here with us tonight? What is your name? Do you mind us being here?*"

I held the recorder out. No going back now. "Who are you?"

No response.

"Why are you bothering a baby?" Reg asked in a protective father's voice.

A loud beep nearly sent the bones right out of my skin. "What the hell?" I shouted.

Reg rattled with the device in his hand. He frowned at the greenish reflection of the display screen. "The EMF reader just went haywire," he said, turning to me in the dark.

"It just spiked at 3.0."

"You've lost me."

"Usually, with the EMF, 0.6 is a big spike and 1.0 is nuclear. There can't be an electrical box in here, but turn on the light a sec to see if there are exposed wires near the walls."

I found the switch, and we both put our hands to our eyes.

"Sorry about that." Reg grimaced.

He scanned the EMF over the walls, trying to find electrical sources. I looked for exposed wires, but we found nothing.

"Okay, turn off the lights again," Reg said. As the darkness invaded, he scanned the room. When he passed over the crib, the EMF beeped at 4.0. His brow creased. "This can't be right." He pulled out his walkie-talkie. "Zoe, I need another EMF, I think this one is broken."

"Be right up, Reg."

We waited for Zoe and listened to the sound of each other breathing. I leaned over to whisper something to Reg. Before I spoke, my breath reflected in the dim moonlight now peeking through the window. My arms broke out in goose bumps as cold air washed over my body. "Reg, did someone open a window?"

"I was about to ask you the same thing."

The cold completely took over the room, and my chest muscles tightened as if someone reached into my lungs and began to squeeze. I started to cough and fought to take deep breaths. Something grabbed my arm and spun me around. I stumbled into Reg who kept me from falling to the floor.

"Aidan? Are you okay?" He sounded far away, like he was in another room.

"Can't ... breathe..."

"Do you have asthma? Where is your inhaler?"

"Don't ... have ... asthma," I wheezed.

"Then get out. Now!" Reg commanded.

As I turned, something brushed past me, and the EMF gauge hit the floor making a loud clatter. The red electronic numbers penetrated the darkness with 10.0. Faint whispers followed me as I kept gasping for air.

"Aidan, get out now!" Reg bellowed as he shoved me through the door.

My chest muscles relaxed, and I gulped in massive amounts of air. Reg came up behind me.

"Careful, don't hyperventilate," he whispered as he patted me on the back.

I massaged my chest and took long, slow breaths. "Reg, what the hell just happened?"

"Something slapped my hand. Are you okay?"

"Yeah, I'm fine. I felt like something was squeezing my lungs."
Reg put a hand on my arm. "Do you need some fresh air?"

"No, I'm okay. I'm sure I just got over-excited. I've suffered from panic attacks before."

"Yeah, maybe," he said as he picked up the walkie-talkie. "Never mind on the EMF, Zoe, we are coming out."

"Reg," I protested. "I'm really fine."

"Sorry, preacher, standard rules. Whenever something physically happens to someone, we go downstairs to discuss it."

We went outside where everyone was waiting in the van.

"What happened?" Zoe asked, coming to me.

"He couldn't breathe, like something had cut off his air," Reg said.

Father Neal stepped close to examine me. "Are you okay, Aidan?" he asked in a low voice.

I waved my hand, a bit annoyed by everyone's gawking. "I'm fine."

Their faces registered more than a little disbelief.

"I'm serious. See?" I took a few deep breaths, parting my coat so everyone could see my chest rise. "Maybe I just had an allergic reaction to something."

"Do you have any allergies?" Darrin asked, fiddling with his cigarette.

"None that I know of, but I mean, I've never lived in an old house, so maybe it was the dust or something."

The looks of disbelief melted into polite skepticism, but they didn't question me any further.

"Let's switch it up a bit," Zoe said. "Kate and Darrin, you're up next."

"You got it, Zoe," Darrin said, taking Kate's arm. "Shall we, my dear Katherine?"

She smiled at him, her scarred eyes relaxed as they went inside.

"So, are they dating?" I asked Reg as he handed me a cup of coffee after we piled back into the van. I hoped he wouldn't ask any more about what happened. I didn't want to talk about it at all.

"Well, they should be, but they are very coy about it," Reg

replied. "I think Darrin wants to, for sure. They should just get on with it. They certainly have shared a lot together."

"Like what?"

He kept sipping his coffee.

"Reg?"

"Not my story to tell, Aidan."

"Fair enough." I sat back against the van wall and closed my eyes. I tried to process everything that just happened; the grabbing of my arm, the shortness of breath. I couldn't find any rational reason for any of it. Thoughts whirled in my head as different teams went in and out of the house for the next two hours. I started to nod off when I felt a tap on my shoulder.

"You and me, P.A.," Darrin said, handing me another digital recorder.

"I'm ready." I stepped outside into the cold. The air shocked me awake. I looked up at the house, and my stomach tensed.

"Let's start in the basement this time, unless you are scared," Darrin teased. "I double dog dare you."

I laughed as the knot in my stomach released. "As long as you don't ask me to stick my tongue to a flagpole."

"Hmmm, the preacher knows his pop culture references."

"A little, my dear Watson."

"Ah, and his late nineteenth-century literature ones as well."

"I can even put a dash of profanity in there too, if you wish."

Darrin laughed. "Always."

We entered the kitchen and opened the wooden green basement door. The stairs creaked as we headed down. Once we hit the bottom, Darrin swept his light forward so we wouldn't stumble.

The layout reminded me of my grandma's basement, but cleaner, with blue painted concrete floors. Stacks of boxes, unused furniture, books, and garden tools lined the walls, leaving the middle of the floor empty except for the heater. A moldy smell soon had me wiping my nose, but didn't cause any more breathing attacks.

"So, do you see where everything is?" Darrin asked.

"Yeah, should be easy. Are you going to shut off your light?"

"Yep, here we go."

With a click, we entered into complete blackness. "Hello, darkness, my old friend," Darrin sang off key.

"I bet you're a karaoke champ," I said, groping in the darkness to orient myself. I touched the cold metal of a support pole.

"Sarcasm in a preacher? Is that possible?" Darrin said from my right.

"It is for this one."

Darrin fumbled around in the dark and then handed me another digital recorder. I could hear him flip out a camera and press the power button. "Well, preacher, start asking questions while I film with the night vision."

I smirked. "What did you think of Darrin's singing?"

"Funny," Darrin grunted.

"Is there anything you want to say?"

No answer. Expected result, I thought.

"Do you want us here tonight?"

My head snapped to the side as something struck my cheek. I dropped the recorder and fell to the floor with a thud. The darkness seemed to press down on me.

"Aidan, are you okay?"

"I think I walked into something."

"Let me see," Darrin said, pulling out his flashlight. He held it up to my face as I righted myself.

"You have a huge red mark on your cheek."

"What?"

"Yeah, you must have run into a pole. Where were you standing?"

"Right by that pole, so it couldn't have been that." I pointed to the general area.

He shined the light where I had pointed. Nothing. There were no shelves, no poles, or anything hanging from the ceiling.

I stared at the beam of light. I knew something had hit me. I could still feel the heat on my cheek, and I rubbed it. It felt rough, like it had been scraped with something.

"You seem to be a magnet tonight," Darrin said, offering me a hand.

"That's me, Aidan the ghost magnet. I wonder if that will work with the chicks."

"It doesn't, trust me."

"Kate?"

He looked at me over the flashlight.

"Sorry, too personal?"

"No, too perceptive."

"Got it. Let's go upstairs."

"Are you sure you're okay? You can take a break, you know."

"I know, thanks, but we can't keep the ghosts waiting."

I followed Darrin to the steps and kept rubbing my cheek, disturbed. What had hit me? I could feel the creeps beginning, like bugs crawling under my skin.

"Doin' okay, preacher?" Darrin said from the top of the stairs.

"Yeah, sorry. I'm coming." I began up the wooden steps, making sure I didn't trip. When I reached the halfway point, something caught my foot and pulled it back. As I struggled to keep my balance, I felt fingers grip my other leg and pulled harder. I fell, face down, onto the stairs, and my chest bore the brunt of my fall. The air in my lungs emptied, and I gasped, struggling to breathe.

Something heavy landed on my back, grabbed my hair, and pulled my head up. As I fought to free myself from whatever was gripping me, I felt something cutting into my forehead. I cried out in pain and punched at the air, but I hit nothing. I kicked into the darkness, but none of my kicks connected.

"P.A.? Are you okay?"

I looked up and saw Darrin silhouetted in the kitchen door, peering down with his flashlight. At the sound of his voice, whatever held me released its grip, and I fell forward with a thud. Darrin gasped.

"Help me up," I croaked.

He rushed down the stairs, and the scraping on my forehead stopped. Darrin's hand, illuminated by the faint light from the basement door, grabbed me and pulled me up. "Come on, let's get you outside."

"No, I'm okay. Let's keep going."

"Rules, preacher, when someone is attacked."

I didn't feel like arguing with him. My whole body felt like I had gone fifteen rounds with Rocky Balboa.

As we walked through the dining room, a glass flew past my face and smashed against the wall. "Darrin, did you see that?"

"No, but I heard it, did a glass..."

The rest of the glasses from the opened china cabinet began to fly toward our heads, some hitting us, and some hitting the wall beside us. Glass shattered and flew in all directions. "Holy shit!" Darrin was frozen to the spot, his eyes huge even in the dark.

"Dude, run!" I yelled.

We ran and dove out the door as other dishes flew toward us. They crashed against the screen door, bouncing onto the floor and breaking into pieces. The sound of faint, manic laughter came from the dining room, and lights began to switch on and off all over the house.

"Well," Darrin gasped. "So much for the wedding china."

I laughed and then groaned. I had no doubt there would be a bruise on my chest. "Don't make me laugh ... hurts too much," I panted.

Father Neal's voice stopped our horseplay. "What happened?"

We related the story to the group as we sat on the stairs leading to the house. Darrin had a slight cut on his head, and a few on his arms. I didn't have any cuts that I could tell, but my forehead burned like it had been lit on fire. "Father Neal, am I cut on my forehead?"

He bent down and took my face in his hands. "There is something scraped into your head, a letter of some sort. Flashlight, Darrin, if you please."

Darrin gave him his flashlight and then lit his cigarette without shame. My body began to tremble, and I almost asked Darrin for one myself, even though I had never smoked. Father Neal shined the light on my forehead and traced the cut with his fingers. His cool touch eased the fiery pain somewhat.

"Hebrew."

"What?"

"The Hebrew letter *nun* has been scratched into your forehead,"

Father Neal said.

I sat on the stairs at a loss for words as the shakes began in full force.

"Aidan, are you okay?" Zoe and Kate asked in unison as they walked up and sat down next to me.

"I gue … guess," I said, through chattering teeth.

They both wrapped their arms around me, warming me a bit with their bodies. It felt nice, homey and comforting. Kate put a washcloth up to my bleeding forehead.

Father Neal stood by us and peered down at me. He looked very grave, face pale and raised a shaking hand to me. "Aidan, I'm sorry. I should not have brought you along. It was foolish of me."

I didn't say anything and stared out into the snow that had begun to fall again.

Father Neal turned toward Zoe. "It appears we have a house possession, wouldn't you say?"

"Yes, Father Neal, I would say." She continued to rub my back.

"Then we must pack everyone up and leave right now," he said. "I will contact some other priests to do an exorcism soon. Something is here that will take more than me to handle. Something that has … been released."

"And the family?" Zoe asked.

"They must not, under any circumstances, stay in the house until we are done."

"Yes, Father Neal." Zoe raised her voice. "Let's pack it up. No delays. Move it."

"Wait, Zoe," Father Neal said, holding up his cane. "Allow me to pray inside for a few moments."

"Alone?"

"Yes, Zoe, alone."

"That breaks our rules, Father," she said, standing up.

"Nevertheless, I must insist." He drew himself up and stood at his full height. I couldn't help being reminded of Merlin, the magician in King Arthur's court.

I could tell Zoe didn't like it, but Father Neal was too powerful of a presence to debate. He stepped behind us and went up the stairs, leaning on his cane. He closed the door right away. Kate stood up to face the house, but I stayed seated on the steps, not yet ready to move.

Upon seeing Father Neal go inside, everyone came out from the van and joined us. We strained to hear what was going on in the house. At first, only a faint whisper of Father Neal's voice, low and commanding, filtered outside, but we couldn't make out anything that he said.

"What is he doing?" I asked, slowly raising myself from the stairs to stand with the others.

"I believe he is binding the spirit from hurting any of us," Zoe said, not taking her eyes away from the door.

I nodded, feeling empty. All my life experience, all my seminary training and ministry dealings had been exposed as a fraud.

"Bound in the name of the Father, the Son, and the Holy Spirit. You are bound and will do no more harm until you are cast from this place." Father Neal's voice had risen to the decibel level of a thunderstorm. A flash of light filled the entire inside of the house and then it was dark again.

I blinked furiously, trying to restore my night vision.

"Whoa," Darrin said, his arm tight around Kate, who clung to him like he was her personal teddy bear.

Father Neal came out of the front door, hunched over a bit. His face was pale, but he smiled at us. "Okay, Zoe, everyone can go in."

The group just stared at him, not moving. The silence stretched, and no one said a word.

"Is anyone there?" he said, still smiling.

Zoe pulled herself into action. "Okay, everyone, let's pack up our stuff." Everybody started moving at once, taking deep breaths as they stepped inside.

Father Neal came down the stairs and walked up to me. He smiled, but there was concern in his eyes. "Will you be kind enough to take me home, Aidan?"

"Of course," I said, looking at the ground.

"Are you alright, lad?"

"Not really. I don't know what to do with all of this. Amanda's murder. The footprints. Attacks in the dark. And not to mention, my lost faith..." The last words escaped my lips before I realized.

Father Neal didn't seem surprised and nodded. "We will talk about these things. All of them." He looked back at the house. "But first, I want you to take me to the cemetery where Amanda was murdered."

"Tonight?" I asked with a growing sense of unease.

"Yes, my son, tonight."

"I don't know if we can. The police have it blocked off."

"I'm sure you'll be able to get us permission."

chapter twenty-one

We drove in silence along High Street with my mind in a blur. The swirling colors and buildings barely registered as I made my way through the deserted roads of early morning Columbus. I wanted to start the conversation with Father Neal but couldn't form the words.

I dialed Jennifer and a sleepy voice answered. "Hey, how did the ghost hunt go?" she asked.

"Fine. Sorry to wake you up, but I need a favor. I need to get into the cemetery."

"In the morning?" she said, confused.

"No, I mean right now."

Silence on the other end. "Jennifer?"

"What are you up to, Aidan?"

"I have someone here who might be able to help us figure some things out."

"Who?"

"A priest, an Anglican priest, who, uh, well, specializes in these sorts of things."

"I'll meet you there," she said, awake and alert.

"No, Jennifer, you don't have to…"

"Actually, yeah, I do. I have to be on sight. I'll meet you there in thirty minutes."

I hung up.

"She's coming, isn't she?" Father Neal said.

"Yeah, she's a bit hard to stop."

He gave me a half smile. "I know the type."

We pulled up to the cemetery and found a parking space across the street. I sighed as I sat back in the seat.

"Aidan? Are you all right?"

I grunted. "No, Father Neal, I'm not all right."

"An eventful night," he said, staring ahead.

I snorted. "Yeah, you could say that. So, you want to try and explain all of this to me? Who are you, might be a good place to start."

He turned his head to stare out of the passenger side window. "Who am I? I'm just an old priest in an older parish." His breath fogged the window as he spoke.

"I don't believe that for a second."

Father Neal turned to me with an eyebrow raised. "And why do you say that?"

"You're kidding, right? After tonight?"

"As I said, a simple old priest."

"Yeah, okay. Fine, then tell me about the Bone Masters or whatever you want to call them."

Father Neal sighed. "No, not yet. You are not ready for that conversation."

"Why not? That's why I came to see you. That's why I went on this whole stupid thing in the first place. I want answers, and I want them now." I banged my hands on the steering wheel.

He gripped his cane with his liver-spotted hands. "I'm not used to being shouted at, Aidan."

The tone of his voice took me by surprise. It no longer had the soothing sound of an upper class professor, but a tone of command like a military officer.

"You're right. I'm sorry," I said. "I shouldn't have shouted, but

I need answers, Father Neal. Please."

"And I'll give them to you ... I promise. However, I can't give you what I don't have. Why do you think I asked you to bring me here?"

"I don't know. You tell me. Whatever you saw in that house scared you enough to come here, am I right?"

He gripped his cane again. "Yes, there's no doubt."

"But why?"

"I don't know, not yet."

"You like that phrase a lot, and it's pissing me off."

"Get used to it. I never give information until I'm sure. But I will tell you one thing. What I saw in that house, well, let's just say it wasn't a normal haunted house. The demon that's scratching that child is only a small part of the problem."

"A demon?"

"Yes and something else." He corrected me.

"What something else?" I pressed.

Father Neal shook his head. "Something or someone I've felt before."

Jennifer pulled up behind us. She wore a long coat and her black hair had been tucked into a Columbus Clippers baseball hat. She got out, and we joined her.

"Good morning, gentlemen."

Father Neal bowed. "Detective, my name is Father John Neal."

She smiled. "Nice to meet you, Father. Detective Jennifer Brown. You think you can help us?"

He shrugged. "That was Aidan's statement, my dear. Maybe I can. Maybe I can't. I make no promises."

Jennifer frowned at me, not amused by my little white lie. "Let's go to the cemetery."

We walked across the street, and Jennifer showed her badge to the cop on duty.

"How's your night, Patrolman?"

"Fine, ma'am. Quiet. Not even a Grand Larcenist about."

She chuckled. "Thanks."

We went inside, and Father Neal held up his hand. "Please allow me to go alone. Wait here." He limped off toward the cross as the snow began to fall.

"He's an interesting guy," Jennifer said.

I nodded, bracing my body against the cold. "That's the understatement of the year."

"Are you going to tell me about the ghost hunt? And what on earth happened to your forehead?"

I shook my head. "Not now. Not here. And don't worry, I'm fine."

She raised an eyebrow. "Oh? And why is that?"

"When I'll tell you, you'll understand."

Father Neal walked around the cross three times and stopped each time behind it. On his third circle, he stopped and raised his hands. His lips moved, but I couldn't make out any words.

"What is he…" Jennifer broke off as Father Neal doubled over with a cry of pain. As we rushed toward him, he backed up as if something pushed him. He kept stumbling back until he reached the pavilion with the grinning face.

Jennifer ran ahead of me and bent down over him. "Father? Are you okay?"

Father Neal grimaced. "Yes, my dear. Just didn't quite expect that reaction. Should've been more careful."

"Reaction to what?" I asked.

He waved me away. "Not now, Aidan."

The ripping cloth sound I'd heard earlier filled the air around us. Jennifer looked around. "I wish I knew what that sound was."

Father Neal stood, pale, but seemed otherwise okay as he walked to the left of the cross. "It's the ripping of the veil. Violent and dangerous."

Jennifer looked at me, and I shrugged.

He turned to her. "I believe we're done here, my dear." Walking to the gate, he looked back at me. "Aidan, are you coming?"

Jennifer ran up to him. "Can you tell me anything else, Father?"

He smiled. "In due time, my dear, I promise. Come, Aidan."

Jennifer looked at me and mouthed, "Call me in the morning."

I nodded and walked back to the car with Father Neal. "Are you going to tell me what that was about?"

"Drive, Aidan," he commanded.

I sighed, and worked the car into the street. Father Neal stared forward not saying a word.

"Okay, look, Father, I want some answers, especially since I got a Columbus policewoman up early in the morning for seemingly no reason."

He smirked. "Somehow, I don't think you minded seeing Detective Brown."

Heat rose to my cheeks. "Whatever, priest. Are you going to explain things to me?"

"Yes, I will. I don't keep people in the dark any longer than I have to except for … well, until I have more information. But, we can start now."

I squirmed in my seat, ready to finally get some answers.

"Tell me when you lost your faith and why."

I gripped the steering wheel. "I don't know if I want to talk about that right now."

"It's a must, Aidan. Without discussing that, nothing else I have to say to you will make sense. You'll not understand the Bone Masters if we don't, nor will you understand what happened tonight. Or why Amanda died."

I touched my forehead. The blood had stopped flowing, but I still felt a sticky ooze come from the deeper scratches. "Fine. What do you want to know?"

"How did you lose it? Tell me the story"

I chuckled as I quoted Brian's words. "Apparently, I read too much."

Father Neal looked at me with a half smile. "My dear boy, no one loses his faith by reading too much. It's usually lost by not reading enough."

"I did."

He waved his hand. "Explain that process to me."

"I guess the best way is to start with my education. I was raised in a home where theology was all we talked about. My dad was a seminary professor. We had Luther for breakfast and Calvin for dinner."

"Seasoned with a dash of St. Augustine?" Father Neal said as I stopped at a red light.

"Yes, exactly. We talked a lot about God, Jesus, all of it. By fourteen, I was reading thousand page systematic theologies for fun. I had all the information I needed to convince everyone of my intellectual belief in God, and I thought that was enough. At least for a while, until I realized I had no feelings for God or deep commitment to Him. I always kept telling myself that just because I couldn't feel God didn't mean He wasn't there. My faith was all rational, logical, and in order. I guess that's why I chose science as my major."

Father Neal scratched his five o'clock shadow. "You felt you could get away from the theology."

"Yeah, I suppose you're right. Anyway, I graduated with a degree in biology. I knew all of the arguments for God's existence from a scientific point of view. At least, I thought I did. I thought that was enough to fill the emotional void I felt. But it wasn't. So I did the only thing I knew to try and fill that ... more knowledge, more understanding, and this time through the ministry. I thought I would be able to find Him in seminary by pursuing ministry."

I couldn't believe I was just throwing all of this out there. I hadn't told anyone, not even Brian. I shifted uncomfortably in the driver's seat.

"If you didn't take Him with you, you wouldn't find Him there," Father Neal said, turning to look right at me.

"Yeah, I guess."

Father Neal nodded. His facial lines deeply grooved from fatigue. "I don't guess, I know. Aidan, I've seen it happen too many times. Young people go to seminary desperate to cling to God, thinking ministry is the way to do that. Really, it's the last reason you should enter ministry, and the most dangerous."

I turned into the church parking lot and pulled into a spot.

"You're right, of course," I said. "But I didn't accept that at the time. I thought if I launched myself into ministry, what I missed in seminary would find me. Didn't happen. Instead, my emotional disconnect suffered when I experienced the worst in Christian lives. The elders want the pastor fired, people backstab, destroy other's characters, and still I searched for God. I had almost given up."

Father Neal nodded for me to go on.

"Then I met Amanda, and I guess I thought I'd met God, too."

He smiled. "You are not the first to fall in love with a girl and think it was God."

"I sure equated the two. I thought the happiness she brought into my life was God. Then my parents died, and she broke up with me. Those two events stripped me of that illusion and exposed the weakness of my faith."

"And so you started questioning your rational reasons for believing?" Father Neal asked, shifting in his seat.

"I'm sorry, are you uncomfortable?"

"Just a bit cold. Do you mind going inside? I have some excellent scotch you might want to sample."

I smiled. "I'm there."

Father Neal swayed a little bit as we walked to the church door. I reached out and caught him. "Father Neal? Are you okay?"

He smiled. "A long night, my dear boy, and in spite of my denial, my body can no longer take such excitement."

Once inside Father Neal's office, he poured two scotches, and we settled into our seats. "Now, finish your story," he said.

I sat back in my chair, looking at the scotch as if it could reflect my story back to me. "I started going back to my reasons for believing ... my logical, ordered, and in-place faith. I found perfectly rational reasons why the Bible was just a book." I pointed to his bookshelf that contained texts on higher criticism of the Bible.

"So, you read Crossan, Ehrman, and the Old Testament critics?" Father Neal asked.

I nodded and then pointed to another bookshelf that contained books by Dawkins, Hitchens, and Schermer. "Then I read those books and found sound, rational reasons to doubt that God existed at all. Belief in Him just didn't make sense to me anymore. There seemed to be perfectly logical and scientific reasons for not believing in him. I equated science and theology ... nice, rational, in place. All of my reading blew that apart. So, when you combine that with everything else, especially Christians' hate for each other, I figured the whole thing wasn't true. So, I guess you could say it was other people's fault."

Father Neal frowned. "It's not good to blame others for our failure to believe, Aidan."

I gulped the scotch and slammed the glass down. "Then who do I blame, Father? God? I would if I thought He existed. He has never made himself real to me in any way. I have never felt Him. There are no rational reasons for believing He exists, so what am I left with?" My voice rose with each syllable until I was shouting.

"Aidan," Father Neal said, holding up his hand. "You are doing what everyone does."

"I'm really in no mood for riddles," I said, throwing myself back in the chair.

He raised an eyebrow. "That much is obvious. You are setting your own experience as the final judge of truth. Therefore, you are setting up science and faith, rationality and spirituality, in opposition to each other. When one fails, the other must be true. When faith failed you, you turned to science."

He took a drink of his scotch, and I jumped back in. "And now science has failed me," I said, pointing to my head.

He raised his eyebrows. "How do you work that out?"

"It's obvious, isn't it? Training in science didn't prepare me to have the air squeezed out of my lungs, to be smacked in the face, to be tripped on stairs or to have Hebrew carved into my forehead."

Father Neal smiled. "It depends on what you mean by *science*. If, by science, you mean the view that everything in the universe has a material and natural explanation, then yes, science has failed you. If you mean science the way it should really be done, you could say that science has rewarded you."

"I don't understand."

"Think about the scientific method. You have a theory, and then you test it to see if it's true. If the tests hold up, you stay with that theory until something comes along that changes it. Am I right?"

I nodded, unable to argue with that reasonable logic.

"You have bought into the idea that what we see is the only way to understand the reality around us. But I hate to tell you, a materialistic view of the world is limited by what it can explain."

"So we should just abandon scientific exploration?"

Father Neal rapped my arm with his cane. "Don't be ridiculous. Didn't you hear anything I just said? Again, you have put things in opposition that shouldn't be. I will hit you with my cane every time you do that from now on."

"Bringing the rod of discipline to a wayward child?"

"I'm just telling you, Aidan, that maybe you are not doubting hard enough."

I had no idea what he was talking about. My chest began to throb, and my head swirled from the strong scotch. I knew what he said was important, but I couldn't quite grasp it. "Okay, so let me ask you this, let's say a demon or a ghost or whatever attacked me. Why was it focused on me? Why didn't it go after anyone else?"

"I don't know the answer to that question. Not yet. It was obviously trying to communicate something. It spoke when I spoke to bind it. But what it said didn't make a lot of sense."

"What did it say?"

"It kept saying 'Nebo darash' over and over again."

Nebo. I lifted up my head as my face went pale.

"Aidan, are you okay? Do those things mean anything to you?"

"Nebo was on Amanda's head when the cops found her."

He stood silent for a moment. "Yes. Yes, it all makes sense now," he whispered.

"What?" I gripped my legs.

"Nothing, continue."

I told him about the note and the vision I had in his office.

"And that is why you asked me about the Bone Masters?"

"Yeah."

"Do you remember your Hebrew?"

"A little."

"Well, the other word the demon muttered, *darash*, means one who conjures the dead for the purpose of conversing or having mastery over them."

I leaned forward. "Then how do I explain Amanda's words *'find him at the gates of the dead?'*" And how does all this fit in?"

Father Neal stared off into space as if looking for answers. "Tomorrow they will go through the evidence of the hunt. I think you should be there."

"Ah, can't. Session meeting tomorrow. I have to be there for this one. They might fire my boss. Long story."

He nodded. "Then meet us in the sanctuary after it is done."

"Why?"

"The Bone Masters. The words scrawled in Amanda's head. There is more that needs to be said, but I need time to think. I don't have the answers you need right now. I know I don't act like it, Aidan, but I'm old. And the confrontation has drained me."

Father Neal's face looked ragged and droopy as if someone had pulled down on his skin. I wanted to object again, but I couldn't. I got up from the chair. "Okay, Father, I'll see you tomorrow."

I watched him rise from the chair, leaning heavily on his cane. "Good night, my boy."

I left his office without saying another word. Father Neal sat back down in his chair, looking out his window into the night as I closed the office door. When I got into my car, I sat in silence for a moment before finally reaching into my pocket for my phone. The white emblem glared in the darkness, telling me I had a text message.

It was from Jennifer. *Need an hour of sleep. I'm going to bed. Hope you are okay.*

I wasn't okay. Far from it. It would have been nice to hear Jennifer's voice. Maybe it would drive away the nightmares.

chapter twenty-two

That is the craziest thing I've ever heard, Brian wrote.

Tell me about it, I replied. *I wouldn't have believed it if I wasn't there.*

So, is your faith restored?

I frowned. A natural question, I guess, but just because I experienced something I couldn't explain didn't mean I was willing to have faith in God. It was too early in the morning to get philosophical with Brian. I wanted to keep it light.

No, why would that be?

Because you just got attacked by something you couldn't see, you stupid asshole.

I laughed. Ashley must've still been asleep. *Yeah, but that doesn't prove anything other than there might be a spirit world. As for God, who knows? It's a huge leap to go from ghost attack to the Christian God, you know.* I chomped on my toast as I typed.

Good point, but come on. There is a purpose behind all of this. You have to see that.

I ran my hands through my hair as Bishop put his head in my

lap. *I do, I guess. But I'm not ready to let go of my doubt or anger. Right now, all of this just makes it worse. I'm confused. I'm angry. I'm sad. I might be falling for a lady cop, and I have met some mystical priest who seems to have one foot in this world and one foot in, I dunno ... ghost land.*

Heh, ghost land?

Only word I have for it.

I rubbed Bishop's head as Brian responded.

Good word for it. Seems like this stuff has always followed you around.

I frowned as I typed. *What are you talking about?*

Have you forgotten that night as we drove back to the city from camp?

I had, in fact, forgotten. In college, Brian and I had worked at a summer camp filled with white, rich kids who wanted a real, honest, "forest" experience, whatever that was. The road from camp was very curvy and more than a bit dangerous. There had been a number of gruesome car accidents along that stretch.

Brian rode shotgun, and I sat in the back while our friend drove. We both looked out the window when a lady in white, riding on a white horse, shining in the darkness, appeared in the woods along the road. We shouted, "What the hell was that?" at the same time, but our friend saw nothing. Right after it happened, I asked Brian to tell me what he saw, and he described exactly the same thing.

He was right. The ghost world was following me around. That thought made me uncomfortable. I had no desire to make any more contact with that place, if there was such a thing.

I hope not, I wrote. *I don't need that complication in my life.*

I know you might laugh at this, but I have a bad feeling about all of it. I think something or someone has an interest in you. I mean, the footprints, the visions, and whatever happened at the house. Something seems to like you an awful lot.

I rubbed Bishop's ears as he started to snore. It was actually a comforting sound, and I needed it. Everything had just become too unreal. I tried to laugh off Brian's comment as I responded. *I think you read too many Stephen King novels.*

Now you sound like Ashley, Brian wrote.

Not pretty enough, I'm afraid.

Stop changing the subject. I'm serious. I really think you are in danger. You can't deny it.

If I had been forced to put this theory into peer review for a scientific journal, I would have been laughed at. I had no evidence other than some personal experiences. But they were powerful ones.

My phone rang. I looked at it and smiled. *Yo man, gotta run. Lady Cop is calling.*

Don't let her put you in handcuffs ... unless you want her to! See ya.

I grabbed my cell phone and answered just in time. "Hello, Officer Brown, how may I help you this morning?"

"It's *Detective* Brown, Reverend Schaeffer."

"Oh, right, forgot," I teased. "What can I do for you, Detective Brown?"

"My boss is chewing everyone's ass out about this case as you might guess. He wants us to go over every lead again, and that includes you."

My heart fluttered. "Are they questioning my alibi?"

"No, they all agree you are no longer a suspect. But they think you may have more information for us."

"So, there are no leads whatsoever?"

She sighed. "No, nothing. Other than the evidence I showed you, we have nothing. Everyone is going nuts trying to figure out what Nebo means. The boss says thanks for that lead, by the way."

"Glad I could help. Believe me, if I could think of more information, I would."

"I really don't know what to do. The press is asking questions. The mayor is involved because it's such a high-profile case, '*bloody murder at a Columbus landmark*' and all that."

"Yeah, I've been reading the papers."

"Thank God no one knows all the details." She paused. "So, are you going to tell me about your ghost hunt?"

"It was fine."

"That's it? Fine? No details?"

"I don't know if I want to share them. You might think I'm totally freaking crazy."

"I already think that, so you have nothing to lose."

I took a deep breath and told her everything that happened to me, including the Hebrew being scraped into my forehead.

She became silent.

"Jennifer?"

"I'm sorry, this is just leaving me puzzled. I don't like it. The stuff with Father Neal last night, just downright crazy shit."

"You and me both," I said. "And tonight, I have to go back to the church to review any evidence they collected from the hunt."

"That sounds interesting."

"I think I would rather go to a session meeting."

"Can I come with you?" she asked, sounding hopeful.

"Are you serious?"

"Yeah, I think it might be interesting."

I had trouble reading her intentions by her tone. "I guess," I said, gently rubbing the painful scratches in my forehead. "Can you meet me at St. Patrick's after my meeting tonight?"

"What time?"

"I don't know. Session meeting will most likely go for hours."

"Just call me."

"I will. See you then." I hung up the phone and stared at a blank TV. I didn't like how I felt right now. I used to have everything figured out, from my faith to my recent bout with agnosticism. I'd drifted into uncharted territory. I had moved beyond my faith, at least I thought I had, but now, I'd started to move beyond my doubt.

To where, I had no idea.

chapter twenty-three

I got to the church a half an hour early. I always tried to arrive before everyone else. It made me feel more comfortable. My own version of surveying the field before the battle.

I decided I wouldn't tell anyone about Mike's affair. What would be the point? If he was on his way out, it was really no one's business, no matter how much of a hypocrite it made him. I felt bad for Sheila and their kids. But maybe knowing would just be worse.

At least, that's what I hoped.

Once I got to my office, I trolled the Internet for the word Nebo. I found nothing I didn't already know. As I went to cross-reference the word, I was startled by a knock on my door. I turned around to see Elder John.

"Aidan, may I speak with you for a moment?"

"Yes, of course. Come in."

He sat down. "You know what we will probably decide tonight, correct?"

"Yeah."

"Do you support the decision?"

"I really don't know what to say to that."

John frowned. "No, I guess you're right. That was badly stated."

"I'll try to serve the church in any way I can, if that is what you mean." I took a drink of water.

"Yes, exactly. God's flock here at Knox will need a shepherd in the coming days. You know how long pastor searches can take."

He glanced at my forehead. Thankfully, I'd covered the Hebrew with a Band-Aid. Before he could ask, I answered his unspoken question.

"I do. Don't worry. I'm not going anywhere." The lie came to my lips almost without thinking.

"Good. I'm sure your faithfulness will be rewarded."

Yeah, like it has been so far...

He patted my shoulder and then looked at my forehead again. "Did you hurt yourself?"

I waved my hand. "Yeah, my dog saw a squirrel or something. Took off after it and ran me into a tree."

John frowned. "I'm sorry, brother, I'll pray for you."

He walked out of my office. I stared at the ceiling for a few minutes trying to gather my thoughts. With a deep breath, I got up and walked toward the conference room.

When I entered, the tension hit me like a developing supercell thunderstorm. If there'd been any Kansas residents in the church, they would have been fleeing for their shelters. No one smiled, and no one looked at anyone else.

Mike entered last and stood at the head of the table. "I call this meeting to order," he said. "And I immediately ask for a replacement moderator, considering the business we are about to discuss. My suggestion would be Rev. Timothy Williams, a friend of this church who is now present with us."

Timothy sat at the other end of the table. He looked like Plato's ideal form of a Presbyterian minister and wore khaki pants, a white shirt and a tie just about everywhere he went. A very sensitive man, he actually broke down crying at a presbytery meeting after we once disciplined an ordained minister for infidelity. Up until meeting

Father Neal, Timothy was the only guy who still gave me any hope for my profession.

"Thank you, brothers. I'll do my best to moderate this meeting in fairness." Timothy paused. "Let's open in prayer. Father, please bring us a spirit of unity as we…"

My thoughts soon lost track of his prayer. I looked up to see Mike gazing at the table with a blank stare. From what I could tell, he was about ten minutes away from losing his job. These men would show no mercy. An unexpected feeling of pity rose up in me, and I stared up at the lights.

Did he deserve to lose his job this way? Over a stupid Sunday school lesson? He probably deserved to lose it for screwing around, but the elders didn't know that. Hell, how many pastors had committed infidelity? The stress of the job could break anyone at any time. Could I really blame him for that? Wasn't my loss of faith and staying in this job the same thing?

I frowned at the unexpected perspective and shifted in my seat as I bowed my head.

"Amen." Timothy looked up at the elders. "Now, the way this meeting will be conducted will be first to let John introduce his motion. It must be seconded, and then the discussion will be allowed to happen. Once seconded, I'll allow five minutes for each person who wants to speak, but we must be balanced on both sides of the issue. John, you may now present your motion."

John cleared his throat and stood up. "Thank you, Pastor Williams. Brothers, it is with deep regret that I introduce this motion."

I would have bet that his depth of regret went about as deep as a paper cut.

"I move that Pastor Mike be removed from the pastorate of Knox church and be given a four-month severance package from the date of termination."

I fought to keep my face composed. I had to hand it to John; four months was generous. Most pastors were given two at most. Some friends of mine had been given only a month to find another position, which, considering how long it took to get a job in the

3 GATES OF THE DEAD

church world, put many of them in serious financial trouble.

Timothy looked down the table at the other elders. "Is there a second to this motion?"

No one raised his hand. John grimaced and looked around at his allies, but they all avoided his gaze.

"Is there no one to second the motion?" Timothy said.

I couldn't believe it. A week before, over half of these men had been rabid dogs about Mike's dismissal. Now, not only did they look reluctant, they looked scared. I expected this meeting to be long and drawn out, but if no one seconded John's motion, it was dead. No discussion would be needed.

We sat in awkward silence for about a minute.

Timothy swallowed hard. "Hearing no second, this moderator declares that the motion may not be brought before this body of elders for a vote." He paused and then smiled. "I would like to take a moment of personal privilege to say that I'm very glad you all chose this route. I'll do whatever I can to help this situation move forward. Things can be fixed by God's grace, and I'm more than willing to be that agent, but only if invited. Now, I turn my moderator duties back over to Pastor Mike."

"Thanks, Tim. I appreciate it," Mike said as he took over the meeting. "Well, guys, I am sure you will be glad to get back to your families earlier than expected tonight. Obviously, we need to have some more meetings soon on how to move forward, and I certainly am in favor of Tim helping us. But for now, let's pray and then we can figure the rest out as we go, if there are no objections."

No one raised any objections, and John stared at Mike with his mouth open.

As Mike closed in prayer, my mind whirled. Did I suddenly have an obligation to tell people what I knew? Could I even prove any of it? All I heard was a conversation. I couldn't even prove that it wasn't his wife Sheila on the phone and that they were playing some weird game.

I bolted for my office at the final Amen. I needed the refuge of my little space. Just as my nerves were starting to calm, someone knocked at my door.

"Aidan?" Mike called out.

"Yeah. Come on in."

He opened the door and sat down. "So, that was unusual, eh?" He leaned back in the chair, hands behind his head.

"To say the least."

"I actually had Sheila calling real estate agents."

"I'm sure." I had no interest in prolonging the conversation.

"I wonder what happened."

"Your guess is as good as mine. Maybe a ghost appeared to them or something."

Mike stared at me for a moment, with no smile, no frown, just blank. Then he laughed.

"That must have been it. Or maybe it was a case of he-who-is-without-sin-casting-the-first-stone."

Strange reference.

He stood up and stretched. "All right, man, you doin' okay? Any more on Amanda's murder?"

"No, not a word." I still didn't want to talk to him, but I couldn't be rude either.

"And how are things with the lady cop? Is she a believer?"

I wanted to ask why it mattered to him. "Well, we are just at the friend stage right now. Not dating."

He nodded. "Are you going to stay here for a while?"

I wanted to get as far away from the church as possible. My stomach churned, and I felt dizzy. "No, got some errands to run tonight."

"Okay. I think I'll stay a bit and work on my sermon. By the way, thanks for filling in at the last minute for me this past Sunday."

"That's my job."

He smiled. "That it is. I'll see you tomorrow."

I gave him the finger after he turned around.

Packing up my stuff, I went outside to call Jennifer.

"Hey, how was the meeting?" she asked.

"Short. Unexpectedly short."

"I guess so. I didn't expect to hear from you for a couple of hours."

"I know. Long story that I'll explain later. Meet me at St. Patrick's in fifteen minutes?"

"I'll be there."

From one strange situation to another...

chapter twenty-four

I pulled up to St. Patrick's and saw Jennifer's Mustang among the ghost hunters' cars.

She stepped out of the car, dressed in hip hugging jeans and an Ohio State sweatshirt. It didn't matter what she wore, Jennifer always had the ability to get my blood pumping. She walked over to me and smiled.

"So tell me, what is this going to be like?" she asked, handing me some coffee from Cup O' Joe.

"I haven't the slightest clue. This will be a first for me." I pressed on my bandaged head.

"Are you all right?" she asked as we walked to the door. "Does it hurt?"

"It does, but it's not that," I said. "It's the meeting earlier. It made no sense at all. And Mike is cheating on his wife."

"What? Are you going to say anything?" Her eyes searched my face.

"I have no proof." I shook my head. "I overheard his side of a phone conversation, that's all. And if I'm gonna be fired, I want to make sure it's for the right reasons."

"I guess you're right. Sucks though." She frowned.

"IFS," I said, smiling a little.

"What?"

"Never mind. Let's go inside."

We walked up the stone steps, and the smell of honey wax hit us as we entered the building. All the lights had been turned off. Four candles, split between the two sides of the door, cast a glow that lit the entryway.

"Where is everyone?" Jennifer whispered.

"In the sanctuary, I think."

We went into the chapel where the team sat before Father Neal. The flickering altar candles illumined the sanctuary. Everyone read the prayers of the Anglican service from the Book of Common Prayer.

Father Neal stood at the head of the sanctuary clothed in the white alb of a clergyman. He chanted the prayers with a passion I had never seen.

"From all evil and mischief; from sin, from the crafts and assaults of the Devil; from thy wrath, and from everlasting damnation; from all blindness of heart; from pride, vain-glory, and hypocrisy; from envy, hatred, and malice, and all uncharitableness; from fornication, and all other deadly sin; and from all the deceits of the world, the flesh, and the Devil; from lightning and tempest; from plague, pestilence, and famine; from battle and murder, and from sudden death; from all sedition, privy conspiracy, and rebellion; from all false doctrine, heresy, and schism; from hardness of heart, and contempt of thy Word and Commandment."

"Good Lord, deliver us," everyone responded in unison.

Murder, pride, fornication, uncharitableness, and maybe the Devil … I hadn't been delivered from any of those in the past few days. I couldn't say "Good Lord, deliver us" because I didn't believe He would. He hadn't been with me in the past, not that I could remember, anyway.

Still, I couldn't deny the beauty of the Anglican service. It had rhythm and form, thoughtful words, beauty and mystery. As I knelt to take communion, knowing I shouldn't, I took the wafer and dipped it into real wine. As I chewed on the wine-soaked wafer, I couldn't help thinking how this way of taking communion seemed right and holy.

After Father Neal gave the benediction, we followed him into his office. I didn't feel sleepy this time, but rather the opposite as if I had drunk four Red Bulls in a row. The light of the room pulsed and flared.

"Okay, everyone," Reg said. "Darrin and I reviewed the evidence." He paused. "You know I don't exaggerate, but I'm telling you all, this is by far the strangest evidence we have ever collected."

Darrin agreed. "And I think we can thank our new preacher friend for that."

I looked up. "What?"

"The spirit or spirits, or whatever the heck was in that house, seemed terribly interested in you," Darrin said, twirling his cigarette.

"Why were they were so focused on Aidan?" Jennifer asked.

Everyone looked at her with raised eyebrows.

"Oh, sorry," I said. "This is Detective Jennifer Brown from the Columbus City Police Department. She is investigating Amanda's murder. I have been helping her a bit, and I told her about this meeting. She is just interested in what you all do." I wished I didn't talk so much when I got nervous.

Zoe came over to Jennifer and offered her hand. "Detective Brown, it is a pleasure to meet you. Welcome to St. Patrick's."

"Please, it's Jennifer. And I'm not here on official business. Just curious."

"Of course, but your help may be required before the evening is over."

Jennifer looked at her, puzzled. "Well, I'll do what I can."

"Welcome, Jennifer," Reg said. "Maybe you can shed some of your luminous knowledge on us."

Jennifer nodded, trying to suppress a smile.

"So, why were they so focused on me?" I broke in, a bit

impatient at the discussion.

"I have my theories, and none are pleasant," Father Neal said, gripping his cane.

"Let's hear them," I said.

"No, not yet. We must view and hear the evidence first."

"Okay, so what did you all find?" I drummed my fingers on the table.

"Many things, actually. The most I have ever seen or heard. But let's all move to the conference room. It has a projector and speakers that will serve us better," Reg said.

As we walked, I grabbed Darrin. "So, what the hell did you guys find?"

"Better that you take it in yourself, preacher man."

"Why is that?"

"Because I barely believe what I saw and heard myself. If someone had told me, I would have said they were crazy."

"Darrin, come help hook all this up," Reg said as we entered the room.

I sat down by Jennifer, and she leaned toward my ear. "They all seem a bit grim," she whispered. "Were they like this last night?"

"No, not at all. They were serious, but not like this. The night went well, other than my getting attacked. Or whatever the heck it was."

She nodded. "They must have found something bad."

"I guess. What could it possibly be? JFK telling us who really killed him?"

She looked at me, lips pursed.

"What? What did I say? You don't believe all this, do you?" I asked.

"I don't know what I believe, but these people don't seem like kooks."

"How do you know?"

She frowned at me. "I'm a cop. Most cops develop a bullshit detector. I might be wrong, but these people don't seem like they are out to fool you. Or us."

"I didn't say they were. I like them, but even the best people can be deluded."

She raised an eyebrow. "Like you?"

Before I could offer a sarcastic response, Reg cleared his throat, and Jennifer turned her attention to him.

"Okay, Zoe," he said. "If you'll get the lights, we can start. Aidan and Jennifer, I need to tell you a bit about how we review evidence. We take everything, audio and video and download it onto computers. That way, we can review everything at once."

"How much do you usually get?" Jennifer asked, more curious than I was.

"Well, the total is usually somewhere around thirty to forty hours of audio and visual evidence. We have the handheld cameras, the motion cameras, the microphones we place in the house, and the digital recorders. So, a lot to go over. Thankfully, Darrin and Kate are on break from school, so the three of us got through it by working nonstop since last night."

"How do you sift through all that so quickly without missing anything?" Jennifer asked.

"We've gotten good at it," Darrin said, smiling. "Plus, the audio is easy. You just look for the humps. When we put the audio on a particular program, we can see if anything has been recorded by the sound waves."

"Ah, got it." She nodded.

"And visually, you can usually spot something out of the ordinary," Darrin said.

"Usually?" I asked.

"Well, we're human, my dear preacher. We have been known to miss things. But in this case, it was not possible."

Reg reached down to the computer and flipped a switch. The screen projected on the wall at the end of the conference table. We watched as the mouse moved around the screen and clicked on a file. "Okay, first the videos. There were only a few things caught that were considered unusual." He clicked play, and a video from one of the night-vision cameras began. "Now, watch the middle of the screen."

A figure crossed over the center of the video.

"Holy shit!" Jennifer blurted before covering her mouth.

"Let's see that again as I slow it down," Reg said. He played it in slow motion, and we saw the figure again, but this time in more detail. It was black and solid and carried something long and pointed in its hands.

"Is that a rifle?" Jennifer asked.

"We believe it is," Father Neal said. "We have looked at this tape quite a few times tonight."

"A Civil War era rifle, to be exact," Kate jumped in. "Look at the bayonet at the top." She took out a laser pointer and shone the red dot at the long knife-like object.

"So, what is a Civil War era ghost doing in this house hurting a baby?" I asked, confused.

"We'll get to that," Reg replied. "But for the record, we don't believe this ghost is doing the hurting. Something is going on here that we've never seen before." Reg went on as if he were giving one of his physics lectures. His very matter-of-fact scientific voice somehow made everything believable.

I looked at Jennifer, whose face gave nothing away. She stared at the screen, fingers on her mouth and lost in thought.

"The rest of the videos are very similar, dark figures moving at a fast pace. We couldn't make out anything clearly, but we saw Victorian Age outfits, Native Americans, and just about every era of Columbus, Ohio."

Reg reeled off each video, five in all. "Now, Jennifer and Aidan, you need to know that we rarely have this type of video evidence."

"What do you mean by rarely?" Jennifer asked, leaning forward.

"Like, we'll usually see something in one out of every ten cases. These five videos would normally mean about fifty cases of work."

Jennifer continued to stare intently.

"There is even more to it," Reg continued. "And here, what we don't see is very interesting." He pulled up another video. "This was taken just after Father Neal walked into the house for his blessing. Notice, the moment he lifts up his cane."

The screen flashed white, and then the video moved as if someone had put it on cartoon fast forward. Dark figures swirled all around Father Neal, but none touched him because of the faint white line that surrounded him. Then the video stopped. "The camera went dead about five seconds into Father Neal's blessing. To do that, it would take an energy burst beyond anything we have ever seen before. These cameras aren't battery operated, they are plug-ins. There's no scientific reason for it to happen."

Reg took a deep breath. "If that was all the evidence we had, it would have been one of the most successful investigations I can remember. But there was more on the audio." He pulled up another program, and a few boxes of wavy green lines dominated the wall. "Let's start with the least impressive. This was recorded during Aidan and Darrin's adventure in the basement. You'll hear Aidan ask the ghost a smart aleck question."

Jennifer looked at me and smiled.

Do you like Darrin's singing?

We waited a few seconds and then we heard it. A low, digital sound.

NO.

"Let me loop it," Reg said.

And then we heard it again.

NO. NO. NO. NO.

Jennifer leaned forward. "How do we know that is not Darrin or Aidan?"

"It wasn't one of us," I said. "Because all Darrin said was 'funny.' I remember."

"Yes, actually you can hear Darrin say that here," Reg said, pointing at a grouping of green lines. "Plus, to answer your question, Jennifer, the frequency is much lower than either Aidan or Darrin's voices. They both register low, but this statement is beyond what can be achieved by the human voice."

Jennifer nodded.

"Now, for the most impressive and, to be honest, the ones that have us all a bit scared. When we get an EVP, it is normally just a few words, scratchy and hard to hear. These next few are, well, different." Reg pressed play, and a male voice came out of the speakers, whispering, but with no distortion.

He is stirring. The Bone Masters have come. Direct us. Show us the gates.

I stared at the screen in disbelief and then looked over at Father Neal. He didn't react. They must have played it for him before we got here.

"And now, the next one," Reg said.

Follow the Path. Go to the Gates. Go to Nebo. Blood is waiting. He is waiting. Open his gate.

My heart raced. "I'm sorry, did that last bit say, 'Open his gate?'"

"Yes, it did," Reg said as his voice cracked. "And here is the next one."

The whole room seemed to hold its breath. A kid's voice, low and frightened played over the speakers.

They want control. They want control of us. Help us. Help us. They want the Grinning Man awake.

I looked at Jennifer. She had her eyes shut.

"And now, the last one." I couldn't help but notice that Reg's hands, steady up to that point, had begun to tremble.

My blood opened the gate. The magician murdered me. Aidan, find him. Save them. Stop him or the Grinning Man will come. I love you. I love you. I wish you could hear me.

I put my head down. Silence crept over the room as I looked down at the table. I could feel everyone's eyes boring into my head, but I didn't want to look up. I didn't need anyone to tell me whose voice that was. I knew it from the moment she spoke.

Amanda.

Her voice assaulted the tightly constructed wall I'd built around my heart. I searched wildly for explanations. Whatever comfort I had found in my unbelief left me the moment I heard Amanda's voice. I couldn't persuade myself into thinking it was my depression or willful delusion. I wanted to crawl back into the comfort of not believing in a spiritual reality. I never grasped until now how disturbing it would be to confront the fact something other than this physical world existed.

I rubbed my face, trying to cover up my unsteady hands.

"Aidan? Are you okay?" Father Neal asked from across the table.

"I … I guess I am. I don't know." I tried to keep my voice steady.

"What does all this mean?" Jennifer asked, the tone of her voice unreadable.

"We don't really know," Father Neal said. "There are a lot of things in here we don't understand."

"Excuse me, Father Neal, but this is the craziest pile of shit I have seen since I've been on this team," Darrin said, twirling another unlit cigarette in his hand.

"Someone has obviously committed murder with the belief that it will give them control over the dead," Zoe chimed in. "Why, how, or what their purpose is, we don't know. And forgive me, but it looks as if Amanda was his or her first victim."

I rubbed my head. "I know you're right. But what about the Bone Masters? And the Grinning Man? What's that about? And the gates? All that has to fit together somehow." I got up from the table.

"I think we have had enough for one night, everyone," Father Neal broke in.

Everyone's eyes widened. They looked as surprised as I felt.

"I would like to talk with Aidan and Jennifer by themselves."

Everyone had too much respect for Father Neal to question him. As they left the room, Father Neal shook every hand, gave them hugs and offered them each little words of encouragement. When the last person left, Father Neal shut the door and turned to us.

I tried not to gasp at the change in his expression. He looked old, weak … and afraid.

chapter twenty-five

Father Neal led us into his office, and he sat down behind his desk. He motioned for us to sit and didn't speak for a while.

"Are you okay, Father?" Jennifer asked.

"Yes, just feeling a little spent. There are things I need to tell you and Aidan. Things I've told very few others. Things I'm not sure you'll believe even when I tell you. However, you were with me in the cemetery, so maybe what you saw will help you believe."

"Try us," Jennifer said.

"I will. I must, it seems. But it will take some time."

"It's okay, Bishop can wait." I sat on the couch across from him.

He smiled, smoothing out some of the grooves in his face. "To understand what I'm going to say, I must tell you a story of my early life." He took a deep breath. "I arrived at Oxford at the tender age of seventeen. I knew pretty much nothing about the world around me, so I was ripe for anything. Of course, like all good Englishmen, I went to the local parish church. But when I got to Oxford, my childlike faith was challenged, and it crumpled pretty quickly. I cast it off willingly and was ready to jump into whatever took my fancy."

No wonder he understood my doubt so well.

"You might think that given the times, I would become a confirmed scientific materialist, but I guess I was too much of a romantic to go that far. I wanted to hold on to some sort of spirituality. So, I looked for alternatives, and I found a group known as the *Golden Dawn*."

"Who is the *Golden Dawn*?" I asked.

He leaned back in his chair. "You might call them modern day magicians, or rather, what they would prefer, scientists of the Newtonian stripe."

"I don't think Newton would appreciate the comparison."

He raised an eyebrow at me. "How much do you know about the history of science?"

"The basics, I suppose. Enough to know that Newton was the first scientist."

He nodded. "And the last magician ... or so people think. Newton's life obsession was alchemy. He considered his scientific achievements as products of that pursuit. Just about everyone during that early period practiced alchemy in one form or another. Tried, I daresay. Science owes its very existence to the magical impulse, and, in fact, the impulse that drives both is the same."

"I'm sorry, Father Neal, that just sounds contradictory," Jennifer said. "There's no logic to it. Magic has to do with stuff like *Harry Potter* and all that. Science is based on rationality, observation, and experimentation."

I nodded in agreement.

Father Neal smiled. "All are used in magic as well, my dear. And keep in mind that I'm not talking about magic like Houdini or someone like that. I'm talking about the desire to control nature, to have power over the elements and unlock the secrets of the universe. Each follows a ritual or experiment. Each wants observable results. Each, depending on the person, wants the power that might be unleashed. To be gods, you might say."

A silence hung over the room. Father Neal reached into his desk drawer and pulled out a bottle of whiskey. He poured himself a glass and took a sip.

"I think Dawkins might disagree with that," I responded.

Father Neal smiled. "Ah, Richard. Yes, he would try. But even he speaks in mystical tones when he describes the process of evolution. It makes you wonder."

"So, the *Golden Dawn*," Jennifer broke in.

He nodded and took another sip of whisky. "There was a fierce war of words between the two strongest personalities in the *Golden Dawn* at the time, Samuel Maters and Aleister Crowley."

"Wait, Aleister Crowley? The same guy Jimmy Page from Led Zeppelin was into?" Jennifer asked.

"The very same, my dear. I met Aleister in 1936 and was drawn to him. He radiated a sense of power over everyone, and, excuse me my dear, his sexual pull on the women was profound. I saw him seduce married women after only five-minute conversations. I'm ashamed to admit it, but as an awkward young man, I wanted that, to have that sort of power and control over women. I fell into Aleister's orbit and sat at his feet."

I tried to picture it. Father Neal, one of the holiest guys I had ever met, sitting at the feet of the man who proudly called himself *The Beast*. I couldn't do it. This gentle old man across from me, who seemed like personal holiness incarnate, had dabbled in magic, seduction, and from the sound of it, illicit sex. I couldn't even begin to bring those two pieces together.

"So, Aleister taught me magic or 'magick' as he called it. He taught me spells that he believed were more like scientific formulas that hadn't been discovered yet. I threw myself into the practice. I'm ashamed to say, I began to participate in many dark rituals. At the time, I wrote them off as experiments, just as any person interested in science might participate in for curiosity's sake."

He bowed his head, cheeks coloring. Now I understood why everyone, including myself, trusted him so much. Father Neal didn't back down from presenting himself as he had really been and didn't hide the truth. No matter what people might think of him. I'd been taught to present one face to the world while hiding my real one, the sinful face, the cynical dark face. The hiding had eaten me alive, and the honesty had turned Father Neal into something different. Something gentle, holy, loving.

"There was a branch of magick that was merely discussed but never practiced. It was darker than anything we ever practiced, the magick known as Bone Mastering or using the dead for magickal purposes. Crowley claimed he never practiced this branch of the art, and I believed him then. After I bowed the knee to Christ, I found out a different story. I saw first-hand what he tried to teach his disciples as well as their goal."

At the mention of Bone Mastering, I began to shake and goose bumps covered my arms. "What's their goal, Father?" I asked.

He frowned. "As for the group, I don't know. I never got far enough. I left them before I got further up and further in. Aleister never told me all of his secrets."

"So how do they control the dead?" Jennifer asked.

"There are a number of different spells, incantations, experiments as they liked to say. Some more powerful and hideous than others."

"How does this relate to Amanda and the cemetery?" I asked.

He paused as he swirled his whisky. "I believe that whoever killed her wanted to start one of the most powerful of spells of control. It's called the *Three Gates of the Dead*. Until Aidan took me to the cemetery, I thought it might have just been a magician urban legend. I'm sorry to say, it's not."

Jennifer took out her notebook and began to scribble notes. "Can you describe this ritual to me, Father?"

"It's brutally simple but effective. The goal is to harness the power of the dead through the use of three sites of power."

"Sites of power? In Ohio?" I asked

"There are plenty of sites here, more than most states in the Midwest. Maybe more than anywhere in North America. For one, the earthen mound complexes in this state are mysterious. No one knows their true purposes, although most of them are one vast graveyard. No one knows for sure, but the American ancients who made the mounds most likely believed these complexes to be *thin spaces* between the living and the dead. From what I've studied in magick, they were right. You don't even need to go that far, however. Any place of the dead will work. The Confederate Cemetery seems to be one of those."

Jennifer tapped her pen on her notebook. "So, a magician finds the sites, then what?"

"You murder a 'defiled woman,' as it were, someone who had sinned sexually. You spill her blood and, as you've seen, carve directions into her forehead. Pardon me, dear, for being so graphic."

Jennifer gave a small smile. She had probably seen too many gruesome sights and heard enough dirty talk from the guys she worked with not to even be remotely offended.

"Thank you, Father," she said. "You are a gentleman. I had forgotten what you all looked like." She winked at me. "But, I have another question. Why three sites?"

"Three has always been a powerful, magickal number. It's a number of completeness. In this case, it is meant to summon the dead in each area for more power, more control for whatever the Master's purpose might be. Such concentrations of power are meant for a purpose beyond the normal, everyday magick."

"What is their purpose?" I asked.

Father Neal gulped the rest of his whiskey. "From what we heard tonight, they are trying to awaken the Grinning Man."

Jennifer and I looked at each other.

"Who is the Grinning Man?"

"His history is long and complicated. I won't go into too much detail, now, other than to say, the rumor is that he is buried somewhere in Ohio, trapped here. I've not been able to find out how or why or even when. That story might be more interesting than my own encounter with him out West. He was, or is, a man who makes Aleister look like a cartoon character."

"How do you know this?" Jennifer asked.

Father Neal leaned forward. "He's the reason I'm in Ohio. I'm here to find him and finish his destruction. I daresay he wouldn't mind finding me either, but for different reasons."

My eyes widened. "How long have you been searching for him?"

"Too many years to count. I've probably overstayed my welcome at St. Patrick's. I've only been able to find traces, enough to make me realize I'm on the right trail. Just when I think I get close, something or someone blocks my view. Maybe whoever is responsible for this ritual might be behind that, who knows?"

"But why have you been searching for him?" Jennifer pressed.

"If someone were to awaken him in this time and place, I shudder to think what he would do. Plus, it's my duty, given to me. I won't back away. I swore an oath. He cannot be allowed to reawaken, or many will suffer."

I frowned. "So, you think Amanda was killed to begin a ritual that will end in resurrecting this Grinning Man?"

Father Neal poured more whiskey for all of us. "I don't think, I know. Everything fits. The unusual power of the dead, the ritualistic nature of Amanda's murder and, more important, the sound of ripping cloth at the cemetery."

"Yeah, what *was* that?" Jennifer asked.

"I told you before. It's the ripping of the veil between the seen and the unseen worlds. The dead are being drawn through that tear and being used by the magician that began the ritual. Or magicians, I should say. There is more than one, as the ritual needs two or more."

I couldn't wrap my brain around anything he was telling us. "It would seem so," I said. "But it might be a copycat killer of some type, you know. Maybe he read about the ritual in a book and decided to try it out."

Father Neal shook his head. "No, this ritual is not written in any available book I know of. And believe me, I know nearly all of them. If it was written down, it is in an obscure book that has never been found. It is always passed from master to apprentice, thus preserving the secret."

"So how did Crowley know of it?"

"Research into various branches of magick, I would guess. He never taught it to me because he kept saying I was not ready for it.

Now, I wonder if it was because he knew that murder was a line I would not cross."

"So, how did you get out from under his influence?" I asked.

He smiled. "By the grace of God and through a man named Charles Williams."

I scratched my chin. "Charles Williams. I've had heard that name before, but where?"

"He is one of the lesser known Inklings."

"Inklings?" Jennifer asked.

"Yes," Father Neal said. "The writer's group of C.S. Lewis, J.R.R. Tolkien and their friends. In fact, Charles was one of the more influential members of the group and wrote quite a few books."

"Interesting," I said.

"Charles pried me loose and led me back to God. Crowley was angry, cursed Charles and me. But nothing ever came of that, of course."

"Why not?" Jennifer asked.

"Because I belonged to Christ, my dear." He smiled and looked over at a painting of a huge man with a dark beard, sitting in a boat, carrying a wooden cup. "Yes, I belong to Him."

I wondered what Jennifer thought about that comment. I didn't want to think about Jesus. It made me uncomfortable. Silence filled the room, and I looked at the painting. "Father, what is that picture?"

"That is the legend of the Fisher King."

"The Robin Williams movie?" Jennifer asked.

Father Neal gave her a half smile. "No, my dear. The legend is way more ancient than that. The Fisher King is the guardian of the Holy Grail in the Arthurian legends of my country. It's a story I've always liked, so my wife painted that for me before she passed."

I tried to tear myself away from staring at the Fisher King.

Father Neal seemed to study us both and Jennifer cleared her throat. "At least we have an excellent lead, Father. Would you mind coming to the station to make an official statement?"

"No, I don't think that is a good idea for you or for me. It's all speculation at this point, and your superiors might think less of you if you come with this theory and no proof."

Jennifer exhaled. "But if you are right about this being the ritual, then we can expect two more deaths. I've got to stop them somehow. That's my job."

Father Neal nodded, his face haggard and pale. "Yes, and I'll help you anyway that I can. But I don't think coming into the station would be that wise. What if you told your superiors you were trying to stop a magick ritual?"

Jennifer deflated. "I see your point."

"So that would mean the next murder would be at a place called Nebo, according to the ritual," I said.

Father Neal nodded. "It would seem so."

Jennifer scratched her scar. "Where would that be?"

"More than likely, it will be some place the Grinning Man has been associated with throughout his long, terrible history. Trust me when I tell you, he's interfered with your country many times." He furrowed his brow. "I'll do my own research and ask around. I may have friends who know."

"Good idea," I said. "We can do some on our own as well. Given that it's from the Bible, there have to be dozens of towns in the US with that name. What else should we look for?"

"You don't even have to look that broadly," Father Neal said in a flat tone. "The ritual must be done within certain boundaries to focus on the control of 'local' spirits. Look for some sort of triangular pattern."

"Yeah, but even if we figure out the location, can we stop the murder?" I asked.

Jennifer looked at me. "We can have the local PD camp out in the area. Or do drive-bys at least. Believe me, we've done that on flimsier evidence than we have here."

Father Neal leaned over his desk. "You must be quick, Jennifer. The ritual will be completed by the next full moon. The magicians want the Grinning Man. But surely, they don't think they can control him," he said almost to himself before looking back at Jennifer. "If he gains the benefits of these ghastly deaths, his power will be breathtaking in its scope."

"I'll get right on it."

Father Neal turned to me. "Before you go, Aidan, may I speak with you?"

"Yes. Jennifer, I will call you later, okay?"

She nodded and walked outside.

"What's up?" I asked.

He took on a tone of authority. "You must be careful. You are in danger of all sorts. The spirit world has an interest in you. You must be careful with your life. And your soul."

I still didn't entirely understand, but I didn't want him to worry. "I will."

"Your doubts make you a target for whoever is doing this ritual. They might use it, but remember your doubts can be used for good or evil. That depends on you. Somehow, you're connected with this in a way I don't understand. Amanda being the first sacrifice was the first sign of what is to come."

"That's comforting," I said, trying to keep from sounding too sarcastic.

Father Neal smiled. "The truth always is. That is why you've got to embrace your doubt like a lover, Aidan. It'll save you and move you in the right direction."

I couldn't keep the skepticism out of my voice. "How is that possible?"

"Thomas' doubts led him to confess our Lord's divinity. We need our doubting Thomases." He smiled while gazing up toward the ceiling. It seemed like he was talking to someone else.

"I wish I could be as good as you."

He eyes bore into me. "You're not me. You're you. Learn to be who you were created to be. Now, go and try to figure out where Nebo might be. I'll work on it from my end." He raised his hands. "May Michael the Archangel guard you by the power of the Blessed Trinity."

chapter twenty-six

The next morning, I drove to the Columbus Library to do some work, my usual midweek ritual that got me out of the suburbs.

As I turned onto Grant Street, my phone rang.

"Hey, Jennifer," I said. I could really get used to her calls.

"How did last night go?"

"Good, I guess. Father Neal told me I was in spiritual danger, then he blessed me and sent me on my way."

"He's an interesting guy and has a fascinating history," she said. "A little old-fashioned for my taste, but I actually like him."

"So do I. What did you think of his story?"

"His personal one or the ritual?"

"Both."

"Well, the personal one was interesting but not nearly as compelling as the ritual. The FBI profiler we brought in suggested that we might find the killer has ritualistic intent. So that didn't surprise me. And the profiler also said the guy will not stop here."

"But Father Neal said there were possible *killers*, not killer."

Jennifer sighed. "Yeah, but I don't buy that. Despite what

Father Neal said, I'm sure this killer found out about this ritual in some obscure book."

"So, you are set that it was one killer?" I asked.

"No, I'm just saying it's more likely. These kinds of killings are usually the work of one psycho, not many. Very rarely do we have a pack of serial killers."

"I suppose so."

"What are you doing?"

"I'm going to the library to study Nebo," I said.

"Aidan, you aren't a cop." She reacted about the way I expected.

I gripped the phone. "I realize that. I'm just curious."

"Curiosity is fine, but stop trying to do our job."

"What do you expect? This was my fiancée, Jennifer. I can't just be a good boy, go along with my church business, and wait by the phone until you come up with something. I've helped before. Who says I can't find something you would never have thought about?"

She paused. "Don't you have a job?"

"Yeah, and everyone thinks I'm doing it right now. If I have to work late tonight, I can."

She sighed. "Fine. Let me know if you find anything."

"I will."

Jennifer lowered her voice. "We need to find something soon, or this case is going to be out of our hands. Scott is running out of delay tactics, and the FBI is going to take over soon. When that happens, the Reverend/Detective double act will come to an end."

"I understand. Talk to you later."

I typed *Nebo* into Google. A broad range of biblical sites came up with variations of the same combination of words about Moses and the Promised Land. I scrolled through five pages of results and found nothing.

I sighed and leaned back in my chair.

What could Amanda have possibly tried to tell me? Nebo was so specific, yet so vague. Without any more information, it was useless.

I pounded on the table and Marge, the sixty-four-year-old

matron of the stacks came up to me. "The Bible frustrating you, Pastor Aidan?"

I smiled. "Well, at least some of the characters inside."

She smiled back and patted my hand. "I understand, but try to express your frustration toward God in quiet."

"Sorry, Marge, just got carried away."

"Don't worry, dear."

As she walked away, an idea struck me. "Hey, Marge, have you ever heard of a place in Ohio called Nebo?"

She pursed her lips. "Hmmm, no, but we have a huge map in the reference section you might want to check out."

I shook my head. I should have thought of that in the first place. As I walked through the book stacks, my conversation with Father Neal about faith and doubt came back to me. I thought about what he said that I should embrace my doubts. I looked at all the books in the nonfiction section, and I considered how many of them contradicted each other. The history books were always being rewritten and updated to debate some other scholar's opinion about a war or certain historical figures. The science books weren't any better. Even in the past hundred years, discoveries that were once considered ironclad realities had been cast off. Rows and rows of books were dedicated to proving opposite things. Libraries were a perfect illustration of human's search for truth and the frustration at never finding it.

Who gets to decide the truth? I wondered. Dawkins? Hitchens? Theologians? Scientists?

I stopped walking as Father Neal's words about science came rushing back to me. I began to realize that even science rested on assumptions that couldn't be proven with ironclad certainty. The universe didn't have a rational order that we tried to figure out.

That idea shocked me. If science relied on those assumptions, so did everything else — history, arts, writing, working, books, and making love. I felt dizzy and sat down in the nearest chair, taking a deep breath.

The map. I had to find the map.

I went to the reference department and found the topographical map of Ohio. I looked in the southeast, Amanda's old stomping grounds, and the possible source of the leaves in the picture.

Small bumps marked the Appalachian foothills surrounding Athens, Ohio. One bump was labeled "Mt. Nebo." My pulse quickened as I wound my way back to my computer. I opened my laptop and searched "Mount Nebo, Athens, Ohio." I clicked on the first link I found — the Athens County Visitor's Bureau website.

I surfed the site and found a link to *Athens' Haunted Places*. As I sped through the text, it seemed Athens had a reputation of being one of the most haunted towns in America. People came from all over the country for ghost hunts, séances, and to suck in the New Age vibe.

As I read down the article, I saw a link to Mount Nebo. *This is it*, I thought. That had to be the place. I printed out the information, packed up my stuff, and headed to St. Patrick's. As soon as I drove out of the parking garage, I dialed Jennifer but got her voicemail.

"This is Aidan. I figured out Nebo. Call me as soon as you can."

I drove as fast as I dared to St. Patrick's. My tires squealed as I jerked to a stop in the parking lot. I jumped out of the car and ran inside.

"Whoa there, Pastor Aidan, where's the fire?" Sue said, looking at me over her glasses.

"Sorry, Sue, I need to see Father Neal."

Her face fell. "I'm sorry. Father Neal received a hospital call this morning. He won't be back until the evening, I'm afraid."

I nearly swore then stopped myself. "Well, tell him I stopped by and to call me as soon as he can."

"I will."

I paused. "Is your computer working okay?"

She brightened up. "Oh, yes, and aren't you a sweetie for fixing it for me!"

"No worries, anytime. I'll see you later."

I got in the car and checked my phone. No messages. I decided to drive home and let Bishop out of his crate. When I got there, I gave him a treat and got myself a beer from the fridge.

I took a sip and parted the curtains in the living room, revealing the lake behind my condo. It looked beautiful, frozen, and white. I put my head against the glass, and my breath fogged the window.

Amanda and I used to walk Bishop around that lake. She liked to feed the ducks and would laugh whenever he chased the birds. They knew their business, so Bishop never caught them. I doubted he would have known what to do with one even if he had.

Amanda, who killed you? Why can't you tell me?

My phone rang, and I jumped. "Hello?"

"Aidan, are you okay?"

"I'm fine, why?" Just hearing her voice made me feel better.

"You sounded a little panicked when you answered."

"Listen, I have something to tell you."

"Me first, because we have a trip to make tonight, and Scott gave me permission to bring you along," she said.

"Where?"

"To a place outside of Athens, Ohio."

"Mt. Nebo," I said.

"How did you know?"

My stomach churned. If Lieutenant Weaver needed to give his permission for me to go, it was because it was a crime scene. I'd been too late. "I guess I'll tell you on the way."

chapter twenty-seven

"Tell me what you found on Mt. Nebo." Jennifer sipped her coffee as she drove. I couldn't help but stare at her. This woman was starting to get into my head. I couldn't figure out if I felt lust, love, or merely infatuation due to the circumstances.

Maybe all of the above.

I looked at the papers I had printed. "Right now, Mt. Nebo has nothing but two roads that join at the top. But the history of the place is intriguing."

"Uh oh, history, you sure you can handle that?" she teased.

"Smartass. The story starts in the mid-1800s with a farmer named Jonathan Koons. Oddly enough, he started out as an atheist but went to a séance and decided to start his own spiritualist movement. Spirits began showing up, rapping on walls, playing music and generally making themselves part of the family."

"What happened next?"

"That's the strange thing. The movement disappeared after the people in the town began to persecute them." I shuffled through the papers. "There are only stories and rumors as to their whereabouts after that."

"Strange. Anything else?"

"Well, according to the Chamber of Commerce, Athens and the surrounding area is widely known for its paranormal activity."

"Of what kind?" Jennifer asked, tucking a strand of hair behind her ear.

"You name it. Creepy cemeteries, insane asylums, haunted college dorms at Ohio University. Oh, here's something interesting. It says the five cemeteries in town form a pentagram."

"What's that?"

"It's a pretty powerful symbol in the world of mythology. Some people say it's evil, some say it's not. Depends on your point of view."

"Interesting. Anything else?"

I skimmed down the page. "Huh, the weird things people come up with…"

"What?" Jennifer looked over at me, and the car swerved. She quickly yanked the wheel back into the lane.

"The Athens area is thought to be a vortex."

"What's that supposed to mean?"

"Well, a lot of the New Agers think there are places of power on this earth where you can tap into energies. Supernatural ones, I guess. You could say they think it's a place where the veil between this world and whatever lies beyond is paper thin."

Jennifer glanced at me. "Gates of the Dead?"

I chewed on my straw. I hadn't thought about that. "You might be right. It would fit with what Father Neal told us. In fact, it all fits."

We sat in silence as we passed the exit for Hocking Hills State Park. I wondered if I would see the same ritualistic acts used on Amanda at the crime scene on Nebo. I shuddered.

"We will probably find the next location carved on this victim's head," Jennifer said, breaking into my thoughts.

I swallowed. "I was just thinking about that."

"Are you ready to see that?"

"Yeah. We have to, don't we?"

"You don't have to look, you know." Jennifer reached over and lightly touched my leg.

"I'll be fine. I was a biology major, remember? I can handle it."

I hope so, anyway.

Jennifer looked over at me with a small frown. The little scar turned down toward her chin. "I've seen hardened men puke at murder scenes. Don't take it lightly."

Not knowing what to say, I turned to look out the window. The road narrowed to two lanes as we drove through the river bottom. Flood plains stretched out from the side of the road, covered in drifts of white. Little hoof prints dented the snow where deer had made their way across the semi-frozen river.

"Aidan, are you okay?"

"Yeah, just looking at the snow and..." I stopped. The field began to fill with indentations as hundreds of human footprints raced toward the car.

"What's wrong?"

The footprints crunched into the snow not fifty feet from us.

"I think we're being followed."

"What?" Jennifer looked at her rearview mirror. "Holy shit!"

Frosted outlines began to appear on the windshield as if dozens of people were running alongside the car. Fogged face prints clouded the glass so I couldn't make out the road.

"Aidan!"

The car shuddered as something began to pound on the roof like large hailstones.

"Over to the side, Jennifer, before we wreck!"

Jennifer swerved off the road into a picnic area and looked at me with terrified eyes as she clicked the power lock button on the door. We gripped each other, and the sound of pounding metal echoed in my head. Jennifer covered my ears, and I did the same for her.

I glanced at the dashboard thermometer. The temperature had dropped from seventy to forty degrees. Our breath came in vapory clouds as Jen dug into my arms. The metal on the roof of the car began to groan. It felt like a bunch of people were stomping on it, making us fear that the car would cave in on us.

"I'm getting out," Jennifer said, reaching for her gun.

"No!" I grabbed her arm. "That's not going to work."

Jennifer pressed her head against my chest as the pounding and thrashing continued. And then it stopped as quickly as it had begun. Deafening silence filled the car.

Jennifer looked up at me, our faces inches apart. Her eyes gleamed in the darkness, and her lips trembled. I swallowed hard.

"What the fuck was that, Aidan?" Jennifer's breath came in short gasps as she clung to me in the cold.

"I don't know. Let's look outside."

She nodded, and we both got out. The face prints had begun to fade, but hand-shaped dents pocked the whole exterior of the car. "Not sure how to explain this to the insurance company. 'Ghosts attacked my car' would invite all kinds of insurance investigators to descend on me." Jennifer's hand shook as she pressed it into a dent.

I looked at her, and we both laughed. The laugh of two people about to come undone. Maniacal. On the verge of tears. She leaned into me, and I hugged her tight. I breathed in her hair and felt her warm neck on my cheek. She pressed against me, and her heat traveled down my body.

"Aidan, I don't know what to think about any of this," she whispered.

"You and me both." I tried to give her a smile.

"Did seminary prepare you for this sort of thing?" She wiped her eyes as tears began to stream down her cheeks.

"What? Attacks by unseen things?" I snorted. "Hardly. The closest thing we ever got to that was talking about whether or not Samuel's ghost was real when it appeared to Saul."

"Now what?"

I shrugged. "I don't know."

We got back in the car. Jennifer gripped the steering wheel as we rode in silence until the GPS voice chirped for us to turn.

We followed its directions until we reached a large hill and drove up the narrow, barely-tarred road. The whole hill seemed to be lit up as police cars, TV vans, and spotlights added their artificial illumination to the scene.

Jen parked the car. "Are you ready?"

I took a deep breath. "Yeah, let's do it."

She gave me a grim smile. "Don't worry if you throw up or anything. I did when I saw my first murder victim. My boss told me everyone does."

"Do you ever get used to it?"

She frowned at me. "You never get used to it. Ever. But you learn to deal with it so you can get your job done."

I nodded.

"They are waiting for us."

I took a deep breath and opened the door. "Okay, let's go."

We got out of the car and walked to the yellow tape. A deputy stood with his arms crossed over his chest. A watcher over the dead. With a Smokey the Bear hat perched on his bald head and a razor-edged jaw, he looked like a recruiting poster for the Athens County Sheriff's department.

Jennifer ducked under the tape, and the deputy put out his arm.

"Ma'am, this is a crime scene. Reporters are supposed to be over there." He pointed to a group of people huddled together, talking.

"Take it easy, deputy. I'm Detective Jennifer Brown from Columbus PD. We are supposed to be here." She flashed her badge.

"Very good, ma'am. And your friend?"

I pulled out my driver's license and handed it over. His eyes darted from my very bad picture to my face.

"Very good, sir. Thank you."

A plain-clothes detective wrapped in a blue coat approached us. "Detective Brown?"

"Yes?"

"I'm Detective Steve Hoover from the Athens County Sheriff's department. Thank you for coming so quickly."

"No problem. Thanks for calling us."

"I figured Weaver would want to know before the FBI. We've been talking about your case, I hope you don't mind."

"Not at all. Can we see the body?"

"Right this way."

He led us around a tree into a clearing. I recognized it immediately — I saw the crossroads from Amanda's pictures and the large smiley face drawn in the gravel.

Amanda knew.

Over the smiley face, two large oak tree branches touched, forming a wooden overhang. A form hung from the tree with what looked like feet dangling over the smiley face.

"I've not seen a killing like this in a long time," Detective Hoover said.

I looked more closely and saw blood on the ground, gleaming in the light. A woman, robed in white, dangled like a broken doll over the smiley face. Her arms and neck had been tied with climbing rope. Open eyes stared up to heaven as if begging for intervention that never came. A bright red and black gash under her throat proved to be the source of the blood as it dripped down on the road.

I shut my eyes. The image of the body burned into my brain. This is what had happened to Amanda. How did she know about this place? How deep had she gotten with whoever did this? What had she thought? The terror must have been beyond imagination. I felt queasy and leaned against a tree.

"Aidan?" Jennifer touched my shoulder.

"Sorry, my imagination just ran away from me."

She nodded as her hand moved to my cheek. "I know, but come with me, you need to hear what Hoover has to say."

We turned our backs on the body and walked to Detective Hoover.

"So, what was the time of death?" Jennifer asked, her pad and pen out.

"About midnight," Hoover said. "The body was discovered around one o'clock by our patrolman. He had been called because someone complained of disturbances. They reported lights rising from here and floating among the trees. They also claimed there were snowy footprints outside of their home. We thought maybe they had a bit too much Appalachian Moonshine, but then we found this." He pointed to the body. "We remembered the APB you all put out in the past day. We all laughed when we first saw what you guys put out there. So, that's when we called Weaver."

"Any explanation for the lights or the footprints?" Jen asked.

"None that we can tell. We think the footprints were a prank, and the light might have been the murderers."

"Murderers?"

"Yeah, at least, we think. There were no discernible footprints, but there is no way one person could have done this by themselves."

Jennifer nodded. "Can we see her forehead?"

"You don't want to look at forensics photos?"

"No, I prefer to eyeball it myself. Thanks."

I tried to remember how to be clinical from my biology labs as we walked over to the body. Detective Hoover pulled over a ladder and propped it against a tree. Jennifer climbed up and bent over the victim's forehead with a magnifying glass.

"Appears to be Hebrew, Aidan. Do you think you could have a look?"

My legs felt unsteady, but I didn't want to look weak. "Sure."

Detective Hoover looked at me and cocked his head.

"Reverend Schaeffer is an expert in occultist ritual and is consulting on this case," Jennifer said as she climbed down.

He nodded. "No problem."

She handed me the magnifying glass. "Are you sure you can do this?" she whispered. "I could just write it down, you know."

I took a deep breath. "I'll be fine. Just hold the ladder, okay?"

Jennifer braced the metal ladder as I climbed up. I avoided the victim's eyes. I didn't want to imprint any more nightmares on my brain. I held the magnifying glass up to the deep jagged cuts.

"It's definitely Hebrew," I said, my stomach churning.

"Do you know what it says?" Jennifer asked.

"Yes, but I don't know what it means. I will have to look it up. The basic pronunciation is '*Nachash*,' although..." I paused as I looked at the scratches.

"What is it?"

"There are some other light scratches under the word, but I can't tell if they're supposed to be a part of the message. They don't look like Hebrew ... or not quite. Strange."

"We thought they were just incidental marks," Detective Hoover said.

Jennifer nodded. "I kind of thought the same."

I swallowed and went in for another look. The light scratches seemed more symbolic rather than an incidental contact with the razor. Something about them seemed familiar, but I couldn't place it. I grabbed a pen out of my pocket, wrote a copy on my hand, and climbed down.

"Did you bring your Hebrew dictionary with you?" Jennifer asked.

I shook my head. "No. We'll have to wait until we get back to Columbus."

Jennifer nodded and turned to Detective Hoover. "You said forensics had been here?"

"Yeah, they've finished the area around the body. They are combing the woods right now."

"Do we have an identity?"

He frowned. "No, not yet. We're working on it. Any possible identifying marks seemed to have been beaten off her."

Jennifer sighed. "Same with our victim. She was a local, so it made it easier to get dental records."

"We are going to have to go statewide for ours. Not too many missing people in Athens County. In fact, none that I know of at this point."

"Can you show us the footprints?" Jennifer asked.

He nodded, his face drawn in a frown. "Yeah, over here. But I'm thinking it's just hillbillies running around."

"Why is that?"

"Well, they're bare."

Jennifer shook her head. "Trust me, they aren't hillbillies. We had them near our victim too. Along with the Hebrew on her forehead, the white ceremonial robe, and the cross-like hanging, it all fits. It looks like the same perp or perps." She glanced at me.

Detective Hoover guided us over to the forest. "When we got the report of the footprints at the farm, the officer investigated and said it must be some sort of prank. Then he found the body, and as we were investigating the area, we found these." He shined his light on the snow.

A now familiar sight greeted me, except for one difference. Instead of a chaotic, jumbled mass, the prints all pointed in one direction, toward the body and the smiley face.

"It's like soldiers marching in formation," Jennifer said, bending down. "Did forensics get any tissue, blood, dead skin?"

"No, and that sort of has them freaked. According to them, with all these footprints, there should be blood, pus, a toenail, something." Hoover shrugged. "They have never seen anything like it."

Jennifer nodded. "Our theory is that the perps wore plastic bags over their feet so they would still leave marks."

I bent down to inspect the footprints. I put my finger in one and received a little jolt of energy, like a bad static shock. I yanked my hand back and looked around. A glint in the snow caught my eye.

"Jennifer, come here," I called out, feeling a rush of recognition. Jennifer and Detective Hoover came rushing over.

"What is it, Aidan?"

"Look."

"Wow, that is a huge f'n ring," Detective Hoover exclaimed. "Sorry, preacher."

"Don't worry about it. And you are right, but the size isn't the issue here."

"What is?" Jennifer bent down for a closer look.

I frowned. "I have seen this ring before. Well, at least one that looks exactly like it."

Jennifer and Detective Hoover both squinted at me.

"Where?" they asked.

"It was on the finger of the secretary at Fields of the Lord Church."

"Are you sure?" Jennifer asked, incredulous.

"Of course I'm sure. How many rings do you see like this?"

"Good point."

Detective Hoover lifted his cell phone and called for a photographer. He hung up and turned back to us.

"Can you give me everything you know about her?"

I told him what little I knew about Jessica, and he walked back to get on the radio.

Jennifer stared at the ring as if it might speak to her. "What do you think?"

"If this is who I think it is, then it's pretty obvious," I said.

Jennifer stared at me. "What, that Daniel Mueller is the killer?"

"Or someone connected to Fields of the Lord anyway. It can't be a coincidence that they both worked at the same church."

Detective Hoover came back as we stood up.

"Jessica Braile, forty-two, was reported missing yesterday morning when she didn't show up for work at the church. Her general description fits the victim. We are going to need dental or DNA to confirm that."

Jennifer nodded. "Let me make a phone call." She walked over to the road for better reception.

Detective Hoover looked at me. "What do you make of all this, preacher? Is this some religious wacko?"

"Is that an official cop term?"

He smiled. "More than you know."

"I have no idea, to be honest with you. I hope not. Religious people already have enough bad press as it is. Adding 'serial murderer' to the list of growing sins might be the final nail in the coffin."

"The final nail?"

"In the current cultural mistrust of religious people."

"Yeah, don't entirely trust them myself, no offense."

"No worries, I hear it all the time," I assented.

"But I can't believe even a religious person would do something like this."

"I know, detective, it's disturbing."

Jennifer walked back to us. "I'm trying to get a warrant to search Ms. Braile's place. We should have a team over there in the next few hours."

"Well, I have some other things to take care of," Detective Hoover said, shaking our hands.

"I'll call when you all can come and look at her apartment," Jennifer said. "We might need to set up some sort of task force for this killer."

"You pretty sure it's the same guy?" Hoover asked.

"We didn't publish the details of the murder in Columbus, so that probably rules out a copycat."

"I would agree with that," I said. "The ritual elements are the same. Same occultist method."

"Detective Hoover, the Sheriff is here," one of the uniformed cops called out.

"Excuse me," he said and walked off.

"Now what?" I asked.

"We go back to Columbus, and then I'll go to Jessica's house."

"No way. I'm going with you," I said. "Besides, if there is more Hebrew there, I might be able to read it. We can stop off at my office and get my BDB."

"Your what?" She gave me a half smile.

"*Brown, Driver, Briggs*. It's the standard Hebrew lexicon."

We got in the car and drove off.

chapter twenty-eight

Jennifer's phone rang as the lights of Columbus came into view.

"Yeah, boss, what's up?" Her face fell after listening a moment. "But why?" she yelled. "It's still our crime scene, why are they there?" She scowled, and her jaw tightened. "That's idiotic. Excuse me, sir." She paused. "Okay, okay, I'll get right over there to help." She hung up.

"What's going on?" I asked.

"The FBI stepped in."

"Thought they had to be invited."

She furrowed her brow. "No. They don't. Weaver was just trying to keep them out of it for now. It means you can't come to Jessica's place after all, so I'll have to drop you off."

"Why can't I go? Can't we use my ID like before?"

She gave a bitter laugh. "We could, but then the FBI will check you out. I don't think you want that."

I sighed. "No, don't really need that now."

We drove in silence until we reached my condo. Jennifer parked the car and looked at me. "Don't worry. I'll tell you everything that goes on."

I nodded and opened the door.

"Wait, Aidan. Can I tell you something?"

Puzzled, I closed the door and turned back to her. "Yeah, of course."

"Listen, I know you were in love with Amanda, and it's been great to have your help on this, especially with the Hebrew..."

"Yeah?" I had no idea what she was getting at. Was she going to tell me that I couldn't be on the investigation anymore? I was too involved to give it up.

"But, well, not sure how to say this." She turned to me, and light from the street lamps caught her green eyes.

I swallowed hard. She was beautiful, smart, and caring beneath the hard-ass, lady-cop exterior. I realized that I had been thinking about her a lot, but my obsession with Amanda blocked it out.

"It's okay, Jennifer, you can say whatever you want."

She took a deep breath. "She didn't deserve you."

That was the last thing I had expected to hear.

"I'm sorry to say it that bluntly, but it's true." She paused and touched my hand. Her warm, soft skin made my pulse race.

"I'm not sure what you mean," I replied, my voice cracked and raspy.

"You did nothing wrong, as far as I can tell, that should have made her leave. I don't understand why she did. These past few days have made me realize that she may not have gotten herself killed if she had stayed with you."

My throat tightened, and I turned to the window. "How can you say that? You don't know. Maybe they would have killed her anyway."

"Aidan, isn't it obvious? She fell in with someone who had a tight grip on her. Whoever killed her controlled her, manipulated her until it was too late to extract herself."

"Amanda was strong, she never would—"

Jen cut me off. "Think, damn it. She knew what was going to happen to her. She told you how to find out who did it."

"I just don't see how..."

"Amanda let herself get this way. She didn't have to go down this road. She had you, a knight who loved her."

I put my head in my hands.

She touched me on the shoulder. "I just wanted you to know. I still would like your assistance on this because I think you can help us. But you don't have to keep doing this, trying to find her killer out of some weird, misplaced guilt."

I looked up, not knowing how to respond.

"Come on, say something."

"To be honest, I don't know why I'm trying to find Amanda's killer. My motives are mixed, I guess. You are partially right — there is a misplaced sense of guilt — but I guess there's more to it."

"Such as?"

"I guess in helping you, I'm trying to find some order or meaning in my life."

She nodded. "I can understand that, believe me, but do you still have doubts after the ghost hunt? I mean, after all we saw and heard there, it was enough to make *me* a believer."

I grimaced. "All we saw and heard is proof that something exists. Maybe ghosts, maybe undiscovered energies that science doesn't know about, or maybe there just might be a spirit world. All that stuff said, there's nothing about God or His existence, much less the specific God of Christianity."

"You are unreal." She shook her head.

"I'm just being honest."

"Are you?"

My brow furrowed. "Yeah, I am, or I'm at least trying to be."

"I know you are trying, but haven't you taken your doubts far enough?"

"Why are you asking me this? You are the one who doesn't believe in any specific God."

"Yeah, but I'm rethinking that."

"Well, I won't stop you, but don't expect me to follow. I have thought and read through this stuff way too much."

Jennifer looked at me in silence, her face locked in an intense stare. "There was a case with this guy about a year ago. He was accused of a rape at OSU. All the evidence suggested this man was guilty. The physical description fit, he had the same clothes, everything. I did my work, my research and arrested him. I had him cold."

"Then what happened?" I asked, glad to change the subject.

"The DNA test came back. He wasn't the perpetrator. It was his roommate who was trying to frame him. I arrested an innocent guy before I had all the facts. Sometimes, even when we think we have all the evidence in hand, we find evidence we overlooked."

"Yeah, but…"

"The Lord wants sheep, not goats." She smiled.

That broke the tension as I laughed. "Where did you hear that?"

"Hey, you aren't the only one who went to Sunday school. Catholics have it too, you know." She paused. "Just think about what I said, okay?"

I nodded. "Thanks. I'll call you in the morning with what I find about Nachash."

"I'm looking forward to it."

I got out and walked to my door. As I fumbled with my keys, I realized she still hadn't left. I turned around and waved. She waved back then pulled out into the street.

Her touch still made my hand tingle, and our conversation set my brain on fire. Amanda didn't deserve me? I guess I had never thought about it that way.

I sighed and took Bishop out. There would be no sleep for me tonight, and not just because I had to know what Nachash meant. I knew that if I shut my eyes, I would see the letters carved into Jessica's head, a woman who had crossed paths with the wrong person, or persons.

I put Bishop back in his crate and headed to the church. Normally, it wouldn't have bothered me to be there in the middle of the night — I often went in to do work when I couldn't sleep — but after everything that happened, I sat in the parking lot looking at the glorified warehouse and my skin crawled. It was as if this building held some kind of dark secret. Maybe more ghosts would ambush me, kill me, or whatever it was they tried to do on the road to Athens.

I shook off the feelings as I walked to my office in the dark. I jumped, and my skin prickled as I heard the heater kick on and blow warm air on my cold skin.

"A little jumpy there, Aidan?" I said.

I turned on the light to my office and looked through my books. John Calvin. Greek Dictionary. Hebrew grammar book. My BDB was usually on this shelf but was nowhere to be found.

Mike had it, I remembered. He'd borrowed it last week. I went down the hall to his office and flicked on the light. The large green cover stood out on his desk.

As I walked over, I noticed the latest book by a well-known, put-together mega-church pastor from Texas. The glow of his white teeth dominated the cover.

Mike wouldn't be caught dead with this guy's book in his office. He'd made so many snide comments about this pastor that even *I* thought Mike went overboard a few times.

I picked up the book and opened it. I read the handwritten note on the inside cover with the inscription:

Mike,

After our talk the other night, I decided to get this book for you so that you could actually read it before you criticize it. This book has meant so much to me, and I want you to understand it. I want us to connect on every level — physically, emotionally, and spiritually — so that when we are together for good, we will be closer than we are now.

I love you so much.
Your lady in red,
Jessica
P.S. I'll wear the ring you gave me forever.

The room spun, and I gripped the chair. I slid to the floor with the book in my hands.

"No, please, no…" I called out.

Mike couldn't be a murderer, could he? Just because he had an affair didn't mean he killed someone, did it? And if he murdered her, did he murder Amanda? No, just because he was an adulterer, didn't mean he killed her. I knew the police would question him. He couldn't hide any longer. The affair would become public. Mike's time would be done, and so would mine, but at least some sort of justice would come from it.

Maybe I'll tell him myself.

I made sure to put the book back under the right pile of papers, positioning it, so the white teeth still gleamed the same way they had when they caught my eye.

I took the BDB back to my office and found Nachash. I realized why it sounded so familiar. Nachash meant serpent. I paged through to the first chapters of my Hebrew Bible to the story of Adam and Eve.

Nachash. Serpent. The words rattled around in my brain.

chapter twenty-nine

"Hello?" I answered the phone as I drove to work, squinting against the rising sun.

"Aidan, it's Father Neal. I'm glad you are up."

"Of course. It's a work day."

"Do you have anything to do this morning?

Yeah, just confront my boss over his affair with a murder victim.

"Nothing much." I didn't feel like getting into it over the phone.

"I have something early this morning, but can you be here in a couple hours?"

"Is everything okay?"

"Well, it depends on how you define that. I would like to talk with you some more about your faith."

"You got it. I'll see you in a bit."

I pulled into Knox's parking lot, and the knot in my stomach tightened. I took a few deep breaths as I walked up to the church and paused before opening the door. No matter what happened, upon exiting, these doors would lead me to a completely different life.

"Hello, Sherry," I said, walking past her desk to Mike's office.

"Aidan, he is on the phone." She rose from her desk and reached out to grab my arm. "He can't be disturbed."

"This is important." I opened the door without knocking.

Mike looked up, startled. "I'm going to have to let you go, my assistant pastor just walked in like there is an emergency." He smiled at me. My fingers flexed as I fought the urge to punch him in the mouth.

He hung up the phone. "Aidan, is there something wrong?"

I looked back at Sherry, standing by her desk, and shut the door.

"You could say that," I replied as I sat down across from Mike.

"Speak to me, and we shall work it out, my young padawan."

Mike pegged me with this *Star Wars* nickname on my first day at church. I always enjoyed the joke. Now, it just pissed me off. Whatever loyalty and friendship we shared before had come to an end.

"*I know*, Mike."

He stared at me, slowly tapping a pencil on his desk. "What are you talking about?"

"The lady in red, the one you were screwing."

"Language, Aidan."

I slammed my hand on his desk. "Fuck you, you arrogant asshole!"

"I really think you should control your temper when talking to your boss," he said calmly, narrowing his eyes. "I'll forgive you if you tell me what you are talking about."

"Let me back up, jackass. I saw the body of a woman last night."

"I hope you didn't fall into sin," he said, his mouth twitching. "She is a beauty."

"Who the fuck are you talking about?"

"Officer Brown, of course."

"It's *Detective* Brown, and it was not her body. So shut up and listen."

Mike sat back in his chair and tapped his upper lip with his fingertips as he stared at me.

"The night of the session meeting a few weeks ago, I overheard your phone conversation."

"Go on."

"I heard you asking someone other than Sheila to wear something red and how much you loved it."

He lowered his hand, and his lips tightened in a thin line.

"Mike, did you kill her? I want to hear it from you before the police come calling. And you know they will. It won't take them long to determine you had a relationship with Jessica."

Mike's face grew pale. He looked like he was going to throw up all over his desk. He got up, his hands on his head, and walked around the room massaging his scalp.

"I didn't kill her, Aidan," he whispered. "This is the first I've heard of her death. I was with another pastor last night."

"Well, at least you won't be going to jail then. But it doesn't matter, does it? It's going to get out that you had an affair, and you know our elders. They're not going to walk you through this with grace and mercy, even those on your side."

"Oh, Aidan, I was stupid. So stupid." Mike slumped to the floor and stared into space, his blank eyes fixed on the ceiling. He held his shaking hands up to his face.

I glanced at the pictures of his family on his desk. I didn't feel sorry for him. He had made his choice. "How could you let this happen?" I asked, not sure I wanted to know.

He moved his hands, and his eyes were red with tears. "It was at the mayor's prayer breakfast. Jessica came with the Fields of the Lord group. She sat next to me, and we talked the whole time."

"She asked me some questions that I needed to look up, so I got her email address. We just started emailing each other, then chatting online. And then last year, when Sheila and the kids went to California to visit her parents, it happened. I went over to give her some books, she offered me some wine and well, the rest you can figure out for yourself."

I stared at Mike in silence.

"It's just the pressure of this job, Aidan. You know what it's like." He looked up, tears running down his face.

I started to have some sympathy for him. Or at least, the

desire to kick him in the head went away. It didn't excuse him, but I understood. This job often isolated people and drove them to extremes. "Yeah, I do, Mike."

"Sheila has been distant. The kids are driving me crazy. Then things went south with the elders. It was just too much. And Jessica … she is, *was*, a wonderful person. I did love her."

"I really don't want to hear this," I said, getting up to look out Mike's office window.

He stood up beside me. "Do I really need to say anything to the elders? I mean, I could get the police to be discreet."

I turned around and looked him straight in the eye. "You don't understand. It's not the police you have to worry about. It's me."

"What do you mean?"

"I have an email that I'm prepared to send out to the elders, if you don't do it yourself."

He looked at me as if I slapped him in the face. "Why would you do that?"

"Because I'm tired of hypocrites."

"And what about you, Aidan? Are you not hypocritical?"

"I am. And that is why I'm writing an email to tell the elders of my loss of faith."

"You're going to tell them?"

"Yes. That's my hypocrisy. And I'm ready to be rid of it."

Mike stared at me as if I had lost my mind. The slow tick of his antique clock filled the silence, ticking away the end of our relationship. I thought about the times we'd had a beer together, watched football, and all of his guidance in ministry. All gone.

"You are serious about this?" he asked.

"I am, Mike. Deadly."

"But our jobs. I have some money saved, but what will you do?"

"I'll figure it out."

He turned to me, massaging his goatee. "I just can't imagine you doing this. You're blowing up everything you've worked for."

"It's called a *spine*, Mike, something I should have grown a long time ago. Besides, don't you mean it would destroy everything *you* have done? I'm fine with that. I'm fine with burning the whole fucking thing to the ground."

"You are an unusual man, Aidan Schaeffer."

"And that is what makes this whole thing ... the church, you, me ... a shitbox."

"Please watch your tongue at least."

I closed my eyes as my blood boiled. "Watch my tongue?" I began to laugh. "Maybe you should have watched your dick and paid less attention to people's tongues."

"That is a very crude way of putting things."

I didn't bother to hide my sarcasm. "Yeah, I'll remember that."

"I'm sorry this happened, Aidan. I'm sorry you were placed in this position." He put his hand on my arm, and I wrenched away.

"So am I. There was a time when I looked up to you, Mike. You taught me so much. Now, I'll do my best to forget everything."

The pager on Mike's desk phone beeped. "Pastor, I have a Detective Brown on the phone for you," Sherry's voice chirped.

I smiled before I could stop myself.

"Thank you, Sherry," Mike replied into the speaker. "Can you ask her to hold for a few moments?" He looked up at me. "I guess your girlfriend is going to be the one to lower the boom."

"Yeah, I guess so."

"How long do I have until you tell the elders?"

"I will give you until the end of the week. I owe you that much for everything you have done for me. You don't deserve it, but isn't grace about what we don't deserve?"

His lips formed a thin smile. "And your email about your faith?"

"I'm going to send it after you tell them."

"That will be a bit much for them, don't you think?"

"Maybe. But they have always wanted control of the church, so now is their chance. We'll both get what we deserve."

Mike grunted. "I guess you're right. It will be good to get all this off my chest. I was getting tired of sneaking around." He looked out the window and sighed.

"What will Sheila do?" I asked.

"You don't know her. She might look like a sweet Southern gal, but underneath, there is a capacity for grudges, and this would be the ultimate betrayal."

I turned to go, and he offered me his hand. "Aidan, please pray for me."

I refused his gesture. "I would if I could, but I don't have any faith left. I will hope things work out for you."

I stumbled to my car and headed to St. Patrick's. I didn't remember anything about my drive there other than a swirl of stoplights and the low drone of the radio. When I arrived, the peace of the building washed over me. I laughed at how this church actually scared me three days before. But now, I just felt utter contentment, like I'd arrived home.

I went inside and knocked on Father Neal's door.

"Come in," his soft, British voice called out.

His face looked drawn and rough, like he'd been up all night, but his eyes shone bright with life. "Aidan, good to see you. You look tired. Is everything okay?"

"Well, something attacked Jennifer's car last night as we rode together, and this morning, I confronted my boss about his affair with the woman who was just murdered." I let out a deep exhale. "And now, I have no idea what I'm going to do about anything."

Father Neal sat with his eyes closed. "How did Mike react to your confrontation?"

"At first, he tried to weasel out of it, as usual, but then he actually admitted his actions. Don't know what it means, but at least he didn't fight it long."

He nodded, eyes still closed, not saying anything. I sat with him in silence for a few minutes.

"What are you thinking about?" I asked.

"The second murder victim. What was carved into her head?"

"Nachash. The serpent."

He nodded. "I wonder where that might be."

"No idea. I was hoping you would know."

Father Neal murmured to himself.

"What?" I pressed.

"Yeah, I know. It's creepy. Any ideas?"

"Not in the least. But we had better find out. And soon."

"The third killing?" I said, feeling chills that had nothing to do with the coldness of Father Neal's office.

"Yes. We must prevent the ritual from being completed. If they do, they'll control the dead and resurrect the Grinning Man."

"How can anyone control the dead, Father? It doesn't make sense. I heard the boy's and Amanda's voices. They can't be controlled, can they?"

Father Neal's eyes slowly opened. "I should modify that statement. They can't control the righteous dead. Amanda and the boy are trying to warn us. But sadly, this ritual will work. Never doubt it. It'll breach the wall between this world and the unseen world with power beyond imagination. It will release the Grinning Man from his sleep, and when he is, everything is in danger, including—"

"Including what?"

He waved his hand. "Tell me about the attack on Jennifer's car."

I ran through what happened. "You think it might be ghosts?"

"There is no 'think' about it."

"So, they were directed by the Bone Master?"

"Yes, I believe so." He played with his cane.

I frowned. "You *believe*? I thought you knew all about this stuff."

Father Neal stood up, limped over to a wooden cabinet, and opened it. Dark amber bottles of scotch, blood red sherry, and other liquors lined the shelf. The good father appeared to have quite a collection. "Do you want one, my lad?"

"It's a little early," I said, realizing how much Father Neal drank.

He poured two glasses of scotch. "After our nights, I think we both deserve to cheat."

I usually made it a rule not to drink before dinner, but the stress of the past week had gotten to me. I reached for the scotch.

"As to your question, about knowing all of this *stuff*, as you put it," Father Neal said, "I was just entering the darker parts of Crowley's world when I met Charles. I don't have as many answers as I'd like. Just guesses. But there are many areas that are dark to me, and for that, I'm grateful. I already see too much."

My brow furrowed at his cryptic statement. "So, Amanda telling me shows she is not under his control?"

He nodded. "It would appear so. But again, he or they don't have full control of the spirits ... yet. That is what makes them dangerous. I felt something had happened last night, but I didn't know what."

"Felt?"

Father Neal swirled his drink. "Aidan, when you have opened yourself up to the other world, you can't turn it off. Yes, I'm under Christ's protection, but the veil has been thinned for me. I feel and see things most people don't. I think you witnessed that at the cemetery."

"Do they tell you things?" I asked, leaning forward.

"Yes, but I don't speak."

"Why?"

"Because I have no desire to communicate with the dead. I don't wish for mastery or control."

I wondered if that explained his unshakable belief in God while my doubts ravaged my mind. Then again, seeing as much as Father Neal might destroy other things, like my sanity. I didn't know which I would prefer. "So is this why you believe in God? You see ghosts?"

"No, not in the least."

"Why not? Jennifer says this situation proves it for her."

"But it doesn't for you, does it?" He smiled.

I frowned. "No."

"And the house? The EVPs?"

"Look, I'm willing to admit something is going on there that I can't explain, but I can't see why all this should restore my faith."

"Good. Very good."

I stared at him with my mouth slightly open. "I'm sorry, I don't understand."

"You aren't believing in God just because you experienced

something paranormal."

I took a swig of my scotch and coughed slightly. "I still don't understand."

"It's Thomas, Aidan. It's all about Thomas."

"Thomas the disciple, who demanded physical proof of Jesus' resurrection and has been looked down on by two thousand years of churchmen and women?"

"The very one."

"Ah, Thomas." I chuckled. "Put your hands here, the demand for proof and all that." I pointed to my wrists and my side. "I can understand exactly where he was coming from."

He nodded. "Most people can."

"No, they can't." I flared. "I have never heard a discussion on faith and doubt in the church. I mean, if you even bring up the subject of doubting your faith, you become an object of either ridicule or pity."

Father Neal sat back in his chair with a groan. "Yes, that's true, I'm sorry to say. Doubt is not an easy thing to talk about. I believe everyone is afraid."

The scotch had gone straight to my head, and I lay back in the chair. I realized that I had missed breakfast and fought through the haze. "Why? Why are they afraid?"

"Because of the nature of doubt itself and all of its complications. Doubt is intellectual, for sure, but you know as well as anyone that it's also emotional."

"Mine isn't." I fought back. "I have read the science books, the historical criticisms of the Bible. My doubts are all intellectual. Many people have the same objections. The problem is people like you who say doubt comes from some sort of emotional distress or weakness."

Father Neal smiled. "Use your head. You know very well from your pastoral experience that people aren't that simple. They're terribly complex in everything they do, and this is certainly true when it comes to doubting their faith. In doubting, or even not believing outright, there is always a mixture of emotion and logic, reason and faith, or lack of it."

We sat finishing the rest of our scotch. I downed what was left in my glass and winced. "So, I still don't understand what that has to do with my not believing in God even though I have seen activity that might be construed as supernatural."

Father Neal spoke in a soft tone. "Blessed are those who have not seen, but believed. You have not let some outside force sway you to or from your beliefs. That's what Jesus wants really, belief in Him, not because you may have had some contact with the unseen world."

"I guess I'm confused."

He stood up. "I'm sure you are, but there are many things here you may not be seeing."

"Father, volumes could be written on things I don't see or get." I laughed.

"That goes for all of us, Aidan."

"I guess," I said, rubbing my temples and staring at the ground.

"Well, let's think about the nature of Thomas' doubt. It's intellectual first, right?"

"Yeah. He demands physical evidence he can touch, see, and hear. The first modern scientist," I said as I cracked a smile.

"You could say that, but really, his doubts are also emotional," Father Neal said. "Think of his situation, Aidan. He was a first century Jew who thought, along with the rest of the twelve, that Jesus would be the messiah who would destroy Rome, lead the Jews to reign over the earth and put them in charge."

"Right, and he lost all of that at the crucifixion."

"Correct. All of Thomas' dreams were destroyed. See how these verses become more complicated and therefore more real? Humans are not able to achieve complete objectivity. So our beliefs, our doubts, our reasons are all dependent on things we can't explain. And of course, emotional suffering makes things even more clouded."

"That is about on par for God's servants," I said, not bothering to keep the bitterness out of my voice.

He stood up, came over to me, and put his hand on my shoulder. "Be careful with your words."

"I'm sorry. I'm tired. It's been a long night and day."

The lines in his face smoothed as he took on a grandfatherly appearance. "Of course. I'm sorry to push you so hard. But hear this, Aidan. Doubters will always be met. Go home and get some sleep. I'm going to give this whole matter some more thought. Maybe there is something I can do to help capture the killer before the last death."

"What are you going to do?"

He turned his back to me. "I'm going to ask."

I didn't dare press him further. I turned to leave, and then he spoke. "We must find Nachash, Aidan. The magicians must be stopped."

chapter thirty

I had no plans to go back to the church, so I drove to a coffee house to do more research. I got a coffee, sat down, and opened up my computer. I had to find out what serpent or Nachash meant to this killer. Someone's life was at stake. I realized the entire Columbus police force was probably thinking through that very thing, but still, it was worth a shot.

I looked up different variations on Nachash and serpent within the context of Ohio. No town names appeared. I tried mountains. No luck. After a couple of hours, I still found nothing of any substance.

"Where is this place?"

My phone buzzed, and Jennifer's name popped up.

"Hey," she said.

I was surprised by the warm rush I felt when I heard her voice. I couldn't deny it anymore. What I felt for Jennifer went beyond just the ordinary lust a guy felt for a beautiful woman.

"Aidan, are you there?"

"Sorry, I didn't catch what you asked me."

"I just wanted to see how you were doing."

"Fine. How did your conversation with Mike go?" I asked without thinking.

I could almost hear her body stiffen over the phone. "How did you know?"

"Well, I was in Mike's office when you called, confronting him on his affair and possible connection with Jessica's murder."

I held the phone away from my ear just in time.

"Dammit, Aidan! First, why didn't you say anything to me? And second, you should have kept your mouth shut. How did you know about the connection?"

I told her about the book I found in Mike's office.

"Well, that fits with everything we found in her apartment. You should have told me about the book immediately."

"I know. I'm sorry. I had to see his reaction firsthand."

"This isn't just a personal thing, Aidan. This is a murder investigation. Mike is now a suspect, especially with his connection to the two victims."

I gripped the phone. "He didn't know Amanda that well."

"But there is still a connection there," she insisted, her voice rising with every word.

"Yeah, but it's not him. I'm positive."

"You can't be positive," she growled. "That's impossible."

"He said he had an alibi."

"I'll have to ask him that when he comes to the police station at four o'clock."

I looked at the time on my computer. In one hour, Jennifer would be questioning Mike. That would prove interesting to say the least.

"See, no harm done," I said.

"Yeah, but if he is the killer he could have skipped town."

"I guess so. I didn't think about it. I just wanted to confront the bastard. I've got my own issues with him."

"Again, you've got to see, this case takes priority over whatever your personal issues with him are." She paused and then laughed. "I bet you shocked the shit out of him."

I grunted. "Yeah, I think I did. And I told him I am going to email the elders."

"Are you really going to?"

"Yeah. I'm going to tell them everything, including my own loss of faith."

There was a long silence at the end of the phone. "When?"

"I told him he had until the end of the week. I try to keep my word."

"That should be fun," she said with a dry edge to her voice.

"Not in the least. But it will finally be over. That's what counts." I changed the subject. "Any dirt on good ol' Pastor Daniel?" I said in my best southern Baptist accent.

"No, he says he has an alibi for last night as well."

"What is it?"

"Don't know. We will be bringing him in tonight at eight o'clock."

"Late night." I got up to walk outside.

"No rest for an investigator of the wicked."

I chuckled. "I guess not."

"Aidan?"

"Yes?"

"Please be careful."

I grimaced. "Why does everyone keep telling me that?"

"Just a hunch, I guess. I'm scared for you. After last night, well, I don't think those ghosts were after me."

I gripped the phone and looked both ways down the street. "I think you are right."

"So, please be careful."

"I will call the Ghostbusters right away," I said, giving her a fake laugh.

"I'm serious, Aidan." The edge in her voice could have cut me in half.

"Okay, okay, I'll be careful. I could say the same to you."

"I'll be surrounded by other cops. I'll be fine. Will you be home tonight?"

"Yeah, might as well be. I'm going to have to start looking for jobs. I think I'll also look at enrolling at OSU for my teaching certificate."

"Don't be so quick to…"

I cut her off. "I don't want to talk about this now, okay?"

"Okay, but later, I want to talk about it with you. Seriously." The emphasis in her voice forced every point home.

"Okay. Breakfast, then?"

"No, I'm coming over. It'll be late, say after Pastor Daniel's interrogation?"

Wow! She wants to come over tonight. To talk about my faith, to be sure, but still, I'll take it. "See you then."

I hung up my phone, trying to comprehend this new development. Did Jennifer get this close with all the people she was trying to help? Was I an exception? Did she feel the same about me, as I apparently had started feeling about her, without realizing it?

My phone rang again. I held it up and looked at the caller ID. Mike.

"Yes?" I answered, my voice devoid of emotion.

"I'm having a special meeting of the elders tonight at eight o'clock to tell them about the investigation."

It felt like a day for shocking revelations, as though someone had placed me in the middle of a soap opera full of unbelievable twists and turns. I couldn't help but wonder if the sun would go dark or the seas turn into blood. "Okay, so what do you want from me?"

"Would you be there? I think all the elders would appreciate your perspective."

I sighed. "Whatever. I'll be there. I have to leave at nine-thirty though."

"I understand. I'll see you tonight."

chapter thirty-one

I'd now been in this conference room three times in the past week which was three times too many. The elders began to file in with puzzled expressions on their faces. Apparently, Mike wanted them in the dark as long as possible.

"Hello, Aidan," Bill said as he sat down next to me. "What is this all about?"-

I wanted to tell him. I liked Bill, and as Mike's friend, I thought he should know. "Well, I have an idea, Bill, but I'm not sure if I should say."

He nodded and held up his hands. "Don't want to put you in a bad spot." He frowned. "Still, Mike usually tells me what's going on, even if he doesn't tell the others."

"Yeah, I know. I'm sorry."

He waved his hand. "No worries, how are you doing with … with everything?"

"I'm okay, I guess. I mean, I hadn't seen Amanda in a long time, so it's a little hard to know what to feel." That was the understatement of the year.

He patted me on the shoulder. "I bet. I'll pray for you."

Unlike most people who said that, I actually believed Bill. He kept lists for people who asked for prayer, pasted them in a notebook, and kept track of each one through notations on how God might have answered.

The room fell silent as Mike walked in with a calm and composed demeanor. I had to admire how cool he was under this kind of pressure. I would have been fidgeting, crossing my arms, or tapping my foot.

"Brothers, I call this meeting to order," Mike said. "Bill, could you pray for us?"

I bowed my head, and then I remembered, when a pastor resigned, he was supposed to call in another pastor for the meeting. Since he hadn't, I figured Mike couldn't stand losing control, even at the beginning of the end.

"…in Jesus' name, Amen," Bill finished.

"Fathers and brothers, you're probably wondering why I called you to this meeting," Mike began.

Heads nodded, and Mike's face became grave. "We have a serious matter before us that we need to consider a course of action for."

Everyone shifted in their chairs, visibly bracing themselves. I would've bet no one expected what Mike was about to say. I still had a hard time believing it. I actually felt sorry for them.

"Yesterday, Aidan came to me with a very grave concern."

He was really drawing it out. I couldn't blame him. The man was about to set an axe to the root of his whole life. I wondered if he had told Sheila yet.

"He has expressed some deep-seated issues that need to be addressed."

Come on, Mike, the longer you put it off, the worse it will be.

"Aidan has told me, and is allowing me to tell you, that his faith is gone. He no longer believes in God and may not be fit for his position at Knox Presbyterian."

The heat rose in my cheeks, and I had to restrain myself to keep from leaping out of the chair. Everyone turned to me. I underestimated Mike, and he checkmated me. Anything I said about him at that point would look defensive. And because what he said was true, I couldn't deny anything. I quickly realized I should have brought Jennifer with me.

"Aidan, is this true?" John Calvin Eisner asked.

"Yeah, John, most of it. I think Mike might have stated it a bit strongly. I don't know if my faith is completely gone. It's at least on life support."

"Why?" Bill asked in disbelief.

I shrugged, unable to look at him. "Lots of reasons, I guess."

"Is there an emotional component to your doubt?" John pressed.

My stomach lurched. "Maybe. If so, I have a good back up on that. Jesus himself."

John's eyes narrowed. "What do you mean?"

"How about the whole, *if you love one another as I have loved you, all the world will know you are my disciples?*"

"I don't understand."

My face flushed. "You don't understand? How completely clueless are you, John?"

He slumped back in his chair as if I had punched him.

"All of you sit here in this room and passive-aggressively attack each other. You cook up little intrigues, conversations, implied threats and plot how best to put your position forward. All that talk about you loving each other is a crock of shit!"

Beads of sweat collected on my forehead. "It seems to me, the men who are supposed to be my spiritual mentors and the leaders of a church shouldn't fail Jesus' test. But you have. So, when I add that element to everything else, it has blown up the rest of my faith."

Complete silence fell over the table. I couldn't remember the last time everyone in this group kept their mouth shut. I fought a mad desire to laugh.

Mike broke the silence. "Fathers and brothers, as you can see, Aidan has some titanic struggles. I think we need to help him, but I think you would agree he can't retain his current position at Knox Presbyterian. This leadership must project strength, not weakness.

We must set a good example for our congregation of unflinching belief in our Lord. Aidan has wandered into weakness, and while we are here to help him, we must all agree he can't take part in leadership at this church."

A second round of silence in the room. Two in the space of five minutes. *Maybe there is a God after all.*

"I would recommend that Aidan be let go, effective immediately, with three months' severance. I would also suggest that he be required to present himself before the presbytery so they may address the issue of his ordination, which is not something we can address here, as that is under their jurisdiction." He took a deep breath. "Can I have a motion?"

No one raised his hand.

"Anyone? Yes, thank you, Bill," Mike said, a flash of triumph in his eyes.

"No, Mike, you misunderstand me. I wish to say something."

Mike faltered. "Go ahead."

"I want to tell Aidan how much I appreciate his candor," Bill said, his eyes full of compassion. "It could not have been easy to share any of those things."

I couldn't quite believe what I was hearing.

John cleared his throat. "Yes, it was brave, but something still must be done. What if the congregation finds out?"

"What if they do?" Bill asked. "It seems like this would be a great teaching opportunity for the church."

Mike stared at Bill. "Bill, the leadership can't show weakness or have questions about…"

"That's where you and I have always disagreed, Mike," Bill retorted. "A Christian leader should lead out of his weakness. It's how Christ is glorified."

"Yes, but it's also clear that leadership must not be tossed about by whims."

"It seems to me that Aidan is not doing that at all," Bill said.

"I agree with Bill. I think you're being too hasty, Mike," Jack, an elder who rarely spoke up during meetings, chimed in.

Everyone except Mike and John nodded.

Bill looked at me. "I don't think the congregation needs to know about Aidan yet, not until we have talked to him. So, I make a motion that three of us — me, John, and Jack — sit down with Aidan over the course of a Saturday morning."

"I second the motion," Jack said.

Mike looked as if someone had smacked him upside the head with a board. I certainly hadn't expected the elders' reaction. I'm sure he hadn't either. They had acted rationally with concern and even love. John frowned, but Bill had trapped him.

"I won't say this is a good idea because it's bound to get out to the congregation," Mike said with a sigh. "But I will bow to the will of the brothers. All in favor?"

Everyone except Mike said, "Aye."

"Very well, the motion is carried. I trust that the brothers named will get a hold of Aidan. Let's pray for God's guidance in this situation."

Mike said a final prayer. The shock of the moment locked up my brain. I didn't even realize the prayer was over until everyone stood up from the table.

The elders filed out of the room while I stayed behind.

Mike stared at me. "Why didn't you tell them?"

"What's the point? If you are going to be chicken shit, so be it."

He nodded. "Thank you."

"You can shove your thank yous up your ass, Mike," I said as I walked out of the room.

chapter thirty-two

I flipped through the channels as I waited for Jennifer to arrive. I settled on a *South Park* episode I'd seen a million times. The cartoon sounds made for good background noise while lying on the couch and staring at the ceiling.

I couldn't believe Mike outwitted me. It wasn't the job. I had already decided to resign and felt just fine. I just hated being outsmarted when I thought I had the upper hand.

I shook my head and opened up my computer.

What are you doing awake? Brian's words popped up on the screen.

Can't sleep. I might ask you the same question.

Ashley is sick. I'm letting her have the bed.

You are a gentleman, sir, I wrote, looking at my phone, wondering if Jennifer would call before she came over.

Ha. Well, she is my wife, after all.

Yeah, good point.

So, anything new?

What a question. *I'm not sleeping anytime soon. Yeah, ghost world is drawing closer to me.*

And your doubts? he asked.

Let's just say I'm more conflicted than ever.

What do you mean?

I recounted the events of the meeting.

I can't believe Mike did that to you. What an asshole.

I can ... now, anyway. That's the way he operates. In the shadows.

And Father Neal, what did he mean, doubters will always be met?

I don't know. He told me that the story of Thomas is the key.

I looked over at my Bible, still open to John 20.

What have you come up with? Brian wrote.

A lot so far ... do you want to hear it?

Yeah, lay it on me.

Thomas had two sorts of doubts that I can tell from the story: *intellectual and emotional. Thomas demands proof. The first scientist,* *the first skeptic, so much for saying the ancients were stupid and* *superstitious. He could really be the patron saint of all those who* *ask questions or express doubts about God.*

Interesting, what do you mean? Brian asked.

He demands physical evidence and historical proof. He doesn't *believe guys who have been his closest friends for three years. They* *keep telling him that Jesus has risen from the dead, but basically, he* *tells them they have their heads up their butts.*

Sounds familiar.

Yeah, doesn't it? So unless he touches Jesus' wounds and puts *his hands in each one, he won't believe,* I explained.

Pretty hardcore.

Yeah, I know. It's amazing how I have never thought about this *before.* I rubbed my head and sighed.

Me neither. I always thought of Thomas as a kind of pity figure, *someone who just didn't get it,* Brian wrote.

I know. So did I until my talk with Father Neal. Now, I'm *starting to think that it's okay to demand intellectual answers.*

We sort of learned that in college, Aidan, Brian said.

No. We didn't. We were taught how to handle others' doubts, not our own. We were taught evidences for faith in Christ, but never how to apply it personally.

Guess I can't argue with that.

And you know what else? I have spent my whole ministry life giving people the wrong answers. I basically told them not to doubt, but to question. But the more I think about it, the Bible is full of people who do just that. I realized I was pounding on the keyboard.

You know, you are right. Gideon laying out the fleece, Elijah complaining to God about being the only one in Israel who believes, Job's continued cries and Jeremiah's constant whining.

And that is just the start. It seems to me that God invites doubts. It's us who can't handle it. Bishop came up and laid his head on my lap.

Wow, Aidan, you have made a lot of progress in the past few weeks. Is it the ghosts?

No, not really. I guess you could say I'm doubting my doubts. I don't know where I am, Brian. I thought I did. I thought I had finally cast aside my faith, but now I'm finding that my questions were superficial.

I didn't think they were.

But they were, Bri, they really were. There is more to this whole issue than I ever realized.

And your faith is coming back?

I looked out my sliding glass door into the unseen blackness. *No, it's not coming back, yet. I'm not done thinking through the story of Thomas. Maybe when I'm done.*

How long will that be?

I laughed. *As long as it takes.*

Are you still going to send the email to the elders?

No, I'm not going to tell them. I'll let Jennifer do that.

I just can't believe the woman he cheated with was murdered. You are sure he didn't actually do it?

Positive. Mike doesn't have the balls to do something like that.

Poor Sheila.

I know.

252

Listen, I need to check on Ashley.

Tell her I hope she feels better.

I will. Lily is still waiting on her candy.

The box sat on my table ready to send.

Ha! I will send it to her. I just forgot.

Don't worry about it, man, she still loves her Uncle Aidan.

Maybe when all of this is over, I'll come down to see you. I might need a good long look at the Tennessee mountains.

A knock on the door startled me out of my online chat.

Hey, I gotta run, Jennifer's here.

WHAT????? Lady cop? What's going on, Aidan?

I grinned. *Wouldn't you like to know?*

You are lucky that Ashley is calling me; otherwise I would force you to explain.

You could try. Talk to you later, dude. Give all your ladies a kiss from me.

You got it.

The wind blew Jennifer's light coconut=scented perfume into the room as I opened the door. Her pink cheeks and green eyes tied my tongue.

"Hey." She grinned. "It's really cold!"

"Yeah, it is," I replied, catching my breath. "Do you want some coffee?"

"Please." Jennifer came in and took off her coat. Her tight black sweater and slacks clung to the curves of her body.

"How did the interrogation go?" I asked as I poured her coffee.

"Well, both their stories corroborate. They were at the same pastors' meeting, and they have witnesses that we are questioning. But so far, they check out."

The tightness in her voice caught my attention as I gave her coffee, and I sat down on the couch. "How is that possible?"

She shook her head and took a seat on a nearby armchair. "I don't know. Maybe we are totally on the wrong trail." Jen chewed her lip as she stared up at the ceiling.

"Well, Mike must have thought so because he felt strong enough to betray me at the session meeting."

"He is so slimy. Maybe that's why we thought he might be capable of murder," she said, scowling.

"Yeah, I suppose."

We sipped our coffee in silence as Bishop put his head on Jennifer's lap, a position I envied.

"So, how are you doing with all of this?" she asked. "How is your faith?"

"I'm not sure. I guess I can say I'm no longer confident about my disbelief, but that's about as far as I can take it."

Jennifer got up from the armchair and sat by me on the couch. The heat of her body radiated as she lightly touched my arm. "Talk to me."

I shrugged. "All we know at this point is that there is some kind of world that we can't see. It doesn't say anything about God or give us any indication that He cares."

She nodded. "Maybe, but it seems to me if the unseen world is real, then maybe God is too."

I put my cup down on the table. "You would think so, wouldn't you? But I don't buy it. I need to see the logical connections, and I don't have those yet."

Jennifer chuckled. "Maybe that's the difference in how we were raised. As a Catholic, I'm used to taking things on faith even when I can't totally prove it. We love a little mystery. It's you Protestants that have to have everything in order."

She had a point. Protestants, especially Presbyterians, clung to systematic theologies like my nephew clung to his ratty *Bruce the Bear*.

"I think you are right." I turned to her, and to my surprise, her face had drawn closer to me so that her lips hovered inches from mine. I could almost taste the coffee on her breath.

"You'll come through it," she said. "You still believe. It's obvious. You just don't know it yet."

I smiled. "Is that right? Glad you have confidence in me." I paused, thinking about what to say next. *Jennifer, I know you recently interrogated me for murder, but I'm starting to have feelings for you. I'll most likely be jobless in a month or so, and living with my brother, but do you want to go on a date?* "Jennifer, I…"

She pressed her finger to my lips. "Shhh. I know."

I stared into her eyes and kissed her without hesitation. Lightly at first, lips slowly moving, and then our mouths opened so that our tongues met. I wrapped my arms around her and hugged her close to me, her breasts pressing into my chest. Our kisses became more passionate, and she climbed onto my lap and straddled me as her soft hair formed a veil around our faces.

We parted for breath, and I stared at her smiling face. "So, do you treat all your former murder suspects this way?"

She gave me a wicked grin and stroked my cheek. "Of course, how do you think I get my confessions?"

We kissed some more and then she put her lips to my ear. "Are you going to invite me to spend the night?"

The words struck me harder than I expected. Did I want to invite her to spend the night? My body screamed, *yes, you do, what the hell are you waiting for?*

I pressed my mouth to Jennifer's warm neck, and her body responded to my touch. She moaned and gripped me to her.

But something else pulled at me, something I couldn't explain. Was it the tattered belief in God? Was it some misplaced leftover loyalty to Amanda? Or was it the strange possibility that both Amanda and God could see me?

Jennifer sensed my hesitancy. "Are you okay? Was I too forward? It's okay if you don't want to." She stared at me in a way I hadn't seen before, unsure, vulnerable, with a hint of hurt.

"No, it's not that. I can't think of anything I want more right now."

"Then what's wrong?" She continued to stroke my cheek.

I sighed. "I don't know. Every part of me wants to take you upstairs to my bedroom and make love to you. My body, brain, and heart are screaming for it."

She moved her head a bit, searching my face. "I hear a big *but* there."

I smiled. "No, it's not big, not big at all. In fact, it's small, but something tells me we need to wait."

Jennifer hugged me again, causing me to fight for self-control. "Okay, I guess I can understand."

"I really like you. Really. I think you can tell."

She pulled her head back so that her nose touched mine. "And I really like you. Don't worry. I understand. It's a little fast, isn't it?"

I laughed. "No, not at all, but I just want this whole investigation to be over first, to get to know each other under normal circumstances, you know?"

She gave me a half smile. "Then I had better go; otherwise, we might not keep to that."

I swallowed hard. "Yeah, I think that's best. I don't have that much self-control."

Jennifer stood and put on her coat. I got up and opened the door for her. She turned to me. I touched her cheek, tracing her soft skin with my fingertips. I kissed her again.

"You keep doing that, and I'm not going to leave," she whispered.

"I'll sic Bishop on you." I laughed.

At that moment, Bishop nudged his head between us and looked up at Jennifer with a face that said, *pet me.*

She laughed. "Hmmmm, I don't think that's going to be possible."

I smirked and rubbed Bishop's side. "Traitor."

"Do you want to have brunch with me tomorrow?" She offered.

"Yeah, say noon at Northstar?"

"Sounds great."

We kissed again, and then I closed the door. Bishop looked at the door and cocked his head before looking back up at me.

"Yeah, I want her to come back too."

chapter thirty-three

As I drove to Northstar Café to meet Jennifer, a legion of questions flooded my head.

Was it too soon to have feelings for her? Was it too weird, given that she had accused me of murder only a few days ago? Did I just like her because I had barely been touched by a woman in the past six months? Was my faith really gone? Even if it was still there, buried under all the hurt, doubt, and questions, did that mean I should still be a minister? None of these questions had easy answers.

I pulled into the parking lot and went inside. Even though I arrived a few minutes late, I didn't see Jennifer anywhere. I figured she probably got caught up with something at work.

I took my seat in one of the booths. A *Columbus Dispatch* newspaper lay on the table, and I picked it up. Articles about Jessica's murder along with speculation about Amanda's killer covered the front page. It amazed me how much the press didn't actually know. I'd never been on the other side of a murder investigation, so I'd assumed they knew more than the average public.

I moved on to the sports page, cursed the Blue Jackets, and

then looked at my phone.

What in the world? Did she change her mind? Did I do something wrong?

I called her, and it went straight to voice mail. Maybe her interrogations brought up some unexpected…

My phone beeped, indicating I had a new text message. I clicked to view it.

Nachash, Nachash, Nachash, Nachash, Nachash, Nachash.

Another message beeped in.

He is waking. He is waking. He is waking. He is waking. He is waking. He is waking. He is waking.

Beep.

He will summon us. He will summon us. He will summon us. He will summon us.

I sat staring at my phone as text messages kept pouring into my inbox.

The final sacrifice has come. The veil will be pierced. The Grinning Man will come.

You cannot save her. You cannot save her. You cannot save her. She is ours.

My heart raced. She? The final sacrifice? No, it couldn't be…

I called Jennifer and got her voicemail once more. "I just got a series of weird texts. I think the third victim has been, I guess, marked. I dunno. Call me please."

I got up and paced around, trying not to think about Jennifer. *No way,* I thought. *She was safe. Surrounded by cops.*

I ordered some food to try to distract my mind. When it arrived, I ate without tasting anything, checking my phone the whole time.

Nothing.

Maybe she turned off her phone and overslept. I paid for my food and sped to her condo.

When I arrived, I was relieved to find no police cars and no broken glass. I drew a deep breath and knocked on the door.

I felt a tap on my shoulder, and I jumped and spun around.

"Aidan Schaeffer?"

"Yes?"

"My name is Detective Nicholas, and I need you to come with me, sir."

Detective Nicholas stood a shade taller than me, but he was built like an Ohio State linebacker. His perfectly-styled blonde hair was encrusted in gel strands, and a gun-shaped bulge stuck out in his well-tailored suit coat. Everything about this guy said law and order.

"Can I ask why?" I inquired.

"You can, but I won't answer until we get to the station."

"Am I being arrested?" I demanded, annoyed with his arrogant attitude.

"No. But you'll make your life easier if you come with us."

"I'll come in, but I'm taking my own car," I said, turning away from him.

"Fair enough," he replied with a wave of his hand.

"Where is Detective Brown?" I asked. "I had an appointment to meet with her this morning."

"We will follow you," he said without flinching.

"I want answers."

He looked back at me, all the muscles in his face tensed. "Detective Brown has gone missing."

My stomach churned, and I grabbed the rail. "How? When?"

"I'll answer those questions down at the station, Reverend Schaeffer."

"Fine." I obviously wasn't going to get any information standing around at Jennifer's door.

I felt like my brain had been invaded by a computer virus. My eyes had gone to the "blue screen of death." All kinds of horrible scenarios passed through my mind. Maybe she had been raped. Maybe she had been murdered. Maybe both.

I raged inside. *Why, God? Why are you that cruel? Do you even care about me? Why do you keep shattering my life this way?*

When I pulled into the parking lot at the police station, my hands started to shake. I took a few calming breaths. I couldn't pray. I couldn't relax. My body started to ache.

I wanted to pound the steering wheel. I had the feeling of being watched. I didn't know if they were the eyes of the ghosts or the detectives. Neither one held any appeal for me.

Chills went through my body as pictures of Amanda and Jessica, covered in blood and a white robe, poured into my mind. *No, God, please not Jennifer...*

Then I realized why they were bringing me in for questioning. They must have known I had spent a lot of time with her, and of course that I was a previous murder suspect. Two strikes.

If that's what they thought, I wasn't going to be a sniveling coward like I'd been the last time. I didn't do anything, and they couldn't just send me to jail.

The police led me into the same interrogation room where I'd met Jennifer just a few days before. The same suffocating space with the same three chairs. I was so focused on Jennifer this time that I didn't let it bother me.

Detective Nicholas came into the room carrying a brown briefcase. He sat down across from me and removed a notepad. Lieutenant Weaver appeared a moment later. His gray eyes bored into me as his lips formed a tight lipped grimace.

"So, Reverend Schaeffer. Is that title right?" Detective Nicholas said. "Or do you prefer Pastor?"

"Aidan is fine."

"Not the first time you have been here, is it?" Nicholas glanced up at me from the notepad.

"No," I replied. "And I'm sorry to see the decoration has not changed since the last time. You guys should hire an interior decorator. Some softer colors and drapes for the interrogation window."

"Yeah, we'll get right on that," Weaver said, acid dripping from his tongue. "Since you have been here before I'm going to dispense with the preliminary bullshit."

"Fine with me. I want to find Jennifer as much as you do. If questioning me will help, then fire away."

His smile went tight. "We hope so."

"And let me just cut the shit and ask, do you guys think I'm a suspect in this?"

Lieutenant Weaver sat back in his chair and examined me. "Yeah, that's about the size of it."

"I thought so."

"Since we are dispensing with the pleasantries, I want you to tell me the nature of your relationship with Detective Brown."

"We're friends, and I was, and I think she is too, hoping for more."

The detectives glanced at each other before Nicholas scribbled something on his notepad.

"When did your friendship begin?" Weaver asked.

"Right here in this room, as a matter of fact. She was the lead questioner when you guys brought me in after Amanda's murder."

"How did things develop after that? Did you initiate contact?"

"I did, but I didn't want to."

"Why not?" Nicholas asked.

"Why not? Because the woman suspected me of murder. Not exactly an invitation to a relationship, would you say?"

"Are you saying you had no interest in Detective Brown?" he asked, leaning forward.

"It depends on what you mean by that. Did I notice that she was a smart, attractive woman? Of course I did. But I wasn't about to ask her on a date."

They both smiled in spite of themselves.

"So, why did you contact her?" Nicholas asked.

"I remembered a storage shed I shared with Amanda, and I thought you all would like to have a look."

"Then what happened?" Weaver pressed.

"I called her, and she visited me at the church the day after. She wanted me to see the murder scene and, well, help with something that was puzzling her."

"What's that?"

"The bare footprints."

They looked at each other. "Why were those bothering her?"

"The same reason they bothered everyone else. There seemed to be no explanation for them."

"So, why did she think *you* would be able to help?" Lieutenant Weaver gave me a hard glare.

"I'm a minister. You know all this already. She said she cleared it with you, so don't bother trying to trap me with it. I guess she thought there was a supernatural explanation."

Nicholas scribbled again on his notepad and looked up at me. "When is the last time you saw Detective Brown?"

"Last night. She came over after my session meeting. We talked for a while, agreed to meet today, and then she went home. I showed up at Northstar, but she wasn't there. I tried calling her a few times; I thought maybe she slept late. So, I had something to eat and decided to head down to her place. The rest you know."

Nicholas stood and began to pace about the room, deep in thought. "So basically, you are telling me that your connection to two recent murder victims and one missing person is just a coincidence?"

"No, that isn't what I'm telling you."

He turned toward me, his face red. "What?"

"Amanda was my ex-fiancée. Jessica was a secretary at a church I visited. And Jennifer, well, she was … *is* the detective investigating the case. All linked. There is the connection."

"Are you confessing?"

"Not at all."

"Then *what*?" Nicholas put his hand on the table and leaned in to me.

"You have all the notes Detective Brown filed, correct?"

"Yes, and you are at the center of all of them."

"Then you know I was at the hospital during Amanda's murder, and I was actually with Jennifer herself during Jessica's murder. So somehow, you have developed this brilliant scheme that I murdered the first two and was preparing to do the same to Jennifer."

I paused to let my words sink in.

"Well, I didn't," I continued. "I like Jennifer, and I want you all to find her. You have all the information you can get out of me, so get started!" I thumped my hand on the desk.

They both looked at me, their mouths slightly open.

"Well?" I said.

"It's not a good idea to yell at cops who are questioning you on the possible disappearance of one of their own," Weaver growled.

I shrugged. "I don't care anymore. I want you to spend your time finding her. I gave you everything I have, now use it."

Before Nicholas could respond, there was a knock on the window. Both men looked up, surprised. "We will be back," Weaver said.

I sat there, slumped in the chair. At that point, the only reason I cared if they arrested me was that it would take away from a real search for Jennifer. I couldn't understand what happened to her. Given the bizarre text messages I received, all the signs indicated that she was the next victim, and it would be tonight at midnight, though I had no idea where.

I looked at the clock on the wall. Two o'clock. I had ten hours, and I was stuck in this interrogation room. I fought the urge to pass out as I drummed my hands on the desk.

Lieutenant Weaver came back into the room. "Why didn't you tell us that you were with someone last night after Jennifer left your place?"

I had no idea what he was talking about, but I wasn't sure if this was another interrogation trick. "Guess I forgot."

"So, who were you with?"

He had called my bluff. I said the first name that came to my mind. "Father Neal."

He tapped his pencil. "Aidan, we have to find Jennifer."

His change in demeanor sent me back into my chair. "I know that."

"She talked about you, you know."

I smiled slightly. "Yeah? What did she say?"

"She really likes you. Of course, being the professional that she is, she never said so, but I could tell."

"And I really like her."

We stared at each other. "Father Neal is in the station right now," he said. "He signed a statement saying you were with him last night."

Interesting, I thought. I wondered if he did some magick trick to implant his name in my mind.

"Now do you guys believe me?" I asked, anxious to leave.

"Yes, we do. But you have to understand, your connection to all of this seems a little strange."

I snorted. "Tell me something I don't know, lieutenant. A few weeks ago, I was just a broken-hearted, single minister with no life but the church." I paused. "What happened with Jennifer? Do you guys have any information?" I was relieved to be able to ask questions of my own.

He shook his head. "All we know is that she didn't make it home last night." He sighed. "Is there anything you can tell us that might help to find her?"

I thought about the footprints. The Bone Masters. Nebo. Nachash. "No, I guess you have everything that she wrote down."

"Only the business parts," he said.

I nodded.

"You're free to leave, Aidan. We never had any real evidence on you."

"Not really a surprise to me." I tried to smile in what I hoped was a good-spirited way.

He gave me a half smile. "No, I guess not. I think Father Neal is waiting for you in the lobby. We told him we were going to let you go home, given his statement."

"Thanks."

I couldn't get out of that room fast enough. I walked down the hall to the main lobby and found Father Neal. His wrinkled face and white hair had never looked so beautiful. He walked up to me and gave me a hug.

"How did you know I was here?" I whispered into his ear.

"*They* told me," he whispered back as he hugged me tighter. "We don't have much time, Aidan. We have to go back to St. Patrick's. Everyone will be there."

We walked out to the car, and I climbed into the back as a long, dark-haired driver turned to me.

"Hey, Preacha. Becoming quite the jailbird, eh?"

"Kiss my ass, Darrin," I gave him a half smile. "Yeah, well, didn't you know? All preachers are either scoundrels or former scoundrels."

chapter thirty-four

The ghost hunting team had assembled in the conference room at St. Patrick's by the time we arrived. Kate, Zoe, Reg, and to my complete surprise, Olan and Edna were there too.

"Oh, Aidan, are you okay?" Edna said as she rushed over to me and put her arm around my shoulders. "We'll find Jennifer, don't worry."

"What are you two doing here?" I asked.

Olan smiled as he gave me a manly pat on the back. "Father Neal is a close friend of ours, and we're unofficial members of the group. We are too old to go on hunts, so we do historical research. We've been keeping an eye on you for him."

Keeping an eye on me? I decided to ignore that comment. All the people in the room made me smile, and I felt a rush of warmth as I looked at everyone. They'd come to help and had probably left class or taken off work to be here.

"Thanks, everyone," was all I could manage.

"Enough speeches. We have work to do, and we're running out of time." Father Neal's voice galvanized us.

The rest of the group looked over text messages and audio from the investigation for any further clues while Father Neal made Darrin bring maps of Ohio into the office.

After several hours of talking and going over Hebrew grammar books, searching for a variant on serpent, we'd gotten nowhere.

"Nachash. For the love of God, what is it?" I said, looking up and seeing that it was five o'clock.

"*Where* is it, is the question you really need to ask. We already know the what."

"It has to be a place close by, right?" I looked at the map of Ohio. Someone had put a red pin in Columbus and Athens and connected them with a red string.

"Yes, to form a triangle, thus completing the ritual," Reg said as he traced over the red lines and looked to the northeast corner of the map.

"How exact does it need to be?"

"Not very, but close enough," Father Neal said as he walked over.

"And it has to be a place of power?" Kate asked, tracing one of the vivid scars on her face.

"Without question," Zoe said, handing Father Neal his coffee.

We all stood, huddled around the map. I squinted to make out features that would qualify as a place of power, though I honestly had no idea what that could be by looking at a simple road map.

I remembered the small scratches under the Hebrew on Jessica's head. Had I missed something? I looked at my hand. The marker had faded. I couldn't make out what I'd written. I wished I'd written it on a piece of paper. I couldn't shake the feeling those scratches would have answered our question.

"What about Moundsville, West Virginia?" Kate offered, pointing at the border of Ohio and West Virginia. "There are Native American mounds there."

Father Neal rubbed his gray stubble. "I thought about that, but how does Nachash fit in? Chillicothe is a graveyard, but there's no serpent connection that I know about. Same thing with the Newark mounds. It's a huge earthen observatory. The complex itself has some interesting associations, but nothing that would help us."

"What kind of associations?" I blurted before I could stop myself.

"Just some rumors of giant skeletons and old Hebrew inscriptions found on the site. Nothing has ever been confirmed so we can discount that. Although, some people have connected it with the Nephilim and magick. It's a possibility, but I don't think it quite fits, because—"

He broke off with a gasp.

"What's wrong?" Darrin asked.

"I'm thick and old, Darrin. How could I not see this? Nachash. It means serpent, yes, but it also means shining magician, necromancer, those who dabble in the black arts. A double meaning."

He placed his finger on a spot in the southwest area of the state then traced to Athens, back to Columbus and downward. "Perfect," he whispered.

"What, priest? Spit it out." I prodded.

He didn't answer as he walked over and grabbed a red book off his desk titled *Weird Ohio*. He flipped through the pages.

"I have found our snake in the grass." He opened up the book and showed us a picture of an ancient Native American earthen effigy mound in the shape of a large snake.

"That's it, that's it!" I yelled. "I can't believe I didn't think of it."

Father Neal began to read. "The Serpent Mound in Peebles, Ohio is the largest effigy mound in the United States. It has recently become of interest in the paranormal community due to its reputation for strange phenomena. The New Age community also holds an interest in the mound as a vortex, like the one in Sedona, Arizona. Shallow caves in the bottom of the hill have been thought to hold gateways to other worlds as represented by the snake's open mouth." He pointed at the snake's head, which was swallowing something. "I wonder what that is."

"Looks like an egg," I said. "I thought you studied all of this, Father?"

Father Neal frowned. "I have as much as I can between

my priestly duties and other things. Plus, there's never been any magickal indication the Grinning Man lay buried there." He looked down at the picture. "My guess is that is where the ritual will be held, at the head of the snake, the opening to the worlds, as it were."

"We have to go. Now," I said, jumping up. "Peebles is about two hours from here."

"Yes," Olan said, laying a hand on my shoulder. "We do."

"But, Olan, you can't..."

"Try and stop me, Aidan, my boy. All of us need to go. Right, Father Neal?"

Father Neal leaned on his cane, taking in each face as if reading some hidden information. "Yes, I think all of us will go, but only Aidan and I must go to the mound itself. It's too dangerous for some of you. Do you understand?"

They all nodded.

"You all promise to do as I say and stop when I tell you?"

"We promise," everyone said in unison, somber excitement in their voices.

"Reg, can we all fit in your SUV?"

"Well, two people will have to sit in the back if they don't mind."

"We will," Kate said, grabbing Darrin's hand as he smiled.

Father Neal nodded. "Then, let's go. We'll call Lieutenant Weaver when we reach the mound."

"Why not now?" I said as I reached for my phone.

"Because I won't risk their lives."

Not knowing what to say, I followed everyone out to the cars.

chapcer chircy-five

I sat in the middle seat between Zoe and Olan. Edna stayed behind to organize what she called "prayer warriors." The knot in my stomach tightened as we drove down Interstate 71 toward Cincinnati. We would have to get on the back-roads eventually, and I hoped we wouldn't run into any slow-moving tractors.

Everyone talked about different things, trying to take their minds off what was about to take place. I couldn't speak. I felt like if I opened my mouth, I would throw up. I tried not to think of the bloodstained cross or Jessica's ring. If I did, my thoughts immediately jumped to what could be done to Jennifer.

Father Neal's voice broke into my racing thoughts. "I think we should pray."

"Aidan? Will you join us?" Olan asked, giving me a sidewise glance. Everyone looked at me.

"No, I can't do it. You all can, but all I care about right now is saving Jennifer, not my faith. I don't want to think about God."

"You have to start now, Aidan. You have no choice." Father Neal turned around in his seat to fix me with his piercing stare.

"Stop it." I looked away from him. A direct look from Father Neal could put the fear of something, if not God, in anyone.

"It's time to draw this poison out of you," Olan said, grabbing my hand. I snatched it back.

"Maybe I don't want it drawn. Maybe it isn't poison to me."

"It is. It has made you bitter, angry, and resentful. And full of doubt. Just like Thomas." Father Neal kept looking at me. "Have you thought about the story like I told you?"

"No. Haven't really had the time." I avoided his eyes.

"You aren't a very good liar, Aidan."

I scowled. "We are driving as fast as we can to stop the murder of someone I ... well, care about, and all you want to do is talk about faith and doubt. Can't you save it for later?"

"No!" Father Neal thumped the console. "It must be now. Haven't you seen enough to understand what we are up against? Nachash. The serpent. Does that penetrate through that thick Irish skull of yours?"

"So, we are fighting *the* Devil, are we now?"

"I don't know about *the* Devil, but *a* devil. And that is bad enough."

"How do we fight the Devil, oh head of wisdom?" I couldn't keep the skeptic derision out of my voice.

"By belief, boy. That is why we must take out your doubt."

"So, how are we going to do that? Is there some kind of operation?" I rolled my eyes.

"Thomas."

"You keep saying that, so will you please explain yourself? I'm getting tired of the mysteries and hints."

"Thomas the Doubter. You know the passage and the nature of his doubts," Reg broke in, rubbing his chin.

"Intellectual and emotional," I said.

"Ah, so you *have* thought about it." Father Neal needled me.

"A little."

"Do you know how Jesus meets Thomas' doubt?"

I was speechless. I had focused for so long on Thomas in that passage, I had never given any thought to Jesus' words. "He meets Thomas intellectually and emotionally."

"The invitation to put his hands in Christ's wounds," Father Neal prompted. "His intellectual doubts met."

"Then what?" I pressed.

"Thomas believes, and then what does Jesus say?"

"Blessed are those who don't see, but believe," I murmured.

"Indeed."

I stared out the window at the white line on the side of the road as it raced by. To his credit, Father Neal remained quiet to let me process.

"Have you put it together, lad?"

"Doubt is always emotional and intellectual, as you said."

"Yes, and what else?"

"Proof can always be had, but belief doesn't depend on it, or shouldn't." It really was that simple. For all my reading, my study, my doubts, I forgot that everything depends on a point of view first.

"Now, lad, given everything you've been allowed to see, which one is it going to be?"

"Do I have to decide now?"

"Yes. You must."

"Why is it so important?"

"Because, if you don't believe, you'll be run over by a spiritual truck. The men we are about to confront are believers of a type way stronger than you. The things they know, the power they have, and it's all *real*. The only way to confront them is to believe in a power much stronger."

"Them? I thought there was only one."

"No, you and Jennifer believed that, but it is not true."

"How do you know?"

Father Neal gripped his cane until his knuckles went white. "Because I have seen them in the spirit world."

"I'm sorry. Can you say that again?"

Father Neal was always extreme, but this was new.

"Aidan, I have told you what I used to be."

"Yeah, but…"

"You didn't believe me. You thought Crowley was a charlatan, doing it only because it got women and men into bed with him?"

"I…" I couldn't believe he was talking about this in front of the group.

"Don't worry, I had to fill them all in," Father Neal said, waving his hand. "Crowley was real, Aidan. His followers are real. They are the men and women in black. All of them have the same purpose. To awaken the Grinning Man. Aleister was obsessed with the idea. I followed him to America to make sure…" He paused and swallowed. "My guess is the Grinning Man sleeps in those caves the book talked about. I've searched for him for years. Now, we've found him, and we can stop him."

"But who is he, Father? Why is this such a big deal?"

Father Neal's eyes pierced mine. "Who he was, originally, I don't know. I'm not sure if anyone does. But the Puritans, the Native Americans, and everyone had a name for him. They called him the Black Man. They thought he was the actual Devil, but I believe he was, or is, only a servant of Lucifer."

"That's a bit racist," Darrin quipped from the back.

"No, Darrin," Zoe jumped in. "He dressed in all black, not that he was black, although, many racist people often equated the two."

"Yes, Zoe, and the Puritans mistakenly equated him with the Native Americans as well. But he was neither. He was a man, but what he is now, even I don't know," Father Neal said.

I decided to change the subject. "When you say you saw them, what do you mean? Who did you see?"

"I didn't see their faces. They had obscured them, but I found them."

"Wait, you actually went into this world? I thought you said it was forbidden," I pressed.

Father Neal looked down. "It is forbidden, but I thought, under the circumstances, I would."

"And?"

"I will not speak of it, Aidan."

"But…"

"Don't ask me any more. Just know I have an idea of what we will face when we get to the mound." He grimaced as if someone had struck him.

"What will that be?"

"I think you know," he said gravely, turning to face forward.

"The final ceremony?"

"Yes. The third gate will open, and the Grinning Man will re-enter the world."

Silence filled the car as we wound our way through the back roads. Father Neal's voice broke the stillness.

"Stop here."

"But we are still a mile from the mound, Father," Reg objected as he tapped the GPS.

"I know, Reg, but this is as close as we will get."

We all got out of the SUV and looked at each other. It was pretty clear no one understood why we were parked so far away.

"Now, it's time for my instructions. Are you all ready?" Father Neal said, his back straight, looking every bit like an old wizard. Not Dumbledore or Gandalf, but more like Merlin, wild and commanding. Everyone nodded.

"Reg," he continued. "Give us an hour. After that, I want you to call the county police, tell them what we talked about. It has to be an hour because if they come earlier than that, they will get more than they bargained for, understand?"

Reg nodded.

"Kate, Darrin, and Zoe, you must pray until Reg makes his call, do you understand? Don't stop. And Olan?"

"Yes, Father?"

"You see the clump of trees in the distance on top of the hill?" he said, pointing.

"Yes, I do."

"That's where the Serpent Mound is and where we will be. After the police is called, I want you to lead everyone up the hill. Carefully and quietly. If you feel any resistance, stop and turn around, do you understand?"

"What sort of resistance?" Kate asked.

"You'll know it when you feel it. There is a barrier around the mound right now that can only be broken by me. If something happens, you won't even be able to come close.

They nodded as they gazed at the clump of trees.

"Good." He lifted up his hands. "May the Power of the Three in One sustain you and protect you." Then he gripped my arm. "Let's go, Aidan."

As we walked down the road, my skin began to prickle, and my heart beat faster. My airway constricted, and I gasped. Father Neal waved his hand and mumbled something under his breath, and I felt better.

"What was that?" I gasped.

"The barrier I mentioned."

"Care to elaborate?"

His gave me a thin smile. "Electromagnetic barriers, you might say, designed to disrupt and paralyze. Reg's car would never make it."

"And humans?"

"Would go into full respiratory failure, as you were just beginning to experience."

The gravel on the side of the road crunched under our feet as I took in his words.

"And how do they do this, exactly?"

Father Neal didn't answer as his lips moved in silence.

"Father Neal?"

He shook his head. "Sorry, my boy, what did you say?"

"I said how do they put up these barriers?"

He limped along. "You might call it a generator, I suppose. They would have generated them, casting a dome around themselves."

"Did you say cast?"

"I did, yes. A spell of sorts, a spell of protection."

"Spell of protection?" I couldn't keep the skepticism out of my voice.

"Yes, *Thomas*, spell of protection."

The clouds hid the moon as we walked up to the earthen serpent. "You know, I might be able to buy the whole God thing again, but this magick business is a bit hard to swallow." I strained my eyes to see Father Neal through the blackness that surrounded us.

He looked at me, surprised. "Don't you remember our conversation about science, magick, and God? And as for how it relates to Christianity, the Bible forbids certain practices, but it never says the cursed things don't work. It just instructs us not to do them. Is that also troubling to you, hard to comprehend?"

I sighed. "No, I mean ... I don't know."

"It's all right, my lad, God loves you anyway."

My throat tightened, but I said nothing.

We walked for about twenty minutes as the darkness closed in around us like a blanket. The lights from the houses that had been twinkling in the distance now disappeared. I could only see a few hundred feet around us as we turned off the road. A sign posted midway up the hill read: *Serpent Mound State Park.*

Father Neal looked at me. "Here we go, lad, up the hill."

The branches of the trees pointed up like bones waving their gnarly fingers in the wind. The farther we climbed, the stronger the wind blew. The darkness engulfed us.

"We are getting close, Aidan."

Father Neal pointed to the left. "The mound is over there."

I could only make out a hump of earth stretching down the hill. "Doesn't look like much," I whispered.

"I know, but trust me when I tell you, it's impressive." As Father Neal moved, I noticed a canvas satchel across his shoulder.

"What's in the bag?"

"Don't ask questions. Let's move."

We walked farther to the mound as the tall observation tower loomed over us. I shivered as a creeping sense of dread hit me. My heart quickened, my breath came in ragged gasps, and my vision narrowed. The telltale signs of a panic attack. I wanted to run, to get away. I turned around, and Father Neal grabbed me by the arm.

"No, you don't really want to run."

"I'm afraid," I heard myself saying, but not quite believing the words, or the meekness of my voice.

"It's all part of their work, Aidan. The fear, the darkness, all of it."

I looked up into the trees. "And the wind? What's with the wind?"

"Spirits ... the spirits are coming to the mound."

Thunder rolled and crackled around us as a ripping sound filled the air.

"The veil," I said, and Father Neal nodded.

As we walked closer to the mound, the temperature began to drop beyond the natural cold of night. My breath, which I could barely see at the start of our walk, had now become a steady stream of gray.

Father Neal slowed down, and his limp grew more pronounced.

"Are you okay?"

"Yes," he gasped. "My knee aches. An old war wound, you might say."

"Do you need help?" I reached toward him.

"No. Thank you, though. I will enter the ring by my own power." His voice was resolute.

"The ring?"

"A concentrated energy surrounding the men who have done all this. It grows more intense from the spirits that are gathering."

At that moment, we heard it. The sound of crunching snow surrounded us in the dark woods. The sound of hundreds of feet marching in step.

"The coming sacrifice draws them, held in the power of the Bone Masters," Father Neal whispered. "They're coming to the mouth of the serpent, to concentrate their power for the Grinning Man. Don't move."

We stood still, holding our breath as the spirits passed around us. With each crunch, I felt certain they would see us, but whether they were too focused on their destination, or Father Neal's prayers protected us, I couldn't tell, and they moved on.

"Now, Aidan, walk right behind me. Don't walk anywhere else."

I might have argued with him in the quiet warmth of his office, but not here, not now. This was his realm, and I could only follow like a kid following his dad.

Each step brought us closer to the mouth. In some parts, the ancient mound rose no higher than our knees. As it stretched down the hill, the hump grew larger. We climbed on top of the nearest earthen coil. It seemed deserted, but Father Neal began to follow the curve.

"We are now on the back of the serpent, Aidan. Shall we find the head so we can crush it?" he whispered, a new strength entering his voice as though he was using all his energy.

"By all means, but how?" I scrambled up after him.

"My guess is this is the tail, so all we have to do is continue in this direction until the end."

I nodded. "Lead the way, priest."

We followed the curvy mound as it wound its way across the open plain. I squinted into the dark to see if I could see the head. Nothing.

As I reached out to tap Father Neal on the shoulder, a hard smack to my chest knocked me onto my back. All the air rushed out of my lungs, and I struggled to breathe. I looked up to see Father Neal stagger, but he caught himself with his cane.

"They know we are here," he rasped.

"What do we do?"

Father Neal crossed himself and said something quietly under his breath as he bent down at my side. He reached into the canvas bag and pulled out something I couldn't see. He touched my arm and then touched my leg. Heat flowed down my arm.

"Thanks. What's that in your hand?"

"Don't worry about it just now. Let's keep working our way to the serpent's head."

As we walked on, the wind beat at us with hurricane force. Father Neal grabbed my arm as we struggled to follow the path. The wind began to howl as if it had become a living being. I thought it was just my imagination, but I started making out voices in the gusts. Faint whispers grew louder and louder as though someone had turned up the volume to a full ear-splitting blast.

The Masters summon us. We will raise him. He will serve us...

A death is coming, we will obey...

I want to see blood, her blood...

Her body shakes and her cries. Mmmmmmm. I hope they cut her now, just to give us a little pleasure. I am thirsty...

"No!" I shouted into the air. My voice boomed as if it had been amplified with a stadium-sized sound system. I felt naked as I sensed invisible eyes turning to me with their full interest.

Why are they here? A voice hissed right next to me.

I felt a hard slap across my face, and I cried out in pain.

They do not belong here! Beat them!

Invisible blows struck my body. Palm prints appeared on my exposed arms, and hands tore at my clothes as I continued to cry out.

"Aidan?" A woman's voice cut through the darkness.

"Jennifer?" I shouted, feeling hope spring up in my chest.

"Over here, they're gone. Help me, please!"

Panic rose in her voice as I ran to the serpent's head, the frozen ground crunching under my feet. The spirits ramped up their attack until my skin grew numb from the invisible slaps.

Another blow to the chest and I went down hard. I looked around for Father Neal, but I couldn't see him anywhere.

"Father, help me!" I didn't know if it was a prayer or if I was asking Father Neal to save me. At that point, I didn't care as I felt something lift me up by my coat and stand me on my feet. I turned around and saw no one. I ran the rest of the way to the earthen egg in the serpent's mouth.

As I approached the mound, I found Jennifer in the center of the egg. They had covered her with a white ceremonial robe and tied her to a wooden doorframe. This was how they planned to hang her.

No one else seemed to be around, and I began to descend the mound. Someone grabbed my shoulder.

"Aidan, don't go to her," Father Neal said. "You will not be able to do it. Let me."

"Come on, there is no one here."

Before I could finish, piercing shrieks tore through the air and brought me to my knees. My ears ached as I tried to crawl down the mound to Jennifer. Gray-colored shadows swirled around me and assaulted my body. I tried to raise my arms and shield myself as two figures struck me at once. I hit face first on the ground, and I tasted the cold grass. Invisible arms pinned me down, making it impossible for me to move.

And then, I heard another voice, a voice of command speaking words I couldn't make out.

Was this actually the voice of God? I wondered. Or maybe some high ranking angel? The voice boomed into the darkness as if pumped through a giant subwoofer.

I turned to look at its source.

Father Neal stood erect, his arms extended above his head, his fingers stretched to the sky. His white hair flew in the relentless wind, and his face had been transformed from a kindly old man into some kind of powerful, angelic warrior. He reached into his bag, and it glowed white. The light crawled up his hand, to his arms and engulfed his entire body. He held up something I couldn't see. Light sprang from him, white, hot, and bright to the point that I needed to shield my eyes.

The world as I saw it turned upside down just beyond the light. Giant thuds hit the ground, and the whole earth shook.

I crawled on my knees toward Jennifer. "Are you okay?" I reached out to her as I rose up near the doorframe.

"Aidan," she sobbed, tears streaming down her face. "Aidan, you're here."

"Let me get these ropes." I took out my pocketknife and began to cut.

"Hurry, Aidan!" the voice of Father Neal roared from the light. "I can't hold them any longer." Then he boomed, "Michael Militant! Come defend us! Father, Son, and Holy Ghost hear my prayer!"

The ground rocked with the force of exploding dynamite.

I cut at Jennifer's ropes with fury until my hands ached. First one, then another. I tried to ignore her wrists and ankles, which were now bleeding freely from chafing. With each tug of the rope, she cried out a bit.

"I'm sorry." I tried to keep my voice steady.

"Don't apologize, just keep going. They could be back." She grimaced as I pulled the rope for more room.

I glanced around quickly. "Where did they go?"

"I don't know. They vanished when you shouted." Her voice became hoarse.

"Maybe they ran away."

"I don't think so."

With a final grunt, I sliced through the rope on her wrists and caught her as she fell forward. I helped her stand, and she shivered as she leaned against me. I took off my coat and wrapped it around her.

"Let's get out of here," I whispered, trying to remain calm.

"I can barely walk," she moaned, leaning on me with most of her weight.

"Is something broken?" I looked down at her bleeding ankles.

"No, my legs are asleep."

"Just lean against me, I'll help you."

"Aidan, it's Daniel Mueller. I saw his face when his hood slid down. But Father Neal is right, there is another."

"Probably another mega-church pastor. Seems to fit. They control people through magick or control people through preaching. I always knew I hated big churches."

At that moment, a deep, familiar chuckle resounded through the air.

chapcer chircy-six

"Ah, Aidan, such a product of your generation. Everything that is immense and corporate is automatically evil. But it's so useful because you ignore the evil that is right in front of you every day."

"Mike..." I shivered.

"Very good, Aidan, very good." He laughed again.

Mike and Daniel, wearing dark red ceremonial robes, stepped into the dying light generated by Father Neal. Mike cast back his hood and smiled at me. Oddly, it wasn't the cold smile of an evil villain, but the smile of a proud father or teacher.

The bright light that had illuminated the whole snake's head had gone out. I looked to my left and saw Father Neal's face buried in the ground. I pressed my fingernails into my palms until they sliced my skin.

"What did you do to him, you assholes?" I ran toward them and hit an invisible wall. My limbs locked, and I stood paralyzed.

"Aidan, you must learn to watch your language," Mike said in a soft voice, wagging his finger at me. "Assholes is so vulgar and coarse."

"Go fuck yourself!"

"Well, the Irish are not known for their refined tongues," mocked Daniel as he stood next to Mike like a bad version of the Grim Reaper.

"Keep them talking," Jennifer whispered in my ear before looking up at Mike and Daniel. "Yes, because that is so much worse than killing people."

Mike smiled as he stood in front of me. "Sometimes sacrifice is necessary to accomplish a greater purpose."

Daniel came up behind me. "Because everyone kills, or would if it served his own desires. Consider it a scientific experiment."

"And what would yours be?" Jennifer began inching closer to Father Neal.

Daniel grinned. "To give Aidan his answers, to meet his questions in a way Yahweh and his disgusting church never allowed."

I felt sick. This whole thing had been about me? For what purpose?

Mike spoke as though he could read my mind. "Behold, Aidan, and you shall see."

He began to chant. I thought it was in Latin, but it was much older and more guttural.

I felt as if someone had removed a filmy wrapping from my eyes. I began to see beings leering at us, some with full bodies and some with half-rotting faces. They filled the air, too numerous to count. The eagerness in their faces looked as though someone had mixed the sins of lust, desire, and pride in a bowl and bathed them in it.

Mike laid a hand on my shoulder. "Now you finally see, Aidan. Now you can place your hands in the side of the Nazarene. Become one of us, one of the Bone Masters."

"Reach out and touch one of them, Aidan," Daniel said with a sadistic grin. "See how real they are becoming."

If I had teeth like Bishop and could move, they would have both lost fingers. As it was, they seemed too intent on me to notice that Jennifer had reached Father Neal and was trying to wake him. I had to keep them distracted. "Guess you're the men in black, eh?"

They both laughed. "Such a bad name," Mike said. "As you can see, it's dark red. It just looks black."

"So, this is what you are, Mike. I knew you were screwing around on Sheila, but I didn't think you were a killer. Or a man in *dark red*."

Mike smiled. "Aidan, there is so little you understand. Such infantile views of good and evil. There is much more, so much more you could learn."

"Amanda and Jessica?" I seethed.

"Tools used for our purposes," Mike said with dry callousness. "And, if I may say, killing Amanda was Daniel's initiation. Took some time, as she was quite committed to you."

I closed my eyes. I knew it would be a long time before I would be able to wipe those words from my mind. "Why? For what purpose? To control Ohio?" I asked. "Hope you enjoy the cold gray skies and declining population."

Mike gave a soft chuckle. "We've been waiting years for this moment. Soon our master will be awake." He paused. "And for you, it's an offer to join us. To become the ultimate scientist, the ultimate knower."

Father Neal's history of magick replayed in my mind. Mike's eyes bored into mine as I stared back, not flinching despite the darkness I saw — the soullessness of a man who had long ago sacrificed his whole self to complete evil.

I laughed in his face. "I'm not joining you, so save your monologues."

Mike licked his lips and ran his hand over his goatee. "I have wanted you to be one of us since I first interviewed you. Such a mind. I had to figure out a way to get you. Think of the power, Aidan. The answers to all mysteries at your fingertips. Our master can give them all to you. And your beautiful lady friend here … she is yours, you know. She would do anything you ask without question."

I shook my head. "You obviously don't know Jennifer."

"No, it's you who doesn't know her. Jennifer has low self-esteem and flings herself at any man who pays attention to her. Why do you think she offered herself to a person she had once suspected of murder? Aidan, she's a total slut. A tramp. A filthy whore."

Mike's jeering was only to provoke me, I knew, but I clenched my fists and fought to keep from punching him.

"So, all of this, the murders, Jennifer's kidnapping, was to get me here?"

Daniel laughed manically. "Yes, and it all worked together very nicely, didn't it?" He pointed to the spirits around us. "And they are waiting on your decision to follow the master."

"Does this master of yours have a name?"

"His name is not to be spoken."

"Like *Lord Voldemort?*"

I felt an invisible whip strike my face. Blood flew from my cheeks.

"Don't mock him or us, Aidan. They don't like it." Mike spat. "If you must call him anything, you may call him the Grinning Man."

I wiped my lip and smiled. "Wow, what a mysterious and threatening name. For someone so damn happy, he obviously doesn't like to be mocked. Like all evil spirits, full of pride."

"For someone who doesn't believe, you talk a lot of filth," Daniel said as he yanked my head back by my hair.

"I always thought you were the one who talked a lot of filth, Mueller. And your neckties. Hideous."

Daniel struck my head and I fell on my hands and knees, blood oozing from my nose, mouth and ears.

"Aidan, come, this is pointless." Mike sighed. "Join us. Make us three and powerful. Take Jennifer. She is yours. Finish the priest and serve the one who is about to wake." Mike turned and faced the spirits surrounding us.

I looked around and finally understood the depths of the power they wielded. Mike and Daniel had summoned ghosts and had broken through the barriers of the physical universe. They achieved something no scientist ever accomplished; they broke the veil between worlds. And they offered it to me. All the answers I wanted to know were right there. I could have them.

A faint glow emanated from over near where Father Neal had fallen. I stared at it, drawing on its strength, and felt warmth return to my body.

"And join the dark side? No, thanks Emperor Palpatine. I'm insulted, Mike," I said, trying to stand. "Did you really think that I would bow at your feet for the secrets of the universe you say you can deliver?"

Two pairs of black boots appeared in front of me. One of them connected with my face. I crumpled to the ground in a heap and spit out a mouthful of blood.

"Regardless of what you choose, Aidan, they will die. It's just a matter of whether or not you will save your own life. Why stand up for something you don't believe in anyway? Why stand for a God who isn't there?" Mike's voice oozed with sympathy.

His words drove deeper than the physical abuse. All the doubts I had experienced rose up like a beast and gnawed, tempted and gripped me.

"Think. All of your struggles, all of your pain, the rejection, the failure, at an end." Mike put his arm around me.

I looked up at the spirits surrounding us. A Confederate soldier with a rotted face leered and shook his gun. A girl in white lifted up her dress to expose a worm-eaten leg. All of the spirits wore a look of starvation, as if only I could quench some kind of eternal hunger in them. I glanced to my left and saw that Jennifer had reached Father Neal. The light underneath him started to grow brighter.

"No," I said.

A ripple of shrieks went through the spirits.

Mike leaned his face in toward me. "I'm sorry, Aidan, I didn't quite understand you."

"Then let me be more clear and direct. In the name of the Father, and of the Son, and of the Holy Spirit, *fuck off!*"

The spirits roared in pain and anger. The Triune name had been too much for them. It had pierced them more than any weapon, material or magick could have.

Mike frowned and shook his head. "Aidan, I guess your mind

is not as developed as I had hoped. You've let me down. You've let science down. You're nothing more than a weak-minded provincial thinker. No wonder your life is a failure." He spat on the ground and waved his hands as if removing a barrier.

The spirits began to descend, hideous glee written all over their rotting faces. I could not look at them, but I began to feel them. Rough bone struck me. Slimy flesh oozed over mine. Hard blows rained down on me, and I cried out in pain.

This is how it will end for me.

Daniel laughed. "Now, Aidan, you will die first."

The spirits pinned me to the ground spread eagle. Mike stood over me and drew out a curved silver knife, perfect for slicing my throat.

I took a deep breath and inwardly crossed myself as Mike began to chant. "So, what will you carve in my head?" I gasped.

"The name of the one you serve, just like your new girlfriend."

"And why would you do that? To complete the ritual?"

"No, Aidan." He smiled. "This is not the end of the Three Gates. That is somewhere else. I'll just carve the name of your god into your forehead. You'll be marked as you meet my master."

"Keep telling yourself that. Your master is a liar and has been since the beginning."

Daniel came down hard on my face with his knee, pinning my cheek to the ground. "And the war will soon be over," he said. "Tonight is the beginning of the end."

The blade pierced my forehead, and I screamed in pain. The heat of the blade, fed by their dark magick, felt like fire on my cold skin.

I closed my eyes. I prayed for the end. I prayed for forgiveness.

The inside of my eyelids grew red. I opened them, and a blinding white light filled everything around us as the spirits cried out in anger. In the distance, I saw Father Neal, silhouetted in the dark, gripping something as he walked toward us. The light seemed to come from an object in his hand.

"Do you think you can fight us with that, old man?" Daniel raged.

"I wouldn't be standing here otherwise, lad," Father Neal said with a hint of humor in his voice.

"The Master is looking for you," Mike shouted. "He is so disappointed. Aleister told him you showed such promise."

"I'm afraid he will have to continue in his disappointment." Father Neal began to lift his arm. He held a cup-like object in his hand. The cup began to glow with a bright light.

"He will find you, you know," Daniel promised.

"I know. I will be waiting, but for now, you will stop. You won't be the ones to bring him back from his sleep."

They both laughed. "We never expected to, old man. We were just supposed to find you and Aidan. Now we will take you."

"If you can."

"If we can?" Mike roared with laughter. "We have already knocked you out with our power. And now the spirits are almost solid. One more death and you'll be overwhelmed."

As Mike turned and pierced my head again, an intense heated gust of air blew past, and Daniel grunted as he was thrown off me. "That thing will not help you, old man," Mike snarled. "It's not magick."

Father Neal continued toward us. "No, Michael, it's not. It's much holier than that."

Another burst of white light and heat went forward, and Mike fell to the ground.

"Back to your abyss! I command you by the power of the Trinity! Await your judgment! The spell is broken by the True sacrifice!"

A roar filled the whole earth around us like the sound of a train and a thousand voices raised in intense pain all at once. Mike and Daniel screamed out. A light brighter than a nuclear blast flashed from the object in Father Neal's hands, and everything went dark.

chapter thirty-seven

I stirred at the light, cool touch of skin on my cheek as a soft voice called to me.

"Aidan…"

I opened my eyes and saw her. Blonde hair, blue eyes, and not a flaw in her face. Ageless, youthful, solemn. She looked like a goddess.

"Amanda! What…"

"Shhh, not much time. He calls, and I must go. I have only been allowed to help you until your task was done."

I couldn't speak.

Amanda smiled. "So now you hold your tongue? Could have solved so many problems between us."

I ached for her. "Amanda, I love you."

"And I love you, Aidan. Now awaken. Jennifer calls to you. Let her take care of you." She paused, tilting her head as she listened to someone speaking. "He is telling me to say to you, 'Good job, faithful servant.'"

Her cool hand touched my face again, and she kissed my eyelids.

"Aidan, please wake up!"

I opened my eyes and saw Jennifer crouched over me, eyes filled with unshed tears. The burning pain in my muscles returned, along with throbbing in my chest and a dull ache in my head.

Jennifer bent down to kiss me, and I moaned.

"Did I hurt you?" she asked, cradling my face.

"No, but they did."

I tried to get up, but needles of pain shot through my body. "That was stupid," I snorted.

"Don't move. The police are on their way. You were amazing, you know that?"

"What, with my smart ass mouth? Yeah, real brave."

"Shut up. You kept them distracted while I went to Father Neal."

"Yeah, you really helped him. If it wasn't for that, I'd be dead. How did you do that?"

She looked away.

"Jennifer? Did I say something wrong?"

"It wasn't me. I mean, I got to him, knelt down and then…"

"Then what?"

"They came."

"Who?"

She didn't answer.

"Jennifer, who came?"

"People."

"Dead ones?"

"Yes, I guess you could say they were dead. At least, they weren't of this earth." Her eyes glazed over as though she were remembering a dream.

"I don't understand."

"Aidan, to call them dead, I can't do it."

"I don't get it. They were ghosts, right? Peaceful ghosts?"

"Aidan, they looked more solid than me."

"I don't understand."

"I don't either. All I know is that when they touched me, I could feel their skin, smell them, even feel their fingers on my shoulders."

She shivered, and tears streamed down her face.

"And they didn't pass right through you?"

"No."

"Then what happened?"

"They touched Father Neal, who looked like, well, like he'd been killed. He was bleeding from his ears and mouth. He had no pulse. I checked him myself."

"And when they touched him?"

"He opened his eyes." She paused. "Then he saw them."

"What did he say?"

She smiled and wiped her tears. "He said, 'is it my resurrection day? Where is He? Where are my ladies?'"

"What did they do?"

"They all smiled at him and shook their heads. Then he looked at me."

"And what did you say?"

She smiled as tears began to flow. "I told him that your soul was in trouble."

It had been. The ugly truth was that I had actually been tempted by Mike and Daniel's offer. My cheeks warmed with shame.

"What happened next?"

She laughed as she wiped away her tears. "Father Neal sighed and said, 'I'd better help the lad.'"

"Well, glad he put himself out," I said dryly.

"Aidan, don't be a jackass." Jennifer laughed as she poked my arm.

Dozens of loud wails sounded in the distance.

"Here comes the cavalry," I said. "Where are Mike and Daniel?"

"They are bound," Jennifer said.

"Where did you get the rope?"

"No rope."

"I don't get it."

She shrugged. "Neither do I. Just repeating what Father Neal said. But they are still alive."

I didn't really know how I felt about that. Part of me wanted them dead, another part wanted them to suffer, and still another wanted to forgive them. Granted, that was the smallest part, but it was still there. And that was proof enough to me that my faith hadn't entirely disappeared.

"What did Father Neal have in his hand?" I asked.

Jennifer shook her head. "I couldn't tell. The light was too bright."

I coughed and moaned again. My ribs felt as if they had been split in half.

"I think I need to go to the hospital," I said as everything went black again.

I opened my eyes to see florescent lighting above me, and I realized at that moment that I wasn't in heaven.

Father Neal peered over me. "Hello, lad, welcome back."

I tried to speak, but all that came out was a froggy croak.

"Here, let me get you some water," he said.

He poked a plastic straw at my chapped lips, and I sipped like a hamster that had forgotten the location of its water bottle.

"Thanks," I groaned. "I feel like shit."

"I'm sure you do. A broken arm, a broken leg, and a broken collar bone. Not to mention two cracked ribs." Father Neal sounded worried.

"Did they have to do any surgery?"

"No, thank Our Lord. But you have been under pretty heavy pain medication for the past day or so. This is the first time you have been coherent in the past twenty four hours." He paused. "How do you feel?"

I canvassed my body. I couldn't really feel anything. "Light."

He laughed. "That would be the medication. It won't always feel like that. They are already starting to wean you off a bit."

"Great."

"The doctor said you will make a full recovery. None of your bones splintered. You'll just be a walking barometer for the rest of your life."

"Ah, come on, that is an old wives' tale."

"Maybe, but it doesn't make it any less true." He chuckled.

I laughed and pain shot through my body. "Don't make me

laugh, please."

His gnarled aged hands rested on his cane as he leaned in close to me. "You did a brave thing on the mound, boy."

"We Irish are known for our mad flights of bravery, you know."

"True, very true." He smiled with satisfaction like I was his own son.

"Father, can I ask you a question?"

He glanced at the door. "The doctors might yell at me, but of course."

"You used magick, didn't you?"

He stopped smiling. "No, Aidan. Not in that situation. What do you remember?"

"You reaching into a canvas bag and bright light shining out of it. You walking toward those assholes, and light shooting from your hand, or rather, what you had in your hand."

He nodded. "You remember well."

"So, what was it?"

He sighed. "I'm sure you'll grow tired of this answer from me, but I can't tell you yet."

"I don't understand."

"There are some secrets you're not ready for. What I had in my hand helped me fight the Bone Masters without using their own weapons against them. I had a weapon of my own, but it wasn't mine."

I couldn't tell if the medicine clogged my head or I just didn't get his point. "Okay, but they used magick, right? Is all of it evil?"

He rubbed his chin. "No, I suppose not. Not inherently. But it is dangerous like an atomic bomb."

"Isn't that splitting hairs?" I said, struggling through Father Neal's vague hints.

"Not at all. There is some magick that is strictly prohibited by Scripture. Conjuring the dead. Seeking knowledge of the future. Any sort that treads on the ground of God is forbidden. In other areas of magick, well, there is more of a gray area."

"Like how much of a gray area?"

"Well, no more or less than how we think of dealing with modern technology. All of it is good but can be used for hideous purposes."

"So, that is how you drove away the spirits? A magickal object? The object was magickal, but not you?"

"Since you are ignorant of these things, I'll pray that God will forgive your blasphemy." The voice of the lion had returned. I didn't know how he could go from a meek and humble priest to an authoritative prophet so quickly.

"I didn't mean to blaspheme, but seriously, I still don't understand."

"Magick relies on formulas used in the right way, chanted in the right sequence." He looked at me and took my hand. "What I said was a prayer to the Trinity, and the object I held responded to the evil around it."

"I still don't see the difference."

"Every difference in the world. Magick, like a science experiment, is a manipulation of the natural environment. Prayer, however, is a direct contact with the One who made the world. You're asking, not manipulating. You couldn't if you tried, anyway. As for the object I held and how it works, you might say, holy reacts to the unholy."

I touched my free hand to my head. Nothing made sense, but it had to be the pain medication. I couldn't concentrate on anything.

"I need to thank you," I said.

"For saving your life? There's no need. That was not me, and you know it from Jennifer's story."

"I know, but that isn't what I meant. You did save something of mine, though."

"Oh?" he asked, his bushy eyebrows furrowed.

"My faith."

Father Neal sat down and gripped the arms of his chair. "You know, you aren't the only one who has struggled with doubt."

"I know." I figured he would give me the whole speech of how many people had struggled with the same thing.

"No, you don't know," he insisted. "I did as well. Still do at times, especially when I'm the loneliest for Judy or my daughters."

Something about the way he said that made me pause.

"Everyone is gone, aren't they? Not just Judy?"

He nodded and closed his eyes. "They all died in the same car crash five years ago. I'm sorry I didn't tell you the whole truth."

We sat in silence for some time. I thought about the people who appeared to him, the ones Jennifer said had touched him.

"Your family came to you on the mound, didn't they?"

"They did. And I wanted to go with them. I must confess, my dear boy, for a moment, I didn't care whether you died or not. Please forgive me."

I nodded. "I saw Amanda."

"I figured you might."

"Do we all look like that when we die?"

Father Neal smiled. "Promising, isn't it? I must say, I was a hunk when I was younger. It will be nice not to have liver spots or these wrinkles. I struggle with the sin of vanity as you can see."

I laughed again and regretted it as the pain meds began to wear off. "Stop it, priest." I paused. "Where is Jennifer?"

"She is being debriefed. She just went in about an hour ago."

"I hope she doesn't get fired."

Father Neal roared with laughter. "My dear absurd Irish boy, there's no way on God's earth they will fire her. Can you imagine what would happen if the press got a hold of that one? Firing the woman detective who caught the men who committed these horrible crimes?"

"But still, I mean, she was ... is, I hope ... in a relationship with a former suspect."

"Well, you never really were a suspect, were you?"

"No, I guess not," I said as I rubbed my head. "Where are Mike and Daniel?"

The lines on Father Neal's face tightened, and his brow lowered. "They're in the county jail. Mike keeps asking to see us both."

"But couldn't they, you know, magick themselves out?"

He gave a thin smile but full of humor all the same. "As I told Jennifer, they are bound."

"By you?"

"Yes, in a way."

"I don't understand."

"Magick, as supernatural as it seems, is also very much a function of the body, a function none of us really uses."

"Like the fact that we don't use all of our brain?"

"That is exactly what it is, actually."

"How do you stop them then?"

"There is a chemical which, if injected into the bloodstream, will alter that part of the brain."

"I'm sorry, but biology was my major in college. I've never heard of that."

Father Neal laughed. "As if the Brotherhood would let the world know about that."

"The Brotherhood?"

"Of magicians, Aidan, of magicians. Charles was one, you know, before he got out. Now, it seems as if all of them have taken the Dark Red."

"But he was a Christian."

"And so am I."

"I don't understand."

"I'm not a magician anymore, but I know all the tricks. *The shot*, as they call it, is a recent invention."

"Okay, so can you teach me to be a magician?" I said, half serious.

"Not going to happen." Father Neal gripped the cane.

"Why not, if some magick is not a sin?"

He frowned. "It's not ideal. Trust me; you are better off without it."

"Well, at least let me be your assistant at St. Patrick's or something. I'm most likely without a job now."

"Now, now, you Irish are way too emotional and jump to conclusions." He tapped me on the arm with his cane.

"I'm not. Once they find out about my doubts and all that, they aren't going to want me around." I sat up a bit. "Besides, I don't want to go back. Bunch of self-righteous, heads up their asses, know nothing…"

"Careful, Aidan," Father Neal scolded. "They are still the men God appointed over His church. Besides, they aren't much different than us, sinners doing an impossible job."

"Yeah, well, they don't need me."

"They are sheep without a shepherd right now. They need someone. Why not you?"

"I can think of a lot of reasons." I laid my head back on the pillow.

"Well, I wouldn't make any decisions while you are still high on pain medication." He chuckled.

"Yeah, I guess not."

We didn't speak for a few minutes. Father Neal frowned as he stared silently at the wall opposite my bed. He seemed to be agonizing over something.

"What's wrong, Father?"

He looked back at me. "Did they say anything that stuck out to you?"

"Actually, I remember them saying something about the ritual not being about the Grinning Man. Something about drawing us out in the open."

Father Neal nodded. "Yes, I remember the same."

"What does that mean?" I slurred, my eyes drooping.

"It's nothing." He smiled and patted my arm. "Go back to sleep."

As the pain medication took effect, I closed my eyes. Father Neal whispered, "Remember the painting in my office, dear boy. We're protected."

chapter thirty-eight

They released me from the hospital a few days later. I healed slowly, but it had its benefits as Jennifer came over every night and took care of me. Over the next several weeks, the pain went from being constant to occasional.

The session at Knox worked hard during my time in the hospital, counseling the congregation after the shocking revelation that their pastor was a murderer. Of course, they had no idea Mike was also a real magician, a fact that probably would have blown their Presbyterian minds.

The elders decided to call a special meeting to plan the next steps. I had healed enough to chair the meeting as the only remaining Teaching Elder.

I got to the church and struggled out of the car. As I hobbled on my crutches, I realized that I could walk, more or less, on my own. Bethany, my physical therapist, said I was making good progress. After a particularly painful session the day before, I told her that she must moonlight at Guantanamo Bay, using her skills to obtain information to keep us all safe. She laughed and ordered me to do some more leg lifts.

I walked into the church and nearly started crying. It was the first time I'd been in that building since the Serpent Mound. I headed for the conference room, but stopped when I reached Mike's office. The nameplate on the door had been removed. I walked inside and saw the cops had left much of Mike's stuff in the office. I wondered if Sheila was going to come and clean everything out. I couldn't imagine what she and the kids were going through.

Voices came from down the hall. They were all waiting for me.

"Hey, guys, sorry I'm late," I said, entering the room.

The elders all stared at me. Each one of them had visited me in the hospital, but I hadn't seen them since I was released. I stared back, not sure what to say. The silence grew uncomfortable until Jim raised his three hundred pound bulk from his chair and the rest of the elders followed. He walked over to me and stuck out his hand.

"Aidan, on behalf of all the Fathers and Brothers, I thank you," he said, shaking my hand.

"Thank me? For what? I exposed our pastor, put him in jail, and brought pain to the church." I sat down in Mike's old chair at the head of the table.

A moment of silence followed. It was coming. I knew it. They would ask me to leave and would begin the firing process.

"As for our pastor, he showed himself for what he really was," John said. "You stood up for what was right. You fought him and his despicable deeds. You are to be lauded."

I swear I will look in his office sometime for the dictionary of 19th century words. My head swirled at their praise.

"As for your doubts," he continued, "there isn't a man in this room who hasn't struggled or still doesn't struggle with the same thing. That just makes you human."

I sat there, numb. These men, most of whom I had actually hated to some degree, were showing me mercy and grace. I didn't understand it. "I don't know what to say."

"Try calling the Fathers and Brothers to order so we can start our meeting." Jim winked.

"Fathers and Brothers," I said with a smile. "I call this meeting to order."

"Now, Aidan," Jim said. "We are going to need to appoint a moderator for our first discussion."

"Sure." I looked down the table. "John, would you mind?"

"Of course not." John cleared his throat. "Fathers and Brothers, the purpose of this discussion is that we need to elect a pastoral search committee." He paused. "But before we do, we need to address the issue of interim pastor."

Uh oh, here it comes.

"In light of everything that Aidan has done for this church and his service over the past three years, I would move that we ask Aidan to serve as interim pastor until such a time as the search committee finds a new head pastor. At that time, he will step back into his current role, which we will then promote to associate pastor."

I stared at John. I had fought with that guy on a consistent basis over every little thing I had tried to change in the church. A guy who I'd always thought was a total asshole. I couldn't think of one subject on which we had ever agreed. Now, he wanted me to take over the church for what would probably amount to the next year, even after I had admitted doubting my faith.

"I don't know what to say."

"Nothing yet," John said, grinning. "The motion hasn't been seconded."

Bill quickly raised his hand, and the floor was opened for discussion.

"Well, Aidan, what do you say?" Bill asked.

"I ... I don't ... can you give me a few minutes?"

I grabbed my crutches and walked outside to get some fresh air. I didn't know what to do. My faith had been restored, but it was still shaky. There were still unresolved questions in my mind about a lot of things. I picked up my cell phone and called Father Neal.

"Hello, my boy," he bellowed.

"I need your advice."

"To the point, aren't you?"

"Yeah, sorry, the elders are waiting for me."

"And what are they waiting on?"

"They want me to be interim pastor and then promote me to associate pastor."

"Well, why not? I can't think of anyone better, and they probably can't either."

"Not sure that is very comforting." I leaned on my crutches.

"Why are you hesitating? Is it still your faith?" Worry crept into his voice.

"Yes. Well, no, not really. I mean, I'm just not sure I want to be a Presbyterian anymore."

"Why?"

"I just ... I felt so unprepared for everything that happened."

Father Neal laughed. "As if I or anyone else was prepared?"

"Better prepared than me."

"Maybe, but that is not a reason to leave your ordination behind."

I frowned. "No, I guess not."

"Listen, you need to take some time to think through these issues. I'm not saying you shouldn't have them, but you are just realizing you have them. You shouldn't make a decision based on that, not right now." He paused. "And in the meantime, you have a chance to serve God's people. You can make the final decision after they find a new head pastor. It would be a more appropriate time, you know, especially after everything Knox is going through right now. They need someone they know and trust. And that's you."

"Okay, priest, you win."

"Good lad. Call me later this week, and we will talk. Cheers."

I walked back into the room, and the elders went silent. I looked each one of them in the eye. "Fathers and Brothers, I accept and will do the best I can for Knox."

chapter thirty-nine

The next week, the weather became unseasonably warm, so Jennifer and I took a trip to Shroom Mound. The mounds seemed to draw me. I'd made her take me to the Ohio Historical Society to learn more about them. Their history seemed shrouded in mystery.

Shroom Mound had been a burial mound looking over a rock quarry in a small city park west of Columbus. Evening winter sunsets could be spectacular as the light mixed in red, yellow, white, and purple explosions of color.

"The doctors did a good job with the stitches," Jennifer said as she traced a soft finger over the scar lines that spelled half of God's name in Hebrew on my forehead.

"Yeah, I guess I'm marked for life," I said. "Can't really be an atheist now. It would be like having a tattoo of an ex-girlfriend on my ass."

She laughed. "One that I would make you get removed."

"So, have things pretty much calmed down at the station?"

Jennifer rolled her eyes. "Oh, it wasn't fun for a while. Weaver is still going on about our dating. I told him that he was my boss, not my dad. He then went on about giving me an official warning until I reminded him that he had five. That pretty much shut him up."

I laughed. "Well, consider it a treasure for your keepsake box to remind you of how we met."

She scowled. "Do I look like someone who has a keepsake box?"

I held up my hands in mock defensiveness. "Is there a way to answer that question that won't involve me getting maced or shot?"

She leaned in close. "No, but it might get you kissed."

We kissed as she ran her fingertips through my hair, and I closed my eyes. "So, interim pastor, how does it feel?"

I gave a half smile. "Weird. The real question is, can you stand dating a pastor?"

"A detective and a pastor. What a combination."

"So, where is *your* faith?" I asked.

She arched her eyebrows. "After all this? I would say at the highest level possible."

"No more vague God of the universe?"

"Not in the least, and I'm looking forward to you telling me more about Him on Sunday."

I faced her and wrinkled my brow. "Really?"

Jennifer hadn't come to church with me since the events at Serpent Mound. I never asked her why.

"Really," she said. "Mom and Dad won't care too much. They will just be glad I'm going back to church."

"I'm surprised you won't be going to Father Neal's church," I countered. "It's probably a bit more your style."

"Yeah, I thought about that. I might ask you the same question."

"I don't know. Part of me wants to, but I'm not ready yet, especially now. I just had my faith restored, and to rethink my church affiliation would be a bit much. Although," I paused. "I'm starting to ask myself those long-term questions."

"And you need time to answer them?"

"Yeah, that would be about right."

"Makes perfect sense, and I'm guessing that pearl of wisdom

came from a certain English priest who is our friend?"

I smiled. "It did. Do you really think I'm *that* wise?"

"No, not in the least."

"If you weren't a girl, I would hit you."

"You could try, but I would break your arm."

"It's already broken, thanks. Great, I'm dating someone who can kick my ass."

"Only when you need it." She moved her arm beneath mine and held onto me. "So, when do you want to do this?"

"Visit Mike in Jail? Today, if that's still good for you."

Jennifer looked out over the quarry. "Yeah, I guess so, but it won't be easy."

"Well, I'll be with Father Neal."

She frowned. "Yeah. I just don't like it. Mike and Daniel are creepy assholes."

"Is that an official cop term?"

"I'm serious, Aidan." She glared up at me.

"You're pretty cute when you're mad, you know?"

"And you are a pigheaded stubborn-ass male."

"And yet, you take care of me." I chuckled.

Jennifer sighed. "Fine. I'll get you in today. Shouldn't be too hard to slip you in, especially since you're clergy."

I pulled out my phone and called Father Neal.

"Yes, my son?" he answered.

"Are you ready to see Mike? It'll be our last chance before they move him."

"Most certainly. Come get me."

"We'll be right there."

We drove to St. Patrick's, picked up Father Neal and went to the county jail. As we entered, my stomach clenched. Jennifer shepherded us through the checkpoints, and we subjected ourselves to thorough searches.

Father Neal limped down the hall. "Well, that's the most touching I've had in a while."

I laughed. "No doubt. Still, better than the airports."

"This way, *Reverends*," Jennifer said, reminding us of our professional identities as ministers in a prison facility.

I smiled. "Yes, ma'am."

She showed us into a room with simple tables and walls.

I grinned. "Aww, honey, it looks just like the room we met in at your station, right down to the plain white paint."

Jennifer rolled her eyes. "I'll be behind the glass. He only wants to see the two of you."

I helped Father Neal into a chair and sat beside him.

"What do you think he wants?" I asked, pouring both of us a glass of water.

Father Neal gripped his cane. "I have no idea. I can't see what he would gain from talking to us. Jennifer arranged with the prison doctor to make sure he gets regular injections of the serum to control his magickal impulse. I'm told he's fighting it, but let's just say he's under doctor's orders." He grinned and took a sip of water.

The door clicked then opened. An armed guard led Mike, bound and shackled, into the room and cuffed him to the table. The patrolman looked at us, nodded and left.

Mike looked put-together, with a trimmed goatee and bright eyes. If it weren't for the orange jumpsuit, I'd have thought nothing had happened between us.

"So, the good Father and his new apprentice. How is everything healing, Aidan?"

I stared at Mike and played with a pen in front of me. This wasn't what I'd expected at all. I thought he would rage at us, curse at us, and maybe even take a swing. Instead, he grinned like a fool.

"I'm fine, Mike. The doctor says everything should be healed up in a month or so."

He nodded. "And how is the church? Do they miss me?"

"Not really. They're glad your ass is gone."

Mike chuckled. "And I'm glad my ass is gone, too. Do you know what a trial it is to pretend to be something you aren't? I've had years of it."

"Well, goody for you," I shot back. "Too bad your true self is going to get you stuck with a needle, asshole."

I leaned forward, and Father Neal placed a hand on my arm.

"Now, Michael, we've exchanged pleasantries, so why don't you tell us why you wanted to speak with us?" Father Neal's tone dropped an octave, and the room seemed to darken.

Mike put up his shackled hands, and his face morphed into a scowl. "Listen, priest, no need to threaten me, I'm just trying to deliver a message."

Father Neal lifted up his cane. "Then deliver it and be done."

The room lightened, and Mike smiled again. "With pleasure. You know, I can't tell you what an honor it is to meet the Mage John Neal."

"My title is Father, not Mage," Father Neal said, giving him a cool stare.

"Yes, yes, you serve the Nazarene." Mike chuckled. "What a disappointment. The Brotherhood had such high hopes for you. Oh well, we know where you are now, and this boy, he's important too. It's been like our own version of Christmas morning lately."

Father Neal glanced at me and then back at Mike. "What do you mean? The ritual failed. Your master still sleeps."

Mike laughed. "Is that so? Have you read the papers recently? Lots of strange things going on lately, don't you think?"

Father Neal gave me a sideways glance.

"Let's pretend I haven't," I said. "Why don't you tell me?"

He rolled his eyes up to the ceiling. "Oh, you know, lions roaming the suburbs, an increase in power outages, grave robbing. Your ghost group is probably busy, yes?"

Father Neal turned pale. "I don't know what you mean, Michael."

"Of course you don't! That's the beauty, isn't it?"

"Speak plainly, or we will leave," Father Neal commanded as the light dimmed again.

Mike looked around, and the smile on his face disappeared. "It's simple. The ritual worked. The Grinning Man has awakened."

"That's not possible. We stopped you." I dug my nails into my palms.

"Yes, Aidan, you stopped us at Serpent Mound, no doubt about it." He gave me a mock bow. "But you were meant to."

A chill raced up my spine as I glanced at Father Neal. His face looked drawn in and he seemed older than I'd ever seen him.

"Come on, Mike," I said. "Nachash, the serpent. That's where the ritual ended."

Mike smirked. "Funny thing about Hebrew words. Their meanings are so tricky."

I ran through my brain trying to sort through other meanings for Nachash.

Mike glared at me. "Think, Aidan, it's not that hard."

"Shining ones," Father Neal broke in.

Mike laughed. "Excellent, priest! We weren't sure it would fool both of you. We figured Aidan would fall for it, but not you, *Father*." He looked back at me. "On the other hand, you ignored other evidence, didn't you? Those scratches on Jessica's head?"

"That was gibberish."

"No, Aidan. It was Aramaic combined with Hebrew. It's an ancient mage trick to imply double meaning. We split the force of the spirits, you see. What you saw at Serpent Mound was only half of what we called up with Amanda's death."

"So, what was the word?"

Mike grinned. "Well, I won't tell you the actual word. I'm sure the good Father knows it anyway. But essentially, we spelled 'The Shining Bone Talker' on her head. Or, if you wanted to be crude about it, 'The Grinning Dead One.'"

"That's a little hard to swallow," I said. "I think you're just screwing with our heads."

Mike stared at Father Neal. "You exposed yourself, old man. You, him, and the thing you guard. The Grinning Man knows. He knows you're here. He felt the power of the thing you possess."

Father Neal leaned forward. "No one possesses it, Michael. It is not a *thing*, it is *Holy*. That is what your kind never understands."

"We'll see about that now, won't we?" Mike laughed.

"I still say you're full of shit." I slapped the table.

"Am I?" Mike's eyes examined me with a half smile. "Look at Father Neal's face. That should tell you otherwise. But if you need more proof, go to Newark Mounds. You'll see."

Mike stood up. "Well, boys, it's been fun. Maybe I'll see you again sometime."

I jumped up and got in his face. "Unlikely, you asshole! Unless it's when I sit in the room to watch your eyes close on your way to hell!"

Mike leaned in close to my face. "Amanda was such a good fuck," he whispered. "Her cries of pleasure made for good magick. It wasn't just Daniel who had her."

"Aidan, no!" Father Neal shouted as I drew back and punched Mike in the face. I got in another punch as Jennifer and the guard rushed into the room. She jumped between us and shoved me to the wall.

Mike laughed and licked the blood as it poured from his nose. "He's back, boys, he's back! And he will find you, she will help him!" He yelled as the guard yanked him out of the room.

Jennifer pointed a finger in my face. "What the hell do you think you were doing? Do you know how much trouble you could have caused? What if he presses charges?"

Father Neal put a hand on Jennifer's arm. "He won't, but we must get to Newark Mounds right now."

She nodded. "I'll see if there is an incident report from Newark while we drive."

We walked out of the jail, and my head buzzed. I couldn't remember ever having the desire to kill anyone, but I wanted to stick a knife in Mike's heart.

"I found a report from the county police in Newark," Jennifer said as we got in the car. "No murder, as I thought, but…"

"Go on, my dear," Father Neal said.

"Well, it seems a hole just appeared in one of the mounds as if someone had been digging there."

"Can you get us permission to be there?" I asked. "I believe it's a golf course, right?"

She nodded. "Yeah, let me make some calls."

Jennifer's voice droned in the back seat as I stared out the windshield.

"Would the Grinning Man actually be buried there, Father?" I asked.

Father Neal sighed. "You must blame me for this, Aidan. I didn't take the Newark legends seriously."

"What legends?"

"Remember when I told you giant skeletons had been found there? And blocks of wood with Hebrew writing? Most people dismissed them as hoaxes, but I should have known better."

I shrugged. "So, what if they're real? What does it mean?"

"It means that Newark is a place of powerful ancient magick, more powerful than I realized. Do you know what the giants probably were?"

"I really don't. I hate to admit."

"And in those days, the sons of God mated with the daughters of men and the Nephilim were born, the men of old, the men of great renown."

I gripped the steering wheel. "You can't be serious."

"If I'd said that a few hours ago, I might have been joking. Now, we seem to know better."

"But the Grinning Man, he's not Nephilim, is he?"

Father Neal gripped his cane. "That is a very good question. I don't know. As I said before, he was human. But as to what he is now…"

His words churned in my stomach as I pulled into the Newark Mounds complex. Cars filled the country club's parking lot.

I shook my head. "Can someone tell me how in the hell someone built a golf course on a major archeological site?"

"Product of the early twentieth century, where no one gave a shit about history." Jennifer snorted. "So, instead of being recognized along with the pyramids, like they deserve, these mounds see douche bags knocking their golf balls around."

Father Neal chuckled. "Feel strongly, my dear?"

"You have no idea. My dad and I have been working for years to get this country club out of here."

A skinny tanned man in a white golf hat walked up to us as we got out of the car. "Detective Brown?"

Jennifer forced a smile. "That's me. Bruce, is it?"

"Yes, ma'am. I'll take you to the altar. That's where the huge hole is."

Bruce walked us down the mounds. As we passed over the green of the ninth hole, he pointed to a mound about fifty feet in front of us. "The hole is up there. I found it a few weeks ago."

"Could it have been made by a backhoe?" I asked.

"No," Bruce said. "No tracks on the course. Nothing. Only thing we found is a ton of bare footprints. Some jokers from Denison University, probably. Little assholes like to come over here all the time and mess with us."

He took us to the altar, and we climbed the hill where a large rectangular hole had been carved into the ground. Father Neal began to walk around the mound, muttering to himself.

"What else did you find here, Bruce?" Jennifer asked.

"Well, ma'am, we found a lot of what I thought was blood. But the police said it wasn't. Just a red substance that looked a lot like blood."

"So what did they say it was?" Jennifer pressed.

"They didn't know, ma'am. But nothing else was amiss, so the police just chalked it up to a weird vandalism case."

I bent down to touch the earthen edges. The smooth dirt shocked my senses as I stared into the hole. Energy seemed to flow from the opening, and the world spun. I backed up so that I wouldn't fall into it, and began to hear whispers, though I couldn't make out what they said.

"Anything else?" Jennifer asked.

"Nope. Good thing you came today. We've got a truck-load of dirt coming to fill this hole in tomorrow morning."

"Thank you, Bruce," Jennifer said. "Would you mind letting us look around?"

Bruce nodded. "Take your time. I want to check out the green for a minute."

"Father?" Jennifer said as Bruce walked away.

Father Neal turned to us. "He was here. Buried right here. He should have been easy to find, but I never could. I'd been around this area so many times and never felt him."

"How is that possible?" I asked.

"The magick of the Nephilim, I would guess. They drew me out. They drew out what I guard. And they found you, Aidan. They won this round. Now, we're all in serious trouble." He shook his head as he stared into the hole.

Jennifer rubbed her scar. "What I don't get is who was sacrificed? If the blood wasn't really blood, how did they finish the spell?"

Father Neal limped over. He went pale and swayed. "No, the red substance was not the blood of a human."

"What?"

He gave me a grim smile as he bent down to the ground. "It's blood of a type. The blood of someone who has erased all their humanity through magick and most certainly had to be a woman to complete the Three Gates."

"But why would she sacrifice her own life?"

"None to sacrifice, Aidan. That's the glitch in the system."

"I don't get it."

Father Neal took a deep breath. "When someone goes far enough down the magickal path, they cease to be human. Even their blood changes. This woman sacrificed part of herself. She died in some way for her master, to serve her master."

"Who is she?" I asked.

The three of us stood on the mound as we gazed over the golf course.

"That is the question, isn't it?" Father Neal said as he leaned on his cane.

"What do we do next, Father?" Jennifer gripped my hand, and I pulled her in close.

"We watch, my dear. And we pray."

FOLLOW JONATHAN RYAN AT:

Twitter:
@authorjryan

Facebook:
www.facebook.com/jryanwriter

Websites:
www.authorjonathanryan.com & www.3gatesofthedead.com

Coming Soon:
3 Gates Series Book II: The Dark Bride